THE
HEAVENLY
SWORD

Alice Poon

The Heavenly Sword

By Alice Poon

ISBN-13: 978-988-8769-54-4

This is a work of fiction. Names, characters, incidents and places portrayed in this book are either fictitious or used fictitiously.

FICTION / Fantasy / Asia / China

Cover Artist: Wenwen
Cover Designer: Silvia Brandmeier

EB167

Published by Earnshaw Books Ltd. (Hong Kong)

In memory of:
Jin Yong
(1924 – 2018)

Author's Note

WHEN I WAS a child, one thing that never failed to light up my humdrum life was the chance to spend my school summer vacation with my five cousins at my uncle's flat in Shaukeiwan, Hong Kong. Even the boring commute by tram from my Wanchai home was a thrill, as in my mind I replayed scenes from Jin Yong's (1924-2018) wuxia (martial arts heroes) novels that I would read whenever I could.

There was a hawker near my uncle's home who lent out the novels for a few cents each. Each summer, the tattered books on loan would keep me and my similarly inclined favorite cousin blissfully occupied throughout the entire vacation.

Jin Yong is a celebrated name for my generation and several subsequent generations of Chinese people. He has been compared to J. R. R. Tolkien of *Lord of the Rings* fame and I do think the comparison is apt in that both authors were endowed with prodigious powers of imagination.

As one of Jin Yong's more well-known wuxia series — the Condor Heroes trilogy — goes through the process of being translated into English and published, his novels have at last begun to gain wider recognition in the English language book world.

My own writing career began with historical Chinese fiction as I have always been a devoted dabbler in Chinese History. As all Jin Yong readers know, his wuxia novels have the marks of well-researched historical settings and casts that include historical characters. The enduring popularity of his novels as well as wuxia C-dramas seems to speak to the proven viability of mixing history with wuxia fantasy.

One day I went down memory lane to revisit my childhood days when my cousins and I, inspired by Jin Yong's novels, used to amuse ourselves by playacting martial arts heroes and heroines. We would spar with wooden ruler swords, don capes of torn towels and hop from chair to chair in imitation of qinggong. Beset with nostalgia, I started toying with the idea of writing wuxia fantasy novels.

That was how the notion of writing the *Sword Maiden from the Moon* duology was first spawned. Later, as more creative ideas developed, the realist in me pleaded for the story to be grounded in a civil war and rebellion that happened in the early Ming Dynasty, while the dreamer in me nudged me to create a female knight-errant as the lead and a magical world where mortals, immortals and demons are staged.

As much as the heroine of my story is imaginary, she is nonetheless inspired by a real but little known woman rebel leader who escaped capture during the Yongle Emperor's reign. I have retained her real name "Tang Sai'er" in the novel and she was also truly a leader of the White Lotus Sect. Information about her life is so lacking, though, that it afforded me much creative liberty to paint her character. Her "Chang'e" side was prompted by a Chinese novel titled *The Unofficial History of the Female Immortal* written by a Qing novelist named Lu Xiong (1642-1723).

CAST OF CHARACTERS

MORTALS:

Tang Sai'er: Daughter of Tang Jun, born in Putai County, Shandong Province. Chang'e incarnate who trains under Zhang Sanfeng to become an expert Wudang martial artist with unique skills. Later appointed as leader of the White Lotus Sect and head of the Sect trio.

Ma Sanbao: A war orphan born in Yunnan Province who's enslaved to serve as a boy eunuch in the Beiping Palace of the Prince of Yan. Later becomes the Chief Eunuch at the Yongle Emperor's Court with the conferred name Zheng He.

Zhu Di: The fourth son of the Ming Hongwu Emperor (Zhu Yuanzhang) titled as Prince of Yan, later the Yongle Emperor. He's the incarnate of a Sky Wolf who is ranked as Deputy General of the North Pantheon and has an immortal twin.

Tang Binhong: Orphaned at two, he is the foster son of Tang Jun and foster brother of Tang Sai'er. Particularly skilled at archery and herbal medicine. Later becomes one of the White Lotus Sect trio.

Dong Yinho: Orphaned at two, the adoptee of Zhang Sanfeng who later becomes Tang Jun's foster son. Specially skilled at Eight Immortals Rod kung fu and qinggong, he is appointed as one of the White Lotus Sect trio.

Zhang Sanfeng: Grandmaster and Founder of the Wudang School of Martial Arts who resides at the Sky Pillar Summit of the Wudang Mountains. Worships the Warrior God Xuan Wu and is half an immortal. (A real historical character fictionalized in Jin Yong's wuxia novel *The Heaven Sword and Dragon Sabre*,)

Pearly: Granddaughter of Zhang Sanfeng who has master status in North Star Qi-Extracting kung fu. She's known as the "North Star Hermit" and later joins the White Lotus Sect as Adviser.

Tang Jun: Father of Tang Sai'er and Head of the White Lotus Society. He eventually joins the White Lotus Sect as Adviser.

Monk Faxian: Father of Tang Jun and Grandfather of Tang Sai'er. Trains under Zhang Sanfeng with Pearly and Monk Yao and becomes a White Lotus Sect Adviser.

Monk Yao: a.k.a. Yao Guang. Chief Adviser to the Prince of Yan and later appointed as the Grand Councilor and Teacher of the Crown Prince in the Yongle Emperor's Court.

Tie Xuan: Commissioner of Shandong who supports the Jianwen Emperor. He is appointed Commander-in-Chief to protect the Shandong capital of Jinan against Zhu Di's Yan army. Tang Jun's good friend.

Yusu: An adoptee of Zhang Sanfeng and childhood companion of Pearly.

Lin San: A merchant born in Putai County, the incarnate of Hou Yi, the ancient King who is famed for shooting down nine Suns to save the Earth from being scorched.

Ah Long: Yinho's favorite acolyte skilled at sketching and using the blow-dart pipe.

Gao Yulan: A favorite qinggong acolyte of Sai'er's.

Gao Feng: Gao Yulan's brother.

Consort Xian: A Jurchen Consort in the Yongle Emperor's harem and an incarnate of a lynx nymph.

Mother Lin: Lin San's mother.

Mother Wang: A refugee. Appointed Farming Unit Overseer of the White Lotus Sect.

Madam Pu: An inn owner and Ah Long's mother.

Fang Xiaoru: Chief Adviser to the Jianwen Emperor. Teacher of Tang Jun.

IMMORTALS:

Chang'e: A Goddess who resides in the Moon Palace under the rule of the Queen Mother of the West.

Sky Wolf: Deputy General of the North Pantheon under the rule of the Warrior God Xuan Wu. He assumes the human form of Zhu Di (Prince of Yan) and has an immortal twin brother — another Sky Wolf who is reborn as the Green Dragon.

Lan Caihe: One of the Eight Immortals of the East Pantheon who is an androgynous sprite skilled at dancing and singing. (Literary Source: *Journey to the East*)

Nezha: Senior Marshal of the North Pantheon. In his previous mortal life he was a prodigious martial talent and youngest son of the Tang general Li Jing. (Literary Source: *Feng Shen Bang* or *Investiture of the Gods*)

Queen Mother of the West: Co-Ruler of the East Pantheon who governs all female Deities in the Pantheon. (Literary Sources: *Classic of Mountains and Seas, Biography of King Mu of Zhou, Biography of Emperor Wu of Han* and *Journey to the West*)

Xuannu the Warrior Goddess: (a.k.a. Jiutian Xuannu, or Xuannu of Nine Heavens) A powerful female Deity of the East Pantheon ranking second to the Queen Mother of the West. (Literary Source: *Shan Hai Jing* or *Classic of Mountains and Seas*)

Xuan Wu, the Warrior God: (a.k.a. Zhen Wu) Ruler of the North Pantheon who upholds justice and is the Protector of the Pantheons. (A revered Deity in Taoism).

Longevity: Ruler of the South Pantheon who controls the life span of mortals. (Literary Source: *Journey to the West*)

Guanyin: (a.k.a. Goddess of Mercy). A Bodhisattva of the West Pantheon. (Literary Source: *Journey to the West*)

Erlang Shen: Chief General of the North Pantheon and ranks second to Xuan Wu the Ruler. (Literary Source: *Journey to the West*)

Jade Emperor: Ruler of the Central Pantheon and Supreme Ruler of all Deities. (Literary Source: *Journey to the West*)

DEMONS:

Green Dragon: (a.k.a. Ao Guang). Originally a Sky Wolf in the North Pantheon. He gets demoted to demon status and rules the East Sea from his Crystal Palace. He has an immortal Sky Wolf twin — the Deputy General of the North Pantheon who is reincarnated as Zhu Di (Prince of Yan). (Literary Source: *Feng Shen Bang* or *Investiture of the Gods* and *Journey to the East*)

Part One

Part One

1

"THE TRICK is to be a needle wrapped in cotton," Sai'er's father said.

Sai'er made a face at his back.

Her foster brother Binhong deflected a flurry of mindless slashes from her sword, then leaping up and making a half spin in mid-air, he slammed his sword down towards her with his full body weight.

Without thinking, she met the ferocious blow with all the qi she could muster. The shock waves from metal slamming onto metal ripped through her arm, and nearly jerked the sword out of her grip. She lurched to one side from the force of the blow, her hand shaking. He took advantage of the opening to bolt forward and in one swipe sent her half-raised sword flying out of her hand and skipping over the ground. With a smug grin, he then touched the wooden tip of the sword to her throat.

"Daughter, you'll never be able to master the Sword-as-Whip technique if you don't work at your neigong," Ba harrumphed, the veins in his temples visibly throbbing. Throwing his bamboo smoking pipe onto the stone table, he mumbled in frustration.

"Neigong needs diligent practice before you can master your qi flow. Qi must be used wisely — in attack, and in defense... If only you would pay attention to what I tell you."

"There you go again, Ba!" Sai'er snapped, her temper flaring.

"You mean I'm thickheaded 'cos I'm a girl, am I right?" She just had to let off some steam.

Constantly losing to Binhong at archery already rankled. In sword dueling, she had a clear edge over him in agility, yet she still couldn't beat him at that either, and the incremental stress she endured was worse than a punch in the guts. And Ba's constant fault-finding just added insult to injury.

"Then how come Binhong catches on and you don't?"

"That's not true, he still can't control his qi flow," she asserted. "His only advantage over me is his brute strength, you know that!" She had no doubt that sometimes her Ba made things up just to irritate her. No way would she believe Binhong understood him any better than she.

You always talk in riddles, Ba! Who on earth can figure you out?

"Aiyah! It's not about physical strength. How many times have I told you? You can take him down if you're good at your neigong."

But what does it mean to be good at neigong? she murmured to herself in exasperation. *Didn't I use my qi to the best of my power?*

A blunt riposte decrying his inscrutable mumble was about to spew from her lips when she caught herself and swallowed it back. Making him lose face in front of his favorite apprentice would not help her case. Worse, it would only add oil to the fire.

Yet for all her rants, Ba was still a Sword-as-Whip expert, as well as a virtuoso herbalist.

Binhong threw Sai'er a sympathetic glance, and kept silent, his eyes roving between the two verbal duelists with a sense of acquired patience.

The Tang home stood among a cluster of straw-thatched cottages bordering the south bank of the main Putai river which fed into the Bohai Sea. It was a stone's throw from the only wooden bridge that straddled the north and south riverbanks. Birthplace to the Tang young and old, Putai was a sleepy coastal county in Shandong province that was almost relegated to oblivion.

The dried mud cottage had a sizable backyard, with a small stable nestling in the north-west corner, a postern gate in the mid-north, and a kitchen and bamboo shed tucked in the northeast. On the south side, a maple and a pear tree were ensconced on either side of the lounge porch. Two small bed chambers squatted in the east and west wings.

Sai'er and Binhong had been using the yard as their training ground since childhood.

Sai'er's Ba had turned the bamboo shed into an apothecary where he treated local patients and dispensed medicinal herbs. That was his favorite nook in the whole house.

Since her mother had died two years ago, he would sometimes sit alone motionless, eyes swimming in tears, for hours on end inside his cherished sanctum. Those were moments she felt less neglected by and closest to him. Her longing to mourn with him together sometimes sent a brittle twinge to her heart. But he seemed to always wear his aloofness like impenetrable armor. She knew better than to expect him to change.

Never conveyed to him in so many words, but the way he had cared for Ma during her protracted illness was not lost on Sai'er. For all the austerity that defined him, he'd made an extra effort to soften his straight-laced mien, cheering and feeding Ma in the last stretch of her life journey.

After supper, Sai'er quietly snuck out through the postern gate, still miffed from the bickering with her Ba. She knew her anger had more to do with hitting a dead end in neigong than with Ba's fumbling for words. Frustration still roiled her mind so much that she almost forgot what she came out for.

Winter Solstice was near, and she wanted to surprise them with a decent festive meal of braised hare meat with chestnuts, which was Ba's favorite.

Binhong was usually the one who brought home wild game or fish. He had been grumbling about the ever scantier food source these days. A month ago he had come back with only two tiny quails and some wild mushrooms. The recent bitter cold spell might have given him another reason to shun the outdoors.

Secretly, she had always yearned to try her hand in tolai hare hunting in the wooded area about a li from their small hamlet. This night seemed a good time to have some fun out. She badly needed something to pick her up.

In the next instant, she was traipsing along the snow-covered, deserted dirt path that led to the forest. Across the forsaken sorghum field to her right, a mass of black shadows hovered sneakily around a campfire right next to a mound of white tombstones. That was a new cemetery built not long ago on land donated by a well-to-do local peddler, primarily for villagers with little means to bury their loved ones properly.

A plausible explanation could be that those men had come out to lay traps for field mice and were just huddling around the fire to get warm. But that didn't stop her from wincing at the sight. She had heard a few gruesome stories of earlier great famines when families had had to exchange their dead babies to eat; when grave raiders had dug up corpses for food.

Pictures of looters gorging on roasted human flesh started cropping up in her mind. The mental images made her guts churn. Stomach acid took no time to rush up her throat. She halted in her tracks and hurled out half of what she had downed at supper. *Guanyin have mercy*, she whimpered, grimacing at the rancid taste of her own vomit. Before she had time to recover from the nausea, a waft of spring flowery scent drifted past

6

her. It was a mix of magnolia and lily fragrance. She swiveled her lantern in every direction to try to get a better look at the surroundings. Not a whiff of anything that should cause alarm. *But flowers at this time of year?!* Anyhow, she greedily inhaled the pleasant perfume, and it helped to calm her frayed nerves.

Now in the midst of a white clump of frost-covered trees, all bathed in hazy twilight, she strained her ears to listen more intently.

Occasional flurries the previous night had blanketed the forest floor with white downy snow, hushing up Nature's lyrical hum. All she could hear was her own thrumming heartbeat and the crackling of brittle branches bracing up to the night draught.

For all she knew, that strange olfactory delight could have come from her overactive imagination.

With that thought, she relaxed her tense shoulders and started focusing on her lookout for hare footprints on the fresh layer of snow on the ground. Winter season had started not long ago, so there was a good chance the animals were still out and about foraging for roots and plants, to fill up their food stash for the long winter.

Tracking hare footprints was something Binhong had taught her the previous winter. For once, she had succeeded in wheedling him into secretly taking her along on one of his hunts. A smile spread across her face when she reminisced that fun outing. She had bagged a couple of wild mallards using her archery skills. Even getting scolded by Ba later for sneaking out couldn't abate the joy and excitement that lingered from that experience.

If only she could have something to show for her lesson!

An unmistakable train of hare paw prints wended its way to the snarly and mossy tangle of oak tree roots straight ahead, some thirty paces from where she stood. Chances were, straggling right underneath that giant tree, was a warren of burrows.

What a piece of luck! She had to muffle an ecstatic scream that almost breached her lips.

Steadily and without a sound, she readied her bow, reached for a shaft in the quiver strapped to her back, and sank on one knee behind a low cluster of withered bushes. Now all she needed to do was wait patiently for the homecoming nocturnal fellows.

The full moon had just peered out from behind the thin veil of cloud. She snuffed out the lantern flame. Shooting in semi-darkness was no challenge to her.

The pallid moonlight swathed her slender shape, throwing a puny silhouette on the white snow. A strange and strong yearning for the moon was something she'd lived with since childhood. It was much like a craving for sweet meats, but more intense.

Her Ma had once made fun of her. "When you were an infant, nothing could calm you when you threw a tantrum except the moon. You craved the moon more than my milk!"

Just as she was getting attuned to the waxen beam, a beastly growl from behind her shattered the drowsy silence. Her limbs froze in response. Whirling around, she spotted a black shape with two glinting dots less than fifty steps away.

In sickening horror, she let her bow and arrow slide from her fingers. Her airways constricted so she couldn't even squeeze out a sound. *Monkey Sage! I'm done for,* she thought, feeling wretched and helpless. She would ease away from the menace, if only her legs would obey her.

As if sensing her distress, the black shape steadily closed in on her.

Her heartbeat slammed on her eardrums. The next thing her ears caught was a sharp whoosh tearing through the air and hitting target. A puncturing noise and a shrill yelp. Another swish. Final gasp. Then silence.

8

The black wild boar sporting sharp fangs had plumped down with its legs awkwardly splayed. Its blood dyed a patch of snow crimson red. The poor beast looked piteously scrawny for a wild boar.

A tall and dark human shape loomed under a shaft of silvery light.

"My surname is Ma. My friends call me Sanbao," he volunteered in a gentle voice.

He happened to be hare-hunting in the area too, having arrived in Putai three days earlier on a family visit.

"I don't know how to thank you, Master Ma," she stammered as her tongue loosened, her pulse settling into a less frenetic rhythm. "You — you've just saved my life."

In a gesture of goodwill, he revealed more about himself. He came from a Hui family, he said, with roots in Yunnan. His uncle and aunt had migrated here from Yunnan several years ago, when the government moved hordes of the Hui tribe to Shandong to make up for its loss of lives during the peasant rebellion against the Yuan Mongol rulers.

"You look so young," he said, quirking an eyebrow, looking truly concerned. "Someone should have accompanied you out here. The forest is always full of nasty surprises."

Crouching down to pry the two arrows from the carcass, he cocked his head and shot a quick glance at the bow and arrow that were lying at her feet.

Sai'er blushed, not even knowing why. She'd never blushed while talking with Binhong.

"I'm fifteen, old enough to take care of myself. Plus I practice Wudang kung fu."

"A hunter and a martial artist! My goodness!" He trained his gaze on her with a mix of curiosity and awe. "I also practice Wudang kung fu. What's your name, and who's your teacher, if

9

you don't mind me asking?"

"My name is Tang Sai'er," she blushed a deeper pink, "My father is my teacher. His name is Tang Jun." She wasn't going to admit this was her first attempt at hare hunting.

"'Sai'er'! I can see you're as brave as a lad, as your name suggests," his lips curved into a wide smile, without any tinge of mockery. He looked genuinely impressed.

"And your father's name is familiar to me. He's one of Master Zhang Sanfeng's students, if I'm not mistaken, and is a Sword-as-Whip expert. In fact, I'm on my way to the Wudang Mountains — Master Zhang has kindly agreed to be my shifu."

It had never occurred to her that her name could be interpreted that way! The compliment certainly helped to break the ice. "Thank you. You're too kind."

The way he was casually striking up a conversation began to disarm her.

"You don't know how lucky you are," she added, her blush fading. "My father told me that the Master rarely accepts apprentices now. You must be someone special. Ba has been toying with the idea of apprenticing me to him."

"Well, in fact it was the personal adviser to the Prince of Yan who recommended me to Master Zhang," he said with hesitation. Or perhaps out of habitual caution. "I—I work in the Palace of the Beiping Princedom." A shade of embarrassment flitted across his face. She couldn't figure out why, but to show courtesy, she nodded in response.

After a short pause, he gushed on of his own volition, "Actually I'm just the Prince's personal manservant. I also fight as a soldier in battles against the Mongols. His adviser, Monk Yao, has been kind and always puts in a nice word for me."

At the mention of the Prince, her heart skipped a beat, defying reason. She had vaguely heard of the Imperial title, but all she knew was that he was one of the Peasant Emperor's sons. Princes. Palace. Princedom. These were such remote and abstract things for simple village folk like her. She had no idea where that strange reaction came from.

But it was plain that she had just met someone from a Palace, someone very close to a powerful Prince. And that someone had saved her life!

Weird reaction or not, this really happened!

Having re-lit the lantern, she couldn't take her eyes off Sanbao's face.

The black woolen high hat fastened under his chin made him look even taller. He had an angled jaw and high forehead, with an angry welt carved in the right temple. Bushy brows hung over soft brown eyes that were young, yet darkly morose. His hooked nose and stalwart build were quite typical of the Hui tribe from Yunnan, if what Binhong had told her was true.

"Then you must be someone of a high rank!" She was now eager for him to tell her more.

"I became a war orphan at the age of ten and was sent to the Prince's palace to serve as his slave. My life practically belongs to him. I'm just his chattel." His voice trailed off as a shadow of deep grief filmed over his eyes. "Enjoy your carefree life while you can, girl. And cherish your parents."

She was trying hard to process what he had just said. *What does it mean to be a Prince's slave?* Without being fully aware, she was deeply drawn to him by some undefined pain in his eyes. All she felt was that they were two lonely people seeking some company on this freezing and inhospitable winter night.

"My mother passed away two years ago," she said with her eyes cast down. "My father thinks I'm a disappointment because I can't do neigong as well as I should."

"Very sorry for your loss, Sai'er," he said with an absent look, as if he was in a faraway place. "Be thankful you still have your father."

In the next moment he regained his presence and looked into her eyes with renewed vivacity.

"Neigong is not that hard. Wudang neigong is all about using controlled qi to disguise power, to give it a soft appearance. Monk Yao is a former student of Master Zhang's and some years ago he gave me a book called *The Secret of Wudang Neigong*, written by the great Master himself. I'll bring it to you if you meet me by the bridge tomorrow at midday."

"Ahh! That sounds wonderful. It's so generous of you!" Heat rose to her face. She heard herself squealing with joy inside.

Holding her in his soulful, obsidian eyes, searing in their intensity, he said, "You're welcome to keep the book as a memento from me. I'll be leaving town tomorrow afternoon. Very pleased to have met you today, Sai'er."

Then, fumbling in his big felt bag, he fished out two dead hare and shoved them inside her hunting sack. "It's getting late. Let me take you home."

"Oh, can you wait for me for just a moment," she said.

Those folks would probably be happy to share some meat. Grabbing the wild boar carcass by its legs, she lugged it across the open field toward the huddling crowd.

2

THE BOOK WAS full of hand-drawn diagrams of the human body.

Of particular interest to Sai'er was the layout of the overarching Ren and Du Meridians and the twelve organ-related meridians. One diagram succinctly showed the course of the Ren Meridian from the chin down the torso center line to the perineum, and the Du Meridian running from the perineum up the back center line right through the top of the head to the nose.

After devouring the book in two days and two nights, Sai'er began to grasp the essence of it all. The crux was to run qi through the Ren and Du Meridians in one continuous loop. Once this was achieved, one could direct qi movement outward and inward at will.

In that duel session with Binhong, she had made the obvious mistake of using aggressive qi while on the defensive. Rather than forcing a hard clash head-on, which was a waste of qi, she should have retracted her qi in order to lessen the impact of the hit, and to give the false impression of a retreat when in fact qi was preserved for new attack moves.

Then, having got Ba's permission, she shut herself up in her own bed chamber for a whole month, practicing qi circulation nonstop from crack of dawn to sundown, only taking short breaks to prepare lunch and supper. The mystery of neigong was finally unlocked.

What Ba had said made a lot of sense now. *The trick is to be a needle wrapped in cotton.* His words actually tallied with what

Sanbao said. *It's all about using controlled qi to disguise power.* Maybe it was really her fault not being a good listener.

She had always been sensitive about how inadequate she was, being a girl, without anyone rubbing this into her face. Ba had named her 'Sai'er' at her birth, three years after her Ma had sadly brought to the world two stillborn male fetuses in tandem, two years apart.

Those two characters in her name literally read as 'rivaling a son'. She had always assumed the name was some kind of stigma to remind her that her birth was a letdown to her father, as she had usurped a son's rightful place in the family. It had made her feel unwanted and unworthy of love all the while she was growing up.

Now that Sanbao had shined a new light on the name, she began to take a liking to it. 'Rivaling a son' could very well mean a daughter was on par with a son! He made her see the nuanced meaning for the first time.

Be that as it might, she still needed to prove her worth to Ba, not least because he always seemed more pleased with Binhong's progress. She had nothing against Binhong, but she also couldn't deny there was keen competition between them where kung fu was concerned.

Which was why she was determined to excel in the Sword-as-Whip skill. It was the only way to win Ba's approval and make him see her worth.

This afternoon, Ba witnessed for the first time how Sai'er effortlessly neutralized Binhong's hard blows.

By retracting qi, she parried with an effective defense. She then countered with a tight series of blows flourished by projected qi, combined with a couple of flying kicks. This unleashed a sudden blast of energy that forced him to back up a few steps. She gained an opening. Like a released arrow, she shot into the space created and touched her sword tip on his throat before he could raise his sword.

Just as easily, she won in all successive rounds. Confidence began to build up that made her feel she could soon master the Sword-as-Whip skill.

She espied a rare grin on Ba's face just before he turned to go back to his writing in the apothecary, which also functioned as his study.

Her preening was enough to stoke Binhong's curiosity and he begged her for the book.

"I'll let you borrow it if you tell me stories about the Prince of Yan," she cajoled with a playful wink.

"Fair enough. What do you want to know?" Binhong was always easy to deal with.

Five years older than she, he had joined the household when the Tangs fostered him just days after his second birthday. His parents had lived in the same hamlet as the Tangs and scraped a living from peddling malt sugar candies and red bean buns.

On his birthday, both his parents had been falsely accused of selling poisonous snacks, after a visiting Court Censor's son had died of food poisoning. The Censor had filed a complaint with the Embroidered Uniform Guard who was in his delegation. A few days later the Guard had ordered the execution of the peddler couple without trial.

These Guards were the Emperor's secret spies and were the highest state powers, second only to the Emperor. Even Ministers bowed to their authority.

That was also the year the Tangs had lost their second male child. Sai'er's parents had given Binhong the Tang family name for his protection.

At the age of five, he started apprenticeship under Ba in kung fu and dispensing herbal medicine. He had hawkish eyes and could hit a swaying willow branch a hundred steps away. Hence his nickname Hundred Steps Archer. From his hard training, he had developed a lean and wiry physique.

"Tell me everything you know about him," she demanded like a spoiled brat, using her fingers to ruffle his tied-up knot until it looked like a bird's nest.

His face melted into a mellow smile, like someone putting up with his puppy's mischief. As usual, he was more than willing to humor her.

"What I know is mostly from hearsay. His name is Zhu Di and he's the fourth son of the Peasant Emperor. Among the princes who were granted fiefs, he got the largest one in terms of area and had the largest army. It is rumored that he had his eye on the throne when the first-born prince died prematurely from illness."

He paused to check if she was bored. Her eyes were glimmering with unquenched thirst. She gestured for him to sit, having already settled on one of the stone stools set around the square stone table, placed just outside the bamboo shed under the cover of a reed canopy.

The sky was turning steel gray and the air was heavy with ice crystals, foreboding an imminent snowfall.

"Gossips run that Zhu Di is by a Mongolian junior consort of the Emperor. It is for this reason that the Emperor bypassed him in the Crown Prince selection, even though he has glorious war victories to show for."

"What is he good at? Is he a warrior, a scholar, a poet or a philosopher? And do people like him as a person?" She shifted on her stool, eagerly awaiting an answer. *From that day on, my life belongs to him. I'm just his chattel.* Sanbao's remark rang in her ears. She had felt a prick on the back of her neck that night.

"I'd say he is a ruthless warrior with a vindictive nature. He doesn't forget a slight. I've heard that people generally fear and loathe him in equal parts."

Ba came out again and sat with them at the stone table. "Hmm, like father like son. The father is cunning and cruel." Pausing, he got up and walked over to the postern door to bolt it close. The door was usually left open during the day as it was the entrance that his patients used.

"As soon as he grabbed the throne, he started purging his high-ranked officials and generals who had been loyal to him, killing tens of thousands. Many were innocent—incriminated merely by blood ties."

The seamless rejoinder surprised Sai'er a bit. *So he was listening to our talk the whole time!* She was just glad she and Binhong hadn't said anything boorish.

After another short pause, he carried on in a voice tinged with fatigue and helpless anger, "Now he fears reprisals so much that he sends his Embroidered Uniform Guards all over to spy on common folks. Ruthless killing of innocents will never end."

Binhong nodded in agreement. "The Prince of Yan takes after his father in cruelty. But the Emperor's choice of his grandson as the Crown Prince must have gutted him. Shandong people can't be more pleased, because the grandson at least gives hope of a more humane rule."

Affected by the remark, Ba's brow crinkled into deeper creases.

"It's ill-fate that there's a history of bad blood between the Imperial family and Shandong people."

Years earlier, in the uprising against the Mongol rulers, Zhu Yuanzhuang had permitted his ally and general Chang Yuchun to massacre Shandong people for daring to put up resistance to his marauding rebel army, almost decimating the population.

The atrocities left deep scars on the survivors.

Since then, whether out of spite or not, the Imperial Court left Shandong neglected and impoverished like abandoned children. Natural disasters like droughts and floods could easily leave afflicted counties starved and bereft.

Sai'er had always felt something was very wrong. She had traveled the previous summer with her Ba on horseback to neighboring counties to hand out to peasants herbal medicines such as astragalus roots, ephedra leaves and cassia twigs, which were good for minor ailments and boosting the immune system.

Scene after devastating scene of poverty and misery had unfurled before her eyes. Some rural settlements of those counties looked achingly lifeless. Layers of flaky yellow dust covered what used to be grazing meadows. Scorched fields stretched on for li upon li under the vicious ball of flame suspended in the sky like a scowling fiend. Malnourished children tottered around naked, faces and tiny bodies caked in grime.

On that trip, while riding into the Yidu county, she and her Ba happened upon an execution-by-slicing in the town square. A local told them that the criminal was accused of treason, just for having written a New Year couplet that was deemed disrespectful to the Emperor.

Ba bade Sai'er avert her eyes. With sickened hearts, they scurried away from the bloody scene of horror. For a long time since, she was not able to shake off the victim's gut-twisting shrieks.

The long-promised peace and plenitude was like one dream too far for Shandong people.

"The county officials are just bribe collectors for the Zhu princes," Binhong seethed, his nostrils flaring. "Yamens feel entitled to skim off farmers' harvests, leaving villagers paltry rations of food."

"Whoever sits on the throne, Shandong's prospects don't look good," Ba added with a languid shrug. "We're supposed to provide corvee labor, taxes and conscripts. But don't expect to get anything in return."

"Isn't there anything we could do to help our poor villagers?" The things Sai'er just heard sounded familiar enough. Aside from having read history texts in her early teens, she had heard her Ma tell folk tales of gross injustices. It was always the ordinary people who bore the brunt of officials' abuse of power. *No power, no justice,* she ranted in sullen silence.

Snow flurries were starting their quiet and ethereal descent. The dreamlike view had Sai'er hypnotized. Snowflakes dancing in mid-air always reminded her of her favorite folklore tale about Lan Caihe, the teenage androgynous sprite among the Eight Immortals. This sprite was a regular performer at birthday banquets held by the Queen Mother of the West. It would happily sprinkle flower petals all around as it sang and twirled to the rhythm of its clappers.

Almost imperceptibly, the luring scent of magnolia and lily wafted in the air to tickle Sai'er's nose again. The image of the sprite dipping into its basket and spraying white petals from the heavens flitted through her mind.

Ba's raspy voice pulled her out of her reverie.

"When people are driven to despair day after day, spiritual belief is the only thing that gives them hope for a better tomorrow. Hope makes it easier to bear hardships."

His gaze landed on Binhong, then moved to Sai'er.

"Children, I have plans for you two in the White Lotus Society. But first you must train up to be expert martial artists. A couple of months ago, I wrote to Master Zhang Sanfeng to ask for a favor — to take you up as apprentices. I suggested for you to learn two specific techniques: Wave Treading qinggong and North Star Qi-

Extracting neigong. But the final decision rests with him. Let's just hope he comes back with a positive response."

The Wudang Mountains! Zhang Sanfeng! In her excitement, Sai'er almost lurched from the stool. She quickly readjusted her posture, hoping no one had noticed. She had longed so much to learn those two famous Wudang techniques. Ba had mentioned in passing this possibility, but nothing concrete had come of it until now! And there was even a chance to see Sanbao again!

But wait, what White Lotus Society? What plans? It was the first time she had ever heard of the Society.

Without waiting for their response, Ba got up and shuffled off to the shed.

As soon as Ba stepped indoors, Sai'er hustled Binhong into her bed chamber. Having closed the lattice door behind her, she pinched him hard on the arm.

"What plans does Ba have for us?"

"Ouch! Not so rough—" he winced.

"What's this White Lotus Society? You know something I don't, isn't that right?"

The way Ba looked at Binhong had roused her suspicion. She wasn't going to let him wiggle his way out of an answer. "Oh, don't be such a girl! Tell me quick!"

"I only know that many years ago Uncle took over the rudderless Society because Zhu Yuanzhang had earlier murdered the Society head when they were jockeying for the throne. When Zhu's reign started, Uncle declined his offer of a Court position. He's stayed low ever since and in his spare time teaches the Buddhist scriptures about the Maitreya Buddha. He may... want us to teach martial arts to the Society students."

There's so much that Ba has kept from me, Sai'er thought with dismay. So that was what all those late-evening capers were about! Her Ma had never uttered any displeasure, if she had even minded in the least.

But could Ba be in some kind of danger? The revelation felt like a nest of snakes had been unearthed. She was hit with sudden spasms of fear and anxiety. She began to see why her Ba was so adamant that she and Binhong learn kung fu. It was as much for self-protection as for the ability to help others in these unsettling times.

"But didn't you once tell me that the Emperor has banned all religious sects?" Binhong was always her chief source of news and information, much as he was the designated healer for all her scrapes and bruises and sprains from kung fu training.

"The Society has long gone underground," he said calmly.

"Do you think Ba is, might be, in any danger?"

"As long as he keeps a low profile, I think he'll be safe."

"I'm sure you're one of his students. Don't even try to deny that. How many students are there? Where do the lessons take place?" Sai'er had always thought the two men were out late for drinking rounds in taverns.

"Umm, I'm not supposed to tell you," he cowered, ready for another pinch. But instead of pinching him again, Sai'er just said in a straight face, "Well then, in that case I won't lend you the book."

"Oh, alright," he gave in after a silent moment. "But don't you dare utter a word that I told you this." He drew his face into a serious frown. "There are about one hundred students now. Near the bridge abutment on the north riverbank, there's a large Buddhist temple that had long stood deserted. We do our thing four times a month there. It's only very recently that we've begun to take on female students."

It was all a bit much to take in in one single day. All the new information siphoned and drained her mental energy. She now had an inkling of how hapless ordinary folks were in the face of oppressive rule.

After handing the book to Binhong, she dragged herself to the kitchen to prepare supper. Cooking was the best way to calm emotions and clear the head.

3

BINHONG SHOWED marked improvement after reading Sanbao's book.

Now the sword duels often ended in ties. They were both ready to train seriously in the Sword-as-Whip technique. Before leaving for the Wudang Mountains, they had to master this technique, because Master Zhang Sanfeng would never accept students with no specific skill under their belt.

Having spent three months training alone in neigong and Sword-as-Whip, Sai'er showed she could lash out her sword as though it were an extension of her arm. Her ability to project and retract qi to and from the sword had been fine-tuned to near perfection. The sword became wieldy like a flexible whip in her hand.

One afternoon in the backyard, newly swept clear of snow, Sai'er and Binhong had their first duel session after a lapse.

Having opened the first round with non-aggressive bouts of sparring, both duelists were ready to show their stuff. Both sank down in their horse stances to summon up their qi.

Binhong lashed out first with a series of direct blows, supported by fluid footwork. Sai'er fended off the blows with retracted qi in an equally nimble dance. In a feint, her left leg suddenly shot out in a flying kick. As he looked to his right, almost instantly her right hand flicked the sword in an electrifying triple flourish with the full force of her projected qi, pounding on his half-raised sword in resounding crackles. On the last vibrating metal contact, Binhong's sword flew from his hand. He uttered a muffled groan from the pain.

Wow, so a qi-empowered sword strike is really ten times more powerful than a pure muscular hit!

Obviously Binhong was still having trouble fusing his hand with the sword through channeling his qi. His counter-hits in subsequent rounds lacked the force and suppleness that bespoke Sai'er's maneuvers, and proved ineffective in reversing the vantage.

At the end of the session, Ba said to them, "If you can master this sword skill along with the Wave Treading and North Star techniques of Wudang fame, you will become near-invincible in the world of martial arts."

If he was pleased with Sai'er's performance, he seemed reluctant to show it on his face.

"Binhong, you still need to practice projecting your qi to the sword if you want to beat Sai'er." Without turning his head, he could read the preening look on his daughter's face. "And Sai'er, vanity leads to failure."

"Listen, Children, Master Zhang has replied to my letter. He's happy to take you both on." He paused to look at Sai'er, "Daughter, he'll be making an exception for you—he's never taken on a girl student before, except his granddaughter. So I think you two had better start making preparations for the journey. It may be wise to start the trip when the snow has all melted."

"But Ba, who's going to take care of you while we're gone?" Scary thoughts began to gnaw at Sai'er. Ba would be living all by himself. What if some bandits preyed on him? Or, heavens forbid, if the Embroidered Uniform Guards tracked down the

24

White Lotus Society and took him to jail? Plus she had never lived anywhere else her whole life, except for last summer's short sojourn in nearby counties with Ba at her side. The thought of living thousands of li away from home was unsettling enough.

"Don't you worry about me, Daughter. One of my students called Lin San lives five huts away from us with his widowed mother. Mother Lin has kindly promised to bring me meals every day. The young man is about Binhong's age and is his good friend. He's also an absolutely gifted archer, the only one who can beat Binhong."

"Binhong never told me," Sai'er pursed her lips in ill-humor. "Who knows how many friends he has? Big boys have so many secrets —"

She felt betrayed and jealous at the same time. She had always presumed Binhong regarded her as his closest friend, other than foster sister. How naïve was she! And how she wished she had his freedom to get out and about! Hare hunting that night, even with the spoils, had only drawn Ba's sharp reproof. But that was not to say the fun wasn't worth it, and she never regretted a single moment of the adventure.

"Sai'er, please don't fret! If I'd known you were interested, I would've told you everything that I learned at the lectures. In fact, I can give you the Lotus Sutra that Uncle handed out in class. How about that?" Binhong tried his best to coax her, so afraid was he that she might throw a fit.

"Daughter, I promise you that when you finish training with Master Zhang, I'll let you attend my lectures and go out on your own. Now you have to promise me that you'll respect Binhong as your elder brother and guardian, and do as he bids while you're on the journey and during your stay at Wudang Mountain."

Once Sai'er's thoughts shifted to her upcoming escapade, her negative feelings all but vanished. She nodded her consent, and inwardly chuckled: *In Ba's absence, I'm the ruling princess, and Binhong is my loyal subject.*

"Ba, how should we address the Master?" Picturing the white-haired hunchback hermit dart around in the mountains almost let a giggle slip. *He must be a hundred and fifty years old!*

"Great Grandba Master, of course. I call him Grandba Master because my father was also his student," Ba snorted with impatience. "Talking of students, didn't you mention some monk when you met Sanbao while out hunting? What was his name again?"

"He's Monk Yao. I only know his surname."

"Yao... If his full name is Yao Guang, then I know him. He belongs to my father's generation. They used to be kung fu buddies at Wudang when they were young." Ba looked as if he were in a trance, going way back in time.

"What was that book again that Sanbao gave you?"

"It's titled *The Secret of Wudang Neigong*, and it's written by Master Zhang. Monk Yao had the book and he passed it on to Sanbao."

"Ahh, I remember now. I was nine, just a year before my father's death. He told me about his days at Wudang, how he became close friends with Yao and Master Zhang's granddaughter. Then he gave me a letter of introduction to take to the Master whenever I felt ready to be apprenticed to him. He also mentioned that book. He said that after Yao left Wudang, the book couldn't be found." Ba looked lost in nostalgia, shaded by some inexplicable sorrow.

"Wow, so Monk Yao was a thief," she blurted out.

"Well, we don't know that for a fact. It's not fair to jump to conclusions just based on our presumption."

"According to Sanbao, Monk Yao is a nice person. The Prince of Yan trusts him enough to make him his personal adviser."

"Daughter, neither is it wise to trust people too easily. The best way is to let time and observation be your guide. You can only judge how good a horse is after it has galloped for a long distance."

She suppressed a yawn with her hand and changed the subject. "Should I trust this Lin San to protect you while Binhong and I are away?"

"Have you forgotten that Uncle is a Sword-as-Whip expert?" Binhong gave her a puzzled look. She rolled her eyes and kept her mouth shut. He irritated her most when he pointed out the obvious and made her look stupid in front of Ba.

"There's no need to worry about me, Daughter. You and Binhong must take good care of each other while on the road, and during your apprenticeship at Grandba Master's abode. Write frequently and don't let me have cause to worry."

That night, Sai'er was just too excited to close her eyes. She got up from bed, lit the bedside oil lamp and thumbed through the stitched bound book containing the Lotus Sutra that Binhong had earlier passed to her.

In the Preface, there was a story of how the Maitreya Buddha attained Buddhahood. She had heard of the Maitreya Buddha in Ba's conversations with Binhong, and she also felt a certain closeness to the deity. She liked that this Buddha was nicknamed 'Laughing Buddha'. In his secular life, he had been the Hemp Sack Monk who always carried with him a large hemp sack full of magical trinkets that he handed out to children.

The more she learned about this Buddha, the more she took a liking to him.

Interest kept her turning the pages of the Scriptures. When she repeated aloud the Guanyin Sacred Chants in the twenty-fifth chapter of the Lotus Sutra, a sense of tranquility washed over her.

At last her eyelids became lead-heavy with tiredness and she drifted off.

That strange magnolia and lily fragrance was in the air again. In a dreamy haze, she heard a melodious sound that seemed to emanate from the empyrean heights. When she listened more closely, she realized it was a beautiful voice singing a ballad:

> Ye men of the world!
> Now are ye born, and soon ye die.
> Yesterday, ye were twice eight,
> And your valor puffed your chest.
> Today ye are as seventy years old,
> Looking feeble and without strength.
> Ye are like flowers of the spring day,
> Blossom in the morning, but fade at sunset.

A blinding flash of white light pulsed through the darkness. Out of nowhere, the ebullient Lan Caihe in miniature form appeared fluttering in the air. It donned a long blue gown with a collar of green leaves, carrying in one hand its signature flower basket. On each side of its head heaped a coiled braid tied with ribbons.

"I'm Lan Caihe of the Eight Immortals and I'm here to deliver a message from the Queen Mother of the West."

"How may I address you, little sprite?" She was looking wide-eyed at the diminutive apparition with a boyish face, about the size of a large magpie. Its large round eyes sparkled like the brightest stars in the sky.

"You can call me Caihe."

"So, Caihe, what's the message?"

"The Queen Mother of the West wants you to know your

immortal identity and your special mission. You were Chang'e
of the Moon Palace in your previous life. The Queen Mother
rules all female goddesses, immortals and nymphs in the East
Pantheon."

*So that's why I've always felt an inexplicable affinity to the Moon!
Chang'e? Can that really be true?* She gaped with wide eyes.

"The Prince of Yan is the Sky Wolf's incarnate. In the immortal
world he used to be a renegade Deputy General who got expelled
from the North Pantheon by Ruler Xuan Wu, the Warrior
God. In the mortal world, the Prince is destined to become the
third Emperor of the Ming. The Deities have predicted he will
tyrannize and torment his earthly subjects."

"Monkey Sage! What has that to do with me? Even as
Chang'e's incarnate, I'm still only a lowly village girl, a nobody,
to be exact!"

"Be patient and listen up, Sai'er." The little apparition drew
itself up to its full height. Even then, it was still no bigger than a
small parakeet. The serious look seemed laughably incongruous
with its childish face. But it went on undeterred, "By the Queen
Mother's order, your job is to rein him in and minimize the
bloodbath he's likely to inflict on earth."

"As I said, I'm only a lowly, starving commoner. The Prince,
or Emperor, is the supreme power on earth! If this isn't a joke, I
don't know what is!"

"Don't worry. When the time comes, everything will fall into
place," it chirped airily. But Sai'er's mind was far from being
eased.

"Is there a plan of some sort that I need to follow? What
exactly is my mission? What am I supposed to do?" Rather than
easing, the knot of apprehension tugged tighter and tighter
around her guts.

"Just take each day as it comes. Be glad that Zhang Sanfeng is half an immortal under Xuan Wu's wing, and he will be of great assistance to you in your mission because the North Pantheon Ruler considers Sky Wolf a disgrace, and is on board with the Queen Mother's plan. In fact, all Pantheon Rulers have endorsed the plan."

"Guanyin have mercy! This mission sounds pretty much like a journey to hell. Please be kind and don't make me do this. Please get someone else to do it—"

"My dear Sai'er, I wish I can change what the Pantheon Rulers have decreed. Besides, didn't you say that you wished to help the villagers? For what it's worth, I will stay close to you and be ready to give you advice when needed. By now you must've become used to my fragrance. If you want me to appear, just call out my name. Remember that I'm visible to you alone, and only you can hear my voice."

"I do wish to defend my fellow villagers against abuse by those in power. But if I understand you correctly, the Gods are pitting me against a ruthless and immensely powerful person who can easily crush me with one finger. This is more like a mission of suicide, to put it lightly." What Binhong had said about the Prince now came back to taunt her.

"I'm afraid there's no way around it."

"Can you at least hint at what will happen to me?"

"Unfortunately, I'm not allowed to reveal your future to you. The Queen Mother's message has been delivered in full," the sprite declared in a solemn tone.

In the blink of an eye, its face brightened into a smug smile. Hopping agilely onto Sai'er shoulder, it sat there without a care, spindly legs dangling loosely. As if trying to beat boredom, it donned an air that encouraged chatting. "But I'd be happy to answer other questions. What do you want to know?"

"So, if I wind up in an untenable situation, will I get any help from you?" Sai'er asked after mulling on how to phrase her question, so she could draw more information without touching on specifics about her destiny.

"I can use my Magic Peach to help you in life-and-death situations, but only for twice. So please be careful not to squander the two chances."

"That's good to know. I'll certainly bear that in mind."

Her previous misgivings about her assigned mission instantly got whittled down a notch. At least she had someone to turn to for help in desperate times.

Before she could utter another word, the sprite had leaped into the air, its long blue gown trailing behind like a blue magpie's tail. It flailed its arm to signal farewell, and shouted: "I've got to run now. Until next time."

4

THE NEXT MORNING Sai'er woke up with the vivid image of bouncy Lan Caihe.

It couldn't be a dream, she mumbled to herself. She pinched her thigh three times, on different spots, to convince herself she was really in her bed chamber. It was no hallucination either. But she could find not even the slightest trace of the sprite. The fragrance was no longer there. Nothing around her seemed different. Yet every scene of the encounter and every word that had been exchanged was as clear as day in her mind.

She figured that Binhong would, more likely than not, laugh at her for being silly if she recounted the anecdote to him.

Should she, or should she not, tell him? Truth be told, she was dying to unload the story on someone she could confide in. The burden was more than she could carry. But, fearing Binhong might pass it onto her Ba, she decided after some more thinking to wait until after they started their journey to tell him. The last thing she would want was to leave Ba home alone and troubled with something that seemed absurd and implausible.

She had always trusted her intuition. It now told her that it wasn't a dream or hallucination. Lan Caihe felt as real as herself. In her previous life, she must've been acquainted with the Queen Mother of the West, the Eight Immortals and other Deities. They all sounded so familiar when Caihe mentioned their names. Of course her Ma had been right. She had indeed come from the Moon!

All of a sudden she recalled the way her heart missed a beat that night when she heard Sanbao mention the Prince of Yan. Somewhere in the deep recess of her mind lurked the specter of a fully armored celestial general carrying a halberd atop an iron-clad black stallion. He looked arrogant, handsome and baleful all at once. She tried hard to recall how she had come to know Sky Wolf, but her mind was a blur. It was like a riddle. But she had a feeling that all she needed was a trigger to bring that memory back.

Days turned into a month. Soon it was well into spring and the last layer of snow had thawed out.

At the crack of dawn on the day of their departure, Binhong and Sai'er said their farewell to Ba, after taking a light breakfast together of millet gruel and salted duck eggs.

Ba had earlier unhitched the two nags that the family had in keeping for years and brought them out of the stable. He had loaded onto the canopied cart bedrolls, warm quilts, bundles of clothes and packages of millet cakes and dried fruit. The horses yoked with the wooden cart were waiting just outside the postern gate.

A quick glance at Ba's languorous movement unleashed an outburst of previously imprisoned emotions. His rheumatism had begun to take a toll on him, Sai'er realized with a lump in her throat. She swiftly wiped away the tears.

"Children, two years is not a long time. It will be over before you know it. But you better use every single moment of your waking time to learn."

She rushed forward to put her arms around his scrawny form. Binhong put his palms together and bowed deeply to him.

Ba patted him on the shoulder and said: "Take good care of your sister."

For the initial leg of the journey, they would travel by grain barge on the Putai River to Jinan city, and then by horse-drawn cart to Zhengzhou at the Shandong/Henan border. From there they would traverse Henan Province diagonally from north-east to south-west, and on reaching Hubei's northern border, they would continue a little further west until they reached Shiyan city, where the majestic Wudang Mountains proudly soared into the clouds.

For land travels, their plan was to ride from dawn to sunset each day, and either bunk over in a cheap guesthouse along the way, or spend the night in their shelter on wheels, whichever option was sensible. To stay within a tight budget, they agreed on only renting one room. Binhong would sleep on the floor.

They made their first stop at a busy pier in Jinan city, capital of Shandong, which was a prosperous trading hub. There were many inns, taverns and guesthouses catering to all classes of itinerant traders. So they had no problem finding a reasonably priced guesthouse to spend the night.

After bidding the guesthouse helper to feed and tend to their horses, Binhong and Sai'er sat down at a grease-stained wooden table in the stuffy dining room to have a hot bowl of noodles before turning in.

"Jinan was always a strategic city that rivaling warlords fought over," the helper said, like a self-appointed history teacher, as he wiped down the table with a dirty-looking rag.

Confident that he had his guests' ears, he rambled on with glee, "The Jurchens had once severed this land from our Song Empire to create the Jin dynasty, but were soon chased out by the Mongols. Less than a century later, Zhu Yuanzhang turned fate around and drove out the Mongols," he looked around circumspectly, and lowered his voice, "but he also spilled Shandong folks' blood. Aiyah, wars are always hell for us common folks, but what can you do?"

Sai'er and Binhong nodded their head slightly as a gesture of courtesy. They both knew the history well and couldn't but agree with the helper's last remark.

Never would any of them have guessed, though, that this place would, in just a couple of years, witness savage civil wars between feuding Zhu Princes.

When the helper left them to pass the meal order to the kitchen, Sai'er thought this was a good time to tell Binhong her strange encounter.

When she finished, she was dying to see the stunned look on his face, and yet all she got was a bland visage. Not even the batting of an eyelid!

"Your mother had consulted a Taoist monk when you were three years old," he said in an annoyingly calm tone. "He had told her and Uncle that you were Chang'e's incarnate, and that you would have to eventually shoulder a mission. But he didn't go into details. He also said that Lin −"

"So Ba had known all along," she cut in, too wrapped up in her own thoughts to care about his unfinished sentence.

"That's the reason why he's been so eager to see you excel in martial arts even though you're a girl. But I'm somewhat relieved to know that you have a sprite and a half-immortal to help you. As far as mortals are concerned, I'm your big brother and will always stand by you. You can count on that."

Sai'er noticed for the first time the sensuous warmth that blazed forth from behind the impassive hard gleam of his eyes, which seemed impenetrable. *Is this a wall to hide the insidious pain of orphanhood?* At the same time, she also sensed a trace of forlorn yearning mixed therein, but thought she might be imagining it.

Out of deep compassion, she leaned over and put her hand over his. He responded with a bashful look, fidgeting with unease as if an unsightly sore had been exposed.

His earlier unfinished sentence came to his rescue. "I was going to say that the Taoist monk also told your Ma that Lin San is Hou Yi's incarnate, and there's unfinished business between you and him."

The bizarre revelation jolted Sai'er out of all somnolence.

Millennia ago, Hou Yi had been the great hero who had shot down nine suns with his magic bow to save the parched earth from total incineration. The grateful people put him on the throne and he selected beautiful Chang'e as his consort. To reward him for his valiant deed, the Queen Mother of the West granted him an immortality elixir. But obsession with power was his undoing. He became a tyrant and abused his subjects at will. So, on the Queen Mother's orders, Chang'e stole the elixir from him and swallowed it. By the time he discovered the theft, she was already floating up to the Moon Palace.

Sai'er knew this fable like the back of her hand. *But what unfinished business?*

As if reading her question, Binhong added with caution, "The husband-wife relationship between you two was cut short unnaturally. According to the monk, you are to let that spousal relationship run its course."

"But I can't marry Lin San—" she almost shrieked. "I—I don't know him. Ah, so you and Ba have known this all along. I can't understand why *you* kept it from me. I've never, ever held anything back from you! You're the one I've trusted without reserve, even though—"

She was so overcome with anger and sense of letdown that she had to bite back a hurtful comment about Binhong's adoption.

As much as she guessed Binhong had likely just followed her Ba's orders to keep mum, she had to let out some steam. *They have no right to keep this secret from me!*

Her near hysterical reaction baffled the helper as he was laying down two steaming bowls of noodles on the table. It also caught Binhong by total surprise. The helper scurried away for fear he might've said something to bring that about.

Binhong clumsily seized both her hands and kept stroking them. Guilt was painted all over his face.

"Please don't be upset, Sai'er. I wouldn't have withheld it from you if Uncle hadn't told me to," he readily confessed. In a loss for comforting words, he did the best he could. "Well, you don't have to marry him if you don't want to. I'm sure Uncle will not force you. Who knows anyway what will happen in two years? When we get to Wudang Mountains, you'll have forgotten all about him, I promise you."

She had guessed right. At last pacified, she made him promise never again to hide any secrets from her.

But he does have a point. Why worry about something that's so far ahead? There are fun times near at hand to look forward to!

After a whole month of traveling on their horse-drawn cart through a mix of beaten and raw terrain in Henan Province, they finally reached Shiyan city in Hubei. There the lofty Wudang Mountains towered above them like a contemplative but good-humored green giant with a benevolent mien.

Their final destination was the Sky Pillar Summit, which was where Master Zhang had built his cottage. But before taking what looked like an arduous climb, they decided to have a good night's rest at a guesthouse at the foothills.

During the Henan part of the journey, one thing that bothered Sai'er was the few times when she and Binhong had to sleep in their cart. In the tight space, Binhong's masculine scent made her feel uncomfortable. For the few times their bodies touched, she felt awkwardly abashed. It was hard to have good, sound sleep. So it was a relief to her when they found the guesthouse. To Binhong too, she was sure.

"I need a good scrub down with soap and water," he declared with a sheepish grin.

"Yes, you most certainly do!" Sai'er wrinkled her nose in jest.

They rose well before dawn the next morning, refreshed from a night of deep, energizing sleep.

Sai'er took out Master Zhang's letter to Ba, which contained his hand-drawn map of the route to take to reach his abode. "Binhong, I think we better lose the cart. Look here, there are two flights of stone steps on the climb up."

He shrugged and stretched his arms, "We won't need the cart any way."

So they each unyoked a horse and carried their own sword and bow and cloth sack cross-strapped to the shoulders.

The lower tier of the mountains was sunken in a dense bamboo forest separated into two groves by a gently inclined rural path in the middle. The east grove nestled in a fern-covered valley, accented by the Dragon Spring Lake, while the west grove draped over a sprawling tree-lined hillock.

Jade green bamboo trees rustled above their heads like rolling waves of green lacquered oil-paper umbrellas. The breeze they generated was cool and invigorating.

The rhythmic horse-hoof clacking chimed with the gurgling of streams, the swish of bamboo leaves and the intermittent bird songs. It was a blithesome change of scene and tempo from the month-long rough ride on dust-covered, tiresome thoroughfares snaking through cities and towns.

When they were halfway through this tier, they stopped by

the edge of the Dragon Spring Lake for a snack break, as they had skipped breakfast to save time. They washed down the millet cakes with swigs of sweet-tasting water from the crystal-clear lake.

Where the middle tier began, bamboo trees gave way to a flourishing mix of pine, poplar, ash, cedar, elm and white mulberry. This part presented a bit of a challenge. It was a long flight of jagged stone steps that were hewn into the steep face of a cliff, with one side looking precariously over a verdure-covered deep ravine. They thought it safer to dismount and walk on foot. Even then, constant drizzles had made the moss-covered steps dangerously slippery, and they were forced to proceed slowly.

At the top landing of the first stairway, the gradient turned gentler for about fifty footsteps and opened onto a lush green meadow laced with sprays of white, pink, yellow and violet wild flowers. The meadow was flanked on one side by a small copse and on the other a large lake so clear that the hilly landscape seemed to be sitting on the bottom like a sunken painting. The lake was fed by cascades flying down a craggy hill on the fringe. Iridescent butterflies were fluttering with abandon all over the meadow.

"I've never seen butterflies as huge as these! This is so unreal!" exclaimed Sai'er as bewilderment seeped into her every pore. Capering onto the center of the meadow, she twirled round and round, humming a folk ballad and imagining herself as Lan Caihe.

Binhong was quietly enjoying the view, just as much awestruck as she.

Abutting the meadow was the second stairway, shorter than the first and with wider steps. This was the final tier.

Throughout their strenuous climb, she was content to lose herself in the verdurous wonder, the refreshing grass and floral aroma and the ethereal music composed by birds and insects. She avoided talking altogether, for fear she might break the magic spell. Binhong seemed equally content to let nature wash over him.

No wonder people call these mountains sacred, she mused. The place felt like a legend carved out of eternity, meant to rejuvenate mortals seeking a break from life's tiresome journey. In this mystical story, Bountiful Nature was at once protagonist and narrator, ready to enchant and heal any willing audience. It was no accident that Taoist monks flocked to these mountains to begin their soul-searching tour.

The higher they climbed on this final tier, the denser the mist became, until trees and ravines and sharp-faced cliffs swam in a translucent whiteness. Their breathing turned into shallow gasps.

As they were groping their way forward, relieved and excited to be nearing their destination, a giant golden eagle darted out from the opalescent white veil and hurled itself at Sai'er's face. She ducked and careened to one side, but had her braid caught in the eagle's razor-sharp talons. It wouldn't let go and tried to yank her down onto the steps. She screeched in pain.

Binhong was about twenty steps below, the two horses trailing behind him. With lightening speed he snatched his bow and an arrow from his quiver and took aim. Twang. The released arrow pierced clean through the eagle's dark brown chest, the sharp tip sticking out its back.

The bird thudded to the ground. Its talons frantically raked the air before it went limp. For some unknown reason, a deep remorse gnawed at him. Had Sai'er's life not been at stake, he'd probably have had second thoughts on loosing the arrow. Looking at the lifeless majestic bird, he felt a strange bond that somehow connected them.

Two imperial guards rushed at Binhong and tackled him.

5

A PEREMPTORY voice behind the mist boomed, "Bring them to me, alive!"

Sai'er and Binhong had their hands bound behind them and were made to kneel on the gravelly landing.

A strong gust of wind blew over and the mist retreated. Above them was an azure sky newly cleansed by rain. Rays of the setting sun brushed a layer of glittering gold on people and scenery, making them look larger than life.

Looming over them was a regal-looking man atop a black stallion, shod in soft leather boots and clad in a luxurious felt tunic underneath a metal-plated vest, hands gloved in gauntlets. He looked dark, witheringly imperious and grim. An imposing entourage of fully-armed guards on horseback fanned out in a half circle behind him.

The tallest of the guards shot daggers at Binhong and growled, "Do you know what you've done? You've just murdered His Highness's favorite hunting eagle!"

Binhong retorted, "The eagle could've killed my foster sister if not stopped!"

"How dare—" Before the Chief Guard could finish his sentence, the solemn-faced princely figure raised his hand, "My eagle is well-trained and would not harm people. You had no cause to kill it."

Sai'er was incensed. Her scalp was still burning from the eagle's deadly pull. "Monkey Sage," she uttered under her breath. Then she spitted out each word in barely controlled rage, "Your Highness's pet eagle was attacking me. This is my lucky day. My foster brother reacted just in time to save me from being scalped. I offer my apology to you for his impertinent response, and I'm deeply sorry for the loss of your pet."

The image of Sky Wolf surged unbidden through her head. She couldn't have been mistaken. She had had a previous connection with him. How she had at once been drawn to and repulsed by that overbearing and chiseled face! *But where, and how were we connected?*

She leaned over and whispered in Binhong's ear, "It's the Prince of Yan."

His sharp wolfish eyes roved haughtily over Sai'er. She did not avert hers and looked straight into his. His mask of stiff iciness melted slightly when their gazes met, as if a memory came up, but reassembled itself in a heartbeat.

"You are free to go. But the lad cannot escape punishment. He will get fifty lashes of the whip," he commanded, expressionless.

"No, you can't punish an innocent person. What crime has he committed?" Sai'er shouted in a high-pitched voice in exasperation. "Why is it a crime to save another person from a vicious attack?"

The Prince of Yan looked stumped for an answer. But pride and disdain only augmented his resolve. "Guards, start the whipping, now!" Sai'er's heart gave a lurch. She struggled to free her hands from the twine, beads of sweat starting to cover her forehead.

"The young lad does not deserve this!" A distant voice echoed in the low-hanging clouds. "Besides, these are sacred grounds. I do not wish to see any trace of animosity here."

The next instant a large white shape seemed to be gliding forward weightlessly on the clouds. On closer look, it was a robust-looking, slightly hunched old man with a snow-white billowing mane and long flowing white beard, his big long ears protruding from both sides of a taut smooth face, illumined by a pair of round, shiny eyes that resembled lapis lazuli.

Wow, so Master Zhang really can fly, Sai'er thought with a burst of triumphant delight.

To her utter surprise, the snobbish Prince turned to the guard holding the whip and said with resignation, "Stand down." Then he dismounted and brought his hands together in a deep bow to the Master, "Master Zhang, I apologize if you take offense at my intended action. I didn't mean any harm to the girl. If it pleases you, I will order the release of them both."

"Ha ha! Do as you please, it's your decision. I'm not asking for a favor!" The Master chuckled, as if he could see through the Prince's mind.

"Oh, no, no. Of course it's not a favor, Master. I want to do this."

"Good, good! I owe you nothing then! Have a safe trip home, son. Farewell now!" He waved his tapered fingers like a child. The Prince snatched the reins of his stallion and swaggered down the steps. His platoon followed his lead in mute obedience.

Sai'er had just set down her belongings in the small guest room on the east wing of the central courtyard. Binhong's room was next to hers. When she came out to the courtyard, Binhong had just stepped in from the backyard, having hitched the horses in the stable and fed them. Together they went in to the sparsely furnished living room to take tea with their new kung fu teacher.

Sanbao was sitting next to Master Zhang, pouring tea into terra cotta cups already laid out on the bamboo table.

He looked up and smiled at her. "Sai'er, Come take a seat. I can't believe we're fellow students!" He gestured for her to sit next to him like she was an old friend. She just hoped no one noticed her dopey smile.

Binhong pulled a long face. She couldn't put a finger on why. He went up and plumped himself down on the remaining bamboo stool. He ignored Sanbao and bowed his head in Master Zhang's direction. "Great Grandba Master, thank you so much for saving us from trouble today. We were lucky that you arrived in the nick of time."

"Haw haw, no problem at all. The Prince was in a bad mood because I had earlier turned down his generous offer. But setting his eagle on Sai'er or anyone else just to let out steam was uncalled for, no matter how angry he is. Tough luck for him that you're a good archer! Haha!"

"But how did you know that he did it on purpose?"

"Can you not see these big ears of mine? Hahaha! I can hear people's whispers from many li away. The Prince's cooing to his eagle didn't escape me!"

"Great Grandba Master, thank you for coming to our rescue," Sai'er said politely. "We're also very grateful that you have accepted us as your students." While gazing at Sanbao out of the corner of her eye, she continued, "You don't know how much this means to us, especially me! Also, my father sends his warmest regards."

"Pray lose the Great Grandba stuff, Children. My students all just call me Master. I hate formalities," he rolled his eyes like an impish boy. With relish, he continued,

"Sai'er, I hear you are quite adept at the Sword-as-Whip skill. Good for you. Its essence is to let flexibility of the sword deceive the opponent. A fragile-looking girl with mastery of this skill is like a double decoy. Softness hides a nasty surprise! If you attain the apex level of neigong to facilitate this sword skill, then you may be able to take down the best of my students yet! Presently, that laurel goes to Monk Yao, the Prince's adviser."

So Ba was right to push me to learn this sword skill.

The white-haired Master swept his gaze around the table and said gaily, "Drink your tea, everyone. This tea is made with water from the meadow lake. The tea leaves are dried bamboo leaves."

He nodded his head at Sanbao and continued, "Sanbao hauls up ten pails of water from that lake every day. Starting from tomorrow at break of dawn, Sai'er, Binhong, you will each haul five pails, increasing to ten after a month. Now after tea, you children go and clean yourselves up. We'll have supper in the Second Hour of the Rooster. Yinho, my adoptee, has prepared a welcome meal in honor of the two new students."

As soon as the Master left the room, Sai'er turned to Sanbao and babbled away, "I can't thank you enough for the book you gave me. There couldn't have been a handier manual for me and Binhong. It totally saved us from a rut in our neigong practice. The drawings make things so much easier to understand."

"Don't mention it. I'm glad you found it useful." He looked her up and down with genuine concern and said, "Are you hurt anywhere? Master Zhang told me what happened just now."

"Oh no, I'm quite alright. Don't you worry about me. I'm really happy to see you again."

"Don't you ever forget that Sai'er is *my* sister," Binhong rumbled with a scowl. "I'd advise you to quit leering at her and keep your distance." He was putting on a more solemn air than he could carry. "If you dare so much as put one dirty finger on her, I'll chop you up in pieces."

"Oh, I'm pleased to meet you, Binhong. I trust Sai'er told you how we had met," Sanbao said politely, ignoring his threat.

"I only know you work for that evil Prince," he kept up with his gruff manner, and added, "Count on it, I'll keep a close watch on you." Then he stormed off to his room in a huff.

"Please don't mind him, Sanbao. He has a softer heart than he lets on." Sai'er was just glad that she was at last left alone with him.

"Sanbao, what on earth led the Prince here, of all places? This must be the remotest corner of the whole wide world!"

"Well, hunting is one of his hobbies. He was on a hunting expedition in the district and thought fit to drop by to see if he could persuade Master Zhang to work for him. He offered him the position of Chief Military Coach in his fief," he paused and pinched his brow. "Probably he was also here to check up on me—"

"I remember you told me that you're just the Prince's chattel. Can you explain it to me and tell me more about him?"

A rugged terrain of pain unfolded across his face, just like that night when they had first met.

"When they captured me, they castrated me and sent me to wait on him. If he's in a good mood, he would play me like a toy. If he's in a bad mood, I'd just be his punching bag."

His eyes glazed over with tears. The last veneer of composure crumbled as he stuttered, "One time, Monk Yao showed up late on the scene—he had flogged me to within an inch of my life."

When his heaving sobs subsided, he drew a deep cleansing breath to force a wry smile. "The only time I could feel alive was when I fought in the battlefield. It's kind of ironic. Killing has become a way to prove my worth to myself—" his voice trailed off.

Sai'er didn't know what to do, except to pat him lightly on his back. She didn't get all the meaning of what he said, but his pain etched itself so deep in her heart that she felt it like her own. She was disgusted with herself for having ever felt attracted to the monster. *How could that even be possible?*

"I'm really sorry to hear this, Sanbao. Thank you for sharing with me. Take comfort that at least Monk Yao is there for you. There has to be a way out—" After a moment of pondering, she said with a spurt of energy, "Hmm, maybe you could persuade the Prince through Monk Yao to send you away on some distant mission. It's just a thought."

Sanbao's eyes lit up at the idea. "How come it has never dawned on me! It's a brilliant idea," then the light dimmed just as quickly. "Thank you, Sai'er. You're very wise. But he'd turn it down on a whim."

"Sanbao, you mustn't give up hope. Perhaps give him something he wants badly. You can do it!" Sai'er was thinking of how Master Zhang had earlier ridiculed the Prince's calculating trait.

"Yes, Sai'er. It's worth a try."

At supper time, Yinho served up a sumptuous meal of salted chicken, braised jicama roots with preserved pork, deep-fried taro root crisps and stir-fried bamboo shoots, with bowls of millet gruel to wash down the greasy food. The tasty home-cooking took the edge off the newcomers' homesick feeling and made them feel welcomed. Sai'er especially loved the taro root crisps.

That night, Sai'er tossed and turned in the bamboo framed bed and couldn't sleep. She sat up and wrapped her arms around her drawn up legs. She so wished to talk to Caihe that she unconsciously mouthed its name.

A flash of light preceded its appearance, just like the last time.

"So, what's troubling you now?" The sprite asked lightly while nestling itself on her shoulder. "Let me guess. You're confused about your mixed feelings towards the Prince of Yan. Am I right?"

"Yes—No—Yes. I don't know—"

"Well, that's because you two have a history dating back to your immortal lives in the Pantheons. Come with me and I'll show you."

Without waiting for her answer, the sprite pinched the sleeve of Sai'er's hemp robe and lifted her up and out the room into the courtyard.

In a twinkle, she was floating up and into the obsidian night sky, spangled with glimmering stars, with Caihe as her navigator. Two sensations alternately dipped her in and lifted her out of a hypnotic trance: her dream-like glide through air like a bird and the sobering kiss of cool breezes on her face, hair and limbs.

"We're going to pay a visit to the Weaving Maid, granddaughter of the Jade Emperor, Ruler of the Central Pantheon. You and Sky Wolf had an encounter on the Queen Mother's birthday, and she heard a conversation between you two."

Caihe's voice was like a resounding echo, as the sprite steered her through billowing folds of clouds. When Sai'er looked down, she saw a foaming, rolling white ocean, with no beginning or end. She felt dizzy like she had had a surfeit of sorghum wine.

When they arrived at the Heavenly Gates, the two Thunderbolt Guards threw a glance at Caihe and let them pass through. As a rule, mortals were not allowed to enter the Pantheons unless accompanied by an immortal.

Having wended through a labyrinth of gilded hallways in the East Pantheon, they found the Weaving Maid in her Silk Palace. She was in the silk-woven aviary feeding her lovely magpies.

Every year, on the seventh day of the seventh lunar month, the magpies would range themselves into a bridge across the Silver River, so that the Weaving Maid could reunite with Cowherd, her husband. The Queen Mother had imposed this as a punishment on the couple for indulging in love and neglecting

48

their duty. Sai'er recalled having felt sorry for the pair.

The place looked strangely familiar. Sai'er remembered that the Moon Palace, her heavenly abode, was just next door.

Caihe told the Weaving Maid the purpose of the visit. When she saw Sai'er, she smiled like a budding flower. "My dearest sister! It's so good to see you."

"It's good to see you too, Sister! Sorry to disturb your work."

"I'm so happy you're here, Chang'e! You don't know how lonely I've been since you left for the mortal world. Now, make yourselves comfortable, you two. About that day, where should I begin?"

6

ON THAT DAY, all the Deities from the Central, East, West, North and South Pantheon had gathered at the Magic Peach Garden to attend the Queen Mother's birthday banquet.

The Ruler of each Pantheon — the Jade Emperor, Supreme Immortal of the Tao, Shakyamuni Buddha, Xuan Wu and Longevity — took their respective opal seats around a large emerald table reserved for them on the high marble dais spanning the north side of the Garden.

At the center was the Jade Pond. Its luscious sweet water had been nurturing the Magic Peach Trees that enwreathed the Garden for celestial ages. A few white cranes were frolicking in the lotus-filled pond.

Festoons of rainbow-like ribbons were hung linking tree with tree. Perching on treetops were phoenixes of prismatic colors wagging their seductive tendrilled tails.

These trees yield fruit only once every three thousand years, and the Queen Mother's birthday falls on the peach-picking day.

The five Bodhisattvas — Guanyin, Wenshu, Puxian, Dizang and Maitreya — along with Xuannu the Warrior Goddess, the Eight Immortals, Three-Eyed Erlang Shen, Sun Wukong, Sand Monk, and other lesser immortals were all comfortably ensconced in floating seats molded out of fluffy clouds adorned with filigrees of silver stars, ranged in a large circle around the

Jade Pond.

Dressed in floral silks and satins, fox nymphs were bustling among the guests, offering cups of heavenly nectar and plates of rare fruit and sweet meats. Everyone was caught up in the festive spirit amidst laughter and banter.

A sudden flap of wings halted the buzz. It heralded the arrival of the banquet hostess, and music nymphs began to play empyrean tunes on their crystal and silver lutes.

The Queen Mother of the West usually resided in the Kunlun Mountains, nestled in the westernmost corner of the universe, and she only graced the Magic Peach Garden to host her birthday banquet.

As befitted her revered status, she made a spectacular entrance, riding with panache on the back of her majestic Blue Bird, its long silvery blue tail wiggling gracefully. Those electrifying eyes of hers could stupefy anyone coming into contact with them. Fox nymphs skittered along to help the hostess dismount and ushered her to the white jade host seat at the Rulers' table.

True to custom, the Queen Mother asked Lan Caihe to perform the famous stomp song and dance accompanied by castanets. The sprite capered and stomped in cadence with verve, showering flower petals on the guests as it hopped around. All the guests loved it and responded with thunderous applause at the end of the show.

"Where's Nezha? Has anyone seen him?" Li Jing, Nezha's father, was asking as he paced impatiently around throngs of guests.

"Not today. He's probably still gallivanting about on earth. Should be with The Prince of Yan," Wukong volunteered with a shrug. Sun Wukong was now a Senior Marshal in the North Pantheon, after he had dutifully accomplished his earthly mission as Monk Xuanzang's personal guard on his pilgrimage to the West to obtain the Buddhist Scriptures.

The Weaving Maid and Chang'e happened to be seated between Wukong and Longevity, who had come down from the Rulers' table to mingle with the crowd.

"Talking of the Prince, or Sky Wolf, raping two fox nymphs is a heinous crime," the Weaving Maid chimed in with her opinion. "Demotion to mortal prince status is far too light a punishment. Hardly what he deserves." She was always a champion of vulnerable nymphs. Chang'e kept her silence, unwilling to be drawn into the conversation.

"I'll never understand why our Ruler pleaded for leniency on his behalf with the Jade Emperor," Wukong sneered with his signature smirk. "No one pleaded for me when I was sentenced to be crammed under the Five-Finger Mountain." He was seemingly ruffled by Sky Wolf's commuted penalty.

"But at least Shakyamuni Buddha interceded for your release and sent you on your earthly mission," the Weaving Maid reminded him. "You should be pleased the success of that mission elevated you to the North Pantheon."

"Unfortunately, Sky Wolf's hubristic nature is hard to correct," drawled Longevity, as he vigorously bobbed his deeply wrinkled enormous head. "Access to too much power in the mortal world will only inflate his already bloated ego, making him a menace to humanity. Now Chang'e has a hard task on her hands."

"She needs all the help she can get," said the Weaving Maid.

"Our Ruler has already assigned Zhang Sanfeng to teach her superior martial arts," Wukong replied with lethargy, looking askance at Chang'e.

Guanyin was sauntering by and stumbled on the conversation. With the kindest smile she muttered softly, "Let's all pray that mercy will prevail over might on earth."

Three strikes of the gong reverberated throughout the entire

Garden. Distribution of the Magic Peaches, the major event of the day, came next.

The Peaches had been plucked that morning and were placed in baskets made with plaited green silk. As usual, fox nymphs helped with handing out the Peaches. Each Pantheon Ruler would get two, while other Gods, Goddesses and Immortals would each get one. A Magic Peach would bestow celestial power on the recipient. With it, a Deity could either wield magic two times or create one mortal being.

When the Queen Mother spotted Chang'e, she descended from the dais, took two Peaches from one of the baskets and approached her with a smile. She gestured for her to step to a quiet side of the Pond.

"Chang'e, as you will soon depart for the earthly realm for a good cause, I'm going to grant you two Magic Peaches. You can turn one of these into a loyal friend in your future mortal life."

Chang'e thanked the gracious hostess profusely and, feeling a bit fatigued, left the banquet early.

Sky Wolf, who had already assumed mortal status as a Ming prince, had snuck unseen into the Garden, using his Magic Peach to make himself invisible. The moment he spied Chang'e leaving the banquet, he bolted ahead of her.

On her way back to the Moon Palace, Chang'e met the Weaving Maid, who had also left the banquet. Chang'e told her about the extra Magic Peach. The Weaving Maid said, "I know Sky Hawk is due to be reincarnated as human soon. Why don't you use your extra Peach to turn him into your mortal friend?" Chang'e thanked her for the prudent advice.

The Weaving Maid parted with Chang'e and headed to her Silk Palace. As she entered the hallway, she found Jade Rabbit squatting in a corner. It was huffing and puffing like mad: "That rascal Sky Wolf has chased me out and is hiding in the Moon

Palace. He's up to nothing good, I dare say. I worry for my mistress."

It was then that she knew Sky Wolf was lying in wait for Chang'e. But it was already too late to warn her. She was eager, though, to find out what Sky Wolf was up to. Immediately, she headed to the Moon Palace.

By then Chang'e was just stepping inside the antechamber. The Weaving Maid tiptoed behind her and hid in the Jade Rabbit's workplace, which was adjacent to Chang'e's antechamber and separated by a wood panel with a latticed upper part mounted with silk. The room was unlit and so, from her crouching position, she could see and hear everything in Chang'e's room without being seen.

"What—what are you doing here, Deputy General? Aren't you already in the mortal world?" Her face went livid with shock when she saw the handsome renegade.

"So what if I am? I have an immortal friend who was glad to transport me here," he said with a preening grin, his eyes riveted on her.

Chang'e blushed a deep pink. She'd always had a soft spot for this good-looking, daredevil of a warrior. He'd also been hankering after her for a long time. Any young goddess or nymph would be flustered by such flattery, and Chang'e was no exception. It did feed her vanity. Yet, his lewd misdemeanors were cause for her to resist his advances, at least on the surface.

"How did you sneak in here?" She was trying hard to put on an indifferent air. "And who's the immortal whom you bribed into taking you through the Gates?"

"Hey, what do you think? I have my Magic Peach," he gloated with a sly smile. "Nezha has always been my good and loyal friend. I thought you knew that. He's happy to do my bidding."

The next instant he was breathing down her neck. Pressing

her close to him, he lifted her chin with a finger, forcing her to look at him. "I know you believed in my innocence. Tell me, sweet maiden, did you miss me while I was gone? I hear you and I will soon meet in the mortal realm!"

She was trembling like a rabbit brought to bay. His look was a mix of condescension and wronged righteousness. That finely chiseled face painted with arrogance was an alluring trap she felt powerless to dodge. His wild, possessive gaze was hunting for morsels of her soul.

The Weaving Maid was whispering to herself in her hiding place, "We've discussed this, Chang'e! Don't give in to his seduction. Don't believe his slick lies."

"Can you look me in the eye and say you did not rape the fox nymphs?" At last Chang'e mustered up her courage and asked the piercing question.

"I swear on my immortal life that what I told you is the whole truth. The nymphs were blindfolded when it happened, and there were no eye witnesses. The rapist was Sun Wukong! That low life framed me because he craves my position as Deputy General. He has always drooled over it, no doubt encouraged by Erlang Shen!"

"Then how come both nymphs pointed fingers at you?"

"That's because they are prejudiced. I've always been saucy with them, like with other pretty nymphs, and so they jumped to conclusions. You have to believe me."

Catching her off guard, he forced kisses on her lips and throat. "I love you, Chang'e! I'll never be able to love anyone else. Say you love me too or I'll die!"

She tried half-heartedly to wriggle free of his embrace. He tightened his clasp on her. Drowning in his lustrous eyes, she could only manage a flaccid struggle. His hand wandered over her lithe body with insolence.

The Weaving Maid cursed in silence in the next room.

Nezha, who was in the hallway keeping an eye out for Sky Wolf, knocked on the door and said under his breath, "The Thunderbolt Guards are making the rounds. I have to get you out of here and back down to earth."

When the Weaving Maid finished recounting the day's happenings, fragments of Chang'e's memory began falling into place to form a whole picture of that single day. All her feelings came roaring back to besiege her. It felt like it had all happened just the day before. She could taste his hot lips on hers, feel his warm, hard body against hers. The tempo of her heartbeat quickened to a dizzying pace. At last she understood that tangled feeling of fitful misgivings and feverish yearning that had afflicted her mortal soul.

Was he wrongfully accused as he claimed? Was it true that Sun Wukong had framed him on the debauchery charge, so he could clinch the position of Deputy General? I was never able to conclude even after the Jade Emperor had delivered a guilty verdict.

"I see you're not convinced of Sky Wolf's crime," the Weaving Maid said. She sighed and shook her head.

"The curse he invoked in his vow is pretty harsh," Sai'er stammered.

He swore on his immortal life. That is a serious oath and its evocation means he can never resume his immortal life once his mortal one ends. His vow will condemn him to an eternal limbo where re-incarnation is not allowed. Why would he do such a thing, except to resolutely avow his innocence to me?

"You feel what you feel. There's no point denying it. I don't blame you," Caihe said with great patience. "But don't worry, Sai'er. Let time and experience guide you. Now let me take you back down to earth."

On their way down, Sai'er asked the sprite, "I remember I used one Magic Peach to create Binhong out of Sky Hawk before my departure from the Pantheons. But where is my other Peach?"

"Ah, good question. This is one thing I meant to tell you but forgot. At your birth, clutched in your little fist was an amber stone. That's your other Magic Peach. Your mother buried the stone in the backyard underneath the maple tree."

When Sai'er woke up in the morning, her eyes were bleary with fatigue, feeling like she had not slept at all. A knock on the door jerked her awake. She knew it was Binhong. "Monkey Sage! I have to haul water from the lake!"

She hated it when she saw Binhong use one hand to lug a brimming pail of water up the two hundred stone steps as if it were just a basket of vegetables. Each step up with the full pail was a physical exertion for her. By the time she reached the top, she had spilled almost a third of the water. Four more pails to go! This was one of those times that she wished she were born a boy.

Binhong finished the hauling of five pails when she was slogging up the steps with the third pail. By the time she finished, Sanbao had hauled up ten pails. The water was deposited in a large man-made pond on the wooded side of the vegetable and millet fields, which were tended by Yinho.

Both her hands were blistered, which would make the days following a painful torture if Binhong hadn't brought with him the most effective minty balm for such sores.

By mid-morning, Master Zhang showed up to watch the three students practice breathing and meditation while taking the horse stance position.

This seemed easy enough, but in reality it was much harder than hauling water. One had to maintain the squat position with a straight back and hands held in front in a circle, and hold this position for a joss stick's burning time, while breathing in and out evenly and keeping the mind blank. The Master would walk around with his wooden staff and would use it to point out mistakes when he saw them.

By the time Sai'er finished the session, every muscle in her began to ache and shake from the exertion.

In early afternoon, they were required to run three times around the vegetable and millet fields at the back of the cottage. Then they gathered in the open field in front of the cottage to do stretches, side squats, front squats, squat jumps, frog leaps up the two-hundred-step stairway, front kicks, side kicks, crescent kicks and back kicks.

The latter part of the afternoon was devoted to sword dueling in the front courtyard. Each student fought the other two in three succeeding rounds, using the Sword-as-Whip technique.

When it was Binhong's turn to fight Sanbao, he became extra aggressive. But Sanbao effortlessly deflected all his offensive moves and countered with qi-empowered winning strikes, which made Binhong grit his teeth. In the final round, Binhong was quickly subdued in the third move.

In a fit of blinding rage, he launched a strike from behind when Sanbao turned his back to sheath his sword. The Master flicked his staff just in time to deflect Binhong's sword. It flew to the ground and ricocheted.

"No honorable swordsman would ever do such a thing," he reprimanded him in a grave tone. "Anger will impede you from attaining perfection in this skill."

Binhong bit his lower lip and hung his head low in apparent self-reproach. Sai'er thought it better to leave him to sulk alone rather than try to comfort him.

Duels between Sai'er and Sanbao turned out to be fights between equals. What Sai'er lacked in physical height and brute strength, she made up with nimble footwork and range control in defensives, and timely and focused projection of qi to her sword in offensives.

"Good work, Sai'er! I didn't know your sword skills were so advanced already," the Master clapped his hands with a grin.

At supper time, Sai'er was so famished that she stuffed herself on fried eggs and stir-fried cabbages, washing it all down with three bowls of millet gruel.

"The eggs taste heavenly. I could live on this alone," Binhong mumbled with his mouth full.

Yinho told him that the eggs were collected fresh that morning from the big fat hens he reared in the backyard.

Binhong topped Sai'er by two bowls of gruel and scraped the dishes clean.

After supper, the Master ordered, "Starting from tomorrow, Yinho and all students will take turn in cooking daily meals."

Alone at last in her room, she found that her muscles ached so much she couldn't even bend her legs while trying to get out of her pants. She would have to sleep in them, soiled as they were. After she finished scrubbing herself thoroughly with a soaked cloth, fatigue caught up with her. She rolled onto the bed and the next instant fell into deep sleep.

Ten days later, one night, before turning in, Sai'er went to Binhong's room to clear the air about Sanbao.

"Binhong, I know you're bearing a grudge against Sanbao. But he's not the bad person you think he is."

"The way you look at him, anyone can see you have a soft spot for him."

"No—that's not true," she faltered, her ears turning hot. "It's just that we understand each other. Listen to me, Sanbao has a painful past. He was made a eunuch in his childhood. It was not his choice to serve the Prince. They forced him. The worst thing is the Prince mistreats him."

Binhong was silent for a moment, shook his head and said, "Sai'er, we all have painful pasts. It's easy enough to make one up. I promised Uncle to protect you. So I must be vigilant around strangers, especially those with close connections to the Imperials. You're young and always too trusting."

"I'm nearly sixteen and I can look out for myself," she brushed him off lightly. Nothing annoyed her more than being treated like a child.

"Remember what Uncle said? You must do as I advise. I only ask that you keep your eyes open. That's all. I know what I did today was rash. From now on I'll keep my temper in check. This I can promise you."

"Are you jealous of him?"

"Why would I be—he's not even a man," he chortled with contempt, lips curving into a smirk.

Do you have to be so mean? "Eunuchs are humans too, you know. I hope in time you'll see him in a different light."

"I just don't see anything in him that I like. He's not even that good at martial arts."

With the rediscovery that Binhong was Sky Hawk incarnate, there were no doubt times when she felt she owed him a big debt of gratitude for his unquestioning loyalty. But this was not one of those times. *He couldn't be more wrong about Sanbao!*

She had always known that once he formed an opinion about a person, he could be as stubborn as a mule. There was no point in trying to win him over.

"It seems we have to agree that we hold different opinions. Good night."

Training activities and the cooking arrangement would become a routine for the next six months.

7

YINHO WAS BORN in the same year as Binhong, only younger by a few months. Like him, he had been orphaned as a toddler.

His parents were from Yidu county in Shandong and had been executed by severing at the waist, on a charge of affiliation to a teacher accused of possessing seditious writings. Affiliation in this case meant that the couple just happened to have attended the accused teacher's lectures for a few times. It was the notorious Embroidered Uniform Guards who had brought on the nebulous charge. These Guards were the Emperor's personal spies who habitually rode roughshod over common folks.

On the day of their execution, Master Zhang was passing by the town square, and the husband secretly shoved a note in his hand. The note said the couple had a two-year-old son, who had been left in the Bamboo Grove Taoist Nunnery in the Yidu suburb to escape the Guards' search. The Master went and fetched the toddler, and brought him here to raise as his own. When the child reached his teens, Master Zhang told him the story of his parents' violent death.

By now, Sai'er and Binhong knew better than to bring up names of the Zhu Imperial clan members in front of Yinho. He would turn grisly dark with wrath. Other than that taboo, he was ordinarily cheerful and easy enough to get along with. His tacit dislike for Sanbao and a growing affinity for Binhong was quite obvious to Sai'er.

He was of tall, lanky build with super long limbs and had learned to master the use of spears in his teens. He was also skilled at Wave Treading qinggong, having attained a master level of neigong through self-cultivation. The Master sometimes called him "Flying Spear".

Six months had come and gone. One day, the Master summoned all three students to the lounge and announced:

"In terms of neigong skill, you've reached medium level, and Flying Spear has achieved master status. From now on, he will be your coach to take you through to the master level. Once you've achieved that, you'll be ready to learn the Wave Treading qinggong. Also, your Sword-as-Whip technique will be dramatically enhanced."

In late afternoon the next day, at the end of the sword dueling session, Yinho came out to the front courtyard to fetch the students and led them out to the pond.

As they were wondering why he took them there, he put the thumb and index finger in his mouth to whistle. Instantly a flock of black and white jacanas flew over their heads and alighted on the surface of the lily-filled pond. The water fowls were so graceful in the touchdown, their long, reedy legs and toes stretching to their full lengths as they descended on the floating lily pads.

They were all rapt with awe.

"The jacanas are our best teachers in qinggong," Yinho beamed with pride. "You've just seen how they can tread on lily pads."

"Are you saying we humans can tread on lily pads like them?" Sai'er asked in wide-eyed wonder.

Instead of answering, Yinho stepped away from the pond,

meditated in a horse stance, leaped forward and upward in one concentrated breath, knees bent and arms spread out, then shot one leg straight out followed by the other as he touched the water, and glided on toes around the pond like he was surfing waves.

After making one full circle, he bounced back to the edge of the pond, without so much as a light pant.

"These beautiful birds are nicknamed lily trotters. Our ultimate aim is to be able to do exactly what they can. But since we don't have wings or long fine toes like the birds to keep us afloat, we must therefore make up by storing qi in our dantian to propel our bodies, enabling us to levitate. So, storing qi in our dantian is the essential second step to get us there. And the first step is to sharpen our meditation capacity."

"Easier said than done. It's for a reason you're called Flying Spear," Binhong scratched his head, puzzled and awed.

Sanbao ignored Binhong's remark and offered his own observation, "In other words, if we perfected our meditation and succeeded in storing qi in our dantian, we'd reach the master level of neigong. Is that right?"

Binhong shot him a caustic look, muttering, "Smart pig!"

"That's right," Yinho replied impassively without looking at Sanbao. He then ordered with a coach's authority, "From tomorrow onwards, you'll extend your midmorning meditation session to early afternoon and cut out the jumping and kicking exercises."

Sai'er wouldn't have believed what Yinho said had she not witnessed his astounding flying feat, as well as the Master's magical cloud treading on the day she and Binhong had first arrived here. The idea of using stored qi to tread waves or clouds fascinated her to no end.

That night, while in bed, all the details of that encounter with the Prince of Yan and the Weaving Maid's subsequent recount of her chance meeting with him in the Pantheons came back to flood her mind.

Did the Prince of Yan recognize me as Chang'e that day? If he did, what was he thinking? Is he still smitten with me? I can't seem to shake off that shameless crush on him. What's wrong with me?

She hadn't revisited these events for half a year. Why did they emerge to bother her now, just when she was about to embark on the most crucial of her martial arts lessons?

Suddenly the Prince emerged in her vision in full leather lamellae armor, snugly ensconced in a golden throne seat on the dais. Next to the throne seat was a huge brass tank in which rollicked a hideous, horn-headed, serpent-like dragon with a thick scaly trunk.

The Prince said to the sorcerer in a long black robe standing at the foot of the dais, "I want victory in tomorrow's battle with sea pirates! I need help from your dragon master."

The sorcerer dipped his head in servility and replied, "His Eminence, Green Dragon of the East Sea, is the ruler of storms and floods. He would be glad to help you, if, in exchange, you could offer him a sacrifice, preferably a beautiful virgin."

"Someone like that?" The Prince pointed his finger at her. She was kneeling in the middle of the gilded palatial hall, bound in chains.

The sorcerer shot her an unnerving glance and nodded, "First she'll have to entertain His Eminence and we'll see if she pleases his eyes."

"Strip her and let her dance," the Prince ordered.

Two eunuchs went up to unlock the chains and roughly undressed her. They put a gossamer cape over her nude body and forced her to join two other half naked dancers in an erotic dance, to the beat of war drums accompanied by nomad tribal music. The Prince's glinting eyes were fixated on her.

Whenever she slowed down in her steps, the eunuchs served her a good dose of whipping. She begged them to stop. But her plea only met with glassy-eyed silence.

As the music reached a climax, the Green Dragon roared out in a grating voice. The bulging eyes of the serpentine beast dilated with lusty excitement.

Gradually the drum music softened. The Prince said to the sorcerer with a hint of remorse. "This woman was meant to be my consort. Can we offer one of the other dancers?"

"His Eminence has made his choice. If Your Highness desire victory, this is a small price to pay."

Her hearing was acute and she caught the dialogue loud and clear. Cold sweat beaded on her skin as she trembled all over. "Please let me go!" Her raspy utters only fell on deaf ears.

A red hot furnace was crackling beside a long wooden altar placed inside the bower behind the throne dais, visible through sheer curtains. The sorcerer was now chanting sacrificial prayers in the bower.

As soon as the drum music stopped, the eunuchs tumbled her to the ground and carried her over their shoulders to the altar. They tied her hands and feet to the four pegs on the edges of the altar.

The Prince stood over her with a manic grin, watching her squirm in curdling dread with perverse pleasure. He looked into her terror-stricken eyes and breathed into her face, "Beg me for mercy."

She writhed and strained futilely at her fetters. It only made him guffaw with abandon.

Finally he gave a nod to the sorcerer. Sai'er looked up and saw an eerie dark cavity where the left eye should be in the sorcerer's face. He waved his wand at the Green Dragon, uttering an eerie chant. The beast made a guttural response, viscous liquid dripping from its sharp-toothed maw. It glided out of the tank and slithered towards the bower.

No! No! Please don't! Help!

She opened her eyes slowly, coming into consciousness with a blurred memory of captivity. Every inch of her body was shaking. The pale light of dawn was prickling her eyes. Her cotton sleeping robe and undergarments were drenched in sweat. She rolled off the bed feebly, trying to feel her limbs. *Let it be a bad dream!* She prayed with all her heart it was nothing more than a sickening nightmare.

This morning, she was just glad that Sanbao and Binhong were there training beside her, providing her with much needed company. She sensed their curious stare, but refrained from making conversation. She tried hard to concentrate, with no success. The nightmare reeled in her mind nonstop.

If she was ever going to make progress in the meditation session, she must discard those degrading and distracting thoughts. But what seemed so obvious and easy a fix was actually no mean feat. It seemed she was no longer master of her own mind.

The same nightmare came back to taunt her for another four nights straight. She felt locked in the despair of wakeful bondage.

For five days in a row, she couldn't get her act together in the lengthened meditation session.

She had never shared with Binhong her celestial trip or her gripping infatuation with the Prince, fearing he might chastise her. Nor was she going to. To talk to him about her immodest feelings for a man was inconceivable, let alone feelings for the Prince, whom he hated like pestilence. There was no way he could begin to understand her nightmares and her anguish.

On the sixth night, she decided to seek the Master's help before going to bed.

It was Binhong's turn to cook. After the meal, Yinho helped him with the washing up. Sanbao retired to his room. So, she quietly followed the Master out to the front courtyard. It was his habit to do a little reading at this twilight time.

"Can I talk to you, Master?"

"Sure, dear child. You look deprived of sleep. Something bothering you? You were awfully quiet at supper." His affectionate smile broke the ice and gave her courage to spill her guts.

She told him all about her first encounter with Lan Caihe, the trip to the Pantheons, the Weaving Maid's recount and, lastly, her nightmares of late, which were interfering with her meditation session.

As he was listening, the light in his lapis lazuli eyes flickered.

"My dear girl, I've been expecting you to reach out. For two nights I saw you sleep-walking outside of your bed chamber, and I surmised you were hit with a hex. It's obvious someone wants to snag your learning progress."

"Who would do such a thing, and why?"

"A reasonable guess would be someone who doesn't want to see you excel in the martial arts. This person is well trained in Shamanist black magic."

So she could safely rule out Sanbao, Binhong and Yinho. Not that she would suspect any of them. As for immortals, of course Caihe wouldn't do such a thing to her.

"Whoever that is, Master, is there a way to undo the hex?"

"I know someone who could do it, but then whoever cast the hex on you would get to identify that person and would turn his wrath on him —" He got interrupted when Yinho came near him with a cup of tea. When he went back inside the lounge, he left the lounge door open.

Sai'er said, "I wouldn't wish anyone to face the Prince's wrath because of me."

"Hmm," the Master was deep in thought. "You did say that the Prince was a main actor in your dreams, did you not?"

"Yes, he was prominently present all the time. In fact, he was the director of the whole drama."

"Then I'm quite certain he's the culprit. Because a hex is only effective when there's emotional connection between the predator and the prey, or when the predator has a portrait of the prey along with the birth date and time. Given the history of your love relationship with Sky Wolf in the immortal world, the feelings you had for each other can easily be rekindled here on earth. A gaze is all it takes to set off the passion anew. Once that happens, he can work with Shamanist black magic to control your mind with a hex, even from a distance. The Green Dragon is his immortal twin, whose usual habitat is the Crystal Palace in the East Sea, which is part of the underworld."

A spasm of gut-twisting fear seized Sai'er at that instant. *He and I did exchange gazes on that day of my arrival! He knew I was Chang'e!*

"If you have a Magic Peach, you can actually use it to eradicate the hex."

Sai'er recalled that she had an amber stone buried in the backyard of her home. But too bad home was thousands of li away. Her shoulders slumped in desolation.

Yinho reappeared at this point. He looked at Sai'er with sympathy in his eyes.

"I couldn't help overhearing your conversation about the hex. I know something about hexes."

"Flying Spear is the person I had in mind," said the Master.

"When he was twelve, by accident he had stumbled upon a book of sorcery in the Xuan Wu Temple inside the forest. I wouldn't have let him practice this craft if I weren't sure of his pristine character. And I didn't mention him because of fear that his involvement might bring him harm."

"Master, you don't have to worry about me. I'll be invoking the power of the Chief General Erlang Shen, who ranks above Sky Wolf — the Prince's immortal — who was only a Deputy. He'll keep me safe," Yinho said with a reassuring smile.

He then led Sai'er to the backyard so as not to arouse attention from Binhong and Sanbao. Within moments, he had set up a ritual altar, with three small burners into which he placed burning joss sticks. He asked her for her year, date and hour of birth, and wrote these and her name on a yellow talisman.

While writing, he tilted his head and said, "When I saw your face five days ago, I guessed you'd been hexed. Over the last few days, I saw you sleep walking in the early hours and was even more certain."

"Thank you for doing this, Yinho. I appreciate it."

"No problem. Doing anything that can rile the Zhu family would give me pleasure."

"How did you know that the Prince was Sky Wolf?"

"Please forgive me for eavesdropping just now." His ears turned red as he confessed. "I also happen to be familiar with names and ranks of the North Pantheon immortals, because Master and I worship Xuan Wu the Warrior God."

"Whatever you're doing, it won't hurt the Prince, will it?"

"Not if he's smart enough to figure out who his opponent is. But how come — I would've thought you'd hate him after what he's done to you."

"It's hard to explain," Sai'er's face became hot with embarrassment. "I want to believe that there's a reason to explain

69

the dark side of a person. Maybe something happened to him in the early years of his mortal life that turned him into the man he is now."

"You have too good a heart. I wish I could believe the same," his face warped into a nasty scowl, so incongruous with his gentle features. "The Peasant Emperor and the Zhu family are the bane of my life. To tell you the truth, I live for the day when I will avenge my parents. He and his descendants will pay in blood."

She patted him on the back, wishing she could come up with comforting words.

Kneeling behind the altar and bowing his head three times, he began the ritual. In his right hand he held a peach-wood sword and in his left the talisman. Chanting incantations, he flicked the sword left and right many times, and then in circles. Finally, he touched the sword tip on the talisman.

Lightening flickered in the maw of the night sky. Gusts of wind wailed as if they were calling on the Pantheons for help. More lightening flashes, followed by a series of rumbling thunderclaps. Then a dog's howling could be heard echoing from way up in the nebulous vault.

Everything went quiet.

Yinho turned to Sai'er and said, "That was Erlang Shen's Howling Dog signaling that the Chief General has acknowledged our petition." He handed her the talisman. "Take this and place it at the head of your bed. The Prince's hex can't touch you as long as you have this by your side at night time. This is the best I can do. The hex can't be entirely erased, unless you use celestial magic."

When she was back in her room, she pinned the talisman on the outer bamboo bed pole at the head and climbed into bed. Her eyes were heavy with sleepiness. As she was lying down, a whiff of air first flicked the bedside oil lamp light, then flipped the paper talisman like an invisible hand. Almost immediately she heard the Howling Dog's vicious snarl in response. Calm and quiet returned.

She fell into deep, restful sleep for the first time since the nightmares began.

The next morning she woke up fresh and well rested.

During the meditation session, with some effort, she was able to push out all distracting thoughts and keep her mind blank for a joss stick's burning time. Her control over her breathing and her mental acuity improved progressively in the following days.

At the end of the third month's lessons under Yinho's coaching, all three students passed the test of meditation adeptness and were able to store qi in their dantian. They reached the master level of neigong.

Of the three, Sai'er's aptitude surpassed her fellow students. She was actually ahead of Yinho in this skill. She knew that her strength lay in her knack for connecting with her inner self, being always a quiet and inward-looking person. Plus she had a perfect object to focus her mind on during meditation: the Laughing Buddha. It was a symbol of hope and positivity that helped to bring peace to her mind. This made it easy for her to direct qi to her dantian at will.

With her impeccable mastery of neigong, she now habitually came out the winner in sword dueling with Sanbao, not to mention Binhong.

The students were now ready to learn the Wave Treading qinggong technique from the Master.

Throughout the time in this hermit's mountain, Sai'er got into the habit of writing her Ba about once every three months, mostly to report on her progress in kung fu lessons and other trivial daily life matters, some involving Binhong. From his replies, she learned that Mother Lin was taking good care of him, which was a relief to her.

At times she wondered what Lin San looked like. It was hard to imagine she had once lived in the ancient world as Hou Yi's consort, before she assumed immortal life as Chang'e. Maybe beauty had indeed been one of her attributes for her to be chosen as a king's consort, and for Sky Wolf to be so smitten with her in the immortal world.

The way her Ba tried to confine her at home had always made her think she was ugly or unlikeable or too unbecoming. Not that she cared a whit about girly behavior or how she looked.

But of one thing she was certain: she had only vague memory of her relationship with Hou Yi and had absolutely no inherited feelings for him. Perhaps in that life she hadn't cared for him at all, powerful though he was. There was no way she would willingly agree to be Lin San's wife.

In this life though, she wasn't sure where she stood with the Prince. If that hex was anything to go by, it appeared that he was still desirous of her. And at the same time he was so threatened by her assigned mission that he felt the need for pre-emptive action to subdue her to his will and to curb her martial powers. No doubt Nezha on his Wind-and-Fire Wheels had been busy delivering news about her to him.

Her thoughts turned to Sanbao and her heart melted. He was like a sad and anxious poet who faced down hardship with steely fortitude without becoming jaded.

Just the day before, he had secretly given her a hand-drawn portrait in which he was handing her a stem of lotus. He had done it up beautifully in ink. All her life she hadn't owned anything of value. The portrait was like the first precious gem gifted to her.

Whenever he looked at her, it felt like a gentle breeze brushing over her heart and made her want to cry. They could both speak to each other's soul when they talked. She cared about him and would do anything to keep him from harm. More than once he had sworn to protect her. *Can this be called love? Does he desire a woman like a normal man?*

Yet she would still suffer an attack of nerves whenever the Prince's image came up. His look was always a mix of condescension and masked fragility, and for unknown reasons this rakish snob clung tight to her heart. *What kind of a person is he really? Is he evil in nature? Or is his vengeful character spawned of some early life trauma?*

She wished she knew more about him, or even came face to face with him.

Both Binhong and Yinho seemed to wear forbidding impassivity like protective armor. But it's easy for outsiders like me to judge. We simply can't fathom what losing both parents to senseless violence feels like, much less how injurious or how lasting such traumatic wounds can be.

8

ONE FINE DAY, the Master summoned the students and said, "From tomorrow for two months, you are to focus on doing frog leaps, ten times daily, from the meadow landing up the two hundred steps."

Having gone through the first year's strenuous physical training, this frog leap session was not too hard. It was vital for increasing strength of the thigh and calve muscles and the leg joints, readying them for the qinggong lessons.

When the two-month frog leap session came to an end, the Master went with the students to the pond and demonstrated to them how to expel qi stored in the dantian to lift the body in mid-air in a successive series of frog leaps.

They saw him spring forward with bent knees in one explosive breath and touch down on one lily pad with one foot, hopping to and landing another pad with the other foot, and another and another. He was leaping around the lily pond as lightly as a jaçana!

Next day he led them to the edge of the forest, where trees were more spaced out. This time Yinho also came. The Master repeated the moves on the pond, only this time he did it on tree branches, swinging from one branch to another like a free-wheeling giant white bird. They held their breath while watching.

"Wow, that's quite an acrobatic feat!" Binhong said, his mouth hanging open.

"Did you know that Master practices frog leaps at midnight every night, while we're all asleep? And he has never stopped his daily ritual of neigong training," Yinho said with unmasked pride.

"Master sets a good example for us," Sanbao said casually. But his remark drew an irritated glare from Binhong all the same.

Physically, Sai'er's small bone frame and light build gave her advantage over the male students in the qinggong practice. She was obviously a natural. But she also knew there was no shortcut to success.

With her superb neigong and persistent practice in frog leaps, she came to master the air-walking skill with relative ease in three months, even bettering Yinho by a wide stretch.

At the end of three months, she was able to do the tree-hopping, though it still needed more practice to reach perfection.

Sanbao and Binhong, whose neigong level was several notches below Sai'er's, lagged far behind her and were still at the pond-treading stage. She couldn't hold back her giggles when she watched them waver, lose their balance and plop clumsily into the water like street jesters. Binhong would go all grumpy the whole day, while Sanbao would look deflated, as if he were begging to be comforted.

Autumn quietly arrived. It was the second one since Sai'er began her apprenticeship here.

By now Binhong and Sanbao seemed to have adjusted to living alongside each other, at least with an effort at civility on Binhong's part. Sanbao appeared to be pleased enough with this development.

Since Yinho had put a stop to Sai'er's nightmares, he took a liking to her and treated her like his little sister, endowing her with the nickname "Flying Sword". He also became close friends with Binhong, often sharing jokes and stories with him.

She had made Yinho promise to keep in strict confidence her nightmares, the hex and the sorcery fix. To her dismay though, he still kept his wary distance from Sanbao.

One cool evening, after supper, Sanbao discreetly nodded Sai'er outside. He wanted to take a walk with her in the meadow.

An outline of a gibbous moon painted itself on the horizon. Homecoming birds gathered inside the copse on the opposite side of the lake, warbling heady tunes. They strolled slowly across the meadow to the lake, and found a smooth ledge on the lakeside to sit down on.

He took a folded letter from his tunic pocket and said in a trembling voice, "This is from Monk Yao relaying the Prince's summons. I have to leave for Beiping tomorrow. The Emperor has just passed away, and his grandson the Crown Prince has acceded to the throne."

Sai'er wasn't expecting the disquieting news. The first thought that jumped to mind was: *Is the Prince going to dispute his nephew's right to the throne? Are the Deities right in their prediction?*

Then her gaze met Sanbao's and reality hit. He had to go back to his demeaning life, no matter how unwilling he might be. Despondency clouded his face. There was no knowing whether they would ever meet again. Tears welled up in her eyes.

He circled his arms around her and kissed her on the forehead, the throat, then on the lips. There was passion and urgency in the kisses. He nudged her onto the grass and looked silently into her eyes. His gaze was tender and melancholic, like the dreamy fine mist in early spring. It strummed every string of her heart. There was nothing more she wanted than caress with her fingers every scab in his soul.

When she looked skyward, the cerulean vault was tinged

with lively orange and red. Blue dragonflies danced with gaiety around them. Giddiness breezed over her like a sheer silk veil.

She opened her mouth to speak, but he covered her moist lips with his. She made no effort to resist. He saw it as encouragement and untied the strings that fastened her upper garment. His eyes explored her soft, nubile curves. A tangle of desires and qualms tantalized her. His teasing touch made her heart quaver like a butterfly's beating wings.

In just a flash, Sanbao stopped cold and grimaced, as if haunted by some affliction. His hand was sliding off her breast when someone approached.

"You son of a whore! How dare you?" Binhong growled like a wounded animal. He used both hands to clutch at Sanbao's shoulders and hurled him off in one violent toss. Turning to Sai'er, he groaned, "Didn't I tell you to keep your eyes open? Some mistakes can't be reversed, do you understand?! Go back to your room, now!"

She was too flustered to word an instant retort. Pulling her garment about her, she glared at Binhong in cold anger.

"You have no say in my choice of friends," a frosty hiss escaped her clenched teeth after a short lull. "Why don't you mind your own business and leave me alone?"

Binhong ignored her and tossed to Sanbao one of the two swords he had brought with him. "You shameless bastard, how dare you? She's already betrothed. If you still have any self respect left, get up and fight me like a man!"

"You don't understand—I love Sai'er, and she loves me. I wasn't going to—" Sanbao was trying to get up, disconcerted. "Do we have to do this?"

"Binhong, you're insane! I'm not betrothed. We haven't done anything!" Sai'er was stumbling over her words.

"Only because I showed up in time. Who knows what

would've happened? I told you this low life was not to be trusted!" Binhong spat on the ground in contempt.

When he turned round to face Sanbao, Sai'er stepped lightly behind him and twined her arms around his waist, using her neigong to clasp him tight. "Go, Sanbao, leave now!"

Binhong relaxed his sword-holding arm and sighed. "Scram before I change my mind!"

Sanbao kicked away the sword on the ground and scampered towards the stairway. He turned around and shouted, "Sai'er, wait for me. I'll come to Putai to look you up."

The next day, Sanbao left at the break of dawn after saying farewell to Master, without waking the others.

After breakfast, Yinho went inside the room just vacated by Sanbao to do cleaning up. He was collecting the bed coverings in a basket when she went in. She sat down on the edge of the bed and said wistfully, "You must be glad he's gone. Maybe not as glad as Binhong."

He didn't answer, but handed her a letter. It was the letter from Monk Yao. "Did you read this? I've found it tucked inside the folds of the quilt."

"No, I didn't. Sanbao told me that it was to convey the Prince's order."

"Read it. He must've dropped it without knowing, while packing up in a hurry."

Sanbao,

The Emperor passed a month ago. The Crown Prince has been enthroned. Our chance in a life time has finally come. Our Prince needs us both to help him strategize on how to snatch the throne from the weakling. You must come back to Beiping at once on seeing this note. His Highness is pleased with your progress on baiting the girl.

Your Mentor,

Yao Guang

Sai'er felt faint when she came to the last sentence. Her chest and throat constricted in utter shock. "Are you and Binhong playing games with me? Did you two make this up?" Indignant denial seemed the only palatable option, as the alternative would be far too bitter to taste. Anger, shame and confusion flooded through her all at once.

When Yinho remained silent, reality started to bite. The piece of paper was no ordinary paper. It was luxurious xuan paper made from blue sandalwood bark, the kind used by the Imperial Court and nobility.

This was a thunderbolt revelation.

Everything Sanbao had ever said to her was one big, fat lie, right from the moment they met for the first time that hunting night! Everything was carefully contrived to trick her! Questions whirred in her head. *Why did he go to such lengths to lay this trap? Why did they target me?*

Yinho answered her unspoken questions, "You pose a real threat to Sky Wolf's worldly pursuits. The Prince certainly knows the strategic importance of keeping his enemies close. In this case, through Sanbao as an agent. It's obvious that the Prince is fully aware of your celestial mission. There's no going round this crucial fact: he considers you his nemesis." Apparently, either Binhong or Master had apprised Yinho of her Deity-assigned task.

Life had to go on somehow, even though she had no idea how to salve her bleeding heart and wounded pride.

Admitting Binhong was right all along was hard enough, not to mention having to face the cruel truth of Sanbao's betrayal, how it wrecked her self-worth. It felt like a layer of her flesh had been peeled off to reveal her squirming organs. She was a crayfish with its carapace removed. All she could think of was running to her mother and hiding in her embrace.

She couldn't look Binhong in the eyes these days, feeling too ashamed of herself.

Sometimes at night she felt like screaming her lungs out, or bang her head on the wall. How could she not detect something was very wrong with Sanbao, when Binhong and Yinho had both tried so hard to warn her of him? So many coincidences! How could she not see the signs?

During the day, she struggled to keep her mind focused on kung fu practices, at times pinching her own thigh to remind herself of the task at hand, which was to complete the apprenticeship.

Winter had tiptoed in and was gone before she knew it.

On the first day of spring, Sai'er seventeenth birthday, Yinho prepared a delicious meal with roasted quails and steamed carp, both her favorite dishes. Yinho had earlier caught the carp in the pond, and the quails were Binhong's hunting spoils.

Yinho was fast becoming Sai'er's close friend, their friendship sealed by the shared secret of the hex. Together with Binhong, they formed an infrangible trio.

After the meal, the Master gestured to Sai'er to meet him in the front courtyard.

"My dear child, I wanted to tell you that you've come to the final session of your apprenticeship," he said in a more-serious-than-usual tone. "You're the one I've chosen to teach the North Star Qi-Extracting technique, because you show the best potential at succeeding. The other reason is that you have a celestial assignment to fulfill and I've been called upon to help you."

"Master, as you're aware, my celestial mission involves the Prince of Yan. There's a question I've meant to ask you. Do you by any chance know about his childhood and upbringing?"

"As a matter of fact, I do. I was actually a witness to his father's rise as a rebel leader in his youth. The father enlisted my help in several of his uprising campaigns against the Mongols."

It turned out that the Prince of Yan, Zhu Di, was indeed the son by Mongolian Consort Gong of the Peasant Emperor, just as the rumor went. She was originally a prisoner of war enslaved by Zhu Yuanzhang during his uprising campaigns against the Mongols.

To his women and children, he was a violent spouse and father with a volatile and explosive temper. He always demanded nothing less than submissive obedience from his family.

After becoming Emperor, he treated this Mongolian slave with contempt and cruelty. Growing up, the child Zhu Di witnessed his father inflicting hurt on his mother. Later in life, the Prince got passed over in the selection of Crown Prince despite his meritorious military feats. In his mind, the obvious reason was that his father looked down on him because of his Mongolian mother.

"The bad experiences probably left him feeling ashamed of himself and resentful of his father at the same time," the Master said with a sigh. "This might have turned him into a ruthless and scheming man."

"Thank you for filling me in, Master. It's important for me to know his background. As Sunzi had said, 'Know your enemy and know yourself; then victory is at hand!' There's one question I've been pondering on. Do you think there's a chance he'll usurp the throne?"

"Ah! So you're well versed in the *Art of War*!" He chuckled as he brushed down his long white beard. "I'd say he's a man of great ambitions. If his desires are bolstered by an urge for vengeance, it's a foregone conclusion he'll do it. I know the Gods have prophesied that he will go down in history as a tyrant. But it doesn't mean one cannot change what's written. We actually have power to change our fate. I hope in time you'll be able to goad him back to the right track."

"I will take your advice to heart, Master. My more pressing goal is actually to help train up my fellow villagers in kung fu so they can protect themselves. They've long been plagued by marauding bandits and abusive officials."

"Fair enough. I applaud your good intent. Now back to the Qi-Extracting skill," the Master changed to a more light-hearted tone. "After you've mastered it, you'll be one of two female practitioners alive. The aim of this skill is to weaken the opponent's neigong by extracting qi from that person, and the prerequisite is that the drawer's neigong level must be above the opponent's." He paused for a moment to let the information sink in.

"Now listen carefully. There's a caution you must take note. If the drawer's neigong is inferior to the opponent's, then forcing this skill will cause the drawer's meridians to burst, causing deadly damage. There's also a cardinal rule in the practice of this technique, and that is, the practitioner must never use it with intent to kill the opponent."

This sounds like a hazardous skill!

Her thoughts jumped to what Ba had told her about Grandba and Monk Yao.

"Master, Ba told me that his father and Monk Yao were good friends initially, but Grandba might have suspected the monk of stealing *The Secret of Wudang Neigong* from your library. So do you know what actually happened?"

"Ah, about that. Actually I was going to say there's a third reason why I want to teach you this Qi-Extracting skill, and it has something to do with Monk Yao. Suffice it to say that I want to train up someone who will be able to surpass him in martial arts. As for the story of your grandfather and Monk Yao, there's someone else who can tell you with more authority."

"I remember that you said Monk Yao's Sword-as-Whip skill ranks topmost. I'll never be able to better him."

"Yes, but when I said that, you still lagged behind him in neigong by a wide stretch. Now that your qi-storing ability has greatly enhanced your neigong level, I'd say as of today you're very close to tying him in a sword contest. So, once you've mastered the qi-extracting skill, you'll stand a good chance in taking the first rank."

"I'm just a bit nervous —"

"Don't be. You, being a virgin, have a definite edge over men in the practice of this skill, because you possess the purest Yin qi, so your body acts like a sponge in absorbing Yang qi from male opponents with lower neigong. After absorbing the Yang qi, your own Yin qi will blend with it to become a perfect and potent qi force."

Arching one eyebrow, he added with a tinge of flippancy, "The catch, of course, is that you have to remain a virgin if you want to be first-rate in this skill. You would lose half the power if you lose your virginity."

Sai'er's thoughts shifted to that day when she and Sanbao were amorously engaged on the meadow. Binhong's angry words rang in her ears, "Who knows what would've happened?"

For all she knew, Sanbao was a fraud, and he might well have set up a trap to violate her! *There's nothing they wouldn't do to stunt my martial powers. Umm, but this would be a good excuse to use to evade Lin San. I'll never want to marry anyone anyway.*

As if seeing right through her mind, the Master said, "Sai'er, we all make mistakes. As Sunzi had once said, deception is a crucial strategy to employ in combat. Be glad that you've just learned that valuable lesson. And if you want to gain something, you have to give up something. Nothing is free in life."

The next day, the Master took Sai'er to the forest. He only mentioned they were going to a grotto that was near the Xuan Wu Temple. He and Yinho were in the habit of coming to this Temple once a month to offer incense and libations to the Warrior God.

There was no clear path that led to the Temple. Underfoot was an endless sea of dried fallen leaves mixed with a thick spread of undergrowth. Sai'er wasn't sure she would be able find the area if she were to come again on her own. Trees and saplings were so dense that sunlight could barely break through the foliage, giving the air a tingling chill and a mossy smell.

The Master stopped by the side of a dawn redwood tree which had the words "North Star Hermit" carved on the trunk. Straight ahead was an almost invisible stone door, hidden in a snarl of vines and climbers. The place had a forbidding and forlorn air to it. The slanting tiled roof and upturned eaves of the Temple could be seen at a distance behind the enclosed grotto.

9

THE MASTER STEPPED up to the door and knocked with his wooden staff.

A long moment passed before the door creaked open. Appearing in the doorway was a young-looking woman dressed in a long, white, wide-sleeved simple robe, in a style that matched what the Master was wearing, except hers was adorned with a purple silk sash tied at the waist. She had eyes exactly like his, round in shape with a purplish luster. In her right hand she held a lacquered seven-string guqin.

A huge black gyrfalcon appeared out of nowhere and was screeching and hovering above Sai'er, as if to check her out for any harmful intent. It seemed to recognize the Master and was content to leave him alone.

"Pearly, I've brought my student Tang Sai'er. As I told you, she needs to train in Qi-Extraction under you," said the Master. Turning to Sai'er, he instructed, "Come here every day for the next three months for your training. This is your coach, my granddaughter. People call her the North Star Hermit."

Sai'er brought her palms together in a deep bow. "I'm honored to meet you, Teacher." When she raised her head, she realized she was looking at a stunningly beautiful woman with alabaster skin and delicate face features resembling ancient great beauties portrayed in ink paintings. Her animated eyes, icy and disdainful as they were, radiated occasional electrifying vibes that could ensnare anyone if she wanted to.

"Call me Pearly," said the Hermit in a bland tone. "Go to the Temple at the back and offer incense to Xuannu, the Warrior Goddess. Her statue is in the alcove inside the Temple. Come back tomorrow morning for your first lesson."

Before she finished the last sentence, she had vanished into the dim interior of her grotto, the stone door grinding shut behind her.

A thin wave of ethereal guqin music wafted out from within. The music stirred strange vibrations in Sai'er's heart. Somehow she felt the player was a lonely soul trying to break out of a mundane shell.

"Pearly's weapon is the guqin. She could kill an opponent with it if she so wished," the Master told Sai'er on their way to the Temple. "Not to mention her Qi-Extraction prowess."

That evening after supper, Sai'er helped Yinho with the dish washing in the kitchen. Bursting with curiosity, she grabbed the chance to elicit an old-time yarn from him.

"I didn't know Master had such a beautiful recluse for a granddaughter!"

"Oh yes. Master has always been discreet about her. He dotes on her, and respects her need for privacy."

"She's so young-looking, and yet she's unmatched in the potent North Star skill."

"You're so lucky that Master has allowed you to learn it from her."

"But why doesn't Master coach me himself?"

"You see, when Master taught it to Pearly, he lost ten years' worth of his neigong, because Pearly, being a female virgin, had the distinct ability, despite her lower neigong level, to automatically siphon Yang qi from a male coach once their respective meridian networks connected. This wouldn't happen if coach and student were both virgins, or both men."

"Oh, I see—"

"Master has taught this skill only to Pearly and two male students, Monk Yao and Monk Faxian. According to Pearly's companion Yusu, the three students are of the same age—" He paused to ruminate for a while, then went on, "They should now be around fifty-seven. Monk Yao and Monk Faxian were both young laymen when they took up apprenticeship here, some forty years ago. Those times were way before me. When I began my life here twenty years ago, Pearly and Yusu had already moved to the grotto. I only heard from Yusu that the three students had been inseparable in their teens."

Sai'er was aghast to hear that her coach was fifty-seven years old. "She looks thirty at most! Umm, Grandba would be fifty-seven if he were still alive." *Ba told me Monk Yao and Grandba had been kung fu buddies at Wudang! So, could Grandba and Monk Faxian be the same person? Ba must've been holding back some secrets!*

"Do you by any chance know the family and given names of this Monk Faxian?" She searched her memory and vaguely recalled that Grandba's full name was Tang Wen.

"No, I don't. But maybe Yusu does."

"I can imagine how ravishing Pearly must've been at seventeen. And she still looks so attractive and full of life."

"Master once told me that it was Pearly's virginity coupled with the practice of the North Star skill that has preserved her youthful looks and physique. The price she paid was a man's love. She has never married."

"A man's love—it must have been either Monk Yao or Monk Faxian."

"If you want to know more, I'd say try to get Yusu to talk."

The next morning, Sai'er rose earlier than usual to get ready to go the grotto. On their return to the cottage from the grotto the previous day, she had purposely engraved tracking marks on tree trunks along the way, so she would be able to find the route this morning.

The stone door was wide open when she arrived. The black gyrfalcon lay sprawled in a pool of blood at the doorstep, an arrow tip sticking out one side of its chest. She stifled a scream. She ran in through the door and found a woman slumped on the floor, dazed and consumed in wheezing sobs.

"Are you Yusu? What has happened? Are you hurt?" Sai'er crouched down to give her a pat on the back, trying her best to stay calm. "I'm Master Zhang's student Tang Sai'er. Please tell me what happened to Pearly."

Yusu looked up with an untrusting and detached gaze. Sai'er had to coax her again and again to make her speak. She stammered, "A band of armored soldiers broke in. They used poison-laced darts on us, tied up Pearly and took her away. They killed our gyrfalcon."

"How long ago?"

"Just a few moments ago. They got away on horses."

Sai'er examined Yusu's limbs, and found a small dart in her right thigh. The poison had paralyzed her. She carefully removed the dart, which didn't go deep. To stop the wound from bleeding, she used her handkerchief to tie around Yusu's thigh. She had to get Binhong to come. He would know how to neutralize the poison.

"My dear, can you be kind and bury Zhou Yu for us? He's like family," Yusu pleaded. "Pearly was devastated."

"Sure, I'll get to it right now," Sai'er was fazed when she heard that name, but held her curiosity in check. Her Ba had told her that Grandba had been nicknamed Zhou Yu, because of his good looks.

When she finished entombing the gyrfalcon under the dawn redwood tree, she suddenly thought of something. She went back inside the grotto and asked Yusu, "Did they leave a message or anything?"

"Yes, yes. Their leader tossed me this note," Yusu jerked from torpor and held up the piece of paper that she had crumpled in her hand.

Sai'er smoothed out the paper and read the note. It said:

> *Master Zhang:*
> *I didn't want to resort to this. But don't worry, we'll treat Pearly well. My only request is for you to join my military force as Chief Trainer. We're going to war against my nephew and his Court. His cronies helped him grab the throne by devious means, and my father had always meant for me to succeed him. So it's in my right to take back what belongs to me. I'm letting you in on this only because I consider you as my friend. If you give me your word of honor man to man that you accept the offer, I'll have Pearly released. All I need is the pleasure of your presence tomorrow morning by the Dragon Spring Lake in the east bamboo grove, at the Hour of the Rabbit.*
> *Prince of Yan*

Sai'er's shoulders slouched and she said in gasps, "I must go and give this note to Master, and get Binhong to come and treat the poison."

Just as she was heading for the door, Master Zhang and Binhong appeared at the entrance. *Master has heard us, thanks to Guanyin!*

Binhong recognized the dart poison as the tendon-numbing

fragrant powder. It was a common paralyzing poison used by Mongols. He administered a concoction to Yusu made of licorice root and chrysanthemum petals and said, "The numbness will be gone by tonight."

Meanwhile, the Master read the note.

After mulling it for some time, he said, "Sai'er, we're going to have some fun tomorrow. My ears have detected that Zhu Di only has six or seven guards with him. So, between you, Yinho and Binhong, you can easily subdue them. If the poison effect on Pearly hasn't worn off by tomorrow morning, I'll need to escape with her on my back using qinggong."

"That sounds great! Good chance to practice what we've learned." Sai'er tried to sound positive. Inwardly, apprehension was gnawing at her. The idea of real combat didn't sound like fun.

"I can't wait to kick some butt. If that bastard Sanbao is there, he's all mine!" Binhong said with barely concealed zest.

Everyone rose before dawn broke. Yinho had sharpened the tip of his spear on a whetstone the night before and was twirling it in the front courtyard. Binhong showed up bright-eyed, with his bow and sword cross-strapped on his shoulders and a quiver of arrows on his back. Sai'er joined them at the first rooster's call and had her sword slung over one shoulder.

The Master was already outside waiting for them at the top landing of the stairway. They marched in single file down the steps. He took only his wooden staff with him.

When they reached the middle tier of the mountain, Yinho scooted ahead of the rest. As he was familiar with the mountain terrain, the plan was for him to quietly scout around the bamboo groves in search of Pearly before the two parties met at the appointed venue. The Prince's men had most likely set up camp in the groves.

The Wudang party of three descended the long flight of steps at leisurely pace. When they approached the bamboo groves, Sai'er espied the Prince, Sanbao and five guards waiting by the lake. Her face turned white with anguish. The Master put a hand on her shoulder to calm her.

After a courteous greeting was exchanged, the Master got straight to the point.

"Your Highness, my granddaughter has nothing to do with my decision not to accept your earlier offer. Therefore, she should not be a part in our negotiation. Your Highness is an honorable man, and taking my granddaughter hostage in order to force my hand is not something an honorable man would do. I therefore implore you to set her free at once, so I can take her back home. Only after that's been done will I be able to talk with you about your renewed offer."

While the Master was engaging the Prince in conversation, Binhong and Sai'er scanned the bamboo vegetation on both sides of the path for signs of Yinho. Sai'er spied him in the west grove bundling the wobbly Pearly along a shaded path. He found a large boulder and they crouched down behind it. Sai'er drummed her fingers on the sword scabbard to send a signal to the Master and Binhong.

"Master Zhang, I appreciate your lecture. But desperate times call for desperate measures. I really need your help badly, and that is the only reason for breaching etiquette."

"It's more than a matter of breaking etiquette. The killing of my granddaughter's beloved gyrfalcon was cruel and totally uncalled-for. Your men also hurt her companion."

"Well, one of your students killed my beloved golden eagle in these mountains two years ago. We can call it even now. Too bad the woman was in the way, so it couldn't be helped."

"I see Your Highness never lets go of your grudge. There's

no point dwelling on the matter now. So be it. Now, would you kindly release my granddaughter?"

"I'd rather first have your verbal acceptance of my offer, or better still, if you'd come with me to Beiping today."

"Can you at least show me that she's unharmed?"

A wall of silence sprang up between the two parties.

"So my word is not good enough for you?" the Prince finally said, his face warping into a canine snarl. "I figure you never had the slightest intention to humor me. Alright. If you're not with me, you're against me. Guards, arrest them all."

Three darts flew simultaneously from blow-dart pipes at the Master, Binhong and Sai'er. The Master swept his staff left and right and deflected them all in one go.

"Sai'er, Binhong, now it's your turn to play," said he.

Binhong rushed at Sanbao pointing his sword right at his throat. Sanbao sidestepped the lunge and countered with a whipping strike. Binhong parried the strike with retracted qi, then, staying low, swept a leg kicking Sanbao's ankle, nearly knocking him to the ground.

Two guards came up to attack Sai'er with their broad knives. She warded off blows from the two, one after another, then countered with a series of rapid, qi-charged whipping strikes. The knives flew off their hands, and they winced in pain from the contact vibration. The Master was nearby and immobilized both by hitting a heart acupoint on them.

Binhong and Sanbao went back and forth with strikes and parries.

Sai'er was waiting for her turn to fight Sanbao. So she was eager to get rid of any obstacles as quickly as possible.

Another two guards charged at Sai'er. She dodged their blades, swept one leg up the chest of one guard, pushing him back a few steps, half-turned and swung the sword at the head of the other, cutting across his temple. The blood splash blinded him as he yelped. When the first one saw the spattering of blood, he froze. The Master put these two at rest with his famous acupoint hit and vanished into the west grove.

A third guard came up behind Sai'er to strike at her head. She ducked, spun around and jammed her knee into his ribcage with a qi-force so strong it sent him flying headlong to the ground, cracking his head on a jagged stone. He passed out.

Binhong still couldn't take down Sanbao after several rounds of hits and deflections.

Sai'er saw the Prince flick his hand. She sensed something was wrong.

When she looked up to the sky, she was just in time to catch a glimpse of Nezha on his incandescent Wind-and-Fire Wheels disappearing into thick folds of clouds. *Monkey Sage! Nezha has called for back-up!*

A group of six armored soldiers were marching out from the east grove.

"Binhong, leave the turtle egg to me," she shouted. When he stepped aside, she leaped into the space left open by him, while he faced the new team head-on.

At this time, Yinho came out of hiding and joined the fray. Between him and Binhong, they tackled the six armored soldiers.

Sai'er glared daggers at her opponent. She sank into a solid horse stance, directing qi from her dantian, and sprang out like a mountain cat, her sword aiming for Sanbao's torso. He fended off the blow and took two steps back, as if wanting to exit the range. She didn't take the bait, and was alert and ready when he bounced right back in and directed a flurry of whipping slashes at her. She dodged the first two strikes and warded off a third when a hit got through to her shoulder. She flinched, but quickly readjusted her stance and resumed her even breathing.

Next she took the offensive with concentrated qi projection. Her sword moved like a sharp, raging whip that was sure to shatter anything on contact. Sanbao didn't even dare to put his sword up to meet the blows. He relied on his footwork to evade the lashes.

Nearby, Yinho tossed, caught and churned the spear while lurching like a drunkard in a dance to show off his slippery Eight Immortals Rod technique, hitting and wounding his combatants unawares.

By this time, two from the new team had been knocked unconscious, another two lying prostrate, moaning and bleeding from blade wounds.

Binhong teased the remaining two soldiers like they were a couple of cornered animals.

From the corner of her eye, Sai'er caught sight of the Prince vaulting onto his black stallion. He whistled to signal retreat.

For the flicker of a moment, Sai'er lost her concentration, and Sanbao bolted out of the fighting range to scamper to the lakeside in the east grove. In a blink, she caught up with him.

They danced in a cadence of qinggong on the mirror-like lake surface, using the stony banks and a sampan that crouched in the middle of the lake as launch pads.

The air quavered in the dappled beams of the rising sun. Birds whooshed in flocks from the trees fringing the lake in a sudden soaring rush.

With ferocious but not deadly aggression on Sai'er's part, they sparred while fluttering about like a pair of jacanas in courtship, their blades clanging and their feet kicking up sprays of glinting waterdrops.

Ripples twirled and lapped the side of the sampan. The lone fisherman in the sampan appeared unflappable as he craned his neck to follow the fight.

Sai'er wasn't going to harm her opponent, even though she could, with ease. As blazing as her rage felt, it was not enough to burn away every instinct she had to keep him unharmed.

Three rounds later, Sanbao sought to retreat from the combat. Tottering away in reverse, he entreated with a splash of grief in his voice, "Sai'er, you misunderstand. I can explain everything." Without waiting for her answer, he sprinted onto the gravelly edge of the lake where his horse was waiting, vaulted into the saddle and trotted off.

Misunderstand? You expect me to believe your lies again, you bastard? I was so blind to walk into your trap.

Binhong raised his bow and was just reaching for a shaft when Sai'er flew to his side and pressed hard on his forearm to stop him.

10

When the three youngsters stepped inside the cottage, the Master was in the lounge having a cup of tea.

He had carried Pearly back to her grotto, where he treated her dart wound and gave her the potion that Binhong had prepared the day before. She was recovering fast, but was aggrieved by Zhou Yu's death.

As they sat down to take their tea, the Master said to them, "I hope you've all gained a little real-life combat experience today. When you return to the everyday world, you need to remember that you should use martial arts as a weapon only when aggressively provoked, and, except in battles and wars where you fight for your own life, you should always leave your opponents a chance to live."

Binhong's ears turned red.

The Master drew his brow into a furrow in deep thought, and after a few moments said in a somber tone.

"I think after today's altercation, the Prince will make every effort to capture me. So, for safety's sake, it is my plan to leave this place with Pearly, Yusu and Yinho in a few days, and go into hiding for a long period of time. Sai'er, Binhong, you're welcome to join us if you like. If you do, I need you to promise that you won't disclose our hideout to anyone when you leave us."

Sai'er looked at Binhong for his lead. He said after mulling for a while, "Sai'er and I would be most happy to go with you. Sai'er still needs to learn the North Star technique. And I could use more practice on my neigong and qinggong. You have our word that we'll keep the hideout location in strict confidence."

"Then it's all set. We'll make the move three days from today."

On the day of the move, things went just as normal during the day. The plan was to go about moving their packed belongings at night to avoid being spied on by Nezha. The whole group met up at the entrance to Pearly's grotto. The waxen moonbeam painted the Temple roof a silvery indigo.

"Grandba, we couldn't find the key," Pearly said with a frown when she saw the Master. "So I asked Yusu to break the lock. She's been to my cousin's cottage this morning to clean it up."

"Good. Not to worry Pearly. I don't think anyone besides the four of us knows the existence of the tunnel. Let's get going then." He turned to Yinho and said, "Don't light the torches until we're inside the tunnel."

The whole group of six snaked their way towards the Temple under a full moon that was occasionally eclipsed by roving clouds. Between Binhong, Yinho and Yusu, they had six wheeled cartloads in tow. Pearly and Sai'er each led two horses, all laden with packed hemp sacks.

Pearly's classic-beauty facial features looked poignantly bewitching in the soft moonlight. Her skin was like delicate, translucent white jade. *What man wouldn't be attracted to her,* Sai'er thought. *Did she love Grandba? What happened between them?*

When they reached the Temple, Master, Yinho and Binhong knelt and bowed three times to the statue of the Warrior God. Upon entering the alcove dedicated to Xuannu, Pearly and Yusu bowed to the Warrior Goddess in deference. Sai'er followed suit.

"Which Pantheon does the Goddess belong to?" Sai'er asked

casually, not directing her question at anyone specific.

After an awkward bout of silence, from Yusu came the drawled reply. "She belongs to the East Pantheon of the Tao, and ranks second to the Queen Mother of the West. Her honorable title is Xuannu of Nine Heavens." Yusu's face had a frigid, sharp-angled contour, which even the mellow moonlight couldn't soften. Her narrow eyes radiated a bitterness that seemed to bite into her own soul.

Since that Pantheon visit, Sai'er could sometimes recall other tidbits of her immortal days as random prompts emerged.

Ah, I remember catching a glimpse of Xuannu at one celestial gathering hosted by the Jade Emperor! When she arrived, she was riding a purple phoenix and wearing a resplendent robe made of multicolor feathers. She carried a long sword with tasseled hilt in her hand, her face emitting a pearlescent luster. Her look was at once graceful and feral.

"Millennia ago, the Queen Mother had sent Xuannu to help the Yellow Emperor defeat the evil monster Chi You in a cosmic battle, giving birth to the Shang Dynasty," added Pearly in a honeyed voice. "She's a Goddess of Warcraft and Justice who has helped righteous heroes with her magic to win battles and wars throughout the ages."

She paused and directed her alluring eyes on Sai'er. "By the way, Sai'er, thank you for coming to my rescue the other day. I should also thank Binhong and Yinho."

Sai'er was pleasantly surprised to hear that. *So Pearly is after all not as cold as she appears.* "Don't mention it Pearly. Master's problem is our problem too. Besides, it was an experience I would cherish." She blushed, floundering in her new coach's attention and charm. "Oh, the Goddess sounds formidable. Thank you for enlightening me." She was careful not to show off her immortal connections.

If I were ever to go to war with Zhu Di, I would like Xuannu's help too!

At this time, the Master called from the entrance of the secret tunnel, "Children, come quickly and follow me."

Behind the altar on which the statue stood was a paneled wall made of redwood. One of the panels was in fact a camouflaged door that opened into a dark, narrow hallway. Once inside, Yinho lit up two torches and gave one to the Master to hold.

Pearly, Sai'er, Yusu and the horses followed close behind the Master in single file, while Binhong took up the middle with the carts in tow, having roped them all together. Yinho bolted the door shut with a crossbar from the inside. He held up the other torch and brought up the rear.

The damp limestone walls, floor and ceiling of the tunnel exhaled a strong moldy odor. Wreaths of cobwebs hung from the ceiling, like in a long-vacated grain barn. Small bats hiding in crevices got startled by the group and flapped their wings frantically. It seemed no one had used this secret path for ages.

After half a joss stick's burning time they reached a fork in the path. The Master turned around and said, "We're taking the left; the right leads to a dead end. But there are some interesting writings and murals on the walls of the right path. Sai'er, Binhong, if you like, you can take a look."

Sai'er was curious and skittered onto that path. Binhong was at her heels.

On the right wall were carved vertical columns of writings in ancient seal script, while the left wall displayed a series of sculpted drawings with eroded paint. The text was still legible. Both limestone walls were reinforced with top and bottom brick ledges.

The text told the story of Xuannu having been sent by the Queen Mother of the West to the mortal world to give help to the

Yellow Emperor, who was in a life-and-death cosmic war against the flesh-eating ogres led by Chi You. These ogres had beastly torsos and iron heads but spoke human language. They had been destroying agricultural lands by invoking droughts, causing a great famine.

In battles, they had the distinct edge of having thick hides which metal weapons couldn't penetrate. The Yellow Emperor's army was on the brink of total defeat when Xuannu went to his rescue, giving him a Book of Sorcery, a Xuannu Sword and a Celestial Amulet. In the end the Yellow Emperor won the battle with the use of these magical tools and got rid of the ogres, and people's lives returned to normal.

The author's name at the end had a suffix that looked like an imperial title. Beside the author's name there was an upward pointing arrow.

The series of drawings on the left wall rendered the storied text in motion. There were three separate images underneath the narrative drawings, each depicting one of the three magical devices.

"What terrible times to live in!" Sai'er mumbled to herself. Her eyes fell on a couple of loosened bricks in the bottom ledge of the painting wall. It looked like someone had dug out the bricks and had shoved them back in haste. But her train of thought was disrupted.

"At least they had a benevolent Emperor to fight for them," said Binhong, peering at the paintings over her head.

"Indeed. It's good to know that deities are there to look out for mortals when disasters strike." Pausing, she turned around and looked Binhong in the eye. "Look, Binhong, I wanted to say I'm sorry for—" Before she could finish her sentence, he interrupted with a feigned jeer, "I thought the word 'sorry' was not in Mistress Sai'er's book. I'm impressed!"

"At the end of the fight that day, before he fled, he said that I misunderstood," she said casually, now that she knew he was not mad at her.

"Umm, I hate so much to say this, but I really can't rule out the possibility that he might be under some kind of duress. Working for the Imperials is no better than sleeping with tigers. That day on the meadow, I saw tears in the sissy's eyes — "

"Flying Sword, Binhong, it's getting late," Yinho butted in as he came up behind them. As Binhong scurried back to join the others, Sai'er whispered in Yinho's ear,

"Yinho, is your Book of Sorcery by any chance the one mentioned in the wall text?"

"How very observant," he whispered back. "Ten years ago when I stumbled on a bundle of inscribed tortoise shells under the altar in the Xuan Wu Temple, I took them back to show to Master. He told me the shell inscriptions are Oracle Bone script dating from the Yellow Emperor era. He also said that many years ago he had seen the wall text and drawings and recognized the text author as a Qin dynasty prince who descended from the Yin imperial clan of the Shang dynasty. After reading the inscriptions, he concluded that it was the Book of Sorcery mentioned in the wall text. He figured that the Qin prince must've inherited the three magical objects and wanted to give a hint about their stash to whoever is fated to find them."

He paused to take a look at Sai'er, and found her totally engrossed in what he was saying. He then carried on with a smug look, "Master deciphered the inscriptions for me so I was able to train in sorcery. He reckoned the Celestial Amulet and the Xuannu Sword are most likely still buried in these walls. That's why he had the tunnel door locked for fear they might fall into the wrong hands."

"Interesting. Umm, whoever had dug out the tortoise

shells must've been stumped by the ancient inscriptions and so mindlessly tossed them away in the Temple. It's pure good fortune you happened upon this treasure." Sai'er was getting all excited. "Oh, I noticed there are a couple of loosened bricks on the left wall," she pointed out the spot to Yinho.

"That looks recent. Very strange. Only Pearly has custody of the tunnel door key, and she said she had lost it... Oh, let's not dwell on this now. We must get going. Master is getting impatient."

After advancing for another half-joss-stick's burning time, the group came to a stop. Immediately ahead, a streak of moonlight broke in through a grilled opening in a bolted wooden door.

Yinho gave the torch to Binhong, went up to remove the iron bar and pushed the door open with some effort, as the hinges were rusty. When the whole group had filed out through the door, Yinho snuffed out the torches, gathered bundles of tree branches and dried thorns and piled these upon the door.

Sai'er squinted her eyes to try to make out the surroundings. It was a quaint wooded area with trees that sported dense foliage, now swathed in a film of mist, with a stream gurgling through it. Frogs, owls and cicadas were performing their nocturnal chorus with zeal.

"We're on the Jade Maiden Peak. On the other side of the forest are a cottage and a Taoist Temple. The cottage used to belong to my grand nephew, the Chief Monk of the Temple. He passed away three years ago, and we're going to settle down there. Let's follow the stream," said the Master, for the benefit of Sai'er and Binhong.

The cottage was the same size as the Master's abode and had six bed chambers, three on each wing of the central courtyard. Everyone was tired from the big move, and all were ready to turn in as soon as their belongings had been unloaded from the carts and horses.

"Sai'er, in order not to waste any more time, I'll begin teaching you the North Star technique tomorrow," Pearly said before retreating to her bed chamber.

In the afternoon the next day, Pearly came into Sai'er's bed chamber and the two sat cross-legged on the bed facing the same direction, with Sai'er in front. Then Pearly used neigong to heat up both her hands. Next she pressed both scorching hands on Sai'er's back, and when Sai'er trembled in response, retracted her own qi, thereby drawing qi off from Sai'er. This was done to demonstrate to Sai'er how the process worked.

"The trick is as soon as you feel a tremor in the other party's body, which means the two meridian networks are joined, you immediately retract your own qi. This way, the other party's qi would be sucked into your network." Pearly patiently explained to Sai'er. "Now let's change positions and you do exactly as I did."

Sai'er heated up both her hands and pressed them on Pearly. But after a long while, she felt not so much as a whiff of a stir in Pearly's body. "I can't feel any tremor," she said dejectedly.

"You're just too nervous. Now try to meditate and heat your hands again."

She did that. Still a failure.

Three days went by, and nothing happened.

On the fourth evening at supper, Sai'er grumbled about her setback in lessons.

"That's because Pearly's stored qi is at a much higher level than yours," the Master said with a grin. "It's natural that happens. You just have to keep at elevating your stored qi level, and eventually you'll get there."

And all the while I thought my neigong had reached an incomparable height! How conceited of me!

Sai'er dug in her heels and for the next twenty days worked ceaselessly at her meditation, breathing and qi-storing.

Life soon resumed its normal beat with the daily Qi-Extracting lessons.

Like the previous qinggong lessons taught by the Master, each day began with warm-up exercises of meditation, breathing and practice of qi-storing in the dantian.

One day, about a month after the move here, for the first time in her lessons Sai'er distinctly felt a quiver in Pearly, faint as it was, and she jumped at the chance to retract her qi.

It gave her an indescribable feeling when Pearly's qi rushed into her, like a storm barreling into her meridians. Thereupon she jerked her hands away, lest she should absorb too much from her coach. "Don't worry! You couldn't have drawn qi from me if I hadn't allowed it," Pearly explained. Sai'er was delirious at her breakthrough.

Thereafter, coach and student continued the practice in give-and-take sequences for another month. In the third month Sai'er advanced to using just one hand to do the job.

All this time, Binhong helped Yinho cultivate a vegetable patch and raise a pen of chickens in the backyard.

It was early summer, and their stock of millet grains was dwindling. One warm day they both wore wide-brimmed straw hats to hide their faces and snuck back through the tunnel to the millet field on Sky Pillar Summit to reap and gather the ripe crop.

Apart from tending to these chores, they also practiced Sword-as-Whip regularly in duel sessions. Sai'er would join them occasionally, and would practice the Wave Treading qinggong every other day.

The Master taught them an additional trick, which was to skip around in nimble, deceptive steps following the Taoist hexagrams. The purpose of this footwork skill was to trigger the defense mode in face of an untenable menace at close range. Sai'er found this easy enough to master, after her hard struggle with the North Star technique.

As the day of departure was drawing near, she was torn by mixed feelings. She had grown so close to the Master, Yinho and Pearly that the very thought of leaving them depressed her. At the same time she missed her Ba and her home village and couldn't wait to return to her familiar life.

11

SAI'ER NEVER felt bold enough to ask Yusu about Monk Faxian, not least because Yusu always appeared less than friendly.

But her curiosity was gnawing at her.

Five days before she and Binhong were due to leave, just after supper, she mustered all her courage and went to look for Yusu. Master, Yinho and Binhong were in the front courtyard playing chess. Pearly and Yusu had retired separately to their own chambers.

Just as she was about to knock on the door of Yusu's chamber, she heard a quarrel start between Pearly and Yusu. Her feet wouldn't move, and she leaned on the door to listen.

"Yusu, I'll be frank with you, I know it was you who stole the tunnel door key," Pearly said in a calm voice. "No one else could've have done it. I didn't expose your theft in front of Grandba because I thought I'd give you time to come forward and confess."

"What if I did? What're you going to do? Report me to the Yamen? Master doesn't have a right to lock up the tunnel in the first place. He isn't the proprietor of the tunnel, nor is he the rightful owner of anything inside it."

Sai'er was taken aback by Yusu's effrontery. She had always behaved demurely enough, if often looking self-possessed and distant. This belligerent side of her was completely new to Sai'er.

"Why are you sounding so annoyed? We've always treated you like family. Grandba only meant well. He didn't want bad people getting their hands on certain objects of great power. After all this time living with me, don't you trust us?"

"Family? Ha! I'm only your servant, just some miserable orphan Master Zhang had picked up in the streets. Don't be so pretentious. The old man only cares about you and Yinho. You're so spoiled that you felt entitled to take Wen from me. It was not enough for you that Yao Guang fell for you..."

"I had no idea you had your heart set on Wen. But you're wrong. From the start I had always only loved Wen, and he had always loved me —"

"You wanted Wen and at the same time you wanted to rank first in the North Star skill. When you chose the latter, you still wouldn't let Wen go and pushed him to despair. How I hate you!"

"No, that's not true. The truth is Wen and I truly love one another, and he... he wasn't attracted to you. That's why he married someone else after he left Wudang."

"You must have been pleased to see him leave that woman later to become a monk, when their son turned ten!"

Sai'er gasped on hearing this. *I always thought Grandba passed away when Ba was ten. So Monk Faxian is really Tang Wen, my Grandba!*

"Well, Yusu, I didn't plan for that to happen. I made a choice to become a master of the North Star skill, and I paid for it by foregoing Wen's love for me. The loss of his love left a permanent gaping hole in my heart. But I've never hurt anyone on purpose."

"Don't sound so noble. You hurt me. If you hadn't seduced Wen with your foxy beauty, he would've fallen for me." Yusu broke down and sobbed.

"Yusu, be fair. I couldn't make Wen turn to you even if I wanted to. Love between two people can't be forced."

"If he so much as held my hand just one time, I'd be prepared to die for him."

"I understand. Love makes us blind to reason. You saw how Yao Guang once threatened to kill Wen and blackmailed me into stealing Grandba's *The Secret of Wudang Neigong* for him. I didn't even blink when I yielded to his demand. All I thought about was Wen's safety."

Calmness seemed to have intervened for a moment.

When Yusu resumed her litany of gripe, a chilly edge tinged her voice.

"Why did you think I stayed with you all these years, when I hated every moment of such a life? It's because I was waiting for a chance for payback. It may surprise you that Yao Guang and I have kept in touch all these years. Monk Yao, as you know, is now the confidant of the Prince of Yan. A year ago he asked me to work for him. My job is to spy on you and Master Zhang. I gladly agreed, because he promised, as my reward, that he'd use shamanic magic to make me look like you and put a love spell on Wen."

"Oh, no, Yusu! Monk Yao did everything imaginable just to curry favor with the Prince. Grandba said Yao learned black magic from a Shaman just to impress his master, despite having been ordained a Buddhist monk. Why would you want to associate with such a reckless opportunist?"

"Why? I think you know why," she snorted with distaste. "You think with all your beauty and music and martial arts skills that you are so special. You had everything easy. Of course it's never occurred to you that someone as lowly as I deserves love too."

She let out a spine-chilling laugh that made Sai'er skin crawl.

"Do you really trust Monk Yao to keep his word?"

"I wouldn't if I didn't know he's desperately lusting after a woman, and he relies on my help to make his wish come true. So it's just a matter of exchange."

Sai'er had to clench her lips tight to muffle a cry. *Oh Pearly, do you realize you're in grave danger?*

She just wouldn't have believed how someone could be consumed with such curdling hatred for so long, if she hadn't heard Yusu's bitter outpouring. She shuddered to think how hatred had twisted Yusu's mind, and how Pearly had been living alongside a snake all this time.

At this point, it seemed that Pearly deliberately raised her voice a notch.

"I just don't understand why you bear such a deep grudge against me, much less why you had to steal the key. I wouldn't have refused you it if you'd asked."

"When Yinho found the Book of Sorcery ten years ago, I heard from him that there were two more magical items in the tunnel walls. I reported this to Monk Yao, and he bade me to uncover them. Would you have given me the key if I'd told you this?"

Ah, Pearly is clever. She's managed to extract the confession from Yusu. It would be disastrous if Yusu managed to lay her hands on the two magical items. Umm, I must consult with Yinho on what to do next.

And it's now clear that Yusu was complicit in the Prince's plot to kidnap Pearly!

Sai'er tiptoed away from the door and went straight to Yinho's room across the courtyard. But he wasn't in his room. So she retired to her own room. She felt really exhausted and, after washing up, went straight to bed.

The next morning, an urgent banging on the door woke her up. The first ray of dawn had just streamed in through the lattice window.

"Have you seen Pearly and Yusu this morning?" Yinho said breathlessly when Sai'er opened her door. "Their chamber doors are ajar and their beds haven't been slept in. I can't find them anywhere!"

"Oh, no! Pearly may be in danger," Sai'er stammered, as the conversation she had stumbled on came rushing back to jolt her out of sleepiness. She told Yinho everything she had heard.

He shook his head in disbelief. "I never would've guessed Yusu was such a conniving person."

"Some people can really act," Sai'er said. Her thoughts jumped to Sanbao. She was still in a fog as to what to believe about him.

"I remember last night when Master and I were at a game of chess, at one point his face twitched and he stopped to listen hard for a few moments. Then he got up abruptly and left us. Binhong and I just went on playing till late."

Sai'er recalled that Pearly raised her voice towards the end of the talk.

"Let's go and find Master and tell him what Yusu is up to."

But the Master was not in his chamber either. They found a hastily scribbled note on his writing table.

> Yinho,
> As Pearly is in grave danger, and our hideout has already been exposed, I had to leave Jade Maiden Peak with her and find another hiding place. Don't worry about us.
> I'm sorry to have to leave you behind, but it's for the best.
> I suggest you join Sai'er and Binhong and start a new life with the Tangs in Putai. They could use your help in their endeavors.
> But before you leave with them, please go and dig out the

two treasures from the tunnel wall. Yusu tried to uncover them, but she picked the wrong spot. Go to the wall with the text writings. The two items are buried behind the top brick ledge. Dig deep and you'll find them. Sai'er will need these in future for her mission. I'll say farewell here.

    Your Master,

    Zhang Sanfeng

While Yinho was reading the note, Sai'er told Binhong the whole conversation she had stumbled on. Yinho showed them the note after reading.

"Thank Guanyin Master took swift action before Yusu had a chance to lay hand on Pearly. And Master's idea is an excellent one." Sai'er couldn't have been happier to read the suggestion in the note.

"Yes, I've always wanted to make such a proposal," Binhong said with a dopey grin. "So glad that Master has said it now. What do you say, Yinho?"

"There's nothing left for me to do here anyway, now that Master and Pearly are gone. Of course I'd be happy to join your household in Putai, if Uncle Tang doesn't mind."

"Oh, don't you worry about Ba. He's easy-going. We're just so happy to have you come home with us. Now you have the deciding vote whenever Binhong and I lock horns!" Sai'er made a funny face at her foster brother.

"Simple, I'll just give you each a good spanking," Yinho laughed like a kid.

The next day the three of them went inside the tunnel with an axe, a pick and a wooden step ladder. Binhong volunteered to do the digging, as he had the strongest arms. The digging was not as hard as he had expected.

"It seems a couple of bricks near the left end had previously been dug loose. That must be the spot where the Book of Sorcery had been found."

After taking out four cemented bricks next to those two loosened ones, he dug deeper behind. Yinho helped him remove the loose earth and bag it. Reaching his arm all the way into the nook, Binhong retrieved a majestic-looking sword encased in an emerald-inlaid scabbard, and a tidily wrapped white jade tablet with Oracle Bone inscriptions.

Sai'er now noticed the upward pointing arrow next to the author's name on the extreme left of the text wall. "Master has the keenest eyes!"

She was puzzling over who could help with the deciphering of the Amulet inscriptions, now that Master was no longer around. *That's of no immediate concern though. I'll worry about that at a later date.* Then she carefully wrapped the two treasures in separate pieces of cloth she had earlier cut out from bed curtains.

The trio spent the following two days packing up and clearing out garbage. They found out that Master and Pearly had together taken one horse, leaving three behind.

Just as Sai'er was about to question aloud why Yusu hadn't taken a horse, Yinho put forward a ready answer, "Nezha could easily have arranged a ride. How complacent of us to believe our hideout was safe!"

Part Two

Part Two

12

BINHONG AND SAI'ER decided to take the same route they'd come back home.

Binhong had wisely put aside a sum of money for the return journey, but it was just a moderate amount. To cut down on expenses, and to save time, they decided to only check into a guesthouse on alternate nights. On the nights without shelter, they would either press ahead or stay in makeshift tents in the open. Balmy summer nights actually made such camping out quite a pleasant experience.

It took almost a month to traverse the greater part of Henan Province.

When they reached Dengfeng county, about a couple of days' ride away from Zhengzhou at the Henan/Shandong border, in early evening they were caught in a heavy downpour and were forced to check into a local inn they happened upon, despite having already spent the previous night at a guesthouse.

The middle-aged inn owner looked ill-humored as she waddled her way to the stable with their horses. When she came back out to register their names, she didn't bother to hide her sulky mood. "I already bolted the gates shut for the night," she said in a huff. "If it weren't for the pouring rain, I wouldn't even think of answering the door. These are bad times. Bandits often show up at this hour demanding a free night's stay."

"But what's happening here, dear Madam?" Binhong asked, not put off by her grouchiness. "We're from Shandong and had left the province to travel for two years. Now we're on our way home."

"Call me Madam Pu," she eyed him with suspicion. "Have you people been hiding in caves? Don't you know there's a civil war going on? The Prince of Yan has waged war on the Jianwen Emperor. Uncle fighting nephew. Guanyin, help us common folks."

When she was done grumbling, she gave out a long sigh and snapped a hand-held lantern to lead the guests upstairs.

While lighting an oil lamp on the round table, she harrumphed, "I hope you people are not heading to Jinan city. They're at each other's throats there." As she turned to leave, she said in a kinder tone, "Oh, if you don't mind vegetarian fare, then come down to the dining room when you've refreshed yourselves. I only serve vegetarian as I'm a Buddhist."

When she had stepped out of the room, Sai'er frowned and said, "Now she's got me really worried about Ba and our village."

"I'd say Putai is safe for now," Binhong said in an even tone. "Our village is just a backwater with no strategic value. It's much too poor for princes to fight over."

When no one responded, he went on to elaborate anyway, "Jinan is the Shandong capital and the transport node for food and military supplies. If Zhu Di gets control of it, he'll have nabbed a strategic military base and can then use it to spring south to the Yangtze region, and on to the Yingtian Imperial Palace. For the same reason, Jianwen must be doing all in his power to prevent that from happening. Hence the fierce fight for supremacy there."

Sai'er was listening carefully to every word he said. She couldn't but agree with her foster brother.

After some reflection, she voiced her own thoughts. "Yes, Jinan is a historic military site, so whoever's in power would see fit to fully provision it. The Yan army must be looking to seize its granaries and arsenals. If they succeed, it would hugely bolster their offensive elsewhere. But common folks' resistance might still sway the outcome."

He took a deep breath. Then, sounding like the big brother, he droned on, "When we reach Zhengzhou, we had better take the river route to go back to Putai, because land blockades should be everywhere over western Shandong. We must avoid the main piers, though."

When she looked at Binhong's firmly set mouth and stubbled jowl, she realized for the first time that the rash and sometimes awkward lad she used to know had grown into a prudent man, one not to be taken lightly. She could almost see Ba's somber shadow in Binhong now.

Yinho, on the other hand, seemed to have imitated Master's lively sense of humor and puerile prankishness. But the way he fidgeted while making jokes betrayed that he was just donning an air of levity to hide his true feelings.

He was wiping his face with a wetted cloth taken from the ceramic basin.

"Master once said that Shandong people hate the Prince because he takes after his cruel father," he mumbled as he dipped the cloth in the basin and wrung it dry, and dipped it in again. Then, with a straight face he added, "Folks are probably begging all deities to keep that stinking turtle egg from the throne. If their prayer is answered, I tell you they'd lug ten roast pigs to each and every temple as offerings, and sing and dance for ten straight days."

Stepping away from the basin stand and, addressing no one in particular, he asked with an impish glitter in his eyes, "Is there a chance of getting a piece of action with this war? After all, we're all from Shandong, and should stand with our folks."

"Even if there is, it's not likely we'll be able to change what is already set in stone," Sai'er said in low spirit, recalling what Lan Caihe had told her.

Yet even if the odds of success lay with the Prince's camp, nothing could stop her from taking him to task, if only to show solidarity with her fellow villagers.

"Perhaps we could give a hand to General Tie Xuan," said Binhong in a murmur, as if he was trying to screen his memory for something. "He's now the Chief Commander in Jianwen's camp charged with defending Jinan."

Sai'er was always amazed at how Binhong gathered street information like this. Now her memory was piqued.

"Ah, I remember Ba praising Tie as an upright man. People call him the 'Iron Face'," she began to perk up. "I don't have a problem with helping him. It's a good chance too for us to gain real battle experience. Hope I'll get to spar with Monk Yao—"

"Yes, some years ago Tie was in Putai and one day he dropped by Uncle's apothecary to get some herbs for his wife's stomachache." Binhong's eyes brightened as if he had stumbled on something propitious.

"At that time he was only a supplies marshal. Uncle and he hit it off in no time, as they are both devout Buddhists. Afterwards they became pen friends, and he was promoted to the post of Shandong Commissioner."

"I'm all for going into this battle," Yinho said with zest, his eyes clouding over with vengeful longings. "Just leave Zhu Di to me, or give me his head." In a beat his expression morphed from light-hearted to almost implacably somber.

Looking at the cloth in the murky water, Binhong wrinkled his nose. Yinho took the prompt and grunted, "Got it!" And he darted out with the basin.

He came back with a clean basin, two pieces of clean cloth and a bucket of water. Then he filled the basin with half the water from the bucket.

Binhong used the bucket to clean his face, leaving the basin for Sai'er. As if thoughts were still forming in his mind as he spoke, he muttered in a low voice, "Let me write to Uncle and see if everything back home is alright. I'll ask him to send his reply and a letter of introduction to a courier station at the Zhengzhou main pier. We'll wait for his response when we get there. If he's safe and sound, then we'll head to Jinan."

"Good! Then it's all set," groaned Sai'er as she was done wiping her face. "Can we go downstairs now? I'm famished."

The dining room looked cozy and quiet with two large lanterns hanging from the ceiling. It only had four square wooden tables with backless benches tucked in. Two middle-aged house guests, who looked like a couple, had taken one table by the stairs and were eating quietly. The other three were empty.

They sat down at the table next to the couple. Madam Pu served up three home-cooked vegetarian dishes and a bowl of noodles for each. They had beancurd laced with sesame and chili oil, stewed lotus roots with fermented bean curd sauce and deep-fried taro root crisps. All three dishes tasted so good they won applause from Yinho the acclaimed cook. This was the first decent meal they had had since leaving the Wudang mountains.

At the next table, the man said to the woman in a hoarse grunt, "We're fortunate to have a pretty daughter. Lin San sure knows how to pick his concubines! If we settle down here in Dengfeng and live a modest life, the bridal money should be enough to keep us comfortable."

Sai'er and Binhong instantly pricked up their ears at the mention of Lin San's name.

The woman shook her head and started her cheerless outpouring. "I've heard his betrothed is a Putai native," she said. "But their wedding has yet to take place, and he couldn't wait to take concubines. Aiya, our daughter is the third one he's picked up in Zhengzhou. Still, she can't ask for more. A large house, good food, fine clothes, and servants. If only the money he makes is clean—"

The husband glowered at his wife but his attempt to stop her burbling met with thoughtless candor. She just gushed right on. "There're gossips that he sells information to the Yan side. The matchmaker and our neighbor both said the same thing. Jinan didn't become a first target for no reason—"

The room was so quiet that it was not hard for anyone in it to catch the conversation.

Binhong's face instantly contorted into a scowl. Apparently he didn't know his archer friend as well as he had thought.

This piece of news didn't come as a surprise to Sai'er. "Hou Yi had a large harem in his previous mortal life," she said to Binhong. "Did you think his incarnate would be any less dissolute? And you wondered why I was so angry about the betrothal!"

But she was sure Binhong was just as worried as she about Ba and his students at the White Lotus Society. If Lin San so much as laid a finger on Ba, she swore she would hunt him down and gouge his eyes out!

Yinho made a funny face at Sai'er. "Wow, your betrothed collects women and bureau secrets! Good job for a past King!" She pulled a long face to feign offense and pinched him hard on the arm, eliciting a yelp.

When they finished eating, the couple had already retired to their room. Madam Pu came round with cups of jasmine tea. Her face lit up when Binhong complimented her on the cooking.

He grasped the moment to ask her for ink, brush, paper

and envelope. When he finished writing, he handed the sealed envelope to her with the request to find a post courier to deliver it to Putai.

The trio was still enjoying their jasmine tea when a sudden loud pounding cleaved through the silence. Sai'er's heart gave a lurch.

Madam Pu pressed the index finger to her mouth to urge silence. They all kept very still. She was clearly not going to answer the door.

Another round of banging. Then a desperate raspy cry wafted through, "Help! Please! I'm hurt!"

Binhong stood up and said to Madam Pu, "Let me go and see what's up. I'll go get our weapons first."

She nodded nervously. He bounced upstairs, came back down with the weapons, and tossed a sword to Sai'er and the spear to Yinho before stepping outside.

When he came back in, he was tugging a half-conscious bald man dressed in monkish garb that was soaked in blood.

"Sai'er, would you mind getting the bag of herbs from my sack? Madam Pu, I need some salted water and clean cloth pads and bands please. Yinho, can you take the horse to the stable?"

When Sai'er came back down with the herb satchel, Binhong had already removed the monk's garment. She saw a deep gash about two inches long on his left shoulder. The inflamed wound was angrily oozing blood and pus.

Binhong took a dagger from his broad belt and asked Madam Pu for a lit candle. He rolled the dagger tip in the flame, saying to the monk, "This will hurt a bit."

The monk nodded. As Binhong was scraping out the rotten flesh with the dagger, the monk remained still and bit hard on his lower lip, while cold sweat beaded on his forehead.

The deft herbalist carefully cleaned the lesion with salted

water, and covered it with sanqi root powder. Then he put a dressing pad on the wound and looped a long cloth band around the shoulder to hold the pad in place.

The pallid-faced monk thanked him in a feeble voice. "I was being chased —" Before he could finish what he was trying to say, a series of hard pounding and hammering rattled everyone in the dining room. The wooden front gates were being rammed open.

Moments later, in barged a group of six soldiers wearing the Yan insignia on the front of their armor. The blood trail that the monk left had led them to the inn.

"Madam Pu, please take the master upstairs and stay there with him," Binhong ordered in a steady voice.

He, Yinho and Sai'er fanned out in one line to face the intruders.

The one who looked like the leader yelled, "The monk is a fugitive. He tried to assassinate His Highness's adviser. If you shelter him, you become his accomplices and we have to arrest you."

"Your Prince is a usurper. If you support him, you become traitors and we have to arrest you," Yinho hollered back.

Sai'er tackled the two nearest her. They put on a lewd grin when they saw their opponent was a delicate-looking young girl. The one to her right jeered and smacked his lips, "Come now, sweet maiden! Give up your sword and lie down. Let me give you a good time."

The other one chuckled in a guttural voice, "Heehee, pretty girls like you shouldn't play with swords. Let me give you something else to play with."

Sai'er was incensed. Sinking into a horse stance, she focused on working up her qi. In a blink, she whipped her sword down on the one to her right in a series of feints followed by deadly flourishes, splitting his halberd in half. He staggered backwards from the violent hit and lost his balance. Springing forward, she touched her heated hand on his chest and drew his qi until he was gulping for air, like he was drowning. When she took her hand off, he crumpled into a wilted heap and passed out. "Thank you for your qi!" she said.

The second one came at her from behind and struck with his halberd. She dodged the blade, rolled over, bounced up and catapulted him into the air with a qi-charged kick.

Crashing onto a table and then landing with a thud on the floor, he frantically scrabbled for his weapon. She leaped over to kick it away and pressed her knee on his throat. While he was choking, she grabbed his right ear, sliced it off and threw it on his face, hissing, "Now play with that! Be thankful I didn't aim for your birdie." He covered the bloody hole with his hand and writhed on the floor moaning.

Yinho let out a short laugh, "Haha, you two don't know who you're messing with!"

All this time, Binhong and Yinho were amusing themselves with the other four soldiers, none of whom was even close as a match.

Binhong teased his two opponents with a series of non-lethal sword strikes. When he got bored with them, he used neigong to slash his sword at them to quickly end the combat, giving both men crippling leg wounds.

Flailing his spear like a whipping rod, Yinho lashed at his two attackers' arms and legs with precise lunges. One of them got his arm pierced, dropped his halberd and bellowed in pain.

The other one had his thigh gashed and was begging to be let go. Yinho roared at him, "Take your wounded and scram! Next time we see you, don't expect to live." As he was scrambling away, Yinho gave him another thrash of the Eight Immortals Rod fame.

Hiding in a dark corner and quietly watching the fight was Madam Pu's thirteen-year-old son, Ah Long. He kept rubbing his eyes to tell himself he wasn't in a dream.

"Ah Long, go to the kitchen and make some ginger tea for the big brothers and sister and bring one cup up here for the old master," his mother shouted over the railing when she saw the room cleared of soldiers.

They took a short rest and finished their ginger tea. Then Yinho suggested, "Let's find out what the master has been up to, shall we?"

Madam Pu had deposited the monk in the room next to theirs. Sai'er knocked lightly on the partly open door, and he beckoned them in. Madam Pu was feeding him ginger tea.

He was sitting up on the bed, leaning against the bedpost. A little color had returned to his face. He appeared to be someone well trained in martial arts whose neigong was deep enough to recover quickly from non-life-threatening blade wounds.

While wrinkles on his face and hands betrayed his advanced years, his shining eyes accented by straight and dense eyebrows beamed wisdom and warmth. Sai'er could picture the perfectly sculpted face in its glorious days of youth.

"Master, I hope you don't mind me asking a few questions," said Binhong politely. "How should we address you? Which province are you from? And which monastery are you attached to?"

The monk's eyes swiveled between the three youngsters' faces and rested on Sai'er's for a while. He seemed to be suppressing a moment of surprise and quickly recovered his composure.

"Not at all. I owe you a big debt for saving my life. My ordained name is Faxian and I'm from Putai, Shandong." His eyes were darting everywhere, as if unsure whether to reveal more. "Most recently I was one of the resident monks at the Lingyan Temple in Jinan. But several months ago I left the Temple to join the Jinan militia to fight the Yan army."

Sai'er gasped at the revelation. *My grandfather?*

"The soldiers said that you tried to assassinate the Prince's adviser. Is that true? And if yes, could you tell us why?" Binhong continued with his probing in as casual a way as he could.

He pondered for a while, and replied hesitantly, "Yes, I did want to kill Monk Yao. Because the miscreant abducted Pearly and is holding her in bondage." His face warped into an angry scowl.

"Pearly is Master Zhang Sanfeng's granddaughter. Monk Yao, Pearly and I used to be fellow students under the Master. But sadly I was not his match, and had to get away."

He was seemingly still holding something back.

I thought Master and Pearly had escaped Yusu's clutches, Sai'er brooded in a fit of anguish.

Binhong and Yinho were just as aghast as Sai'er on hearing the news.

"That's really bad news. Master Faxian," Binhong then said. "The three of us here are also students of Master Zhang's. Actually we left Wudang not long ago. Pearly had been kidnapped once before, and as a precaution against more threats, we moved from Sky Pillar Summit to Jade Maiden Peak to hide. A few days before we departed from Wudang, Master Zhang took Pearly with him to look for another hideout because the one at Jade Maiden Peak had been exposed. We never thought Pearly could possibly be caught again—"

On catching the additional details, and seemingly relieved in learning the youngsters' background, Monk Faxian now appeared less guarded, his eyes emitting a ripple of warmth.

"Ah, I'm so glad to have met you all, my Wudang fellows! As

a matter of fact, after locating the detention camp where Pearly was held, I decided to rescue her. I disguised myself as an old woman, claiming to be her aunt bringing food to her cell, and bribed the guards with sorghum wine. Once Pearly saw it was me, she disclosed that she had deliberately played the victim and allowed Yusu to take her hostage. Her aim was to spy out the Yan camp for General Tie of the Jinan garrison."

He paused to catch a breath. When he found them all hanging on his words, he went on at greater ease, "But on leaving the Yan compound, I found Monk Yao waiting for me. I tore away and fled Jinan by boat, but he chased after me with a contingent. Shortly after I got off at the Zhengzhou pier, he caught up and challenged me to a duel. That's when I got stabbed. I managed to get away and rode all the way here."

Ah, that makes much more sense now, because Master couldn't have allowed Pearly to be caught again, thought Sai'er. It was uplifting to know Pearly also joined the fray against Zhu Di.

One question Sai'er was itching to ask was whether Master Faxian's secular name was Tang Wen, who supposedly had died many years ago according to Ba. But she just couldn't bring herself to do it, lest she might embarrass him. Anyway it was not a good time to ask personal questions now.

From his bravado though, Sai'er could glean where his heart belonged.

"I think we have to leave as soon as possible," Yinho warned. "The soldiers will definitely call for backup and come for us again."

"You're right, Yinho," said Binhong. "Zhengzhou doesn't look like it can hold back the Yan soldiers. Nothing could stop them coming a second time. We need to be on our way before dawn. Master Faxian, would you be able to ride with us to Zhengzhou? I was thinking maybe we could all disguise ourselves as street acrobats, just to throw any spies off the scent. Our plan actually is to join General Tie's army in Jinan."

"I'm sure I'll be fine after a night's rest. And thank you for the kind offer. But as I'm now a fugitive, it would be best for me to lay low for a while. My plan is to seek refuge in the Shaolin Buddhist Monastery just a short way from here. When it's safe for me to travel, I'll go back to Jinan. Maybe we'll meet again one day soon."

"Alright. Perhaps that's all for the best. We'll leave you to rest then. Take good care and stay safe. Farewell now, Master."

13

"Wow, so you got your good looks from your grandfather," said Yinho with levity when the trio returned to their own room. "If I were a woman, I'd fall for him."

"Binhong, has Ba told you any stories about his father?" Sai'er asked, brushing aside the joke.

"Nothing more than what he'd told us both that day when he told us of Master's acceptance letter," Binhong shrugged in reply. "But I did feel there was bottled-up anger in him. My impression was that he lied about his father's death just to get you off his back."

"From what Yusu disclosed, Tang Wen left his family to become a monk when his son was ten. Grandma and Ba must have been devastated. I know Grandma died shortly after — Ba's anger was understandable."

Sai'er might have accepted that Monk Faxian was her grandfather, but something still barred her from using the term *Grandba*.

"If you look at it from another angle, love sometimes makes people do insane things. I guess your grandfather just couldn't bear living a lie and so tried to find escape in a monastic life. He didn't mean to hurt his family." Yinho tried to sooth Sai'er, as best as he knew how.

"Yes, I can see that he'd rather be honest with his feelings than pretend to be a loving husband and father," said Sai'er in a resigned way, her miff somewhat abated. "Living with a guilty conscience was probably the price he paid for regaining freedom."

Binhong appeared pensive. A few moments passed before he finally came out with what he was thinking.

"True love is about sacrifice and letting go." A melancholic shadow eclipsed his face as he continued, "Master Faxian married a woman he didn't love in order to assure Pearly he was moving on, just to ease her guilt and worries. This is something Yusu could never understand."

He paused for while to look at Sai'er, before resuming. "He knew he couldn't make his wife happy, but still gave her a son. The sad reality was: his heart couldn't chime with hers. He became a monk not for his freedom, but to do penance for hurting his family."

Sai'er couldn't help gaping at Binhong in admiration. *And I've so often chided him for being insensitive.*

She could only pray that Ba could find it in his heart to forgive Grandba. After all, he only did what he thought best for the love of his life. And he did try to atone for his wrongs. *Who am I to judge his actions or motives?*

For the first time, she learned something about spiritual love, such as the love that let Grandba's and Pearly's hearts beat as one, despite their being separated by physical distance. Their hearts always chimed like a butterfly's pair of wings, with joy, harmony and to the same attuned rhythm. *Maybe 'this' is called true love.*

More than at any time before, she was now ready to welcome her beloved grandfather into her heart. After all, from the moment she had laid eyes on him, affection began to creep up on her like a clinging vine. That familial bond was something latent in the blood, a bond that always stood up well to the test of time and separation.

Her thought then shifted to her feelings about Sanbao. Prompted by Binhong's remark made in the tunnel, she had accepted the argument that the Prince had strong-armed Sanbao into spying on her. She was cleaving to the notion that that day on the meadow his urge to protect her had prevailed over the plan to ravish her as ordered by the Prince.

After all that initial knee-jerk reaction to that letter, she now realized how much she had missed him all this time. Their mutual attraction had sprung from little more than a shared humanity, a pure longing for company and tenderness. There was never any artful pretense. She convinced herself that all the ache and anguish she had witnessed on his face couldn't have just been for show.

Yet, at the back of her mind flashed a big warning sign. Her superb North Star skill that she had struggled so hard to achieve was contingent on her virginity being kept intact. That meant love and a happy family was not in store for her as long as she was saddled with the mission. *But what simple girl doesn't cherish that simple dream?*

She thought of Pearly and tried to find solace in her example. Yet her guqin music vibrated such a heartbreaking note of wistfulness that it pricked Sai'er's heart just listening to it. It was apparent that she yearned for something she knew was denied her. That was the price she'd had to pay for the single-minded pursuit of her ideal.

As Sai'er was preparing to turn in, someone knocked lightly on the chamber door.

Yinho opened the door. It was Madam Pu and Ah Long.

In one breath, Madam Pu poured forth the reason for the late-night visit.

"I apologize for disturbing you at this hour. But I understand that you will be leaving before dawn, and it's something that can't wait. To cut it short, we understand you're planning to join General Tie's army. My son Ah Long would very much like to tag along as an assistant or aide to you all. His dream since he was little was to become a martial artist. Sadly, my husband passed away when he was still an infant, and he never had anyone to look up to. If you would be so kind as to take him under your wing, we would be forever indebted. There's no future for him in this poor county. If you agree to let him join you, teach him kung fu and make a useful man out of him, then Guanyin will bless you all."

Binhong looked to Yinho and Sai'er for their opinion. They looked at each other and both nodded their consent.

Madam Pu told them she had a two-wheeled enclosed cart ready, along with men's clothes and cloth caps for Sai'er's disguise, and bags of millet cakes, dried plums and peanuts. The cart could serve as their cot at night.

They were to travel as a group of vagrant acrobats, with Binhong as the group leader. He was to ride one horse, while the other three would ride on the cart hitched to two horses.

With Sai'er's help, Ah Long made two vertical banners with the group's name "Flying Spear Kung Fu" painted on in black ink. He also drew an eye-catching picture of a spear-wielding martial artist at the top of the banners. He beamed when she gave him a pat on the back for a job well done.

A little less shy now, and before leaving the room, he mustered up all his courage to tell Yinho that he would like very much to learn the Eight Immortals Rod kung fu.

"Wow, someone has just become a coach," Sai'er teased. "No more excuse not to act grown-up."

They arrived Zhengzhou safely after four days' travel. This was twice the usual time to travel from Dengfeng to Zhengzhou, as they deliberately avoided beaten tracks and took circuitous paths through sparsely populated villages and hamlets.

When they reached the city gates, the banners on their boarded cart caught the interest of the bored sentry guards. They directed a barrage of questions at Binhong. On which days is the show on? What kind of show? Where?

It was a good thing that Binhong had been to Zhengzhou on an herb-handout visit with Ba a few years back. He told the guards the first performance would be in the afternoon the following day and the venue was in front of a teahouse that he remembered was named 'Long De', located right on the edge of the city square.

The guards knew the place well and let them pass without further questions, only warning them that there was a night curfew.

Residents of the city seemed to be carrying on with life just like on any ordinary day, as though the war raging in Jinan was happening in another universe. Restaurants and teahouses buzzed with loudly chatting patrons. Street vendors peddled their wares with zest like tomorrow would never come. Zhengzhou looked like a safe haven, as least for now.

The next afternoon they gave their performance in the city square, right in front of the Long De Teahouse.

As soon as Ah Long began striking the small brass gong that he had brought to draw attention, guests at the Teahouse swarmed to the upper storey verandah to catch the show. Curious passers-by also pressed close, thronging the square.

Yinho started the show with a solo performance of Eight Immortals Rod kung fu. Twirling around like a drunkard dancing, he tossed, churned, swung and thrust his spear in cadence with his lurching steps. Then, using his qinggong and the spear as an aid, he vaulted to the eaves of the teahouse, and from there sprang to the roof of the next building like a grasshopper, and leapfrogged across the next two, before hopping in reverse direction back to the teahouse roof ledge.

As soon as he touched ground again, the enraptured audience rewarded him with vigorous applause. Ah Long gaped as if he were in a trance.

Dressed in men's working garments, her hair coiled into a bun and wrapped in a white square cloth, Sai'er performed a Sword-as-Whip stunt with Binhong. She was blindfolded in the dueling. They had done this for fun many times during their years at Wudang.

Her parries to Binhong's strikes were entirely timed based on her sense of hearing. The tight series of back-and-forth thrusting and deflecting kept the audience breathless. At one time her left foot got tangled in the hem of her pants and she tripped as she fended off a blow. She swerved to one side, but was nimble enough to immediately reset her footwork. The crowd gasped. Lightning-fast movements of their swords whistled like bursts of sharp wind gusts. Spectators let out sighs of awe.

Lastly, Binhong showed his masterly archery skills. He asked Ah Long to serve as his target and went up to a fruit vendor to buy a couple of tangerines. He put one on the lad's head. Standing fifty yards away, he raised his bow and aimed. Twang! The tangerine split into two halves. Sai'er saw Ah Long's face turn ashen white. A round of hearty handclapping followed.

Ah Long recovered from his shock in no time and skittered around happily with a bowl to collect money from the audience. When he was done counting the coins, he proudly announced, "We've earned two silver coins and fifty-six coppers today!"

By the time they were ready to get back to their cart, which had been parked in an alley adjacent to the teahouse, the sun was sinking down into the sea of darkness.

An uneasy feeling, like a premonition, grazed Sai'er.

As they approached the wagon, they saw a white-robed woman darting away from the alley across the square onto the main street. Sai'er couldn't help calling out to her, "Pearly, is that you?"

No answer came. She just disappeared into the home-going crowds.

"Are you sure it was Pearly?" Binhong asked.

"I'm not sure--I didn't see the face. But Pearly likes wearing white."

Wait! Could it have been Yusu? She had plans to impersonate Pearly.

The thought gave her the jitters. Immediately she jumped up onto the cart and checked her baggage. "Monkey Sage! The Xuannu Sword is missing! That woman is —"

Before she finished the sentence, Ah Long had sprinted away and broken into a run through the milling crowds. Yinho was on his heels. Sai'er got a peek of Yinho leaping onto the roof of a house and lost sight of him.

After waiting an eternity, Sai'er was relieved to see the two return. Yinho was carrying Ah Long on his back and a crestfallen expression on his face.

"What happened?" asked Sai'er, rattled.

"Yusu blew a dart at him, and she got away when I was propping him up. It's the paralyzing fragrant powder," Yinho said, while laying Ah Long down on the wagon floor. "Binhong, do you still have that antidote potion?"

Binhong nodded, fumbled in his sack and fished out a vial. While he was tending to Ah Long, Yinho said, "When I caught up, at first I thought the woman was really Pearly. While I was

ALICE POON

hesitating, she blew the dart, and I realized too late that she was in fact Yusu. She looked exactly like Pearly, the face, the hair, the skin. That's some kind of shamanic magic. We have to be extra alert from now on."

"Umm, I think I should write Grandba to warn him of this," said Sai'er, recalling Yusu's bitter outpouring.

"We're going to the courier station tomorrow to collect Uncle's letter. You should be able to find a courier heading to Dengfeng," Binhong said.

"Yes, I'll do that—" Sai'er said absent-mindedly, wrapped up in her distractions. "I wonder what's so special about the Xuannu Sword? I wish Master had told us."

"He said you'll need the Sword and the Amulet in the future," Yinho reminded her of what the Master said in his farewell letter.

"Maybe Lan Caihe could tell you something about the Sword?" suggested Binhong.

"Ah yes, thanks for the reminder. I've almost forgotten my sprite friend! Too bad I've lost the Sword now." Sai'er felt ashamed. It was her fault not guarding the treasure well. She must somehow think of a way to get the Sword back, because it might make all the difference to her mission.

By the next morning Ah Long had recovered from the temporary debilitation and returned to his bubbly self, to the great relief of everyone, especially Yinho. His dark baggy eyes showed he'd barely slept.

After taking millet cakes for breakfast, the four of them headed to the Zhengzhou main pier courier station. These courier stations were normally only for government use, but private citizens could get postal services they needed by greasing the palm of station clerks.

Ba's reply had arrived. Binhong paid the dues and picked up the envelope. Much to her relief, Sai'er found a courier who

135

was heading to the Shaolin Monastery and handed him her letter along with the necessary fee.

Looking around, Sai'er noticed that boatloads of people who looked like refugees were swarming the main pier, with lots of luggage in tow. They'd probably fled the Jinan war zone.

After skimming through the letter, Binhong summed it up for Sai'er and Yinho.

"Uncle is well. He's given us permission to join General Tie's army using the introductory note. He says that a few months earlier Lin San had moved from Putai to Zhengzhou but Mother Lin insisted on staying behind to take care of Uncle." He paused to look at Sai'er, and met a blank gaze.

So Lin San is a step ahead of this stampede. He must be well informed!

Clearing his throat, he went on matter-of-factly, "He says to tell Sai'er that her betrothal to Lin San was her mother's wish, and that he looks forward to her wedding. I'm to continue to act as Sai'er's guardian while in Jinan and make sure she's safe. Uncle is glad that Yinho is with us and he welcomes him into the family. Finally, he bids us keep safe and obey General Tie's orders to the letter while in his army."

Sai'er had somehow known all along the nagging issue of her betrothal would come back to bite her. Not that she believed Ba would force her to wed Lin San if she didn't want to. But if that was Ma's wish, it could be a bit tricky to refuse. Anyway, with the Jinan battle right in front of her, she couldn't but push the issue to one side for now.

How she wished she could have a chat with Caihe! With the tight sleeping space shared with the young men, she had to be creative to eke out some privacy.

14

THE NEXT DAY they decided to leave Zhengzhou for Jinan at sundown.

They would try to catch a grain barge at an obscure pier a few li downstream from the main pier. Yinho went and got the grain barge docking schedule from the cashier at the Long De Teahouse.

As Yusu had managed to locate their cart, it was certain their whereabouts had been exposed. So leaving as soon as possible without the cart was the only sensible option. *The Yan army must get no intelligence about our destination or our plan to join General Tie's army.* To dodge Nezha's surveillance, it was thought sensible to buy four sets of Taoist robes and caps for disguise purpose, using the performance money.

How can we lose you, Nezha? Sai'er hissed under her breath with frustration.

By the time they reached the pier, the sky was dark with heavy rain clouds, the air laden with moisture. That was fortuitous for them, as Nezha's vision would be hampered in such weather.

Binhong negotiated the fare with the barge helmsman. The barge had just unloaded all its cargo and was heading back to Jinan. The helmsman was happy to take the passengers and horses on his home-bound empty vessel. All four of them, dressed as Taoist monks, boarded the barge with their horses.

It was going to be an overnight trip, and the destination was a small pier ten li upstream from the Jinan main pier.

As soon as they settled down in the hull, a flash rainstorm broke out. About half a joss stick's burning time later, the sky cleared. A freshly bathed full moon peered out from the inky boudoir.

Binhong, Yinho and Ah Long had all drifted off into deep sleep during the downpour.

Sai'er couldn't sleep. Her mind was saddled with muddling emotions and thoughts. She went up to the deck for some fresh air. The rain-soaked deck was empty. At last she was all alone.

Leaning on the railing to look out, she was overwhelmed by wistfulness. Right in front was a sheer veil of translucent dark, illuminated by a wrinkled moon in the water. Was she staring at her own crumpled dream?

From her sleeve pocket she retrieved the portrait that Sanbao had sketched and looked at it through misty eyes. Suddenly, a profound sense of loneliness welled inside and spread like mercury to the tips of her limbs.

What is to become of me? How am I to evade marriage with Lin San? If I do get my way, will I have a future with Sanbao, or will I grow old alone, like Pearly?

Her thoughts then hovered around more practical problems. Would she get the Xuannu Sword back? How could the Sword and the Amulet help with her mission? Why was Nezha willing to serve the Prince?

As her troubled thoughts whirled and wheeled, she whispered Lan Caihe's name. In a beat, to her panting joy, she caught a whiff of the familiar floral fragrance.

"Caihe, is that you? I've missed you so much!"

The blue-robed sprite leapt out of the immense darkness onto the railing and sat there with its bare feet dangling over the water, as at home as a neighbor dropping by for tea.

"I see you're sad, my dear Sai'er," chimed the sprite. "Don't be. You are destined to give hope to the oppressed in this mortal life, short as it is. Follow the Maitreya Buddha's teachings and love and compassion will fill your heart. Do not let yourself be trapped in worldly obsessions. They are but flowers in the mirror, moon in the water. When you see color, it's not color at all. When you don't see color, everything is infused with it."

The little sprite sounded like a veteran Buddhist to Sai'er, much as it belonged to the Tao Pantheon.

"Ah, my dear Caihe, that's a level of wisdom that's beyond me. Can I ask a more down-to-earth question? Must I wed Lin San? What's this nonsense with letting our previous spousal relationship run its course? There was hardly a relationship to speak of. Being Hou Yi's consort was little more than being his plaything for goodness' sake!"

"Ah, be that as it may, I'm afraid your spousal years fell short of the fated number and there's a need to make it up. But don't worry. You're not required to consummate the marriage, because your mission requires superior mastery of the North Star skill, which only a virgin can achieve."

"That's good to know. But how come Hou Yi got reincarnated? I thought he was condemned to the underworld for eternity?"

"The Deities are merciful and gave him a chance to redeem his previous sins. But it looks like he's been squandering this one rare chance. Greed will be his undoing. Anyway, I can assure you he's too preoccupied with his pretty concubines to care about you. Your time with him will be short. Oops, I'm already telling too much."

I guess I'll have to take this as good news.

"Oh, Caihe, can you tell me something about the Xuannu Sword? I'm sorry I was too careless and gave Yusu a chance to steal it from me."

"Well, let's just say the Sword is in good hands. There will come a time when you'll need to use the Sword and the Amulet. But not in the near future. The Xuannu Sword is one of a pair of magical swords that belong to Xuannu the Warrior Goddess. She gifted one to the Yellow Emperor to help him win a cosmic war. This is all I can say."

But the Sword is in Yusu's hands! This little creature is really evasive when it's talking about the future. All those riddles!

"Now that Master Zhang has gone into hiding, I don't know who can help decipher the writing on the Amulet, or how to use it."

"Don't worry about that just yet. In time someone will emerge to offer help."

"Alright, in due course. There's one more thing. What's been puzzling me is that Nezha chose to work for the Prince. If my memory serves me right, he was decent as a Senior Marshal in the North Pantheon. Now he's a real nuisance, spying on us all the time."

"You see, as much as the Prince claims that Nezha is his buddy, they are not that close. And it is for a different reason Nezha agreed to help the Prince. That reason is that Nezha owed the Green Dragon an old debt, because a long time ago Nezha had killed his third son by accident and the Green Dragon abducted his parents in revenge. Out of filial piety, Nezha offered his blood and mangled body in exchange for his parents' safety. But later, the Taoist Immortal Taiyi resurrected him and the Jade Emperor granted him immortal status. That, however, gave the Green Dragon an excuse to reject Nezha's act of self-destruction as reparation. Of late, he has reminded Nezha of the old debt and coerced him into helping the Prince to satisfy it."

"Ahh, that explains it! So at heart Nezha is not a villain after all." Sai'er was wondering if there was a way to persuade Nezha to change sides.

Tired from standing for so long, she slowly sank down on her haunches with legs crossed, and pondered aloud, "That sounds like Green Dragon and the Prince are somehow closely connected. It probably goes back to their immortal lives. So what was their relationship?"

"Hmm, that's a long story." Caihe leaped onto Sai'er's lap and reclined against her thigh in repose. With eyes closed, it drew a deep breath and unspooled the thread of history.

"Green Dragon and Sky Wolf had been immortal Sky Wolf twins. Sadly, at the time of their birth, their birth mother, a lynx nymph who had had an affair with an old sky wolf, was so shocked by their ugly faces that she disowned the infants and left them at the entrance to the fox nymphs' quarters. Two fox nymphs found them, and each picked up one of the twins and raised him separate from the other. So, while growing up, they were not aware they were twin brothers."

Caihe took a break, as if deliberately to create suspense. Sai'er stared at the sprite, round-eyed with anticipation. With preening delight, the hermaphrodite resumed the story at a measured pace.

"In their youth, the twins turned out to be very good-looking, and many maiden nymphs were attracted to them. One day the older twin, that is, Green Dragon, got drunk and bullied a group of the Jade Palace maids into dancing naked for him. This was reported to the Jade Emperor, who got furious over this brazen act. So, as punishment, he demoted him to demon status in the East Sea underworld.

"Meanwhile, Sky Wolf the younger twin sweet-talked his way to the rank of Deputy General in the North Pantheon. But eventually he got demoted to the mortal world because of debauchery, as you well know. By chance or design, the two twin brothers met on earth and were reunited."

Sai'er gave out a sigh of satisfaction. "Ah, now the whole picture is much clearer to me! Thank you so much for the back story."

Sai'er also recalled Master Zhang saying that the Green Dragon had command of storms and floods. That unfortunately meant he would be the Prince's most formidable ally, apart from Monk Yao. It didn't help that the hex experience still kept haunting her. She would give anything to have that memory erased.

"Caihe, I have one last question. While at Wudang, I grew close to Pearly. She's now in the Yan camp trying to snitch intelligence under cover. I've been wondering if she's also on a celestial mission?"

"The answer is no. What drives Pearly is her keen sense of justice and compassion, thanks to her upbringing under Master Zhang. She willingly gave up true love to pursue justice against evil. Xuannu the Warrior Goddess is her role model."

"I truly admire Pearly. We're fortunate to have her on our side. I can see why my Grandba fell in love with her," said Sai'er, her eyelids drooping from fatigue.

"I better leave now. You need your sleep for your battle in the coming days. Till next time, my dear."

Before the first ray of dawn aroused sleepy earth, the barge had moored at a small pier in Jinan.

Yinho and Ah Long were to share one horse. The thirteen-year-old bubbled over with excitement when he was told of the group's destination. He was just too young to understand the meaning of war. Still, his sprightly mood helped to kindle the group's spirit.

They started the land leg of the journey at the west-central part of the city, which was where the Daming Lake was located. Many poets had written about the beauty of this lake, fed by a web of crystal clear underground springs. Large pink and white water lilies wove through the mirror-like lake and the periphery was festooned with swaying green willows. Jinan was also the birthplace of renowned Song poets Li Qingzhao and Xin Qiji.

Sai'er had often formed mental pictures of the place from what her Ba had told her. He had the good fortune of being taught history and poetry in his adolescence by the famous Confucian scholar-official Fang Xiaoru, now the Chief Adviser to the Jianwen Emperor. It was one of the places she had often dreamed of visiting.

Instead of water lilies and willows, now afloat on the lake surface and strewn haphazardly by the lakeside were mounds of human corpses and horse carcasses, beset by ravenous armies of squawking crows and gigantic buzzing flies. A dark and putrid miasma hung above the once resplendent lake.

The odious stench nauseated Sai'er. Cold sweat beaded on her back as grisly reality ahead stared her in the face. She had to kill, or be killed or maimed, or taken prisoner, which would be far worse than being killed. Never had she imagined she would have to contend with her own fear before actual fighting even started.

Having passed the west side of the lake, they headed south to the city center, where General Tie had built up defense fortifications around the nucleus of the city.

Sai'er felt sure that this time Nezha was not on their tail. Latching onto that positive thought as an escape from debilitating fear, she bade the others not to stall and be vigilant, as they had now entered a battle zone and might come under attack any time. Black storm clouds teeming above provided some sort of cover.

Garrisoned ramparts loomed out of the semi-darkness. Coming into view was a semicircular swathe of medium-height thick brick walls topped with a crenellated parapet, the entire stretch punctuated by watch towers and skirted all round by a wide moat. Behind this outer layer perched the main, taller bulwark, made of gigantic slabs of stones and crenellated.

The surroundings were a vast expanse of flat land, purposely cleared of woods and dwellings. Even without much military knowledge, Sai'er could see this was a wise defense strategy, as the barren openness not only offered a clear view of any encroaching army of invaders but also denied the enemy convenient cover and supply of firewood for their armory.

Binhong waved a white cloth as the group approached the central gates. Sai'er spotted vigilant bowmen lurking behind the crenels with hand-held crossbows.

Moments later, a commander shouted out the order to let down the suspension bridge.

The group rode through the bridge and the outer gates. At the entrance to the inner ramparts, Binhong and the others dismounted and he handed the sentinel guard Tang Jun's letter of introduction. They waited for a reply from General Tie.

15

THEY FOLLOWED the guard's lead across two large training compounds into the barracks at the rear.

The door to General Tie's private chamber was wide open.

With a robust muscular build and a swarthy, bearded face, the general looked stolid and intimidating. When Ah Long saw his face, he flinched like a frightened puppy and held Yinho's hand tight.

"So you're Tang Jun's daughter, and you his foster son," he directed his gaze at Sai'er and Binhong, seeing through Sai'er's Taoist guise at first glance. Then he turned to Yinho and said, "You must be Master Zhang's adoptee, and this little fellow here, your admirer."

"I would have treated you all to a big welcome feast had we not been in war time," he said, lifting his eyebrows and curving his lips in a facetious smile. "I hope you don't mind having delicious millet gruel for a welcome breakfast. Dear fellows, we'll talk after you've filled your stomach."

And thus he had broken the ice.

After breakfast, General Tie led them on a tour of the inner and outer battlements. Behind the barracks lay the city's beating heart, comprised of shops, restaurants, apothecaries, butcher houses, vendor stalls, granaries and hamlets of private dwellings. Further afield were farmland and forests. He showed them the whirlwind catapults that were ranged at intervals on the outer wall terrace.

"These machines can hurl projectiles in any direction. We use them to fire incendiary bombs and pots of burning tar," the general explained.

While touring the inner defense walls, Sai'er noticed that they were manned by a front line of crossbowmen, supplemented by a second line of archers.

"The crossbows can fire volleys of bolts and can inflict serious damage, but they're expensive and training takes longer than archery. Nimble archers can fire incendiary arrows and are just as valuable as crossbowmen," said the General.

Then he walked them through the armory. Racks of different kinds of weapons and artillery ammunition lined the three walls of the room. "The most commonly used are broadswords and halberds," said he. "So, what kind of weapons are you kids good at using?"

"Sai'er and I use double-edged long swords, and Yinho uses a spear," Binhong replied.

"That should be useful in close range combat. I've heard you and Sai'er are adept at Sword-as-Whip kung fu. That's really impressive. Yinho, I would suggest you exchange your spear for a halberd, because it's a sturdier weapon for attacking."

"Yes, General Tie. That's a good idea," replied Yinho with alacrity.

Sai'er, Binhong, Yinho and Ah Long were assigned one cubicle with four pallet beds in the barracks. For practicality, Sai'er continued to disguise herself as a man.

Sai'er and Binhong spent the next three days practicing archery in the training compounds, competing with each other in the firing speed of successive shots. Yinho taught Ah Long the basics of spear wielding and gave him the task of sketching the catapults.

On the fourth day, the Yan army mounted an assault on the garrisons. Armor made of lacquered rhinoceros hide was handed out to the three young people. They were to stand ready with their weapons on the inner rampart terrace.

Three siege towers on wheels carrying bowmen and ammunition took up front position, followed by cavalry troops. Foot soldiers brought up the rear.

As the battalion approached the moat, the whirlwind catapults fired volleys of stones and firing bombs at the siege towers, engulfing one in a sea of flames and forcing soldiers inside to clamber out. These met with sheet after sheet of incendiary arrows fired by archers behind the inner walls. In a matter of moments, they flailed and floundered like a flaming mass of porcupines.

General Tie, who was watching the battle scene with the three youngsters, nodded with relief. "The siege tower that's on fire is the one with the battering rams," he said.

The other two towers managed to come to the edge of the moat to drop two separate moat-crossing bridges. Catapults fitted inside the towers fired projectiles at the outer walls. The sturdy brick walls hardly budged.

Soldiers wearing helmets with red tassels and lamellar armor and wielding machetes and halberds sallied out from the siege towers. They began pouring onto the two bridges like waves of fire ants.

Pots of burning tar and oil were flung at them. Dozens of singed bodies plunged shrieking into the moat.

Choking odors of fire smoke and charred human flesh filled the air.

Those lucky enough to escape the scorching liquid, some

seventy to eighty of them, managed to leap over the parapet onto the terrace of the outer walls.

"Allow no one to get near the drawbridge gatehouse," shouted the vigilant Commander Su.

"Now let's see what you can do, young people," General Tie said to the trio. "Leave their leader General Zhang Yu to me."

One after the other, they hopped onto the outer wall terrace to join the combat.

Yinho skewered the first opponent who charged at him with a mace like a wild bull, and retracted his halberd laced with bloody bits of organs.

Turning sideways, he churned and swung the weapon at two others with bewildering speed and force, slicing both with the crescent blade before they could dodge.

Having drawn up qi to his arms, Binhong whipped his sword at the two who aimed their halberds at his torso, warding off the hit and with a backward swipe, slashed the throats of both. Blood splattered on his face and armor.

Three Yan soldiers wielding machetes closed in on Sai'er, probably thinking the puny girl was an easy target. She stood stock still, sword raised, and worked up her qi. Pew, pew, pew. Blindingly fast whiplashes caught them dumbstruck. Before they came out of their daze, blood spurted from a cut nose, a severed arm and a gashed leg.

Leaping up in mid-air, Binhong lunged at a couple of attackers nearby, cutting them down like melons. Three more encircled him. His qi-driven triple-slash split open the bellies of two, their stinking innards spilling through the gashes. The third one skittered away like a lizard.

One somersault and Yinho jumped to the rescue of a garrison soldier, fencing off a would-be lethal hit. With a beguiling drunken spin of his halberd followed by a head-on stab, he pierced the chest of the attacker, who instantly fell with a screech. Three other aggressive ones hemmed Sai'er in. To dodge their strikes, she deployed nimble hexagram footwork and leaped about evasively. Then she launched a series of ferocious downward swipes of her whistling sword, and cracked their kneecaps, at once crippling them all.

She looked over her shoulder and spotted General Zhang Yu aiming a halberd lunge at General Tie's back as the latter tried to readjust from a stumble. She spun around and made a flying leap over the heads of those in her way, just in time to ward off the deadly blow.

Landing on her feet, she flicked her sword in a tight triple-strike with crackling force. The last hit caught the handle of her opponent's halberd. The vibration on metal contact jerked it out of his hand. He tottered backwards from the impact. She used the opening to kick him down and extracted his qi till he slumped to the ground, unconscious. He was going to live, or so she thought.

A garrison soldier, with blazing hatred in his eyes not dissimilar to Yinho's, sidled up close and, to Sai'er shock, began hacking at the prostrate general with his broadsword. When he was done, squirts of blood splattered on his face and armor. A frenzied howl emitted from his twisted mouth showing scarlet-stained teeth.

Sai'er forced herself to watch the lunatic murder in cold blood, trying hard to swallow her fear. She did it to have the violent image seared onto her memory, so she could get used to the notion of ruthless killing. In combat there was no room for mercy. Hate was a handy aid.

In her dazed state, she felt a faint rush of wind behind her. The blade of a mace fell a hairsbreadth away from her left shoulder. No sooner had she turned around than a second swing homed in at her throat. Binhong bolted out of nowhere to flick away the mace just in time. With another quick thrust of the sword he cut down the attacker.

"Sai'er, are you alright?" His deep voice calmed her frayed nerves. "Yes, yes. I'm alright," said she, face livid with shock.

Between them, the trio tackled and subdued about half of the invaders. Not one of them even panted from the exertion.

The retreating Yan soldiers scrambled back to the siege towers to retract the bridges and the invading battalion beat a hasty retreat. The wounded and surrendering survivors were being taken prisoners. Mutilated bodies emitted shrill cries. Bruised faces puckered with pain and dread. The terrace was swathed in a cloying, metallic tang of blood.

Wars turn people into subhumans, allowing no room for mercy, Sai'er mused with quiet resignation as she watched the defeated squirm and writhe pitifully.

General Tie's army gained the upper hand, until the next battle rolled around.

Commander Su made a quick count of his own men and ordered them to clear the terrace of the dead and wounded. He went up to General Tie to report the number of casualties, flustered and a little addled.

"Well done, Commander Su! You should be proud of your men," said General Tie. The commander flashed a smile of gratitude. "I can't take credit, General Tie. Without the help of these esteemed guests, our casualties would be much higher."

Turning to the trio, General Tie said to Sai'er with genuine admiration, "Sai'er, thank you for saving my life. I owe you a big debt." Swiveling his gaze onto her comrades, he added, "Young people, you've opened my eyes today! We're all very grateful for your help. Please join us in my chamber for a meeting tomorrow morning."

At the military meeting held the next morning, General Tie revealed that Pearly had just sent in her pet eagle Zhuge Liang with the urgent message that the Yan camp were talking of flooding out Jinan city with swells from the Yellow River.

He threw the floor open for suggestions of a defense strategy. Instantly a somber silence draped over the room. The military elite realized the danger they were facing. Flat land was indefensible against flooding.

Sai'er froze from recalling what Master had said about the Green Dragon. The water demon had total command of storms and floods at his fingertips.

A deputy commander proposed to abandon the fortifications and retreat south to Tai'an city. General Tie shook his head. "If we give up one inch, the enemy will advance a foot."

"But our citizens will be trapped and their property destroyed if we don't retreat," said a junior marshal whose face was white as paper.

Silence was so thick that a knife could cut through it.

"General Tie, I must warn everyone that the Prince has the Green Dragon as an aide," Sai'er said, breaking the silence. "For all I know, the evil demon is absolutely capable of churning up the Yellow River to wreak havoc anywhere. The question is whether the Prince would think it worthwhile to flood a resource-rich city like Jinan."

Yinho nodded with a deep frown. But Binhong, who had never heard of the Green Dragon or the hex incident, drew a sharp breath like everyone else. He glared at Sai'er with questioning eyes. She avoided his accusatory gaze.

If retreat is not an option, then deceive and entrap!

In a deep voice, General Tie boomed out his order. "We shall not retreat, but will fake surrender. The plan is to invite the Prince and his troops to come within our walls to accept our surrender and take over the city."

He paused to look round the room. Satisfied he had the group's undivided attention, he elaborated further:

"But we must wait for the Prince to send us the threat first, because if we acted right away, we could blow Pearly's cover. With the Prince's favorite general now dead, he probably can't wait to teach us a lesson. Meanwhile, we'll use the time gap to set up the trap."

Ah, so I'm not the only one who's thought of using deception.

The General was betting on the Prince's flood threat being just a bluff, as his ultimate aim must be to plunder Jinan's abundant food and armory resources rather than to inundate the city. General Tie based his bet on the informed guess that the Yan camp's protracted siege tactics had exhausted their own food and supplies.

Sai'er couldn't believe that the General and she were of the same mind.

"General, may I ask a question? I didn't see Monk Yao or Ma Sanbao at the battle. Are they not with the Yan battalion?" Sai'er couldn't figure out why the two hadn't shown up. Truth be told, though, the real reason for asking was that she missed Sanbao badly and hungered for any shred of information about him.

"Ah, my scouts told me they were both sent back to Beiping a month ago to defend the fort there, because Imperial troops from Yingtian had laid siege to Beiping," replied General Tie.

That night, back in their room, Binhong wormed a confession out of Sai'er.

"But why did you feel you had to hide it from me in the first place?"

"You're as stubborn as Ba. I just didn't think... you'd understand a girl's complex feelings," Sai'er stuttered, flushed with embarrassment.

"Sai'er, who was the one that said to never keep secrets from each other?"

Ah, beating me at my own game!

"I'm sorry — I should've let you in on the hex story sooner."

"I always knew you had mixed feelings for the Prince," he said with sharp exhalation. "I trusted that if I left you alone, you'd in time sort it all out."

"I guess I felt ashamed that he had such great power over me. I didn't want you to see my weakness."

"It was hardly your fault. That bastard! Stooping so low as to use hex. Good thing Yinho knows how to work sorcery." Deep frowns crinkled his prematurely roughened forehead.

Trying to sound as gentle as he could, he ended up whispering, "I wouldn't know how to answer to Uncle if something happened to you —" Clearing his throat, he added, half pleading, half demanding, "From now on, no more secrets among the three of us? Alright?"

Relieved he was let off the hook, Yinho hastened to affirm, "Right, right! No more secrets!"

Sai'er gave an awkward nod. If she was being absolutely honest, she was still enmeshed in lingering passion and abject fear for the Prince, hard as she had tried to untangle these confounding emotions. Sometimes she wondered if submissive fear was addictive. Binhong thought it wasn't her fault. But wasn't it really?

Two days later, an envoy from the enemy camp approached the outer walls with a white flag. He shot an arrow with a letter attached at one upright plank of the drawbridge, and then rode away.

As expected, it was the Prince's letter warning the General

of a man-made flood. With the loss of General Zhang Yu, the vengeful Prince was anxious to bring Jinan to its knees.

General Tie's invitation letter, sounding reluctant and helpless, was sent out three days later.

At the entrance of both the outer and inner ramparts, a heavy suspended wooden grille with spikes ranged at the bottom had been installed using a pulley and winch mechanism, with the release lever secured by a latch. Normally, ropes would be pulled to raise the grille, and gradual release of the ropes would allow the grille to drop steadily. In case of emergencies, striking the latch with a hammer would result in a precipitate fall.

The plan was to trap the Prince and his vanguard in the passageway between the outer and inner walls after they came through on the drawbridge. Crossbowmen and archers would hide in watch towers and along the rampart parapets and ambush the trapped soldiers as well as those left outside the outer grille. The Prince would be captured alive.

As soon as Yinho heard the Prince would be coming, he volunteered to take charge of the outer grille release. Commander Su would handle the inner grille. Timing control and coordination between the two would be critical. Both grilles must be dropped at almost the same time once the targets were inside.

Sai'er and Binhong would join the bowmen and archers in the main watch tower.

The day of surrender finally arrived.

Moisture-laden clouds hung heavy in the darkening sky. The Yan cavalry troops roared towards the main gates in three columns. On approaching the moat, the left and right columns stopped their advance, while the middle column merged into a single file and trotted with insolence across the lowered drawbridge. White flags fluttering outside all watch towers offered a note of welcome to them.

Sai'er spotted the fully armored Prince at the rear of the line. Even at that distance, she could make out a familiar smirk on his lordly face. Her heartbeat slammed in her eardrums. This was the man who had wanted to prostrate her by any means, even abetting his bestial twin to rape her. What happens in a hallucinatory hex is often a reflection of the creator's real desire, Yinho had told her.

Yet the words he had spoken in her Moon Palace still strummed like soft music in her ears: "Say you love me too or I will die!"

Still, she would never go anywhere without taking the talisman with her.

Binhong moved to the opposite side of the watch tower to catch a better glimpse of the incoming horsemen. She was at his heels in a state of angst. She wished more than anything for the trap to work. Yet a faint premonition made her jittery.

Having gathered in the passageway, Yan soldiers in the vanguard spread out to allow space for their Prince to come through.

Just as the Prince's black stallion approached the outer grille, it suddenly balked and reared up with a shrill screech. Sai'er looked up just in time to catch a glimpse of the Wind and Fire Wheels slinking into the thick clouds. Apparently Nezha was keeping watch.

The stallion's shreak alarmed the soldiers in the passageway. In a flash, both grilles plonked down with a heavy thud. The stallion's snout got snagged in the spikes, and the Prince, out of desperation, jerked the horse away with violent force, instantly ripping off a chunk of skin and flesh from its face. The stallion squealed in agony. He used his reins and spurs to whip the mangled animal across the bridge, just in time before it was hauled back up.

Meanwhile arrows and bolts rained down on the trapped soldiers.

The Prince changed horses with one of the cavalry soldiers and waved a retreat in the beating rain.

It was not possible to catch the look on his face. But just picturing his murderous fury sent a frisson of danger down Sai'er's spine.

"It was so close. We were just an inch away from nailing him," said Yinho in low spirits when the trio got back to their cubicle.

Darn! Our 'needle wrapped in cotton' strategy almost worked.

A bad omen hung in the air. The Prince was not one to take such humiliation lying down. The failed attempt to capture him was going to foreground a monstrous backlash, Sai'er thought glumly.

16

TWO DAYS LATER, a secret message from Pearly, written in a shaky hand, advised General Tie that the Yan army was directing its forces to capture the neighboring city Dezhou, which had abundant grains and supplies, and their next target was Liaocheng, through which the Grand Canal coursed. Once they got hold of Liaocheng, they could quickly swing south using the Canal to the Yangtze region. So, for the next while, Jinan was safe from further attacks.

"That makes strategic sense from the usurper's viewpoint," said Binhong. "His ultimate goal is Yingtian and the throne. So getting around the iron-clad fortifications of Jinan is obviously the more sensible choice. Once he seizes the throne, the whole country will be his anyway."

Sai'er had to admit that Binhong's thinking was getting sharper by the day.

"The Prince isn't that smart. Someone must've given him this sound advice," Yinho sneered.

"No doubt it's Monk Yao directing the show from Beiping," Sai'er said. "But I do worry about Pearly. I wonder how she's doing."

The answer to Sai'er's question came a couple of days later. While practicing neigong with Binhong and Yinho in the cubicle, a soldier came in to hand her a folded note, just delivered by the eagle. He stood by to await a reply.

It was a personal letter from Pearly, smeared with blood and seemingly written in a shaky hand. The letter read thus:

> Dear Sai'er,
>
> About a month ago, on the Prince's sudden order, Monk Yao and Sanbao left for Beiping in a hurry. Once they left, the Prince asked Yusu to harass me... daily. But Yusu is a loud mouth, so I could extract from her all the information I wanted.
>
> Four days ago, he was in a foul mood, no doubt because he was almost caught by General Tie, on top of learning.... that you and your friends had lent Tie a hand. He bade Yusu to torture me... with finger crunchers. Apparently he's still angry that my Grandba refused to join his army. Yusu took it upon herself.... to also mar my face with burning joss sticks. But they knew better than to cross the line – they couldn't afford to enrage Monk Yao, who is the brain behind this entire war. Fortunately, they suspect nothing about my new pet eagle Zhuge Liang.
>
> You might be happy to know that Yusu has given.... the Xuannu Sword to Nezha for safe-keeping.
>
> If you get a chance to see your Grandba, please tell him I'm fine. My Grandba is in hiding and it's best not to look for him.
>
> Pearly

Sai'er's hands couldn't stop shaking. *No, no! This is not happening to Pearly.* Shivers ran down her spine just picturing beautiful Pearly being disfigured and humiliated. The only consolation was that the Sword was now in Nezha's hands, as foretold by Caihe. But when her thoughts turned back to Pearly, she couldn't help weeping aloud.

Binhong grabbed the letter to read. Yinho stood over his shoulders to catch a look.

Binhong cradled Sai'er in his arms and stroke her back. "Our job here is done. Let's go and rescue her tonight and take her home with us."

Yinho was quick to jot down a few words on a scrap of paper alerting Pearly to expect them tonight and gave the note to the soldier. The soldier inserted it inside the bell that the courier eagle carried on its talon.

After saying farewell to General Tie, the trio and Ah Long left the city fort.

An autumn crescent moon smiled behind a smoky screen of gossamer clouds.

All dressed in black for camouflage, the group dismounted from their horses about two hundred yards from the Yan compound. Having hitched the horses to trees in the copse just off an open field bordering the eastside of the compound, they crept westwards along the south border of the camp site.

Sai'er had scanned a layout drawing of the compound just before their departure from the city fort.

The compound lay on the southeast side of the Daming Lake. There were five horizontal rows of tents, with sentry guards stationed at both ends of each row. Their siege towers and military horses were kept in the open field to the east of the compound and were heavily guarded by sentries. The west border abutted a dense pine grove that extended westwards along the south bank of the Lake. Their escape route would be through the pine grove.

A waft of discordant guqin sound gave them some hint as to the spot of Pearly's detention tent. Sai'er estimated that it lay in the middle of the last row of tents. The obvious choice was to sneak up to the final row along the west border.

Yinho had bought Ah Long a blow-dart pipe in Zhengzhou, and the lad had been practicing its use while idling in the city fort.

Now he moved forward like a stealthy cat, and blew drug-laced darts, one at a time, on the five sentry guards at the west end. His movement was swift as the run of quicksilver, so none of the guards got a chance to alert another.

The dimly lit night provided good cover for the rescue team despite the ominous, throttled quietness.

Sai'er and Binhong moved swiftly along the edge of the grove towards Pearly's tent, while Yinho and Ah Long snaked their way back to the copse to fetch the horses.

Once inside, Binhong cut down the only guard with one single stroke. Sai'er saw Pearly seated at a table on which lay the guqin, her thin ankles bound with ropes. Zhuge Liang stood protectively on a perch by her side.

Her delicate face looked inflamed with ugly black spots and welts and her eyes were swollen. Her fingers were a mangle of twisted shapes. Crusted blood stains and burn marks daubed her white dress. Tears prickled Sai'er's eyes when she saw her coach in such pitiable state.

Yusu, looking like Pearly but with an infuriating smug expression, was seated on the other side of the table.

Just one glance at the imposter and blinding fury surged in Sai'er. She hadn't been aware that rage was always dormant like latent cinders in a corner of her heart. It just lay in wait for a flint to spark a deadly flame.

She grabbed Yusu by the collar and flung her to the ground. Yusu cringed as she stepped forward menacingly. At that moment, nothing gave Sai'er more pleasure than watching Yusu's comically frantic look. Rolling her over, she slapped her palm on the woman's back to extract her qi with a single mind till she gagged and the light in her eyes dimmed. The provocation rule in the use of martial arts as a weapon that Master had set flitted across her mind, but she just willed to push it aside. Never had she imagined that overpowering another person could give her such a kick out of it.

Pearly said feebly, "Don't kill her, Sai'er."

Pearly's tender voice arrested Sai'er's murderous mood.

"You owe your life to Pearly," Sai'er grunted at the prostrate Yusu. "Do you understand?"

While cutting the ropes that twined Pearly's feet, Binhong said gently, "Good thing you tipped us off with your guqin. But how did you—"

She pointed at her eagle.

Then Sai'er asked, gazing at her coach's disfigured hands, "How did you manage to write the letter?"

"I used neigong to grip the brush with my mouth," Pearly replied calmly.

"We must get going," Binhong said as he helped her strap the guqin across her shoulder. She placed a leather glove on her other shoulder and Zhuge Liang hopped onto the glove without any prompt.

Sai'er seated Pearly in front of her on the horse and trotted off. The group rode through the pine grove and headed straight to that small pier where the foursome had previously alighted. They waited until dawn to board a Putai-bound vessel.

It was mid-afternoon the next day when the group of five arrived at the Tang cottage.

Sai'er's Ba was not expecting them when he heard knocking on the postern door. When he opened the door and saw the visitors, he appeared fazed, because Sai'er was dressed in men's clothes and was a lot taller than two years ago. Then he saw

Binhong and cried out, "You're back!"

"Yes, Uncle, we're back! You're looking well."

Ba turned to take another look at Sai'er and tears filled his eyes. Sai'er dashed forward to hug him tight, tears cascading. "Thank Buddha you're all safe," he patted her back. Then, looking disconcerted, he added, "Daughter, we have guests."

"Oh, let me introduce. Ba, this is Yinho, Master Zhang's adoptee, and the young lad is Ah Long, his apprentice."

"Ah, good! Welcome to the family, Yinho, Ah Long. Please feel right at home here. Binhong, why don't you show them to the guest room to set down their belongings. And this madam is…"

"She's Pearly, Master's granddaughter and my coach," Sai'er was praying the presence of Pearly wouldn't upset Ba.

"Ah, Pearly. Welcome to our humble abode," he said warmly, then added with genuine concern, "Are you hurt? It looks like you need medical care."

Sai'er felt relieved and said, "Ba, Pearly was tortured in the Yan camp, and yes, we need to take care of the burns on her face and her crushed fingers."

"Thank you kindly, Teacher Tang. I'm sorry to be imposing on your hospitality," Pearly said with a mellow gaze into Ba's eyes, as if trying to find traces of Grandba there.

"Please call me Jun, and don't be a stranger," Ba said politely. "I was once your grandfather's student too. Only I never had the pleasure of meeting you while I was there. You must be tired from the journey. Why don't you get some rest in Sai'er's room before we all have supper together? After supper, I'll take a good look at your wounds."

Binhong had just come back out to the yard with Yinho and Ah Long, and Ba asked him to move the spare bed from his room to Sai'er's, so Pearly could lie down a bit.

"Sai'er, why don't you make tea for everyone, while I run along to Mother Lin's place to ask her to prepare more food for supper," said Ba with barely concealed joy.

Sai'er felt immense comfort to be back home, as she hitched the horses in the stable and gave them water and hay. Everything looked and smelled familiar.

The maple and pear trees seemed to have grown a little taller. Pots and woks in the kitchen were exactly the way she had left them. And Ba looked pretty much the same, except his shoulders had stooped a bit.

Yet, so much had happened in her life in just two short years that this place felt at once very familiar and a little strange. It was like meeting an old friend after a long lapse, and all it took was a little catching up to warm her heart and rekindle the bond.

Mother Lin was a kind, matronly woman who was a superb cook. On Ba's insistence, she stayed to have supper with the whole gang. She showed special affinity for Sai'er, quietly piling the best cuts of meat into her bowl during supper.

Sai'er had a vague memory of Mother Lin coming to visit her Ma. According to Ba, when she was around seven, the two women had made a verbal pact for Sai'er to be betrothed to Lin San.

"Sai'er, I know my son doesn't deserve you," Mother Lin said, while helping Sai'er with dish washing in the kitchen. "But if you're so kind as to forgive his taking concubines and consent to wed him, I'll call him back from Zhengzhou right away and have him buy you a new cottage here."

Sai'er had been preparing herself for this moment since that last meeting with Caihe on the barge. So she said with a patient smile, "Mother Lin, I can't thank you enough for taking care of my Ba these last two years. As for the wedding, this was always my Ma's wish, and I must obey it. I know it will please Ba too. So please go ahead with planning the ceremony as you wish."

When Mother Lin had left, Ba carefully examined the burns on Pearly's face and her bashed fingers.

"I have herbs that can completely heal your burns, leaving no scars," Ba said with a knitted brow. "The bad news is, from the look of it, your finger bones are broken, and unfortunately I can only give you medication to ease the pain but I have no way of restoring them to their original state."

"Oh no! Does that mean she's maimed for life?" Sai'er blurted out in utter disappointment.

Pearly appeared calm enough when she heard Ba's diagnosis. The way she had been enduring the excruciating pain without so much as a groan just astounded everyone around her.

Ba diluted a handful of sanqi root powder in warm water and spread the white paste onto two cotton pads. After cleaning the mutilated digits with salt water, he wrapped one pad around each of Pearly's hands and said, "This should clear up the inflammation, but it's only palliative. I'm going to brew some dried longan tea for you. It'll help you sleep through the night. Tomorrow morning I'll tend to your burns."

When everyone had retired to bed, Sai'er went to Ba's bed chamber for a chat.

"I've missed you, Ba," said Sai'er, gazing into his eyes to try to reach his soul.

"Life was hard without you, Daughter." Ba replied. He didn't evade her gaze, but met it with reddened eyes. "I know you want to know why I told you your Grandba died when I was ten. The reason was, when you were a kid, I was still furious about my father leaving us in my childhood. For a long time in my youth, I pinned the blame of my mother's death on him. So when you asked, I felt a simple lie would be much easier than facing the truth," he paused to wipe away a teardrop.

"As you grew up, your Ma helped me see I was wrong. When she died, my heartbreak made me realize that my father had suffered no less from his stunted love. And in my heart I forgave him. But I was too much of a coward to admit to you that I had lied. For this, I ask for your forgiveness."

Sai'er leaned over and patted him on the back, saying softly, "Ba, I understand. There's nothing to forgive. I'm so glad that you've forgiven Grandba. We are and always will be family. That's all that matters." She sniffled, sucking back tears and broke into a smile.

"Oh, I almost forgot. I actually met Grandba on our way back from Wudang. Binhong probably didn't mention this in his brief letter to you. Grandba had tried to rescue Pearly from the Yan camp but learned that she was an undercover spy. Then on leaving the camp, Monk Yao stabbed him in a fight. He fled to Dengfeng and that's where we met. I knew who he was but I didn't reveal my identity. He's now recuperating in the Shaolin Monastery there."

"I'm relieved to hear that he's safe. Obviously Pearly and he are still in love. We haven't seen each other all these years, but I've missed him and have been praying to Buddha to keep him from harm." He paused to take an intense look at Sai'er, then said, "Sai'er, you're a grown woman now—"

"Ba, Mother Lin and I talked earlier. She seemed nice and kind and I've asked her to go ahead and plan the wedding."

"Ah, that's good to hear. I was worrying you might object. Lin San turned out to be not as honest as I had thought, but to honor your Ma's wish—perhaps you could be a good influence on him after you two become man and wife."

"In the end, one must take responsibility for one's actions. I can't change anybody for that matter. But I think I know how to handle him. Lan Caihe assured me that it'd be a union in name only. Ba, you don't have to worry about me. I'm a grown-up now."

"Ah, Binhong had mentioned your strange encounters with a sprite," he said casually. After a pause, a thought hit him and he added with affection, "Oh, before I forget, your dowry. Before your Ma passed away, she told me she had hidden a yellow amber stone underneath the maple tree, and she meant it as your wedding dowry."

"Good thing you mentioned it, Ba. The stone is actually a Magic Peach that the Queen Mother of the West gifted me before my reincarnation. Umm, I wonder if it could heal Pearly's fingers... Well, we shall find out tomorrow."

When she stepped out of Ba's chamber, a cozy feeling of gratitude crept over her. At last he had willingly let her into his heart.

As soon as the first streak of dawn crept in, Sai'er rose from bed. She glanced in Pearly's direction and noticed her deep, even breathing and serene look in sleep. Her marred skin didn't alter her delicate face features. Straying strands of hair from the rich dark mane scattered untamed around her temple.

Under different circumstances, this strong-willed woman and Grandba could've been sharing a simple happy life, Sai'er thought with a wisp of sadness.

Sai'er tiptoed out of the bedroom and went into the backyard. No one else was up yet. She fetched a small shovel from the stable and began digging into the soil around the maple tree. In just a short while, a corner of some red shiny fabric caught her eye. Using her fingers to scrape away the dark soil, she uncovered a small red satin pouch. She unfastened the drawstrings and retrieved a glittering yellow stone the size of a copper coin.

Having stashed away both pouch and stone under her pillow, she shuffled to the kitchen to prepare breakfast.

Later in the morning, hosts and house guests had a simple breakfast of millet gruel and salted eggs in the lounge. Sai'er took it upon herself to spoon-feed Pearly.

After eating, Yinho gave a spear lesson to Ah Long in the backyard, and Binhong practiced Sword-as-Whip by himself.

Ba had earlier prepared batches of a herbal mixture made from arnebia root, dang gui, sesame oil and beeswax and carefully applied one portion on Pearly's burns.

Sai'er went and fetched the amber stone while Ba was unwrapping the sanqi root paste pads from Pearly's hands. Her fingers were still a woeful lump of squashed bone and flesh.

"Pearly, I don't want to raise your hopes, but I have this stone which is supposed to work magic. It's a gift from the Queen Mother of the West. Shall we see if it works?"

Pearly's face lit up when she heard the mention of the Goddess.

She palmed the stone in one hand and waited, closing her eyes tightly in a prayer to Xuannu, her patron deity. Sai'er chanted the Guanyin Sacred Chants for her. The men and Ah Long were all milling about and watching with anxious anticipation.

Under their very eyes, one by one the mangled digits firmed into shape, all the blood-crusted slits and lacerations slowly scabbing over. She tried to flex the newly mended fingers, and they bent and unbent with stiffness at first, then with greater ease.

She quickly passed the stone to the other hand. The same thing happened.

"Thanks be to Guanyin!" screamed Sai'er in joy. She looked towards the sky with her hands clasped together and murmured, "A million thanks to you, Queen Mother, for your healing gift!"

Pearly was too stunned for words. Grateful tears spoke for her. Rising from her seat, she snuggled on Sai'er's shoulder and wept like pear blossoms drenched in rain.

The group was totally dumbstruck by the miracle and everyone exhaled a big sigh of relief.

Five days later, marked improvement showed on Pearly's face. Ba said it would probably take a few more doses of the arnebia mixture to heal the skin completely.

The next day, Pearly bade farewell to her friends, taking with her the remaining batches of the arnebia paste. She said she was going to find a Taoist nunnery in the Yidu environs where she could go into recuperative retreat. She would write to let Sai'er know the location once she'd settled down.

"Jun, Sai'er, I owe you both a great debt, and hopefully someday I can repay it," Pearly said in earnest.

After a short silence, her face shone like an iridescent flower that reminded Sai'er of graceful Xuannu in the Pantheons, and she spoke in a distant echo, "The Prince will inflict more cruelty and harm on anyone who opposes him. There'll be more violent clashes ahead. You've done well so far, Sai'er. But greater challenges lie ahead."

"Thank you, Pearly—" Sai'er's voice trailed off, much awed by the spectacle. She wondered if that was the Goddess herself speaking. Once out of her daze, she said her fond farewell. "Please take good care of yourself, Pearly. Remember to write."

With Zhuge Liang perched on her shoulder, Pearly rode off on one of Ba's mules taken from the backyard stable.

17

As PROMISED, Mother Lin told Lin San to come back to Putai as soon as possible for the wedding. She also demanded that he buy a cottage in the same hamlet as a wedding gift for Sai'er.

Lin San hurried back on hearing from his mother. He bought a large cottage on the north bank of the river, near the lecture temple where Ba taught Buddhism to the White Lotus Society students. The wedding took place on the first day of spring, Sai'er's eighteenth birthday.

For Sai'er, the whole business of the wedding was enormously tedious. The formal rituals of taking note of wedding gifts and sending "return gifts" prior to the wedding, of dressing in a bright red robe and skirt and donning a gaudy headdress on wedding day, of bridal tea-offerings to elders from both households, of kowtowing to the ancestry plaques, and of being ushered from table to table at dinner to accept guests' wine toasts.

The day just wasn't over soon enough.

When wedding guests had finally all left, the bride and groom retired to their bedroom which was newly decorated with embroidered scarlet bed curtains and beddings. The glaring colors and decor irked Sai'er and made her head spin. She just hated red.

Lin San wore a bland look, his eyes glassy and cold. At the wedding feast earlier, disdain and ennui had been written all over his face.

Dead tired from the day's bustle, Sai'er sat down on the edge of the bed and stretched herself out. No sooner had she removed her headdress than he leaned on her and tried roughly to kiss her on the mouth, his breath reeking with liquor. She averted her face and he began to claw at her robe. He had sinewy arms and large hands and with the least effort pulled off her bridal robe and pinned her down on the bed.

"Don't you dare touch me. Go and sleep in the guest room," she grunted in a low-pitched voice.

"But you're my woman—mine to use in bed," he slurred and looked at her with a sly smile. "Not to mention I bought you with a lot of money."

Straddling her with knees at her hips, he tore open her flimsy top undergarment with one tug. As she bucked and strained against his clasp, he ran his hand over her bared breasts, and scoffed, "You little whore! What decent girl would live in the mountains for two years? Did you lie with that wimp Binhong? Maybe that long-limbed ape too? If I find you're no longer a virgin, I swear I'll tie you up and whip you every day."

He gave out a chilling laugh. Hiking up her skirt with one hand, he unfastened his pants with the other, his eyes bulging in excitement.

All this time, Sai'er endured the revolting grope in silence and worked up her qi. Then in one violent smack, she jammed her fist into his eye and shoved him off the bed. He croaked like a raven, palming his darkened eye in shock.

Bounding up, she shot out one leg and kicked him onto the floor. Ramming one knee onto his neck, she planted her heated palm on his chest and began siphoning his qi. He gasped for air, but she wouldn't let go. Not until his eyes rolled all the way back into his head did she release him. The massive loss of qi would leave him weak and impotent for a long while.

"I didn't want to do this. You forced me," she said in a cold voice. "Now go to the guest room. I don't want to see your face here ever again. If you want to play, go back to your concubines in Zhengzhou."

"You'll be sorry —" he spat out the words even as he choked.

Sai'er recounted the incident to Binhong and Yinho the next day at Ba's cottage.

"That should teach him!" Yinho snickered. "I pity him though for having a tigress for a wife!"

For that comment, he got a rough shove from Sai'er.

Binhong eyes spewed fire when he heard what had happened. "He had the nerve to vilify you, and me, after all he had done? Son of a whore!"

Sai'er couldn't help rubbing it in, "Weren't you two buddies before? I had thought you would defend him for old times' sake."

"He fooled me," he simmered with self-directed anger, blushing to the nape of his neck. "It's now clear he's not only treacherous, but a wicked devil too. Sorry you had to go through this."

"Well, I had been mentally prepared. Hou Yi had been known for his abusive ways. The good thing is, the marriage is just a ritual to make up the time of that ancient union."

"Ah, I see. I was worried you might lose some of your North Star power if he — But now I fear he might take revenge —"

"I had no choice. He was too aggressive. I had to repulse him once and for all," Sai'er shrugged. "Let's forget him and talk about how we can train up the White Lotus Society students."

"I can teach Sword-as-Whip," Binhong replied, only too glad that Sai'er changed the subject.

"And I Eight Immortals Rod," Yinho added.

"I'll teach Wave Treading qinggong then. The backyard in the new cottage opens out onto a large tract of grassland. I thought it would be ideal as training ground. What do you think, Binhong?"

"That's a good idea. The cottage is just a short walk away from the lecture temple, so students can go to their training on lecture days. The lectures are now shorter and offered ten times a month, because long lectures tend to bore the students. Uncle said about one hundred male students and twenty female students would like to train in martial arts. The number could go up. We'll see how it goes."

"Good! Let's come up with a schedule so Ba can announce it to the students."

The cities of Dezhou and Liaocheng had previously been lost to the Yan army but General Tie had since recaptured them, taking advantage of high army morale that the Wudang trio had inspired. Jinan still remained impregnable.

As a whole, most of Shandong province was off limits to the Yan army, for now. General Tie was promoted to Minister of War. The Yan camp decided to leave this province and focus on capturing other provinces to the west.

At the start of the civil war, the Prince of Yan had proclaimed that his campaign was a righteous one taken to eradicate evil ministers from the Imperial Court. He was fooling nobody though, as all could see his real goal was the throne. The Jianwen Emperor and the loyalists called him and the Yan camp criminal usurpers.

Yet it could also be said that Jianwen had always been wary of his uncle's political and military clout. He couldn't wait to retract Zhu Di's powerful princedom and other princes' fiefs. In short, it was the power-obsessed Peasant Emperor who had sown the seeds of hatred among his offspring by trying to divvy up power. He obviously only ended up invoking bitterness and vicious rivalry between them.

By this time, the Yan campaign was entering the second year. The two feuding sides still drew a tie, with massive deaths and casualties on both sides. The Yan camp had captured a few provinces in northwest and central China. But the rest of the country was still firmly in Jianwen's grasp.

Lin San had not reappeared in Putai since the wedding night. Sai'er surmised he would take at least half a year to recover from infirmity.

So that allowed her to devote all her attention to the training program.

Mother Lin didn't appear too perplexed, as she had probably foreseen the match was anything but a compatible one from the start. She still treated Sai'er and her Ba with kindness and understanding. Which was the best outcome Sai'er could've hoped for. She was only too willing to perform all household duties as a filial daughter-in-law should.

With Sai'er now living in the new home, the chore of cooking at Ba's cottage fell to Yinho, who gladly took up the duty as recompense for board for both himself and Ah Long. Binhong, as usual, kept busy by helping Ba with dispensing herbal medicine and medical ministrations.

The martial arts program turned out to be very popular among Society students.

As the civil war dragged on, counties, towns and villages all over the country were forming their own militias to defend their communities. Many of these places were pro-Jianwen and were ready to ally with local government forces to fight off the Yan army should the latter encroach on their boundaries. In other places, bandits' marauding became so rampant that self-defense on the part of locals was a must.

In the case of Putai, it was for self-defense that the Society students wanted to train in martial arts. Cases of venal tax collectors fleecing local farmers were not uncommon. Corrupt censors backed by the Zhu princes assumed they were entitled to extort bribes from villagers. Local shop merchants also lived in constant fear of being plundered by bandits.

Trainees were grouped into three classes, with each coach taking one class, and the classes rotated between the coaches at the end of a month.

After six months, the coaches reshuffled the classes so that trainees' aptitude matched with the appropriate class. The aim was to come up with three specialized groups: a spear group, a sword group and a qinggong group.

Ah Long shrieked with excitement when Yinho made him an assistant coach. Anyone could see how he doted on the kid, whose affections had rubbed away his acerbic edges.

It didn't escape Sai'er that a light danced in Yinho's eyes whenever his tender gaze fell on his protégé.

To Sai'er's delight, Ah Long volunteered to make six copies by hand of diagrams in *The Secret of Wudang Neigong*, so that each group had two copies to pass around. He was truly talented at sketching.

"Little brother, we all admire your work!" praised Sai'er on one occasion. The lad blushed and simpered shyly, "I only want to be useful."

One female trainee named Gao Yulan from Sai'er's qinggong group was from a family who owned a small printing shop. Two years younger than Sai'er and endowed with a super nimble gait, she was a fast learner and well liked among students. Her older brother Gao Feng, a reserved and quiet young man of the same age as Binhong and also a bright trainee, was in the sword group.

Yulan took the initiative to have the book's text block printed, so copies could be made available to all trainees.

Like Yinho, the Gao siblings were also born in Yidu county. A couple of years ago, the Gao family moved here to start a printing press, to take advantage of Putai's lower cost of doing business.

Yulan was fond of telling Yinho about their birthplace. Yinho's memory of the place was a blank page, and appreciated her painting it with words.

"My Ba once took me to a place in the suburb called Rocky Ridge. It's a ridge of steep craggy mountains with the bottom half hidden in a bamboo forest. We went up to the crest of the highest hill via a long steep path. There was a flat landing at the top, fringed on all sides by strange-shaped boulders. From there, we took in a breathtaking view of sprawling groves of pear, linden and white mulberry trees to the east. The west side looked out on the whole Yidu county. Ba said it was a natural site for building a fort. But I just loved the scenic vista."

"That sounds really beautiful. I look forward to seeing it one day," said Yinho with yearning in his eyes. An aching sense of loss was palpable in that yearning to see his birthplace.

"Me too. I wonder how Pearly is doing. The Bamboo Grove Taoist Nunnery she settled in is located there," muttered Sai'er, as she re-read the letter Pearly had earlier sent her.

Kung fu training on the meadow outside Sai'er's cottage had become a routine by now.

Most of the trainees acquired a more robust physique and were noticeably more positive and upbeat about life in general, even as living conditions remained harsh and resources scrimpy.

The classes had now swelled to two hundred trainees, since the program started a year and a half ago.

All the trainees adored the three coaches, especially Sai'er, who was not as harsh and rigid in her ways as Binhong and

Yinho.

Often in after-session hours, she would chat with trainees from all three groups and encourage them to read the Lotus Sutra as a way to attain inner peace.

"Inner peace is crucial to your neigong training, and reading the Lotus Sutra is the best aid to go into meditation mode," she would tell them. They were already well-versed in Maitreya Buddha's teachings from Ba's lectures and so were eager to read the Sutra on her suggestion.

Now the Yan usurpation campaign was entering its third year. On New Year's Day, a massive black cloud of locusts swarmed the sky of Yingtian and ravaged more than half of the farms in rural areas, sending a dark omen to the capital.

The two-year stalemate between the feuding sides finally broke and a reverse of fortune for the Yan army came as a nasty shock to most people in Shandong.

In early spring, on Monk Yao's advice, the Yan army looped around the stronghold of Jinan city to capture resource-rich Dezhou and Liaocheng again, along with several southern counties of Shandong. Zhu Di's troops barreled straight south to the Huai River, and further onto Yangtze River in a massive offensive, winning battle after battle.

By early summer, the last Imperial bastion Yangzhou put up only weak resistance and succumbed in just a couple of days. It was now just a matter of days before Yingtian was forced to capitulate.

When the news of Yangzhou's fall reached Tang Jun, Sai'er was on a home visit. Her Ba's harried expression weighed heavy on her heart.

At supper time, the dining table was moved to the backyard for the family to enjoy the balmy evening breeze. Yinho had whipped up several delicious dishes, but nobody except Ah Long could work up much of an appetite.

"Ba, please stop worrying. Let's just take one day at a time," Sai'er tried her best to placate him. For a long time she had seen it coming, but the prospect of seeing Zhu Di claim towering victory still galled her to no end.

"It's our collective fate," Ba breathed a long sigh. "If history teaches us anything, it's that the heavens like to send tyrants to the world from time to time to test commoners' resilience."

"Uncle, do you think your former teacher Fang Xiaoru will be in trouble?" asked Binhong.

"As Jianwen's Chief Adviser, Fang has been Zhu Di's archenemy right from the start. General Tie is obviously in a bind too."

"If — I mean when Zhu Di sits on the throne, there's nothing more we could do except bow to his reign. Dogged resistance will only bring more deaths and prolonged pain and chaos." Binhong said with a crestfallen expression. He was only being honest.

"Yes, when Jinan surrenders, it's time for us to hunker down and just pray that the new Emperor will show magnanimity."

"The number of refugees fleeing the captured counties is rapidly on the rise," Yinho said with a miserable look. "Vagrant beggars are flocking to Putai, not that taking flight now will improve their fate. Very soon, our county's food will run out. I think we should start planting root vegetables in our yard."

"Good idea, Yinho. Please come to my cottage to plant all you want," Sai'er said, glad that Yinho changed the subject. "The front and back yards are pretty much unused. I'll help you dig a pond in the backyard and we can plant lotuses. We all love stewed lotus roots. Umm, we can even carve out plots on the grassland and mobilize our trainees to plant millet crops. When we have a steady yield, we can feed those who haven't enough to eat."

"You always come up with brilliant ideas, Flying Sword!"

"But I just took your idea and tried to grow it. Two brains are always better than one," Sai'er said, slightly abashed.

18

In the sixth month of the year, Jianwen's Chief General betrayed him and opened the Southern Gates to the Imperial Palaces, letting Zhu Di's Yan army through. Jianwen set his Palace on fire, killing his Empress and Princes, while he himself vanished into thin air.

Three days after entering Yingtian, Zhu Di declared Jianwen dead and acceded to the throne as the Yongle Emperor, to a cacophony of dissenting voices from loyalist Court officials and scholars.

Unabashedly, he professed that Empress Ma was his birth mother, which conferred on him legitimate surviving heir status. He falsely accused Jianwen of forging the Hongwu Emperor's will to grab the throne from him, and claimed without grounds that the Hongwu Emperor had handpicked him as the successor.

He then proceeded to have all official records of the four-year Jianwen rule eradicated, making it look as if the reign had never come to pass.

Next to go on the chopping block were the heads of all consorts, palace maids and eunuchs who had served Jianwen. None was left alive. He stayed his hand in purging all loyalist officials only because he knew better than to stir up too much resentment before he was firmly rooted.

In utter despair, Fang Xiaoru conveyed news of all this in a final letter to Ba, his favorite student.

Fang was arrested at his home almost immediately after he sent out the letter. Word on the street intimated that he and his whole extended family were thrown into the Court-operated, heavily guarded prison in Yingtian, awaiting trial for treason.

People understood it wasn't so much treason as dogged support of the Jianwen side in the three-year bloody feud between uncle and nephew. That the real usurper should accuse the legitimate ruler of usurpation was simply ludicrous. Be that as it might, the farce got shoved down people's throats anyway.

When Ba showed the letter to Sai'er on her regular home visit, she could immediately call it the charade that it was, having personally heard from Master Zhang about Zhu Di's past.

She began to see what lengths Zhu Di was ready to go to when it came to seizing absolute power. Nothing was beyond him. Nothing was too debased. For all she knew, he was prone to subjugate others to his will using violence. Absolute power in his hands only meant worse was about to come.

As Sai'er came to grasp a more lucid view of her immortal lover's character, the passing of each day blighted her inherited passion a little more. Her past amorous feelings were being given a good sluice down. If anything, this came as a welcome relief. At least this was her immediate response to the nasty turn of events.

"Sai'er, Binhong, I think you two should pay General Tie a visit," Ba said at supper time, his face drawn and haggard.

"He's not going to respond well to the news of Zhu Di becoming Emperor. Try to persuade him to give up resistance for the greater good of Shandong. Also for his family's sake."

At the break of dawn, Sai'er and Binhong set out in their Taoist guises for Jinan.

By the time they arrived at the pier near the Daming Lake, it was early evening. The sky was teeming with obsidian storm clouds. The air was sultry and stifling, permeated with the miasma of gore and violence.

Half-way through their horse-back ride to the city fort, Sai'er's pulse hammered hard as she saw mutilated corpses and horse carcasses daubing the open field that stretched as far as eyesight could reach, blotching the earth dark red. She hated to have to face it, but she knew she and Binhong were too late.

In a blink, clouds of dust whipped up by horse hooves barreled towards them. Flags with the Yan insignia fluttered into view. They couldn't but rein in their horses. There was no place to hide in the open field.

Clad in shiny breastplate armor etched with the single character "Yan", Sanbao looked fierce and imperious atop a grey stallion at the front center of the three-column troops. At the rear were two wooden cages on wheeled carts, hemmed in by infantry soldiers.

He snapped at the reins and put up one hand to halt the battalion when he saw the two lone riders.

Sai'er nearly lurched from her saddle at the sight of him. She squinted to try to make out the prisoners with cangues around their necks. General Tie was in one, looking vehemently defiant like a provoked lion. When her gaze fell on the other caged prisoner, her heart plummeted to the ground. It was her Grandba.

She gagged from roiling emotions as she struggled to snuff them out. Binhong had his hand on the sword hilt, obviously as stunned as she. But this situation called for anything but brazen effrontery. As in sword dueling, a defensive move called for retraction of energy.

"General, may I please have a word in private?" Sai'er mustered all her charm to utter those words in an alluring tone, dismounting as steadily as she could with eyes fixed askance on him, even as her heart was thudding like war drums.

He hesitated for a brisk moment, then threw one leg over and hopped to the ground. His eyes hardly betrayed any emotions, but as he looked past Sai'er's guise and recognized her, his stiffly set jowl registered the faintest twitch.

They stepped away from the troops and headed to a nearby lianliu shrub bush where they were out of earshot.

"Sanbao, I've missed you," Sai'er began. "How have you been?"

"I'm fine. And you?" he uttered the scantiest of words in the most guarded tone, his eyes unblinking. He was keeping her well at arm's length. She tried hard to conceal her fidgets.

"You said you were going to look me up, but you never made contact in the last three years," she said, attempting the guilting tactic, wanting desperately to break his wall of ice.

"I heard you got married," he was determined not to be put down.

"It was my mother's wish..." she was floored, not quite knowing how to explain herself on the spur of the moment. "We don't live together," she added emphatically, casting down her eyes in a fit of discomposure.

"Sai'er, I've been locked in a difficult position—" He trailed off. "There are things that are hard to explain."

Sai'er looked up again and stared him in the eye.

"Last time we saw each other, you said I didn't understand. What didn't I understand? That letter that you accidentally left behind clearly tells me you had been a fraud, but I persuaded myself you probably had your reasons. Did Zhu Di coerce you? That day on the meadow, I felt your keen desire. But why did you stop cold?"

"Look, what I say or not say won't change the reality," his voice stiffened, brow pinched. He could barely conceal his internal turmoil as he prattled on. "I shouldn't have let my emotions rule my head. I had a job to do. Like now, I'm only doing my job. Can you understand that some people do what they have to do just to hang on to life?"

"Are you saying nothing ever happened between us?" she whimpered as Sanbao's indifferent tone began to chisel at her self-confidence. "When you kissed me, did you not feel anything at all? I don't care a whit that you're a eunuch. I'm in love with you."

It was this same man who had panted for her and roused her with his hot lips and calloused but gentle hands. Intoxicating pleasure had sent her to vertiginous heights. She had felt his hardness. In the heat of the moment, she had been ready to forsake her mission and give herself to him.

But standing in front of her now was just a cold hard carapace emptied of feelings.

"I — some things are out of my control. My master is the Yongle Emperor and I have to do whatever he bids me. I failed him with you because I was too weak. Because of my failure, you went on to become a super master of the North Star skill and used it to bolster Tie's resistance. I can't possibly fail him again. Let's face it: you and I are not meant to be. We're on opposing sides."

His face contorted in agony for a beat. In the next his jowl tightened, the face contour once again taut and ruthless.

His blade-like words pierced Sai'er's heart and slivered it strip by strip, inflicting the maximum torture. She could taste raw blood on her tongue. Desperately searching for a plausible excuse in his eyes, she only found they were sickly hollows, as if all emotions were congealed in the ice of callousness. *Why is he cutting me off?*

Her vision was blurred as she fought back tears with whatever was left of her pride. Sniffling hard, she pleaded with the greatest humbleness she could command:

"The monk you've captured is my grandfather. I beg you, for old times' sake, to please let him go. You already have General Tie. You don't need another prisoner to answer to your master."

"I'm afraid I can't. The Emperor has somehow heard that Monk Faxian is a key loyalist to Jianwen and has specifically ordered his arrest." His eyes darkened and his voice assumed a chilling timbre now. "If I could give you one piece of advice, it would be to get yourself and your father into hiding at once, before trouble comes knocking on your door. I can't promise to let you off next time I see you."

With those last words, he turned his back on Sai'er and strode slowly back towards the stallion, his shoulders sagging as if weighed down with an invisible load.

"Sanbao," she called after him, fumbling in her pocket for the portrait that she always carried with her. "Will you please take this back?"

Her outstretched hand holding the piece of paper trembled like a willow sprig in the wind. She wasn't sure what she was feeling. There was just the maddening urge to do something, anything that might smash his icy front and stab his heart.

He halted in his tracks, and then stomped ahead without turning around.

The tear-stained sheet glided from her hand, flitting to the ground like a dying butterfly.

She tried to feign calmness on the way home, her head spinning into a void, and she was too upset to share the conversation with Binhong. He just rode alongside her like a mute.

When they reached Ba's cottage, Ba and Yinho were in the backyard planting some turnips and jicamas. She recounted what had happened in Jinan in the briefest way possible, not going into her private dialogue with Sanbao except for his last bit of advice.

"I think Uncle and you should take his advice. Why don't you two go to Yidu to find Pearly? Maybe she knows a good hiding place. Yinho and I can hold the fort here," Binhong said with deep concern in his voice.

"Umm, the Rocky Ridge might be the answer. Yulan said that the hills are partly embedded in a bamboo forest in the Yidu suburb. Her father only stumbled upon it by accident when he was hiking in the area. But it'll be like leading a hermit's life," Yinho said with sadness, his usual levity missing.

"But what about Monk Faxian? How can I hide when my father rots in prison? He might even be sentenced to death," Ba covered his face with both hands, his voice a reedy rasp.

The air was weighty and Sai'er's heart was constricted. She could not go into hiding. Not when her Grandba's life was hanging by a thread. She had to think of a way to get him out of captivity. After mulling for a while, she made up her mind.

"Ba, please listen to me. I'll get Yinho and Yulan to take you to the Rocky Ridge and help you settle down. You'll be safe there. Binhong and I will try to catch up with Sanbao's troops to get Grandba out. I'll talk Sanbao into releasing him. As soon as we get him out, we'll join you at Rocky Ridge, alright?"

Sanbao had at least volunteered the advice. She was imagining a thin ray of hope in that gesture. *He still cares enough to give it.*

Having little idea how she'd go about the rescuing feat, she could hear the feigned bravado in her words, as she prayed hard Ba would listen to reason. Her prayer was answered.

"Ba, please take this with you and guard it with your life. It's a magical treasure from the Wudang Mountains," she said, handing him the white jade tablet before she left with Binhong.

Once again Sai'er and Binhong disguised as Taoist monks set out for Liaocheng, which was certainly where the Yingtian-bound Yan troops were headed, as the city was a mid-way point on the north-south Grand Canal route linking Beiping with Yingtian.

They galloped at top speed towards Liaocheng as time was racing against them.

Sai'er was turning one thought over and over in her mind: *there's only one way to force the release of both Grandba and General Tie.* She kept fingering the amber stone that she had in the inside pocket of her Taoist robe, as if to seek reassurance from it. This task allowed no room for bungling, as two lives were involved. Above all, her beloved Grandba's life was at stake. It had to work.

When they approached the main pier in Liaocheng, from a distance, she spotted some of Sanbao's troops and horses filing onto the gangway of the first one of three four-masted war junks aligned on the shore.

Sanbao was standing on one side directing some soldiers to move the two prisoner carts toward the gangplank of the middle junk. The rest of the soldiers and horses were waiting to board the third junk.

Sai'er and Binhong, having tied their horses to a poplar tree, perched on a high vantage point of the mound overlooking the pier. Sai'er espied crossbowmen taking up positions on the upper decks of the first war junk.

The moment was now or never. She nodded to Binhong to create a diversion with the third war junk, which was yet to load passengers.

He had brought along three small paper packages of gunpowder equipped with fuses that Ah Long had pilfered from the Jinan fort armory, and had attached each to the tip of three of his arrows. He struck a flint to one, nocked the arrow in place, aimed and released. It hit the center of one of the sails and at once set it alight in a small explosion.

A stray gust of river breeze helped fan the flame, and in a beat, tongues of fire lapped up the adjacent sails. The masts and bamboo-strip sails were crackling up in smoke and fire, and sparks and charred debris rained onto the wooden decks below.

Someone shouted in a frantic call for help, "Quick, someone fetch water! Put out the fire!" Instantly, the milling group on the shore dashed towards the burning ship in a bedlam of disarray.

A series of qinggong leaps catapulted Sai'er from the top of the mound down to where Sanbao was standing.

Before he could react, she slapped her heated hand on his back, and hissed under her breath, "You know what I can do. Don't make me do it." Swiftly she snatched his sword and threw it into the bushes at the foot of the mound. His soldiers around them were at a loss as to what to do.

To demonstrate what she was capable of, she began drawing qi from him, but stopped short of causing any real harm. He buckled and sank down on one knee, obviously dumbstruck by how fast his qi was exiting his body, and how masterful Sai'er had become in her specialized skill.

"Order your men to throw their weapons on the ground. Those crossbowmen on the ship too," she commanded in a loud, coarse voice.

"Do as she says, now!" he hollered as his face turned morbid white, his voice quavering.

Clanging and thudding of metal instantly swelled into a tumultuous clamor.

"Get them to step back. Now hand us the key to the cangue locks."

Binhong was right behind Sai'er. He snatched the key from Sanbao's guard and stepped to the cages. With a couple of qi-charged sword strikes he splintered several slats in both. Then he opened the cangues on both Monk Faxian and General Tie and let them out of the cages.

At this point, General Tie recognized Sai'er and said in his usual booming voice, "Sai'er, take your grandfather away to safety. I will not come with you, because I cannot give the new Emperor cause to harm my family. Thank you for the thought all the same."

"If you insist, General Tie. Take good care then," said Sai'er in a dubious voice, fearing the worst for the General. But there was nothing more she could do.

Turning to Sanbao, she said, "We need you to come with us for a short walk before we release you."

To warn the soldiers ashore and the crossbowmen aboard against any wayward moves, Monk Faxian tumbled one defiant soldier to the ground and palmed his back, drawing qi from him until he passed out limp.

Then he snatched a horse nearby and picked up a sword from the ground. He kept watch while Binhong and Sai'er had Sanbao pinioned with a rope and walked him to the mound above the pier. Then he sprinted off to join them.

When they reached the spot where the horses had been hitched, Sai'er bade Sanbao walk a hundred paces away from them.

The trio swiftly mounted their horses, and together they whisked away from the mound.

At this time, one of Sanbao's guards climbed up the mound via a shortcut carrying a bow and a quiver of arrows.

The guard aimed the first shot at Binhong's back and missed.

The second arrow was aimed at Sai'er. The shot went off before Sanbao could yell a stop order. It hit the small of her back. She promptly rolled off her horse. Binhong careened to snap up the reins of the horse.

Monk Faxian, who was behind her, at once pulled to a stop,

jumped down and took a quick look at the arrow wound. He used the sword to split off the shaft and carried Sai'er to his horse. Having carefully propped her on the saddle, he swung up behind her and spurred the horse into a gallop.

Binhong turned around on his cantering horse and loosed an arrow, aiming at Sanbao, who was giving the guard a tongue lashing. The arrow hit the guard instead. Binhong directed both horses to speed up to draw even with Monk Faxian.

19

As Sai'er was unconscious and her wound still weeping blood, Binhong and Monk Faxian decided to stop over at an inn on a side street leading to the city square of Liaocheng, satisfied that no pursuers were on their tail.

Monk Faxian was known to the innkeeper through his Jinan militia connections and got a room almost immediately.

As soon as they entered their rented room, they carefully laid Sai'er down on her side upon the bed. Monk Faxian went out to find an inn helper and returned with a basin of warm salted water and wads of clean cotton cloth.

Both Binhong and Monk Faxian knew their priority was to get the arrowhead out before infection set in, but they were wary of the danger of unstaunched bleeding. She was wheezing softly and her chest was almost still. Her face was turning bluish white like glacial ice.

Sai'er lost consciousness right after the arrow hit. The last sensation she had was one of withering pain shooting up her spine.

She was reeling weightless as her soul divorced from her body.

Her spirit hovered on the edge of the Bridge of Forgetfulness, the place for the good souls to await a drink of Meng Po's soup of oblivion, so reincarnation could start on a clean slate.

She winced at the sight of souls bobbing in and out of the foul-smelling, viscous Blood River below the Bridge, hands flailing and faces twisted into beastly shapes. They were the ones who had done evil deeds in their mortal life, and hell guards had pushed them into the river, where they were doomed to flounder and sink into deeper levels of torturous hell.

Having floated away from the grisly scene and back to her stiff cold body, Sai'er saw the tiny blood-drenched figure curled on her side in a fetal position, stray tufts of black hair clumping on her temples. The blue-grey Taoist robe on her was splotched with rust-color congealed blood. The Taoist cap was missing. It had probably fallen off when her grandfather lifted her up from the ground.

This image was being carved onto her spirit's mind. She realized she was no less vulnerable than a fetus upon its entry into the world. In her twenty years, she was just a pathetic mass of blood and flesh shuffling aimlessly through life until disaster struck.

The previously pulsating mass was now making a silent and unceremonious exit from the mortal world. She mocked herself for her futile existence, not having left a tincture of good on earth before the light in her extinguished.

Then it struck her that she was destined to return to her immortal life in the Moon Palace. She breathed a light sigh of relief. But how was she going to answer to the Queen Mother?

Swirling in the air like a kite cut off from the string, she listened in on her grandfather's talk with Binhong.

"I think one of her arteries has been punctured," said Monk Faxian with a deeply creased brow. He was looking at the half-dead girl with woeful red-rimmed eyes, his face twisted in pain.

Binhong was pacing the room in utter distress. "I knew it was not good," he said, exhaling a long sigh, flustered and defeated. Dropping on his knees the next moment, he bleated like a lamb, "What are we going to do? Guanyin, please have mercy…"

Her heart ached to see their distressed, tear-streaked faces. She tried to comfort them, but no sound came out of her mouth when she spoke.

Becoming listless, she flew back to a happier place—her childhood.

Ma had just finished washing dishes in the kitchen. She was sitting on a bench by the maple tree in the backyard, trying to catch the receding natural light to mend one of Ba's blue cotton robes.

The wide-eyed seven-year-old sat on a low stool next to her and wheedled her into telling the legend about Red Jade from the Song Dynasty. It was her favorite story.

Red Jade was no less a heroic and intelligent warrior than the iconic Yue Fei in defending the nation against the nomadic Jurchens. She had humble beginnings, working as a woman wrestling performer in taverns in her younger years. Meeting the general Han Shizhong one day changed her fate. He married her and from then on the couple fought ferocious battles shoulder to shoulder.

Soon she rose through the ranks to the post of Commander. She won several crucial naval battles using war drums and flags to direct her soldiers in concerted and well-timed attacks. These battles were won against an enemy ten times the size of her army. Her strategic feats drew the Emperor's praise, and he granted her the noble rank of "Lady Protector of the Nation" on her own merits.

Sai'er remembered all the details of the story, as she used to make her Ma tell it again and again.

Ma looked at her with tender eyes and teased, "Why do you

like the story so much? Do you want to be a warrior like Red Jade? But don't you want to be a wife and mother?"

The girl answered with starry-eyed confidence, "I want to be the Lady Protector of Shandong."

From that time on, she had thrown her heart into learning martial arts from Ba.

Revisiting the cozy home scene sent her emotions pitching and rocking like waves.

Her mother's voice washed over her like gentle crooning rain, stirring up deep melancholy. Sai'er was at her deathbed. "Take this and guard it well — it's your father's portrait that I engraved in the clam shell he'd given me as an engagement present. Please take good care of him after I'm gone." The young man etched on one valve of the shell had kind eyes. His birth date and time was carved on the other valve. Tearing up, she secured it on a red string and wore it around her neck.

She had never properly mourned her Ma's death, and the dark specter of grief caught up with her right this moment, as if Sanbao's betrayal wasn't heartbreaking enough.

It might as well be. A man's love and family life wasn't in her destiny anyway.

The dam to her pent-up tears finally broke. She needed so much to bawl to her heart's content.

When the torrent of tears subsided, she couldn't help but wonder if she'd be able to find her Ma in this strange limbo, or whether she'd already been re-incarnated.

But somehow a voice inside her head kept droning on, "You have unfinished work to do on earth."

In the next instant, she was back inside the rented room in the inn.

Desperate to placate the turbulent storm that was raging in her mind, she began chanting the nerve calming Guanyin Sacred

Chants.

Very slowly, her eyes flickered open into narrow slits, her vision foggy. Her fingers gave the faintest of a twitch as she tried uncurling herself from the fetal posture bit by bit. Something was lodged in her lower back but she didn't feel any pain. A light purr escaped her parched mouth to draw attention. When her vision cleared, the first thing she saw was Monk Faxian's smiling tear-stained face.

Binhong was so startled that he gave out a dry, raspy cry.

She fumbled in her robe pocket and fished out the amber stone. The bleeding had miraculously stopped for some time. She gestured for Binhong to place the stone on her wound as she lay on her stomach.

Shortly thereafter, the arrowhead came loose and Binhong tried with a light hand to twist it a little. It got easily dislodged and slid out smoothly. In the next moment, the bloody raw wound gradually scabbed over.

As Binhong and Sai'er had both witnessed the power of the stone in Pearly's case, this didn't come as a total surprise. Still it pushed credulity to the limits, as Sai'er had been just one little step away from slipping into the world of the dead before being hauled back.

But for Monk Faxian, this spectacle was nothing short of a miracle. He watched the entire process with a gaping mouth. Meanwhile, he kept stroking Sai'er's tousled hair, cooing as if she were an infant, "My little tangyuan, you're my precious sweetie. I must thank Buddha every day for bringing you back."

"Grandba, I love you! Ba has missed you," Sai'er gripped his hand and wheedled. "We want you to come home to stay with us and never leave again."

"Precious, you're my love, and you saved my life!" he said softly, his lips quirking with emotions. "If only you knew how much I wished it was I who got shot and not you. As for coming home to stay – I did make a serious vow to Buddha to serve him for life – "

"But we *are* family. Family stays together," she insisted.

"My sweet girl, you're always a part of me, and I you. Nothing will change that," he coaxed patiently. "I've missed your Ba too. Look, why don't I come with you for a short family reunion? How does that sound?"

Grudgingly, she nodded her head, well aware her babbling wasn't going to get what she wanted. *But at least Ba will get to see him.*

Binhong was kneeling by the bedside, thoroughly shaken up and was now reveling in a cathartic release, big grateful teardrops escaping his puffy eyes.

"Don't ever do this again. You scared me to death!"

"I love you, Binhong!" She threw her arms around Binhong's shoulders and pecked his cheek. "Can you get me some water and something to eat? Oh, some clean clothes too. We need to get out of here and head to Rocky Ridge right away. This is not a safe place to linger."

"Can't you stop ordering me around just once?" he grumbled with a dopey smile.

She then chanted her gratitude to Guanyin and the Queen Mother, aware that she had just used up all the magic allowed for the stone, her Magic Peach. She only hoped that her life was worth using the celestial magic.

Two days later they were in the bamboo forest at the foothills of Rocky Ridge.

Yulan had led Yinho and Ba to a serene spot on the flank of a hillock attached to the Rocky Ridge western foothills. A gurgling stream fed through the landing. The access to this place was completely shrouded in a dense thicket of bamboo trees and overgrown fern bracken. It was Yulan's father who had shown her this secluded but habitable retreat.

Yinho had lots of experience in building cottages from his Wudang days, and with help from Ba and Yulan, was building a simple shelter using bamboo poles, lianliu branches and reeds, which were in abundant supply in the lush vegetation all around. Meanwhile they lived out of makeshift tents made with canvas.

Sai'er, Binhong and Monk Faxian would never have found the place if Yinho hadn't come outside of the hidden sanctuary to look for fruit and stumbled on them.

The crisp early autumn air, sweetened by the crisp scent of bamboo leaves, buoyed everyone's spirit. Glittering rays of sunlight filtered through the bamboo shade and bounced off the running stream to dapple the new found habitat, giving it an aura at once sprightly and tranquil.

Sai'er was especially elated to be among family and close friends, having gone through her life-and-death ordeal. A new sense of purpose suffused her heart and soul.

Upon arrival on the scene, Binhong and Monk Faxian immediately offered help to Ba and Yinho. They were bundling together bamboo poles using lianliu twines to make into the fourth wall for the hut, having already constructed three. The newcomers helped with weaving a roof out of reed stalks to put over the trussed up walls.

Yulan served everyone bamboo leave tea, much heartened by the amiable atmosphere.

"How would you all like a supper of roasted game?" Binhong asked. When no one raised any objection, he scooted off like a jaunty kid with his bow and quiver.

Ba had probably been eagerly looking forward to this moment of reunion. When he did meet Grandba face to face though, he appeared a little awkward, not knowing where to place his hands. Nothing strange about that. After all, they had been separated for thirty long years.

Sai'er eyes prickled with tears when she saw them finally embrace each other, both choking up. With that hug, Ba renewed the father-son bond with Grandba, the long painful grudge over his absence finally laid to rest.

That evening, Yinho made an open fire to roast the grouses and rabbits that Binhong had earlier caught. Yulan had brought from Putai one large sack of millet flour and another of taro roots. She made millet cakes for supper. As Grandba was a vegetarian, she served him a dish of steamed taro root strips to chow down with millet cakes.

"Ah, I almost forgot," Yinho said with a mouthful of roasted meat, "last night we heard guqin music coming from downhill. I went to check it out and guess what, I found Bamboo Grove Taoist Nunnery where Pearly resides. It's only about fifty yards to the west of the access path. She looked well. We talked just a bit as it was late and the Nunnery was closing its doors to visitors."

"That's great. I was going to search for the Nunnery," Sai'er said with excitement. "Has she heard the bad news of Zhu Di becoming Emperor?"

"I didn't ask. She'd not be pleased —"

When Grandba heard Pearly's name being mentioned, his face lit up at once.

"Sadly, there's little more we can do now, especially when some of us are fugitives. Pearly is in danger too," Grandba said with a long sigh.

On their way here from Liaocheng, Sai'er had briefed him what had happened to Pearly in Jinan. The three had also agreed to spare Ba from hearing of Sai'er's near-death story.

"Well, hunkering down is not being passive," Sai'er spoke her mind after a moment of meditation. "There's a time to strike, a time to step back. I'd like to think that to step back is to prepare for future action."

As soon as those words came out, Ba threw her a smiling and prideful glance. His eyes beamed. It was as good as a loud accolade from him. She felt she had finally become the son he had never had!

"But how are we going to fight Zhu Di's colossal Central Army?" Yinho asked, frowning.

"If we can come up with some hit-and-run plans, we may work like horseflies and still do lots of damage to the Shandong Yan army and city and county governments." Her thoughts were running wild as she called to mind how Red Jade had crushed enemy troops ten times her army's size. She stared at her portion of roasted grouse without seeing it.

"It might be a good time to organize ambushes against local officials while Zhu Di is busy with setting up his new Court in Yingtian," Binhong added his own thoughts, taking a wider perspective. "We can work from counties to prefectures. In the longer term, we can make it our goal to take back the whole of Shandong."

"We can form a permanent rebel army out of our trainees," Yinho said with verve as his face brightened, taking hint from Binhong's views. "I'm sure they're all eager to join."

Sai'er was amazed that Yinho had spoken her mind.

"I had some experience with ambushes and small raid tactics while serving in the Jinan militia." Seemingly roused by the youngsters' animated talk, Grandba also threw out his ideas. "One effective strategy is to target and assassinate the top man in a military or administrative unit. It's one way to induce their underlings to switch allegiance. At the very least, it will throw them into chaos. But then one also has to be prepared for reprisals."

"Umm, we must avoid Jinan city, as the Yan side will arm it to the teeth against insurgents after General Tie had shown his mettle there," Sai'er murmured as if in a trance. She could feel it in her bones that a serious venture was taking shape even as she spoke.

"At the same time, we need more recruits for the White Lotus Society," Ba drawled after a bout of silence. "The number of our trainees is still too low. I was thinking of drawing new students here in Yidu. But the problem is we can't do this openly."

"We could ask Pearly to request some lecture space inside the Nunnery," Sai'er said after some thought. "The cloisters would provide the best cover."

"You really can think fast, Commander Flying Sword," Binhong threw her an admiring glance.

"I wonder if we could start building up a command center here," said Sai'er, too wrapped up in her own thoughts to notice Binhong's compliment. "Yulan, tomorrow we need you to show us that stronghold you had mentioned."

"Of course. I'd be happy to be the guide," Yulan replied with alacrity. She might seem quiet and withdrawn, especially when in a crowd, but she was a good listener and an intelligent judge of people.

20

NEXT MORNING, after inspecting the site with the whole group, Sai'er couldn't but agree with Yulan's father's remark.

It was indeed a military commander's dream of a perfect stronghold. The irregular-shaped boulders surrounding the flat landing were like a natural crenellated battlement from which crossbowmen, archers and catapult handlers could launch attacks in sheltered positions. At the same time, the altitude offered an unobstructed all-round view of the low-lying lands. In short, it was a fortification hard to attack but easy to defend.

At a lower level, there were winding pathways leading to two adjacent flat hilltops, one on the east and the other on the west. The east and larger one had a natural catchment area fed by small cascades and occasional heavy rainfall. These looked ideal as wing forts to accommodate a stable, a kitchen/granary, tents and an armory.

"Wow, this could work as our permanent base," Yinho blurted out. To his surprise, no one disagreed.

"The hardest part would be the transport of mules and supplies up the only access that's long and steep," said Binhong, the brain who could always see pitfalls in a plan.

Yulan, who had kept her silence all this time, spoke up. "Ah, actually there's a gentler sloping access that leads up the eastern annexing hill. The entry point is well hidden behind a dilapidated mass of graves at the eastern foothills of Rocky Ridge."

"Perfect. Thank you very much for the pointer, Yulan," Sai'er said, her mind spinning fast to prioritize things.

"Perhaps we should worry about transport when the time comes. Our immediate task should be to see if we could recruit more new students. I spoke to Pearly earlier. She sought permission to use the prayer hall for our lectures and got it. Also, she said there's a large front yard that we could use for martial arts training. The nuns never use it."

After a short pause, she went on when no one spoke, "In parallel, we should start building up an arsenal of weapons, especially catapults. Ah Long's sketches will come in handy. We need to source the materials and manpower to carry this out."

In the month that followed, Binhong and Yinho scoured the nearby woods for tree trunks and sturdy branches and stashed them in the hideout for future use in building transport carts and weaponry.

One evening, shortly after the group had eaten a simple supper of millet gruel and boiled taro roots, Pearly showed up unexpectedly, bearing shocking news.

Sai'er offered her a cup of bamboo leaf tea, sensing something ominous. A macabre air pervaded the space as Pearly began to speak.

"Fang Xiaorou's family and relatives, to the ninth degree kinship—over eight hundred innocents—have been beheaded in Yingtian," her already brittle voice crackled like desert sands being whipped by violent gusts. It was a wail of bitter disgust.

"The entire process took many days to finish. Zhu Di forced Fang to watch every single execution. He's now ordered the arrest of all of Fang's students."

Everyone in the audience gasped in terror. Yulan gave out a

stifled scream. Ba scrunched his hand into a fist and unleashed a surly growl. Even the talkative Yinho went silent, looking wan and hollow-eyed. Losing his usual sangfroid, Binhong rapped his knuckles on the bamboo table so hard it wrenched out of shape.

"I'm just thankful that the Tang family and close friends have taken refuge here," Pearly added after a pause.

A tense silence hung in the air, safe for a few wistful cicada chirps. Treading lightly for fear of disturbing the quiet, she went on in a barely audible voice:

"It's said that Zhu Di had summoned Fang to write the inaugural address for his new reign, but Fang responded with a caustic refusal, calling the Prince a traitorous usurper in front of the whole Court. Zhu Di just went berserk."

If a few days earlier Sai'er had still been hesitant about the notion of bringing on a rebellion, she was now in no doubt that that would be the only way forward.

"It's useless to cower now. Zhu Di will come for us sooner or later. Not only the few of us whose guts he hates, but the entire populace of Shandong, given what happened at Jinan. He's not given to forgetting a slight, let alone a public loss of face. We have two choices before us: one is to arm ourselves for defense or even attack. The other option is to sit still and be slaughtered like pigs."

Sai'er swept her gaze around the fire-lit camp and found everyone was hanging on her every word.

Bolstered by the encouraging sign, she laid on the table what had been brewing in her mind for some time.

"I'll go back to Putai and persuade our trainees to join our cause. We'll call our new faction the White Lotus Sect, and will base our command center in the Rocky Ridge stronghold. Our initial objective is to take control of as many Shandong counties and prefectures as we can outside of Jinan, through whatever means that's available to us.

"We'll probably start out with planning the assassination of top men in counties, while at the same time building up an army and an arsenal. As we grow in manpower and weaponry, we'll engage in skirmishes with the Imperial Army. Our ultimate goal will be to take back the whole of Shandong. Is everyone here with me?"

Everyone in the audience nodded silently.

"I propose to make Sai'er our Commander-in-Chief. Is there any objection?" Monk Faxian said in a steady voice, his face beaming with confidence and pride.

"No objection," the group murmured.

"Thank you all for putting your trust in me. I promise I'll give it my very best," said Sai'er with gratitude. "Obviously I can't do things all by myself. So, with your agreement, I'll make Binhong and Yinho my Deputies, and Yulan my assistant."

The trio eagerly bobbed their heads.

Swiveling her eyes to the seniors in the group, she ventured, "I would also like to invite Pearly, Grandba and Ba to act as Sect Advisers. We could really use their wisdom and guidance."

Pearly and Grandba almost spoke at the same time. "Sai'er, you can count on our full support." Tang Jun flashed her daughter one of his rare smiles and grunted, nodding vigorously. "The title sure sounds fancy!"

Sai'er secretly rejoiced at reaping the additional benefit of getting Grandba to stay on longer.

As Yulan wanted to go back home to Putai to break the news to her father of her intention to join the Sect, she asked to accompany Sai'er on the trip. Yinho also came along as he needed to appoint someone in Putai to take charge of the farming enterprise there.

The farms would be an important food source to sustain the Sect through the movement. Fighters would need to have their stomachs filled.

Binhong would follow a couple of days later, as he had gone into town to persuade a couple of blacksmiths to coach blade forging. Monk Faxian had known them from his Jinan militia connections and had made the recommendations.

On the journey, Sai'er saw droves of refugees streaming from every direction towards Putai, which was one of the more remote counties where key government posts were not yet filled by new personnel sent from Yongle's Court.

"Yinho, do you know what's happened to the Putai magistrate?" Sai'er asked.

"The last I heard was that he'd resigned for fear of being accused of treason by Zhu Di," Yinho said with dismay.

"Can't blame him, I guess. But Putai people seem pretty calm despite that."

"Thanks to the militiamen who've been keeping order in their own communities. You know a few of our trainees are militiamen."

They found themselves getting in the way of the straggling crowd, and so moved to the side of the dirt path to allow the vagrants to pass.

Most in the moving crowd were frail women and children in dirty rags, with hollow gazes and defeated looks. The drawn-out civil war had killed millions of able-bodied men, leaving behind starving women and children in the war-torn towns and counties, now fleeing from home and seeking safer shelter and food elsewhere. They probably hadn't even heard that a new Emperor had just ascended the throne who now owned every inch of the nation's land. It was anybody's guess if he'd even care a whit about these wretched souls.

"I was thinking of calling a meeting of all our trainees and militiamen in Putai."

"Good idea. With any luck, we might just take over Putai," Yinho said with zeal. "If that works, we can repeat the process with Yidu, and other counties."

"On second thought, we could use the help of these women to do farming on the meadow fields, releasing our trainees to work on the weaponry."

In the next beat, Sai'er had already moved to the front of the crowd and she called out in a loud, clear voice, "Dear folks, I have a few words to say. If you're looking for food and farm work, please go to the old temple on the north bank of the Putai River and wait for instructions outside the temple. We could use your help."

When they arrived at Ba's cottage, it was late morning the next day.

A grim portent grabbed Sai'er by the throat when she saw the postern gate ajar, the smashed cross bolt lying splintered on the floor.

"Ah Long! Ah Long!" Yinho yelled at the top of his lungs. "Oh, no!"

The teenager was sitting on the ground with his back against the peach tree, his head lolling on one side, his neck and torso roped to the tree trunk and hands tied at the back. Dark, crusted blood smeared his clothes and caked around his stiff body. Blood-stained sharp knives and pincers were littered on the ground, along with a small urn of embers.

On closer inspection, a deep gash stretched across his throat from ear to ear. Deep lacerations, burns and black bruises marred his face, limbs and fingers. Brutal torture before his end was all too evident.

Yinho bawled his lungs out. "I shouldn't have left you behind all alone. It's my fault, it's my fault," he kept hammering his chest as if that'd relieve him of his pain.

Yulan cried helplessly along with him.

Sai'er first retched on reflex, then gritted her teeth so hard her jaw almost broke. Trying hard to swallow her tears, she patted lightly on Yinho's back, and moaned, "It's not your fault, Yinho. Please don't do this to yourself." Then with vehemence, she croaked, "Whoever did this will pay, I swear."

She went to take a look at Ba's apothecary. The drawers in the herbs chest were all in disarray. Fortunately Ba had packed up most of the herbs and carried them with him to Rocky Ridge. Then she took a round of inspecting all other rooms. It looked like someone had overturned the rooms in a search for something. But there was nothing valuable in those rooms. So it couldn't have been the work of bandits.

The only explicable scenario was that someone badly wanted to know the family's whereabouts and had tried to torture the kid into revealing it.

"Yulan, please stay with Yinho and look after him. I'll be back in a little while," said Sai'er, while her mind spun over the possibility of the hideout being exposed. Before stepping out, she asked, "Yulan, did you tell Ah Long where you were taking Ba and Yinho to?"

"No, not the exact spot," replied Yulan. "But Ah Long had probably heard the mention of Rocky Ridge."

Sai'er's gut feelings told her that Ah Long had stoically sealed his lips, and for that he died a gruesome death.

She had an inkling of who had done the grotesque deed.

She went straight to the Lin cottage across the river. When she entered the lounge, Mother Lin was slumped in a chair, weeping quietly.

"Po Po, what happened?" Sai'er asked gently.

"He's a beast! My son is a beast," she babbled through tears when she saw Sai'er. "He was searching for your father like crazy. He said Master Tang is on the Court's Wanted List and there was a reward for catching him. I don't know what's gone into him. He wants to sell out his teacher and father-in-law. He's a shame—"

That was pretty much what Sai'er had guessed.

"So where is he now?"

"He's staying at the Dragon Inn near the main pier. He was asking for you the moment he stepped in late last night, and said to tell you to meet him there."

"Don't worry, Po Po. Let me handle this."

So the bastard wants to see me. He has the nerve...

"Sai'er, I know you hate him. But he's still my son. I beg you—please let him live," Mother Lin beseeched in a hoarsened, wearied voice.

"Po Po, he tortured a kid to death. That sweet kid is also someone's beloved son, and our precious friend. The cruel act is not forgivable. I can promise you I won't kill him with my hands, but I can't guarantee someone else won't."

In the backyard, several trainees were digging a pond for growing lotuses. Mother Lin had begun planting jicama and taro in the front yard. Outside on the meadow, other trainees were planting millet seeds in the recently tilled plots.

Seeing her farming plan in full swing gave Sai'er a brief moment of satisfaction. But it didn't ease the grief that weighed like a load of lead on her. Ah Long was only sixteen. How was she ever going to explain his tragic and violent death to Madam Pu? And the mere thought of the excruciating pain that Yinho had to endure was enough to break Sai'er's heart. To Yinho, Ah Long was his light and hope. She understood.

Before she left, she called out to one of her group's trainees and asked him to notify all other trainees of a meeting to be held outside the temple the next morning.

Sai'er went to the county's only coffin shop to buy a simple coffin made of thin planks. By the time she returned with it to Ba's cottage, Yinho had calmed down a bit. With Yulan's help, he cleaned up Ah Long's body and dressed him in clean clothes.

"So who do you think did this?" Yinho asked Sai'er in a gravelly voice.

"No doubt it's Lin San. Mother Lin confirmed it. I can't tell whether he's after the Court's reward placed on Ba's and Grandba's capture, or whether he's doing this to get back at me. Maybe it's both."

"That heaven-cursed son of a whore! Wait till I dig him out, I'll tear him to pieces with my bare hands," Yinho gritted his teeth hard, blue veins protruding and prancing on his temples.

"Yinho, he's a cunning and dangerous scoundrel, and he may have accomplices," said Sai'er, fearing Yinho might do something rash and stupid in his grief. Should Yinho get harmed by Lin San, she wouldn't be able to forgive herself. She must try to distract him.

"Listen, we have a more urgent task on hand. We're going to host a meeting with our trainees and the refugees tomorrow morning at the temple. Yulan and Yinho, I need you two to notify as many of the militiamen as possible of the meeting."

"Sure! We'll get on it right away," Yulan said without hesitation, immediately catching Sai'er's intent. Yinho couldn't but nod along.

After a moment's contemplation, Yinho said with an animated glint in his eyes, "I've been thinking, perhaps we need to show the attendees some supernatural feat if we want to convince them of our power, so they would willingly follow our lead."

"Thank you, Yinho! I was going to ask you to do a little sorcery show at the meeting."

Sometimes Yinho's instinct was so close to her own that it bewildered her. She exhaled a breath of relief, somewhat appeased to see the dawn of some positive energy in him.

"Let's hold a Buddhist vigil for Ah Long tomorrow evening after the meeting," suggested Yulan in her usual thoughtful way.

"Yes, let's do that," Sai'er concurred, as she remembered that Madam Pu was a devout Buddhist. "Binhong will be here by then."

21

The MEETING attracted a larger-than-expected turnout outside the lecture temple on this early autumn morning.

The sun beamed its lukewarm rays on faces whose expressions ranged from hope to despair, with misgivings and confusion filling up the middle ground.

Naturally, the trainees were the most optimistic ones. But the misery that Sai'er had observed the day before among the refugees still clouded their vacuous eyes this morning. The militiamen in the crowd weren't sure what to expect from a twenty-year old woman, who was supposed to talk about the newly formed White Lotus Sect.

Yinho had hastily nailed six planks of wood together to make a temporary platform.

Sai'er had been jittery all morning. She had spent the previous night rehearsing her speech and only dozed off near dawn. Once she stepped onto the platform, she knew there was no turning back.

"My dear folks, I'll start by thanking you all for your presence here. My name is Tang Sai'er and I am the daughter of Tang Jun, founder of the White Lotus Society. I'm sure he is no stranger to many of you. For those who belong in the various county militias, Monk Faxian should not be a strange name. His secular name is Tang Wen, and he happens to be my long-lost grandfather."

A low murmur rose from the audience. It sounded like approval.

"Before I go into the main topic of today, I have to share with you a piece of heart-rending news. Ah Long, a sixteen-year-old beloved trainee of ours who lived at my Ba's cottage, was brutally tortured and murdered yesterday. It's obvious to me that the murderer wanted to force out of the boy the whereabouts of my Ba. I'll explain the reason in a moment. But you can see this is just the kind of monstrosity, by no means isolated, that Zhu Di and his allies are capable of."

From among the trainees came an outcry of shock, followed by weeping and sobs. Everyone in the training classes had loved Ah Long, and the agitated response came as no surprise to Sai'er. The rest of the crowd let out a loud collective moan and shifted in an uneasy squirm.

"As you may or may not be aware, the Jianwen Emperor has lost the war with his uncle Zhu Di, who has now enthroned himself as the Yongle Emperor. Sadly, he is now conducting a bloody purge of Jianwen's Court and supporters. Fang Xiaoru, the Chief Minister, has been sentenced to death by slicing. His kinsfolk to the ninth degree, totaling eight hundred and seventy innocent people, have already been beheaded by Yongle's order. Our beloved General Tie, who staunchly defended the Jinan city from the Yan army, has been imprisoned and will likely face a charge of treason."

Delivered with an impassive voice, Sai'er's straightforward recount on the situation galvanized the crowd, extracting gasps and grunts of disgust. The overwhelming response took her by surprise, but gave her self-confidence a strong boost.

"Now the new Court has issued a Wanted List aiming at hunting down all who had dared to fight off the Yan army. My father's and grandfather's names, among others, are on that list.

They've gone into hiding, and for now, they're safe."

Exhalations of relief streamed from the crowd, as they perked up for more news.

"This meeting is not about my family. It's about the fate of all Shandong folks. Let's face it. In our people's and our ancestors' blood always ran a deep hatred for the murderous and tyrannical Zhu Yuanzhang. Just as we thought his grandson, the gentle Jianwen, was going to put things right for us, another Zhu tyrant surfaced. This civil war has once again torn open that old wound in us. After his humiliating defeat in Jinan, Zhu Di is not going to spare us. We would be in denial if we thought otherwise."

"But what do you propose to do?" someone from the audience shouted. "We're only common folks. How can we stand up to the Central Army?"

"Fair question," Sai'er said calmly. "I, for one, do not believe that hunkering down is the answer. The answer is in arming ourselves up and preparing for a long-term struggle with the Yan faction in Shandong. My family and friends all agree with me on this. For this purpose, we have formed the White Lotus Sect. My grandfather has nominated me as Commander-in-Chief, and I have appointed Binhong and Yinho as my Deputies. These positions will need your ratification once you've joined our Sect and sworn an oath of brotherhood. Our immediate task is to build up an army and an armory, and we'll need every bit of your help in sourcing materials and in weaponry manufacture. If we stand together and fight as one, there's a chance we'll keep our enemies off the boundaries of Shandong."

A wave of nodding heads surged, amidst an assenting murmur.

Swiveling her gaze to the corner where the refugees huddled together, Sai'er saw fit to address them now.

"Dear folks from out-of town, I know you've trekked all the

way here from other counties to look for shelter and food. You're in the right place. Let me reassure you that you're welcome to set up tents along the foothills. We would ask that you help in our millet farming work. Wages would be in the form of a small portion of the crop yields. By working in the fields, you will not only ward off hunger, but also keep our army fed. We would most appreciate your contribution."

The vagrants had been silent until now. From their corner rose a collective guttural sound that promptly turned into an animated burble.

At this point, Yulan and Yinho went around doling out millet cakes to the attendees. The stricken vagrants bowed in deep gratitude as they put out their trembling hands. Trainees and militiamen gladly gave up their portions to pass to the hungry lot.

By now, most of the militiamen in the crowd had dropped their earlier misgivings and were showing enthusiasm about joining the Sect.

One swarthy man with a thickset build stepped forward in a swagger and snorted, "What makes you so special to deserve the post of Commander-in-Chief?" He deliberately thumbed his nose at Sai'er in contempt. "I dare you to a one-on-one sword duel with me. Do you accept the challenge?"

Sai'er was fully prepared for such a challenge, well aware that her gender and age would leave some doubting her ability in martial skills and leadership. Out of the corner of her eye, she saw Yinho covering his mouth to hide a quip. Without being prompted, he threw a sword Sai'er's way.

"I gladly accept," she said in a flat tone, without the faintest of inflection, at once catching the sword and hopping off the platform.

In the instant the brawny man took to unsheathe his sword,

Sai'er had already propelled qi from her dantian to her wrists.

Her eyes glued to her opponent, she pointed her sword straight at his throat. Feeling threatened, he brought his sword up in reflex to fend off the suspected onrush.

With a quick turn of the wrist, Sai'er flipped her sword down to the exposed lower parts and gashed his thigh, eliciting a loud yelp.

Then she backed off a couple of steps to let the man recover from his shock, and engaged in a series of non-lethal hits and parries timed to a hexagram footwork dance, to amuse herself and entertain the audience.

Just as the man began to let down his guard, she launched her deadly triple-strikes to send his sword hurtling to the ground, and touched the sword tip to his throat.

The final act drew a loud applause from the crowd, but it hardly raised eyebrows among the trainees.

Almost invisible to the audience, Sai'er's sword had slid back into the scabbard and she was standing on the platform again.

By this time, Yinho had set up a simple altar on the side and had inserted three lit joss sticks into a small urn.

"My dear folks, I hope what you're about to see will leave no doubt in your minds that I have the most capable Deputies that any leader could hope for. Binhong, my foster brother, is the chief strategic brain in our Sect and he's now at our hideout mapping out our Sect's future course of action. Yinho here is going to show you his special gift of supernatural powers."

This time Yinho was going to invoke the power of Sun Wukong, Senior Marshal from the North Pantheon, the one and only Monkey Sage.

As Yinho flicked the peach wood sword left and right, then in wide circles, he began the sorcery incantations. The cerulean gates of the Pantheons above slowly slid open, and a gentle breeze drifted forth, accompanied by a whiff of empyrean music. Wukong rode on his Somersault Cloud in descent. Flipping over several times to cover the great distance, in the blink of an eye the Cloud landed the Monkey Sage on earth in a luminous aura. Magic Rod in one hand, he was garbed in golden chainmail armor with a sash at the waist. His animated red eyes darted around to get a sense of bearing.

When he spotted Sai'er, he dipped his head in greetings. She bowed in response, a bit apprehensive that he might be annoyed with her habit of calling his name in vain. She also wondered what Yinho would request of this mischievous immortal.

"We bid you a warm welcome, Venerable Sage!" Yinho said respectfully.

"What would you have me do?" Wukong's blinking red eyes swept around before settling on Yinho.

"I was wondering if you could create ten clones of my deceased pal Ah Long, endowed with super powers?"

"Ten only? Is that all? You've got it," he said, then turned to face the crowd. "I hear Sai'er is going to lead the White Lotus Sect for a just cause. Folks, do yourselves a favor. Follow her lead. You can trust her to have your interests at heart." As he spoke, he scratched his fuzzy head several times, gamboling around in a playful mood.

Sai'er remembered that Wukong had always been nice to her, even though he had never bothered much with manners. She now wondered if Sky Wolf's accusation against this warm-hearted immortal could really stand up to scrutiny.

Having pulled out a tuft of his golden hairs, he spread the tuft out on his palm, picked up one bristle and blew into it. A life-size teenage boy in the exact likeness of Ah Long burst into life, dressed in the same robe and wielding the same spear.

This time, the jaw-dropping response came not only from the

crowd, but also Sai'er. *Yinho can be really creative*, she thought. *At the very least this could work to distract him from his grief.*

The bouncy immortal repeated the process for nine more times. Now ten clones of Ah Long were frolicking around in front of the dazed crowd, drawing cries of immense awe.

Then Wukong instructed the clones in no uncertain terms, "You are to follow orders from Deputy Yinho."

Wukong then handed Yinho a gold wrist band and a small yellow pouch, and said, "You can shrink them back into bristles by rubbing this band twice. Keep the bristles in this pouch. Always wear the band on your wrist and keep the pouch close to you. Rub the band once and they'll appear and be at your service. But don't ever trifle with them. Only summon them when you're in the gravest danger. Remember you can use their service only once."

Yinho and Sai'er bowed deeply to Wukong and thanked him profusely for his gracious help. Just as he was about to leave, Sai'er tugged his sleeve lightly and gingerly whispered, "Wukong, may I ask you a personal question?"

"Ask away."

He and she stepped to the side for some privacy.

Sai'er ruminated for a moment, then posed her question. "Do you remember why Sky Wolf was demoted to the mortal world?"

"Yes, of course! For the rape of two fox nymphs," Wukong replied without hesitation.

"Well—he told me a different story. He said that it was a trumped-up charge, and that you... framed him. He even swore on his immortal life."

"What? I framed him? How original!" he blinked friskily and chortled in good humor. "Haha, I've heard him swear, let's say, more than once!"

Then he went on in an unwonted serious tone.

"Chang'e, there's an easy way to affirm he's a liar. Nezha happened to pass by the fox nymphs' quarters on the day of the crime and caught Sky Wolf red-handed. Nezha told me this himself. He didn't volunteer to be a witness because his father had warned him to keep clear of the affairs of both the Green Dragon and Sky Wolf. If you get a chance to talk to Nezha, by all means ask him. He's known to be honest."

"Thank you for being upfront with me, Wukong. I appreciate this piece of information."

"No problem at all. I want my name cleared too."

One leap forward and he was atop his Somersault Cloud again. In a series of acrobatic flips, the Cloud and he vanished into the cerulean vault.

22

SANBAO PASSED many a sleepless night after that last encounter with Sai'er in Liaocheng.

Not a day went by without his wondering whether she was alive or dead or permanently disabled. That image of Sai'er getting shot kept taunting him day and night. It was never meant to happen, and he cursed his guard for his rashness. Every day he prayed to Buddha to keep her alive and well.

He had never loved anyone like he loved her. She was a seductive rose who didn't mind flaunting her deadly thorns. But that didn't change the petal-soft essence of her soul. It was this aching softness that he wanted so much to protect.

She was the one who treated him with tender kindness and genuine empathy from the first time they met. With the depth of her naked and innocent emotions she had kindled the flame of desire in him that he'd long thought snuffed out by raw cruelty. She'd hauled him up from the fathomless pits of self-loathing and let him see light in humanity again.

Having captured General Tie and incarcerated him in the Yingtian prison, on top of shattering the Jinan resistance and snapping several other victories, he'd finally regained the Prince's trust. To his relief, the Prince only gave him a slap on the wrist for losing custody of Monk Faxian.

His decisive defeat of the Jinan stronghold also earned him

the title of Chief Eunuch, and the honorary name of "Zheng He", conferred by the new Emperor himself. Above all, his master now allowed him access again to the Imperial bed chamber and often consulted with him on military strategy in private.

His uncle and aunt were released and Sanbao at once installed them in a new mansion in the Yingtian suburbs.

No doubt this was all due to the final victory of Zhu Di's usurpation campaign and his recent ascension to the throne, which put him in a rare cheerful mood. But it didn't mean he'd given up purging whom he deemed as traitors. Monk Yao was now charged with issuing a Wanted List. A bounty was offered for the capture of Monk Faxian and Tang Jun.

Whenever Sanbao looked back on the days right after his departure from Wudang, he would still cringe.

The Prince had grilled him for days on his failure to take Sai'er's virginity, and then had punished him by ordering the imprisonment of his uncle and aunt. Sanbao could endure the flogging, but this stinging penalty had really frayed his nerves, as his uncle and aunt were his only family left.

Those days were the worst since his excruciating early-teen years.

The bone-breaking waves of pain as the knife slid across his groin had been hellish, but the physical pain had only lasted a few months. It was just a scratch compared to the mortifying sense of shame and loss that had mutilated his self-worth. But that was far from the worst. When he was used as a sex toy, that double wallop of shame mercilessly impaled his soul, driving him to a couple of suicide attempts.

The merciful break came when he enlisted in the military in his late teens. From then on, he gradually learned to squeeze those putrid memories into oblivion. *The only way to live is to forget the past*, he somehow convinced himself. Killing in battles became the perfect escape valve for his untamable inner tempest. Now the memory of the Prince's grilling again stirred in his mind.

"Are you telling me you failed your mission because you have feelings for her?" the Prince grunted with an illegible expression, in a restrained puff.

"Your Highness. I beg for your forgiveness," Sanbao stammered as he fell on his knees, nerve-wracking anxiety coursing through his limbs.

A raven-dark shadow shrouded the Prince's glacial face. Eerie silence echoed in the chilly bed chamber, so ominous that it made Sanbao's skin crawl.

"So, you two enjoyed the frolic?" came the barbed question.

"I — we care for each other. I couldn't bear to hurt her," Sanbao almost wailed at this point.

"You mean you love her? Are you really content with this *love* without gratification of the flesh?" the Prince cocked his head in a jeering sniff.

"I — I care for her well being. I don't need to possess her."

With the faintest twitch of his eyebrows, the Prince glared at Sanbao with a murderous glint of scorn and sourness in his eyes.

After a pause that felt like eternity, the Prince finally exploded in an inhuman, bone-shattering howl, "Failure cannot go unpunished. Guards, go and arrest Sanbao's uncle and aunt. No release until I order it."

Then he rose from the chair and, in a fit of unhinged fury, whisked the leather whip off the hook on the bedpost.

After he had let out his steam with the lashing, he growled like a provoked tiger, "This is for your impudence! I let you get away with your half castration so you can carry out my order. Was I not merciful enough?" He thrust the blood-stained whip on the floor in a huff and panted menacingly into Sanbao's welted face, "Didn't you owe your life to my mercy?"

Yes, your cruel mercy, Sanbao had wept in his heart.

A moment later, with a flick of his hand he'd hissed, "Let him work at the chamber pot cleaning station."

Sanbao had never been forthcoming with Sai'er that he had sexual urges and could function like a normal man. During the castration process, the drunken knifer had only cut out his testicles, leaving his member intact. The Prince of Yan and Monk Yao were the only ones privy to this.

Sanbao had never dared to let anyone else in on this secret, much less the shameful truth that he had been the Prince's catamite as a kid. Yet that latter truth was an open secret to other eunuchs, whose jealous and spiteful tongue-wagging wouldn't spare him.

Sanbao realized too late that it was not so much the mission failure that had riled his master as the candid confession of his feelings for Sai'er. How he wished he had never said those words. His blundering honesty had hit a raw nerve in the Prince.

The only reason the Prince had ordered him to defile Sai'er was that he wanted to foil her attempt to master the North Star skill. That Sanbao would dare to develop feelings for her was something that had never entered his cold calculations.

There was only one way for him to keep his uncle and aunt alive, and that was to do whatever he could to lick the Prince's boots. Sanbao knew his biggest asset was his fighting prowess, and the Prince could still use that.

Slowly and painstakingly he had clawed his way back from that low point, gaining credits from battle after battle in the Prince's throne-grabbing campaign.

Even so, there was no predicting what his master was up to next.

Despite all, he was still grateful to have found genuine

friendship in Ma Huan, a fellow Hui who recently joined the league of eunuchs and was fast becoming the new Emperor's favorite chamber eunuch, as he was cheerful, well-read and had a flair for foreign languages. At least there was now someone to talk to within the frosty walls of the Palace.

Chief Eunuch or not, life in the Palace was like having to keep knife-edged balance on a thin line above a sharp-rocked chasm. But at least the promotion had stopped all idle gossips among the eunuchs' lot in regards to his woeful history. Now he was treated by some with submissive fear and others new-found respect.

While he dawdled away reminiscing the besotted dalliance with Sai'er, Ma Huan came in to deliver the Emperor's summons. His immediate presence was required in the Audience Hall. A wan expression clouded the young eunuch's usually bright-eyed face. Sanbao could smell something rotten.

This was the day of the trial of Chief Minister Fang Xiaoru for treason. The Emperor was personally conducting the trial.

Dressed in a bright yellow silk imperial robe embroidered with nine dragons and donning the Emperor headdress with jade bead strands hanging front and back, Zhu Di was ensconced in the glitzy golden throne seat on the high dais, looking darkly intense and imperious.

Below the dais, Ministers with eyes fixated on the tips of their boots ranged in two columns, leaving the central aisle for passage.

Sanbao stepped to the front of the dais and read out the Imperial Order for the prisoner to be brought before His Imperial Highness, to be tried for treason.

Two Embroidered Uniform Guards dragged the old man in chains screaming and kicking along the central aisle right up to the foot of the stair to the dais. His grayish hair was a matted mess and his white hemp mourning robe was splotched with dark red stains.

"The usurper has murdered our Emperor," he shrieked as he was forced to kneel on the hard marble floor. "As subjects, we should all mourn his death…"

Pity and dread taunted Sanbao when he laid eyes on the haggard-looking but truculent Fang. The Ministers all tried to avoid eye contact with the prisoner, who was struggling to appear dignified even if he could barely hold himself upright.

"Has the prisoner considered my request to write an inaugural address for my reign?" the Emperor asked with a stern face.

"Prisoner, answer His Imperial Highness," urged Sanbao.

"My answer is still the same," Fang drawled in a low voice. "The person sitting on the throne has no legitimate right to it. There is no new reign and thus no call for an inaugural address."

"Get the prisoner ink, brush and paper. He will write the address," the Emperor insisted with a deep flush, barely hiding his ire.

When the writing tools were brought before Fang, he took up the brush and wrote the words, "The Prince of Yan is a usurper."

This stung the Emperor right where it hurt. His face at once warped into a scathing scowl.

A dagger of fear stabbed at Sanbao as he knew nothing good could come of this escalating bitter exchange.

"If you refuse to write the address, I will sentence your kin to the ninth degree to death right now," howled the Emperor, his face darkening into a reddish black.

"Go ahead!" said Fang. "You can kill scholars, but you can't take away their dignity. All conscientious scholars pledge their allegiance to the Jianwen Emperor."

Sanbao flinched when he saw the familiar manic glint in his master's eyes. The next thing he heard was his frenzied bellow.

"Jianwen was the true usurper, and you were foolish enough to conspire with him. I hereby declare Fang Xiaoru guilty of treason. He's sentenced to death by slicing under the Great Ming Code." Pausing to shoot a venomous glance at Fang, he then curved his lips in a demonic grin, "But before your execution, I grant you the pleasure of watching the collective beheading of your kin to the ninth degree!"

"Might as well make it ten," retorted the recalcitrant Fang with a smirk.

"Alright. As you wish. In addition to kin, your students will also be exterminated."

Helpless tears coursed down Sanbao's face. In the battlefield, even if his life was constantly threatened, he could still defend himself and survive. Here, people could be crushed like ants, through no wrongdoing except by being akin to an alleged criminal.

Even for Fang, what serious wrong had he committed to deserve death by slicing? He was just being loyal to the previous Emperor. That was all.

History was filled with cases where rulers newly endowed with absolute power had every chance to win hearts and minds through simple acts of human decency. But more often than not, they foolishly chose to stamp out dissenters with heinous violence, sowing seeds of hatred which would only sprout into backlashes and retaliation in time.

Damming floods is never the answer, mused Sanbao in a grim mood. *It's a pity so few rulers have the wisdom of Yu the Great.*

He remembered Sai'er's suggestion for him to try to get posted to faraway places.

I must give this further thought. As long as I'm near this bloodthirsty man, there'll be no peace in my life.

A total of eight hundred and seventy-three folks from the

Fang clan came under the axe in the following days, with Fang in the audience.

An eagle hovered in the sky during those executions. On the last day, a sprite cooed to the big bird and tied a note to its talon. It disappeared into the rolling clouds, heading to Yidu.

The blood that splashed all over the Yingtian city square soaked so deep into crevices of the flagstone ground that it was impossible to scrub clean afterwards, leaving a fetid miasma that imbued the vicinity.

No one dared to walk near the square at night any more. Stories of headless ghosts wandering in the neighborhood went around like wild fire. Many citizens decided to move away from Yingtian, just to be well clear of the site of atrocious mass murder.

Monk Yao, now the Grand Councilor, had been preoccupied with mountains of administrative work at Court since Zhu Di's enthronement. In particular, he was charged with overseeing the destruction of Court records and documents related to the Jianwen reign. Historians could just presume that the four-year reign never existed. Sanbao felt his mentor was aware he was doing a disservice to history, but had no choice but to follow the Emperor's orders.

Finding him at rest in the front yard of his residence after a long day's work, Sanbao sat down at the stone table to have a chat with him.

"You look dispirited! Anything wrong?" Monk Yao was always keen-eyed as an owl.

"His Imperial Highness has personally tried Fang Xiaoru. Fang's clan has been wiped out— "

"I heard," said the monk with a long sigh. "If you only knew how hard I had tried to persuade the Emperor to spare Fang. Sadly, I can't change what's already predestined for Zhu Di.

Mark my words, Sanbao. Everyone in this life has to pay for his evil deeds in the afterlife. No one is exempt. Not he, nor I."

"Any news on Monk Faxian and Tang Jun?"

"Ah, you'd be happy to know that Tang Sai'er has shown up in Putai, according to Yusu's intelligence. Yusu is now working with Lin San to get Sai'er to cooperate with us."

"But there's no way Sai'er is going to cooperate," Sanbao blurted out, while exhaling a cathartic sigh of relief on the news that Sai'er was alive and well. After a pause, he continued, "She loves her Ba and Grandba more than her life. Besides, her union with Lin San is in name only. I doubt she would heed his advice."

As soon as the words slipped out of his mouth, he realized how much he had wanted to share the secret of the unconsummated marriage. His beloved Sai'er was still a maiden and her North Star skill was intact. That was all that mattered.

Monk Yao shot Sanbao a knowing glance and said, "With or without Lin San's help, Yusu will come up with something." He then shook his head slowly and added, "As your mentor, I have to caution you. The Emperor considers Sai'er his favorite, and her taking a combative stance has whetted his desire. He certainly can't stand another man being amorously involved with her. You're treading in dangerous waters."

"He's my master, Teacher. I'm a loser at the outset. Not to mention my uncle's and aunt's lives are in his hands," said Sanbao with sagged shoulders, but in his heart he was stubbornly saying something else. *Sai'er is part of my soul. No one can separate us.* For her protection though, he had thought it best to let her believe there was no hope for their love.

"I can see that. But the Emperor is not stupid. With your intelligence, you probably figured out for yourself that for all his histrionics, he was actually pleased you failed your mission."

Sanbao had always admired his mentor's acute perceptive

power. Once again his incisive judgment enthralled him.

After a moment of rumination, Sanbao collected himself and broached the main objective of his visit.

"Teacher, I need your advice on one thing. Do you think it would be a good idea for me to ask the Emperor to send me on an overseas mission? I was just thinking that this is one way to keep clear of the Emperor's wrath."

"Ah, good thing you brought this up. In fact, the Emperor and I have been discussing plans of sending envoys to foreign countries on diplomatic missions, bearing gifts and the latest news of the new Yongle reign. I also agree that you'd be a lot safer if you stayed away from the Palace. You had better let me handle this, lest the Emperor should suspect your motive if you make a direct request."

"Perhaps you could suggest to him to let me conduct a search for the Jianwen Emperor in neighboring countries," said Sanbao, recalling Sai'er's advice to give Zhu Di something he badly wanted as a bargain chip.

"Hmm, good thinking," Monk Yao bobbed his head. "You do understand your master well."

"Teacher, I'm so grateful for your help!" Sanbao felt like a load had been taken off his chest. At last he could see light at the end of the long dark tunnel. With gusto, he added, "I'll start reading up on shipbuilding, sailing and maps. Oh, I have tons to learn."

"Indeed! Start with a visit to the Longjian Shipyard on Qinhuai River," advised the mentor. "The largest fleet of treasure ships in China's history is being built there even as we speak."

The news lit up Sanbao's face instantly. He wouldn't believe it if it came from anyone other than his respected mentor. A frisson of surprise and thrill ran through his blood.

Then he asked with a sheepish look, "Teacher, can I join you when Yusu reports back?" Speculation on what Yusu might do with Sai'er had been taunting him. He had to find out one way or the other.

"You know I wouldn't refuse you."

"Teacher, I have another favor to ask," he said with an earnest look. "For a long time I've cherished the wish to be converted to Buddhism. Would you consider taking me as your acolyte?"

"Ah, I thought you'd never ask," the Monk chuckled. More than once he had hinted that Sanbao had the innate wisdom to imbibe the Buddhist Scriptures.

Sanbao knew very well this would please his mentor. He had to do everything in his power to strengthen the bond with his only protector in Court. To successfully clinch the job of envoy, he must get his mentor's unwavering support.

23

SAI'ER SPEECH was a huge success.

Without exception, all militiamen and trainees who were present took an oath of brotherhood and joined the White Lotus Sect before noon that day. If they'd earlier harbored any doubt at all, Sun Wukong's magic stunt had wiped it all away.

The trainees quickly got to work and helped the refugees set up tents along the foothills abutting the meadow. Yinho then assigned a mature woman named Mother Wang from the group to be the Farming Unit Overseer.

In the afternoon, Yinho and Yulan were busy with organizing all Sect members into different function units according to their professions or skills. Sai'er had directed them to group members into one of four units: Strategists, Weapon Crafters, Scouts and Assassins. She also appointed Binhong head of the first couple of Units, and put Yinho in charge of the remaining two, naming Yulan as the go-between for the two Unit Heads.

When evening came, Yinho and Yulan headed back to Ba's cottage to make supper, and to await Binhong's arrival.

Sai'er made up an excuse for not joining them, saying she would return in time for the Buddhist vigil to be held that night. Before she left, she said to Yinho, "I'm sure you don't need reminding, but we do owe Madam Pu a note of condolences and a clear explanation of the circumstances of Ah Long's murder.

Please assure her in the letter that the Sect leaders will not rest until his unjust death is avenged." Sorrow and guilt weighed on her even as she spoke.

When she arrived at the Dragon Inn, she swept her gaze around and decided that the brightly lit and half full dining lounge would be the best place to meet Lin San.

This inn was something like an outlandish costume that fitted poorly. Its gaudily sculpted façade, conspicuous amidst drab and sooty buildings in the backwater county, was complemented by showy redwood tables and chairs and silk lanterns in the interior. Its exclusive clientele consisted of high ranking officials and wealthy merchants, who habitually splurged on escort services offered by local courtesans and prostitutes.

She stepped up to the reception counter and asked the inn owner, a squat middle-aged man with a goatee, to deliver a message to the guest named Lin San, that Tang Sai'er was waiting for him in the dining lounge. The owner scanned her from head to toe and made a snide remark with a smirk, "Isn't it a bit too early for your trade?"

Sai'er seized the man by his collar with such aggression that he almost gagged. "Watch your tongue, fatty!" she hissed. His face flushed and he coughed a few times to catch his breath. As soon as she loosened her grip, he scrambled away and crawled up the stairs to do her bidding.

She sat down at a table nearest the inn entrance and waited.

A moment later, Lin San appeared. He took the seat opposite her, looking infuriatingly smug.

"I didn't expect you to be so prompt," he said with a furtive grin.

"Let me make one thing clear. I didn't come on your bidding. I came to seek answers," she glared daggers at him.

"What do you want to know?" he harrumphed with self-importance, his eyes darting around.

"Why did you kill the boy?" Sai'er asked under her breath with gritted teeth.

"What is he to you? Just some good-for-nothing street urchin..."

"So you admit to the murder," she cut him short in an irate voice. "Just so you know, Ah Long was my best friend's apprentice and my buddy. I knew you're incapable of human decency, but I didn't know you were such a beast." She struggled to keep her voice steady and emotionless.

"He was a stubborn kid," he shrugged his shoulders with apathy. "I tried every method to make him talk."

"You still haven't answered my question. What did you want with him?"

"Why don't you calm down and hear me out?" he said with exaggerated nonchalance. "Look, Sai'er, I know you and I are not meant to be a couple. Believe me, I'm fine with that. Like it or not, we're now in a new era with a new capable ruler. The only way to get ahead is to pledge loyalty to the heavenly mandated supreme ruler."

"Please spare me your lecture and get straight to the point," Sai'er couldn't help but roll her eyes. The only reason she was putting up with his nonsense was to find out what dirty tricks he was up to.

"Alright. Monk Yao has issued an order for the arrest of Monk Faxian and your Ba. There's a huge bounty offered for their capture. In the eyes of the Emperor, they are traitors. So I'm just doing what's expected of a good citizen. The reason I wanted to see you was to ask whether you'd be interested in partnering with me. No doubt you know where they are." His eyes couldn't stop blinking as he talked.

Had Sai'er not been so caught up in her fury, she would've been able to see through the artful guile.

"Ah, what else could I expect from you?" Sai'er grunted with irritation.

"You knew very well Monk Faxian is a wanted fugitive. You had some nerve kidnapping him out of captivity. Why would you want to be on the wrong side of power? As for your Ba, he's unfortunate to be a former student of Fang Xiaoru's. Right now the Emperor is angry with Fang and wants his students rounded up, but I think he'll show leniency once his anger subsidies, if it's your Ba's safety that you worry about."

Sai'er couldn't be bothered with explaining to the bastard that Monk Faxian was her Grandba. The lesser he knew, the better.

"My father was your teacher once, remember? What makes you think I would sink to your level and betray my own father?"

"So you're not going to help me with this? Not even if I say I'll let you have the bigger cut?"

At this point, the inn owner approached with a fawning smile, bringing a ceramic pot of tea and two porcelain cups. "Please forgive my intrusion, Master Lin. I thought you and your guest might want some jasmine tea." Gingerly he poured tea from the pot into the cups and quickly slinked away.

Lin San lifted the cup near him and took a sip, gesturing for Sai'er to have a drink too. She was really thirsty and in two gulps drained the floral scented tea.

"You can go to the eighteenth level of hell! Listen! I would have slashed your throat with my sword the moment I saw you, if not for the promise I made to your mother, you depraved child murderer. But mark this: even if you can walk out of here alive today, it doesn't mean you can elude your well-deserved retribution."

"Calm down, Sai'er. No need to get so uptight." His words

seemed to be drawn out with an echo to Sai'er's ears. "You're still valuable to me. I'll treat you well—"

"What do you mean—"

Before she could finish her sentence, her limbs suddenly went flaccid and when she tried to stand up, her knees buckled and she slumped to the floor. She tried to speak but her tongue didn't listen to her. *I've been poisoned! That squat head!* Her hearing capacity and vision were still good. She had no doubt the jasmine tea had been laced with the infamous fragrant tendon-numbing powder.

Then Lin San came round to her and lifted her up in his arms. He carried her up to his room and put her on the bed. She glared knives at him. He responded with a snort and a devilish grin.

"Much as I want to have my way with you, I have to restrain myself, only because you're the favorite of our Emperor. I wouldn't want to cross him, now would I? But it doesn't mean I can't allow myself a little pleasure."

Sai'er opened her eyes wide and wriggled limply on the bed, as Lin San ripped off her robe and started fondling her. She screamed till her throat singed without making a sound.

"Relax! I said I would treat you well. How could I not? Those close to the Emperor want to use you as a bait to entice Monk Faxian and your Ba out of their hole. So netting you means a step closer to the bounty, hehehe! Hmm, you do have smooth skin..."

"You dirty little man, lay off her!" Pearly yelled as she entered the room. She scowled at Lin San and then asked in a sullen voice, "Did you find the white jade Amulet?"

It immediately dawned on Sai'er that this was Yusu in Pearly's guise. She was just glad that she had earlier entrusted Ba with the white jade tablet.

"No, I turned the cottage inside out but there was no sign of it. She doesn't have it on her either," he replied in ill humor.

"You're a fun wrecker. Why don't you help me wrap her up and put her in the carriage. How long is the dose effective for?"

"It's enough to keep her still for three days. Don't worry. I have enough doses with me to last the whole journey to Yingtian. We better get going at the break of dawn."

The horse-drawn carriage took Lin San and Yusu and their prey to the Liaocheng main pier, where they boarded a courier junk bound for Yingtian.

On the second night on the junk, inside the hull cabin where Sai'er laid bound on a straw-filled pallet, Lin San and Yusu were having a lavish supper prepared by the crew's cook, specially hired by Lin to cater to all their meals.

"Let's drink to our almost accomplished mission," Yusu offered a toast to Lin, who eagerly drank up the sorghum wine. Then he helped himself to another filled cup.

"I've been wondering. How were you able to find me?"

"Easy. I have eyes and ears all around," Yusu said with a smug smile.

Damn you, Nezha!

"Your plan to use that urchin as bait was perfect. This hot-headed bitch was easier to fool than I thought. So, we're agreed on a sixty-forty split, right?"

"Only when Monk Faxian and Tang Jun are caught. The bounty is on their capture. But there's no reason to believe they won't come for the whore. Come, have another cup. You deserve to relax a little."

Moments later, Lin San was so drunk he slumped facedown on the table.

A glimmer flickered. Sai'er's throat constricted and almost gagged.

Yusu had taken out a serrated dagger from her boot. She walked calmly round to the motionless figure. Using both hands, she thrust the blade deep into Lin San's back. He let out a shrill cry and rolled onto the floor, his eyes wild with terror.

Again with both hands she yanked the dagger out and kicked him into a supine position. He squealed in agony. With the blood-dripping dagger she slashed his throat, setting forth a wide spray of blood. A guttural sound emitted from his gaping mouth and he fell silent, eyes in a blank stare.

Sai'er watched the dispassionate murder in cold sweat. Never had she imagined Lin San would die at Yusu's hand, and in such a savage way. She was not exactly a believer in karma, but her perception might be changing. *Perhaps the heavens do have eyes!*

Moving swiftly, Yusu lugged the corpse out the cabin and Sai'er heard a loud splash at deck level. When she came back in with a pail of water, she had already cleaned herself up and changed into a fresh white robe. She cleaned up the blood stains in the cabin in a few short moments.

"What are you staring at?" She glared at Sai'er with hateful, steely eyes, most out of character with that lovely face of Pearly's. To the stone-hearted Yusu, roguish Lin San was as dispensable as an innocent sixteen-year-old. Anyone who stood in her way deserved to be indiscriminately crushed like an ant.

But what is she after?

As if she heard Sai'er unsaid words, she began her monologue with a deadpan face.

"I wanted Lin San to find the Amulet and he failed. He didn't deserve to live. Besides, he has no place in my personal plans. So the sooner he was out of the picture, the better. Now I'll tell you why you're an important quarry for me. Monk Yao wants bait to net Monk Faxian and Tang Jun. The Emperor wants you in his bed, much as he's never said it aloud. For this reason, you're a valuable item. Now that I've got you in my hands, the two most powerful men under heavens will be in my debt."

After a brief pause to rivet her gaze on Sai'er, she snickered, "To settle scores with your North Star coach, I've never swerved from my ultimate goal, and that is to get Monk Yao to cast a love spell on Monk Faxian, my beloved Wen." Then she spread her lips in a burst of malicious, high-pitched laughs, entirely uncharacteristic of the woman she impersonated, which was eerie to watch.

Sai'er could sense that hatred had cauterized the nerves and sensibilities of this lovelorn woman. That prickly conversation between Pearly and Yusu at the Jade Maiden Peak cottage rose to the front of her mind and sent chills through her veins. Yusu would stop at nothing to ensnare Grandba.

The boat trip to Yingtian would take a little less than a month and felt like one endless journey.

Every day, Yusu would feed Sai'er some millet gruel mixed with boiled taro root. Every three days, she would administer a dose of the tendon-numbing powder. Sai'er couldn't walk more than a few steps without Yusu's help. Paralysis aside, she was becoming weaker in constitution.

She knew if she didn't do something to help herself, her body would give in to deterioration. So, seven days into the trip, she tried to slowly and painstakingly work at moving her qi through her meridians, so she could channel energy to her muscles.

Once she started the regimen, it was easier than she thought. This was because in the recent past, her extraction of Yang qi from male opponents had significantly bolstered and perfected her store of potent qi, which actually enhanced circulation.

As was her normal routine, Sai'er would go to the common latrine to move her bowels in the late morning. Yusu hated going to the putrid, dank and feces-smudged cabin except for her own needs, and so didn't mind letting Sai'er crawl her way there to do her business. This was the only time she would let Sai'er out of her sight.

On mornings she got fed the drug, she would use that time to induce vomiting by shoving two fingers deep into her throat.

Towards the end of the trip, she felt her energy returning and was on way to resuming strength and flexibility of her limbs. But she still feigned infirmity.

All this time she was worried sick about her folks back home. With some deep thinking, she convinced herself that Binhong and Yinho could be counted on to do what needed to be done for the Sect. She prayed hard that her Ba and Grandba wouldn't walk into the trap set for them.

Meanwhile she kept her mind busy figuring out how best she could play her hand when she confronted Monk Yao and Zhu Di.

When she thought of her stupidity in discarding the only love token she had ever had, she couldn't help castigating herself. But when she seriously weighed her options, she realized she hardly had a choice. In all fairness, she had long chosen her path. Wasn't it her childhood dream to become Lady Protector of Shandong? Even if she hadn't been charged with the celestial mission, she still would have taken the route of leading Shandong folks out of misery.

Now that she'd willingly taken up the reins as leader, romantic love couldn't be anything but a taunting rainbow. Every conscientious choice carried a price. It was a price she was ready to pay.

24

BINHONG HAD arrived home the night before.

Yinho had briefed him on Ah Long's tragic death, the Sect member initiation meeting, the registration and swearing in, the recruitment of refugees as farmers, the sorcery stunt, the clones, the grouping of members into four function units and the appointments of unit heads.

Yulan had cooked a simple supper of stewed lotus root and stir-fried noodles with mushrooms. After having supper together, they had lit up candles in the backyard and chanted the Heart Sutra in vigil rite held for Ah Long.

A veil of sorrow had draped over Binhong as he was reminded how volatile life could be. Death. Loss. Pain. They could pay an unwelcome visit any time. Nothing could bar them from stepping over the threshold. Witnessing the friendship between Yinho and Yulan had made him miss Sai'er all the more.

The sky was still an inky veil when Binhong rose from bed. He had barely dozed off during the night as he'd been worried about Sai'er, who hadn't come home at all.

When he stepped into the backyard, he could hear the sound of pottery clinking coming from the kitchen. Yulan had stayed the night to keep Yinho company. She and Yinho were already up and making breakfast.

The first shafts of light broke from the sleepy vault of darkness to paint the distant mountains golden red.

Binhong had always loved watching sunrise in quietude on the rooftop, before the rest of the household stirred. Sai'er had usually been the one to rise from bed after him, and she would climb up the wooden ladder to sit beside him for a while before making breakfast. Those moments of quiet company had been precious. From the time when they were small kids, he had readily taken on the duty of protecting his foster sister. He took the responsibility so seriously it verged on obsession.

This place he called home somehow seemed different after she moved to the Lin cottage. Her vivacious presence had withered into dregs of bland memory. Every room, every nook, every inch of space had breathed her scent, but now the air seemed to have turned stale. He still could not accept that she no longer lived here. *Damn that Lin San!*

Binhong had brought along Zhuge Liang, which he'd placed on a wooden perch hung from the maple tree. The bird's job was to function as the Sect's official courier. Bird and man had bonded well on the journey from Rocky Ridge. No surprise there. Sky Hawk and golden eagle should have natural affinity for each other.

He picked up a ripened peach from the ground and let the large bird peck it out of his hand. When he muttered to the bird what was on his mind, it seemed to understand him and snuggled its head affectionately against his neck. He was just so grateful for this new companion.

"No sign of Sai'er?" he asked in a hoarsened voice when Yinho came out from the kitchen.

"No. Not to worry. She probably decided to stay overnight at her own cottage."

"But you said she didn't say where she was headed," Binho said with a frown. "If she was going to her own cottage, she would have said so."

"You're right. Actually, I was expecting her to come home last night, because she said she'd be back in time for the vigil," Yinho said with a bashful look. "I just wanted to say things to ease your mind. My gut feeling is that she went looking for Lin San."

"Probably Mother Lin knows where Lin San is. We can go and ask her after breakfast," said Yulan thoughtfully as she placed bowls of millet gruel and a dish of steamed salted eggs on the backyard table.

This morning, a wave of anxiety pounded him head-on. He couldn't shake off the feeling in his bones that something bad had happened to her.

After making a stop at the new cottage and talking with Mother Lin, the three of them headed to the Dragon Inn. The inn owner hemmed and hawed when asked whether Lin San had been seen leaving with a young woman of Sai'er's description.

From his shifty-eyed behavior, Binhong could tell he was hiding something. But if he was bent on keeping what he knew to himself, there was nothing much they could do.

They went back home dispirited, being worried sick about Sai'er. From what Mother Lin had told them, they were certain that her disappearance must have something to do with the Court's Traitors Wanted List and the related bounty.

"My gut tells me that bastard Lin San has Sai'er in his hands," Binhong muttered to himself. Yinho nodded sullenly in agreement. They both knew Lin San's sudden appearance in Putai couldn't be anything but a bad omen. It was not difficult to join the dots, given the rogue's notorious track record of avarice. The word 'kidnap' tickled their minds.

In the afternoon, while taking the coffin to the cemetery near the copse to conduct a proper burial, they met Mother Wang the

Overseer. She was in a maudlin state when she accosted Yinho.

"Deputy Dong, I have something bad to report." She kneeled on the dirt path, wailing. "Someone from the Yamen came to our tent site this morning and demanded us to pay taxes. They said the visiting Censor from Court sent them. When we said we couldn't pay, they brought in a gang to pull down our tents and tie up our girls!"

While propping her up, Yinho asked, "Are they still there?" He was apparently flustered at being addressed by his surname, and with a title.

"Yes, they're wrecking the tents right this moment. Please do something to stop them!"

"What gives them the right to extort money? That land has no registered owners," Binhong intervened in a grumpy mood, his voice in a rumble.

"Oh, this is Deputy Tang. He arrived last evening," Yinho made the introduction.

With stricken eyes, the wizened woman bowed deeply to Binhong and stammered in a shaky voice, "Deputy Tang, I'm sorry to trouble you like this. We just have no one to turn to. They say they're going to sell the girls to brothels. My little girl is only thirteen. Luckily I was able to sneak away to get help." She broke into heaving sobs again.

Binhong bristled at what the oppressors were up to. *These women and children are victims of the civil war who hardly have enough to eat. The officials are just animals!*

"Don't worry, Mother Wang. We were on our way to bury a loved one. Why don't you help Yulan here to do the burial for us, and let me and Deputy Dong go to the tent site to sort things out. Is that alright?"

She bobbed her head with relief and gratitude.

Yinho and Binhong exchanged a glance and they leaped their

way in qinggong to the tent site.

Upon arrival at the scene, Binhong saw a number of trainees in a scuffle with the Yamen runners who were forcibly tearing down the tents with rakes and hoes as ordered by a grim-looking Embroidered Uniform Guard.

A group of screaming teenage girls had their hands tied behind their back. Older women and children were bawling in helplessness.

Binhong went up to the Guard and said under his breath, trying hard to damp down his anger, "Master, these are starving refugees from other counties. They just want a basic shelter here. Can you be kind and leave them in peace?"

The Guard was livid and frothed at the mouth, "Who are you to talk to me like this? I'm carrying out orders from the Honorable Censor. Step aside and hold your tongue, or else I'll have you thrown into prison."

In the vista of Binhong's mind suddenly unfurled the long suppressed image of his parents being executed by order of an Embroidered Uniform Guard on a trumped-up charge of poisoning a Court Censor's son. Over the years, he had tried his best to pretend that part of his life didn't exist, in order to live like a normal person. The wound might've been invisible, but the pain did not die and was always crawling just beneath the surface. A fit of scalding fury now fired him up, stoking the dormant pain. That in turn fueled his living ire.

Without another word, he unsheathed his sword and with a quick flip, touched the tip on the Guard's throat, and said, "Tell your men to stop what they're doing, now!"

The Guard froze at this unexpected maneuver. When Binhong swiveled his gaze towards Yinho, who was yanking a runner off from a girl he was molesting, the Guard took one stealthy step back and drew out his broadsword.

A flurry of hits and parries later, Binhong launched the qi-charged triple-strike, slashing the Guard's right cheek, right shoulder and arm, his broadsword promptly bounding out of his hand.

Binhong latched his sword on the Guard's neck and ordered, "Call your men to leave at once!"

This time, the Guard couldn't but submit and did as he was told. In the matter of a few moments, the intruders had left the site.

Fortunately, only a couple of tents had come undone and needed repairs. The trainees lost no time in helping to mend the damaged tents.

When Mother Wang returned with Yulan, all she saw were smiles breaking through tears and a site returned to order. Grateful tears flowed.

As Yulan wanted to head to her father's home, Binhong and Yinho accepted Mother Wang's invitation to have a simple meal of steamed taro roots with her family.

On their way home after supper, Yinho unloaded his worries on Binhong.

"After today's event, there's a good chance people from the magistracy will retaliate. A trainee told me earlier that a new magistrate will take office in a couple of days. No doubt he won't dare ruffle the Censor and will certainly side with him. It'll be a matter of time before they clamp down on us. The defenseless women and children are not safe from their claws."

"I have the same feeling too," Binhong replied with a pensive look. "Maybe it's time to set our assassination plan in motion."

The next evening, Yinho went to the lecture temple with Binhong with the aim of introducing him to the Strategy and Weaponry Unit members, whom Yinho had earlier summoned.

Binhong told the hundred and fifty Weaponry Unit members

that they were required to move to Rocky Ridge in Yidu and to train in weapon forgery under two expert blacksmiths. Upon arrival, they were to first report to Pearly at the Bamboo Grove Taoist Nunnery.

Then he briefed the ten Strategy members, who had all studied *Great Learning*, *Doctrine of the Mean* and *The Art of War*, on an outline of the Sect's near- and long-term objectives, and asked each of them to submit to him a guideline for the governance of Putai.

On the following day, at a meeting of the Scouts and Assassins, numbering a hundred and seventy respectively, Yinho told them about the assassination plan that he and Binhong had hacked out the previous night.

He then briefed the Scouts on the mode of action.

The Scouts immediately set out to work. They were required to gather as much information as they could about the layout of the Magistracy Yamen compound, the approximate number of security guards manning the sleeping quarters of top officials and what time of night security was at its most lax. They were free to use devious or coercive means to achieve the end, as time was of the essence. The Chief Scout was to present the layout plan with security information within two days.

Yinho had personally assessed the seventy Assassins on that day of the initiation meeting. Out of them, he now selected four, two being top-notch Sword-as-Whip fighters, one of whom was Gao Feng, and two superb qinggong trainees, one being Gao Yulan.

He went over with the four chosen ones every detail of the assassination plan, including a back-up course of action. Their targets were the Censor and the newly appointed Magistrate. As soon as the Chief Scout came back with the crucial intelligence, the four would take immediate action.

Two days later, Binhong and Yinho met with the Chief Scout and the four Assassins at the lecture temple.

The Chief Scout placed on the worn-down altar a hand-drawn sketch showing the Yamen compound layout and shared the intelligence his team had gathered.

In the rear courtyard, the Magistrate's bed chamber and the guest bed chamber, now occupied by the Censor, stood adjacent to each other, facing a dining lounge and a study on the opposite side. This residential area was separated from the front judiciary hall by a large central courtyard flanked by runners' quarters on one side and guards' quarters and prison cells on the other. Servants' quarters, a stable and a kitchen were tucked away in the backyard in the rearmost part.

Six well-trained bodyguards were assigned as sentries to keep watch in the rear courtyard that the bed chambers fronted onto. Their watch would begin at the First Hour of the Dog and would end at the First Hour of the Rabbit the next morning.

The Magistrate had only recently moved into the compound. His family was to arrive a month later.

Having brooded for a moment, Yinho said, "It looks like the best time to attack is right after the guard watch ends at break of dawn."

"I agree. But the job has to be done really fast, and must be finished before the servants start their daily service routine," said Binhong.

Binhong was not one who could easily trust another person. But he felt confident that Yinho could be relied on to execute the plan without fail.

25

As head of the Scouts and Assassins, Yinho considered it his duty to lead the task.

Since Ah Long's death, Yinho had been tamping down his feelings of violent anger and hatred. Somehow he felt this assassination attempt could at least help dilute the bitterness that clogged up his senses. If he couldn't gouge out Lin San's heart with his own hands, the next best thing would be to witness the murder of those who deserved to die.

Much as he was grateful for Yulan's well-meant consolation, he couldn't fool himself. The savage truth was, the loss of Ah Long had plunged him into pitch darkness, a fathomless well of debilitating guilt and loneliness.

The love between him and Ah Long was much more than that between mentor and protégé. Poor Yulan didn't understand it, nor did anyone else, except maybe Sai'er. Ah Long had been an honest and sweet boy whom he would have died to protect. Yet he'd failed to protect him and he hated himself for it.

In their own world, their love had been tender, shameless and mutually pleasing. He could not hope to find another like Ah Long, nor did he want to find another. That was why he had come up with the idea of creating clones. Having the clones close to his body at least somewhat assuaged his sense of loss.

His lover's brutal death had also mercilessly scratched open the old-time wound that he had thought healed. That visceral pain of losing both parents to vicious power had sadly only been lulled to sleep. It was very much alive and kicking. The violently torn scab was just too painful to bear. *Why do the heavens have to be so cruel to me?* This was a question he kept asking.

Who would avenge his parents' and Ah Long's unjust deaths, if not he? Who should answer for all the unjust civilian deaths under the inhumane Great Ming Code and Da Gao, if not the heaven-cursed Zhu family and their cohort?

The group of five was all dressed in black with their faces covered with black cloth masks.

Steel-grey clouds were teeming in the sky above, effacing the remnants of moonlight. The Yamen compound was in the center of the county, mired in a warren of busy streets and sleazy back alleys, now deadly quiet in this lightless predawn.

Five spectral dark shadows made a flying leap over the fence wall and onto the tiled roof of the front judicial hall. A foot accidentally kicked loose a ceramic tile from the upturned eaves; it plummeted to the ground, cracking to shards. The apparitions lay flat on their stomachs, hardly breathing for the next instant. No stirring in the premises, except for a cat's soft purr.

A few moments later, they trod with the lightest footfall past the roof of the runners' quarters, always on the alert for the slightest sound coming from beneath.

When they came close to the rear courtyard, Yinho gestured for his team to lie low while he craned his neck to scan the ground below. Their timing was perfect. The sentry's watch had just ended and the courtyard was empty.

The two swordsmen and Yinho leaped to the ground, while the two qinggong experts remained on the roof. Their qinggong skills were at a level where they could each push or carry another person in airwalking, so their job was to help the swordsmen in retreat.

Yinho knew very well that it was the first time the two swordsmen were required to kill and that they might get cold feet. So he was there to give them reassurance, as much as to keep watch on them and provide back-up when needed.

The two had now separately entered their respective target's chamber.

Yinho held his breath and prayed.

A shuffling sound emitted from the Magistrate's room, followed by noises of a physical wrangle and objects falling and clashing. Yinho couldn't wait any longer. He charged into the room.

In the ebony darkness, he saw a gleam reflected off something shiny. It looked like white silk. He lunged forward and grabbed the silk-robed target by his hair, yanking him away from the beleaguered Gao Feng.

With his drawn dagger he sliced the target's throat in frenzied anger, his mind filled with the image of the hateful Lin San. Gao Feng stood dazed for a fleeting moment, then collected himself. He picked up his sword from the floor and thrust it into the dying man's bulging belly.

When the two came out to the courtyard, the other assassin stood trembling like a leaf, his hand and sword dripping blood.

"Did you do it?" Yinho asked. "Yes. I think so," came the shaky reply.

"Let's get out of here, now!" Yinho ordered. No sooner had he leaped up to the roof than he realized the two swordsmen were so scared that they couldn't jump. So Yulan and the other qinggong trainee had to hop down to grab them by the arm and haul them up.

A servant stumbled into the rear courtyard. Startled into

wakefulness when he spied moving black shadows, he shouted at the top of his lungs, "Bandits on the roof! Guards!"

Torches flared in the central courtyard amidst commotion. The six sentry guards had sprung from their rooms with broadswords in hand. One after another they clambered up the only ladder to the rooftop and started an uncoordinated chase.

By this time, the group of five had already bounced from the fence wall to the ground outside the compound. Slanting shafts of dawn light began shooting from the horizon. Cockerels were not shy to perform their morning call.

Like gusts of wind, they whipped down the main street, which was still deserted except for a couple of noodle hawkers who went about lighting up their stoves. Shop owners who happened to peer out from the dark interior and spot the fleeing shadows quickly slammed shut their oil-paper-covered lattice windows.

At an intersection, they sprinted into a shady back lane and skimmed along the guttered alley.

As soon as the guards lost sight of them, they gave up the pursuit. They didn't even bother to interrogate the hawkers for pointers to track down the fugitives.

Putai people, with the exception of the few snobbish rich who always bootlicked the officials, were known to be protective towards their own.

As soon as the team reached the lecture temple, where Binhong was waiting, Yinho asked the swordsman whose assassination target was the Censor what had transpired.

It turned out that he had murdered the Embroidered Uniform Guard who happened to be bunking in the antechamber. The Censor who slept in the inner room, according to his report, had probably escaped unscathed through a back door.

After recounting the entire episode to Binhong, Yinho suggested that the next step was to lay low and watch for the response of the Yamen. Binhong agreed.

About ten days later, the Chief Scout reported to Yinho, "My men who use a Yamen runner as snitch told me that the Censor quietly left Putai yesterday. The compound is now without lead. Which means Putai has no governing head."

"Brother, I think the time has come for you to take the helm," Yinho said to Binhong with a grin.

"We ought to call a meeting of our Sect members and let them decide," Binhong replied. "In any case, it won't be appropriate for me to occupy the position of Magistrate. I think it's best for the White Lotus Sect as a whole to rule over Putai, with me acting as agent."

"I'm sure Sai'er, for one, would approve of that. I'll call the meeting."

Yinho had always looked up to Binhong as his older brother, even if they were the same age. He always admired him for his cool-headed sagacity, but it was for his selflessness that Yinho idolized him. Sometimes he felt sorry for Binhong when he saw him discreetly cast a pining gaze on Sai'er.

The proposal to appoint Tang Binhong as Agent for the White Lotus Sect to govern Putai was put to the vote at the meeting. The vote was unanimously in favor.

Led by Binhong and Yinho, the Sect members marched to the Yamen compound to initiate the takeover.

Yamen runners and guards had long been unhappy at their jobs because of the paltry pay and low social status. The officials were too busy stuffing their own pockets to care about the workers' welfare. So carrying out orders was more often than not a matter of going through the motions.

They had heard of the Sect's formation and the sorcery stunt and were already silent supporters. The trio's names were well known to them. Someone had probably tipped them off about the Sect's intended takeover of the Yamen. So when Binhong informed them of the proposed arrangement, they accepted without fuss.

With the help of the Strategy team, Binhong immediately set to working out a new manpower and salary structure for all Yamen personnel. Having gone through the account ledgers, he was satisfied that a raise in workers' pay was feasible.

Next, at Yinho's suggestion, he went to inspect the county granary with the head runner who had custody of the latchkey to the barn door. The head runner told Binhong and Yinho that on the new Magistrate's agenda the priority plan was to auction off all the millet and sorghum grains in the open market to the highest bidder.

"The stored grains are the fruit of Putai farmers' hard labor," Yinho seethed with gritted teeth. "Most of the populace don't have enough to eat. How could that heaven-cursed even think of doing such a disgusting thing?"

Binhong then ordered for one-third of the granary store to be distributed to the homeless, the beggars, and the refugees.

After ten days on the job, Binhong finally took the time to sit down in the apothecary to write a full report to be sent back to the Advisers at Rocky Ridge.

"So, what next?" asked Yinho as he plumped himself down on a stool across the writing table from Binhong.

"Repeat the process in your birth county, Yidu," Binhong looked up from his writing. "You will head up the operation there, naturally. But that's not as urgent as finding Sai'er."

"I agree our top priority is to find Sai'er," Yinho said with a long sigh. "But, as for Yidu, please don't count on me to lead. Let's face it. Administration is not my thing—I'm better suited to be a cook! But seriously, I want nothing better than to train up my Assassins. The best thing would be for you to head up Yidu and get one of your Strategists to oversee Putai. Oh, I'm sure you have this in mind — in your report, you might want to alert Uncle Tang and Monk Faxian to the suspected kidnap of Sai'er."

Sai'er had disappeared for a month now. Yinho missed her not any less than Binhong.

He knew if he told her that Ah Long had been his true love and that Yulan and he weren't meant to be, she would understand. Somehow he would have to break the truth to Yulan. But that could wait.

In his early days as a member of the Tang household, a sanguine feeling of belonging in a family had surged through his entire being and had truly elated him. Uncle Tang treated him like a foster son, no different than Binhong. Both Sai'er and Binhong loved and cared about him like true siblings.

As kind as Master Zhang was, he always acted more like an affectionate coach and mentor than a fatherly figure, and Wudang was more of a shelter than a real home to him.

Those days as a new Tang family member up until Ah Long's death were the happiest in his life.

But the heavens can give you one precious thing and just as well take away another.

After a spell of silence, Yinho muttered as if to himself, "If you were Lin San, where would you take Sai'er?"

"The Court has offered a bounty for the capture of Monk Faxian and Uncle. Obviously Lin San is after the bounty and is using Sai'er as bait."

"Yingtian!" Both uttered the same word at the same time.

"You're right. I think we'd better tell the Advisers the truth," Binhong said with a sigh, as he took up the brush pen again. "Perhaps we should ask them to come out here so we can plan a rescue together."

"Yeah, then at least we can act as a group," said Yinho, knowing Binhong had been worried sick about Sai'er, but had tried to appear strong.

I don't understand why he keeps his feelings for Sai'er bottled up all these years.

Clapping Binhong on the shoulder, he added with reassurance, "Now that we have Putai under our control, at least we can see to it that they're safe here."

Outside the apothecary, the sky had turned obsidian black and strong winter gusts began to thrash. In a heartbeat, hailstones the size of pebbles came roaring down.

An involuntary tremor raced through Yinho. He prayed hard to both Xuan Wu the Warrior God and Xuannu the Warrior Goddess to keep Sai'er safe.

Ba, Ma, Ah Long, I swear to the Deities that I will make the Zhu family pay for your unjust deaths!

The next day, the last but one day of the eleventh month, Binhong sent Zhuge Liang off to Yidu with his full report.

On the day following, Binhong received Sanbao's note, delivered by the maid from the Ma household. After reading the note, Yinho and Binhong hugged each other in cathartic sobs.

Part Three

26

A COLD WINTRY gust chafed Sai'er's face as Yusu led her up the steps onto the main deck.

As anchors were being lowered, she squinted to take in the on-board and riverside activities while pulling her collar tighter around her neck. Her legs wobbled from lack of use, and she had no choice but to lean on Yusu for support. For that, she met with an irritated glare.

Plumed with feathery clouds, the pale blue sky lolled in the lukewarm cuddle of the late afternoon sun, unruffled by the human dramas below.

Two crewmen threw lines onshore for the junk to be moored. A pier worker looped the ropes round two separate bollards. Another two crewmen hefted a gangplank over the junk's gunwale.

Bleary-eyed passengers began pouring out from their cabins. Having been cramped in cubbyholes of the pitching and tossing vessel for nearly a month, they were all, like her, hungry to scuff solid earth with their feet.

From ancient poems, Sai'er had heard of the Peach Leaf Pier. She could now see that it had bloomed into a transport hub on the famous Qinhuai River, an offshoot of the Lower Yangtze.

Crowds thronged the Pier. Porters were busy unloading passengers' luggage and loading for the return journey a plethora of goods ranging from bolts of silk and fine pottery to exotic fruits. Idling ones tried to solicit hirers.

Spruce and neat travelers with servants in tow were exiting their lavish horse-drawn carriages, all eager to get onboard. Families and friends, equally dandy looking, appeared in droves to bid leavers farewell. Peddlers in the vicinity were pitching their precious curios and fragrant jasmine flowers. Hunched over empty docks were a few fishermen leisurely wiling away the hours with their fishing rods.

So this is the Imperial Capital, now the seat of the Zhu clan's supreme power, with enviable prosperity to boot.

If no one had told her this was Yingtian, she would've believed the place was some sort of imaginary 'Peach Blossom Spring' utopia. In all her life, she had never encountered such a poised display of affluence. She had assumed that abject deprivation — the kind of existence she was familiar with — was the only reality.

Yusu gave her arm a squeeze and hustled her ashore toward an ornate horse-drawn carriage that stood waiting in front of a fancy porcelain ware shop. Sai'er played along and limped all the way.

The driver gave Yusu a deep fawning bow and helped her and then Sai'er into the canopied enclosure.

After snaking through a labyrinth of busy streets and obscure lanes, the carriage turned a corner and came upon the Imperial City Gates. The sentry guards let them through without questioning when Yusu flashed them a gold-plated pass.

The carriage trundled down a long quiet street. The half-parted curtains framed a running row of late autumnal golden trees — cypress, gingko, elm and others. The vehicle rounded a bend, whereupon a cobble-stone path unfurled along one side of the Mochou Lake. Pulling back one curtain panel, Sai'er espied the azure lake decked in pink lotuses, insouciant like a pampered mistress dawdling in daydream. Sprucely ranged weeping willows and a scatter of finely sculpted pavilions with green roofs and red pillars cuddled the limpid body of water in a possessive hug.

Sai'er wouldn't have known the name of the lake, which literally meant 'insouciant', had she not heard Yusu utter their destination to the driver at the Pier. She had never set foot in this part of the country. To her, the pristine, polished beauty of the place was simply a fantasy.

They stopped at a grand-looking lakeside mansion, where a pair of sculpted unicorns perched on stone plinths guarded the scarlet moon gates. A lacquered plaque with the words "Yao Residence" painted in glittering gold stared down with authority from atop the gates.

A servant answered Yusu's knock on the door and led them through a front yard that looked untended, with fallen leaves clumping in corners and untrimmed hedges in disarray.

For the residence of a Grand Councilor and Teacher of the Crown Prince, the reception hall screamed modesty and stinginess, unwitting or not. Only two unadorned high-back host chairs flanking a worm-eaten square table squatted against the back wall, on which hung a pair of dusty calligraphy scrolls. On either side of the hall ranged three plain receiving chairs separated by side tables.

Astride the hall entrance was a single pair of guards armed with broadswords. It was hardly the kind of security expected in the abode of the second most powerful man of the nation.

Still, the set-up of the hall smacked of authority and power, one where state matters likely were discussed and supplicants' petitions heard.

The servant disappeared into the deeper recesses to announce the visitors, and came back out discreetly with two cups of tea.

No sooner had Sai'er taken a sip than she saw Monk Yao and Sanbao emerge from the inner parts to take the host seats. She almost spewed out the liquid she was swishing in her parched mouth.

Sanbao's face turned pale when he set eyes on her, and then looked nonplussed on catching sight of the fake Pearly.

"Yusu, I see you've brought a guest," Monk Yao opened the conversation. When Sanbao heard the name, he seemed even more befuddled. Monk Yao probably had not told him about the Shamanist magic that could alter a person's visage.

"Excellency, this is Tang Sai'er, daughter of Tang Jun and granddaughter of Monk Faxian," Yusu crowed, her face reeking of rakish impudence.

Sai'er wondered if Monk Yao had a special trick to distinguish this fake from the real one. After watching her closely the whole time while aboard the junk, Sai'er had noted one significant trait that betrayed the impersonator, and that was her habit of compulsive nail-biting, which had grown worse since her Wudang days. Pearly was never given to this habit.

"So what do you propose we do with her?" The Grand Councilor shot Sai'er a piercing glance, brow pinched.

"Well, it may not be apparent to you, but she's been drugged and is our hostage now," she said with apparent impatience, as if deriding Monk Yao's slow grasp of things. "All we have to do is wait for the two traitors to turn up. Then we can pimp her to His Imperial Highness."

"Ah, that sounds like a plan," said the old man with squinted eyes. "I reckon you've disposed of Lin San?"

"He was not of much use," she trailed off with a little hesitation.

"No matter. He's not important. So, what do you want in return?"

Now Yusu was flustered. The Grand Councilor was not as slow as she imagined. She glared daggers at Sanbao, plainly reluctant to divulge her secret wish to anyone other than the old man. Obviously she could trust no one except Monk Yao.

She pretended to take a slow sip from her cup.

An awkward moment of silence passed. Then Monk Yao drawled, "Very well! Guards, lock the girl up in our cell. Do not mistreat her."

"Don't you want me to watch over her?" A shade of disappointment flitted across her face.

"Hmm, Pearly was under your watch, wasn't she? And where is she now?" Monk Yao took a jab at her. He certainly wasn't one Yusu could easily manipulate as she hoped. "If you'd like a word in private, please meet me in my study."

With that last invitation, Monk Yao rose to leave the hall. Sanbao was at his heels, turned around and threw Sai'er an intense glance, with the faintest quirk of his brow. She gazed back. Sparks flew from their eye contact.

When Yusu rose from her seat, Sai'er tried to make a scene. She lunged at her, pulling her hair and clawing at her chest. Yusu whined and cursed. The guards pried Sai'er away and had her hands bound.

She had pinched the gilded pass and slipped it inside her robe.

The cell was just a bed chamber with iron grilles installed over the two latticed windows. The double-panel door was fitted with a padlock on the exterior. The guards deposited her on the bed, lit an oil lamp on the table and locked the door. One stood sentry outside the room and the other left.

Sai'er had always had mixed feelings about Monk Yao. From Sanbao's description of him, he sounded like someone with a sympathetic heart and even kindness. She had no doubt that he had taken Sanbao under his wings out of compassion and genuinely wanted to protect him.

Yet he had also unethically bullied Pearly into stealing *The Secret of Wudang Neigong* from Master Zhang, had no qualms about wounding Grandba, once his Wudang buddy, and stooped to using Shamanist black magic to buy Yusu's loyalty.

Did he still have a soft spot for Pearly? Had unrequited love forged him into an iron-hearted opportunist and power monger?

But being an intelligent man, why did he choose to serve an erratic and cruel ruler?

There could only be one plausible explanation. Yao must've happened to meet young Zhu Di when the latter was down in the dumps. One needed a clever, mature listener. The other, while nursing a heart wound, desperately needed to feel needed. One chance meeting at a critical moment thus sealed their fated alliance.

Having now met him in person for the first time, the impression left her none the wiser. He seemingly disliked Yusu, the hard-hearted ingrate. But how come he could still work with her? Was it out of pity, or cold calculation?

People sought power to amass wealth. From the drab ramie fabric of his monastic robe and the shabbiness of his residence, Sai'er could tell that wealth was the last thing this strange man was after.

A man of shady character or not, she knew she couldn't possibly bet on his mercy. After all, he was Zhu Di's confidant, who was still on the hunt for her loved ones.

The thought of escape had already spawned in her mind when she was still on the junk. She must find a way to flee as soon as possible, praying she could somehow forestall her Ba and Grandba coming to Yingtian. Binhong and Yinho should've figured out where she had been taken.

She leaned down and took a porcelain shard from the lining of her boot and used it to saw the twine that tied her hands. That day when Yusu had murdered Lin San, a cup had dropped from the table during their scuffle and broken to pieces. She had picked up a shard and hidden it away. But the feat of cutting with hands tied was harder than she had imagined.

In a joss stick's burning time, all loops of the twine gave way. Her wrists were scratched raw, her thumb and index finger bruised.

She took a sweeping look around the room. The two windows were both barred with iron grilles. The only hope for escape would be through the door.

She tried to call to mind the last look on Sanbao's face. Was there a message for her? She would certainly hope so. Meantime there was nothing she could do with the sentry guard right outside the door. She might as well lie down and take a rest.

But the discomfort of her soiled clothes clinging onto her unwashed body kept her awake. A sniff of herself was enough to turn her stomach. She would kill for a proper bath.

Soon, the twilight that filtered through the papered windows gave way to inexorable darkness, save for the lonesome flicker of lamp light.

As she hovered between wakefulness and slumber, the sudden sound of boots hitting cobblestones jolted her alert.

Cocking her ear, she heard Sanbao demanding the key and ordering the guard away on an errand. Then a click in the padlock. His familiar silhouette glided through the door. She bounded up from the bed.

"Come quick. A horse is waiting in the front yard," he said with urgency in his voice, gesticulating for her to move faster. "You've got the gold pass, right?" She nodded, amazed he had seen through her little ploy earlier. "Here, take this cape. It's getting chilly."

"Thank you for this," she stuttered in a whimper as she flung the cape over her shoulders. With one foot over the threshold, she turned back and pleaded, "Can I ask you please to send a message to Putai to warn my folks not to come?"

"Don't worry about that. I have a couple of courier pigeons that I had brought from my uncle's home. I'll send a message addressed to Binhong care of my uncle's house maid."

May Guanyin bless you! I owe you a big one! She wanted so much to say those words aloud and to hug him there and then. Instead, she threw him an abashed smile, her lips quirking with emotions, and flounced off to the front yard.

Vaulting onto the saddle, she found the gates already opened. Without another moment's delay, she set the horse to a canter. As she moved to the rhythmic stride of the mount, she felt something jiggling inside the cape. She reached into the right-side pocket and found a dagger. In the left one was a silver ingot.

The lustrous full moon was a godsend. She traced her way back to the City Gates with little difficulty. In her agitated state, she thought she heard light crackling and rustling sounds coming from behind her, but when she turned around, she couldn't detect anything. As far as she could make out, it was probably her horse's footfall echoes mixed with the crack of fluttering branches.

At the Gates, imitating Yusu, she flashed the gold pass at two half asleep sentry guards. One of them waved her through with a big yawn.

Aided by her impeccable memory, she managed to trace the original route back to Peach Leaf Pier through the web of outer city streets.

Unlike during the day, the Pier was now almost deserted in the silvery opaqueness of the night.

A small rowboat was bobbing by the stilts of one of the docks. It gave her an idea. Hitching the horse to a nearby gingko tree, she grabbed the tether, hauled the boat up and lugged it to where the horse was.

Curling up in the cozy space of the boat with the cape wrapped snugly around her body gave her a palpable sense of security. Sanbao's musky scent that the cape gave off soon glided her into a sensual dream.

His hot breath was on her neck and ear. Sealed in a breathless space of darkness, they let words of longing float, unspoken, in the air. His piercing eyes roved over her body and pinned her in place. An involuntary tremor tore through her. Her cheeks were like live embers. Lips parting, she wriggled and begged for his kiss.

Someone gave her a rude shove. Her eyes slowly opened into slits.

27

A CIRCLE OF torches flooded her space, almost blinding her.

When her eyes strained open again, the disgusting grin so incongruous with Pearly's face morphed into a hunter's triumphant smirk.

"Did you think you could fool me?" she snickered with infuriating contempt. "You flatter yourself too much. I let you get away with the pass, certain that your naïve little lover would play the hero. Unfortunately, neither he nor Monk Yao would ever have guessed the sentry guard was under my pay."

Before Sai'er could utter a word, Yusu grabbed her chin, squeezed her mouth open and force-fed her a spoonful of the tendon-numbing powder dissolved in water. "There. Just to make sure there're no more surprises. Guards, tie her up and take her to the carriage, but take care not to leave one little scratch on her porcelain skin. No one can save you from the consequences of such a crime. We're going to the Chaotian Palace."

Sai'er noted those burly men holding torches all wore the Court-designated Embroidered Uniform. These Guards reported to no one except the Emperor. She had probably underestimated Yusu's special position in Zhu Di's Court. The imposter had likely gained his trust with the theft of the precious Xuannu Sword. Sai'er wanted to kick herself for not guarding it well. Knowing it was in Nezha's hands somehow gave her a little consolation, though.

Remorse was futile now. She was being taken straight into the lion's den. Her fate was near. She felt it in her blood and bone and pulse, in the crackle of nude branches and caw of the ravens.

The first time she had seen him in person was five years earlier at Wudang Mountains, when she had had a first taste of his wicked streak. Not long thereafter, he had given her the chills in the hex. Then in the Dragon Spring Lake melee, they had had a brief and arm's length encounter. The last time she had set eyes on him was at the battle of Jinan, where, even from a distance, she could sense the venom of his wrath as defeat had shamed and chafed him.

At none of those encounters had she felt completely helpless, save for the hex episode, which thankfully was only vicarious and soon effaced by Yinho's talisman. But this time she was alone, drugged and utterly vulnerable, while he was in the almighty, indomitable position of the Supreme Ruler. For the first time ever, she was to meet him one on one. The daunting sense of being bayed like a quarry grew with each heartbeat. Her body felt clammy with cold sweat.

But she still had a clear mind. The drug would lose its effect in three days. If she could somehow bide her time till then.

Four men with deadpan faces roped her and carried her to a carriage painted in black and hitched to a couple of dark grey horses. No wonder she hadn't been able to detect this apparition.

They placed her on a pallet covered with a pink embroidered quilt. Both sides of the enclosure were curtained with heavy dark fabrics to completely block out views. She caught the rhythmic clopping of horses' hooves on the stone-paved streets. Guards on horseback tailed them like a spectral platoon from hell.

The journey took about the same time as her trip from the Pier to Mochou Lake. She had a sense that Chaotian Palace was not far from Monk Yao's residence, because the Emperor would naturally want the Grand Councilor close at hand.

Yusu was seated beside the carriage driver. Sai'er heard her order the man to head straight to the Inner Palaces.

Upon arrival at the Imperial Palace Gates, the Guards carried Sai'er from the carriage to a waiting palanquin, borne by four wan-faced eunuchs.

She was taken straight to the Inner Palaces at the rear of the Palace compound. On entering, the eunuchs hustled her to a screened bath area inside some ornate chamber, where palace maids undressed her, scrubbed her down and washed her hair in a tub of warm scented water.

When that was done, they doused her with a rose perfume before dressing her in a sheer embroidered white silk gown with no undergarments. She insisted on covering herself with the cape. They then braided her hair into a loose plait and tied it with a red ribbon, dusted her face with fragrant rice powder and tried to smear rouge on her lips, which she adamantly refused.

Never in her life had she been treated to such pampering luxury. With her present limp body, resistance was out of the question. She might as well lay back and let things be.

Once the grooming was over, they ushered her to a spacious antechamber that was bedizened in gold. It looked uncannily familiar. Dragons in relief curled tightly around thick columns and looked down at her with hostile eyes.

Zhu Di looked regal on the carved high-back chair, placed on a foot-high dais. He was dressed in a yellow silk sleeping robe and didn't wear any formal headdress. His hair was coiled in a bun secured by an ivory hairpin, his chin hidden in a tuft of ebony beard. The austere face decreed total prostration of anyone in his presence.

The maids left Sai'er in the middle of the chamber and

withdrew.

Drowned in the heady fragrance of burning sandalwood chips that emitted from several copper urns placed around the chamber, she felt trapped and disoriented.

He was holding her in his drilling gaze. She remembered how she had been drawn to and befogged by that haughty, handsome and inscrutable face. But the memory was also mottled by shades of misgivings. Meeting his dark and moody eyes now, she gasped at how they crackled with the same power and masculinity as before. It liquefied her into a puddle.

He rose slowly from his seat and walked towards her. He stretched out his hand and gave her waist a gentle nudge, guiding her to the carved seat beside his throne chair. Her breath caught when she felt the heat from his firm hand. Even with her dulled senses, she realized she was supposed to fear him.

"Do you know how long I've waited for this moment?" he asked, his eyes reaching right into her groin. "We are meant to be together. Don't you remember our sweet moments of love in the Pantheon days?"

If he had said these things before he flashed his wolfish maw with Fang Xiaoru and others, she might have swooned over the honeyed words. But now he'd just provided her with chips to wager in the stalling game.

"Love?" she sneered with a deliberate cold smirk. "Do you love somebody by casting a hex over her? And by sending a spy to sully her? Is that what you call love?"

A twitch in his lips. A short pause later, he said in a reedy voice, his face crumpling in bruised pride, "You gave me no choice. I did that to scare you from taking the wrong path. Why would you want to take my enemy's side? Do you have any idea how much that hurt? If you have feelings for me, you wouldn't want to go against me."

"Maybe your greatest enemy is you," Sai'er retorted in a sarcastic tone. She wouldn't let him twist the truth around.

He got up, kneeled at her feet and folded her hands in his huge palms, "Sai'er, I've always loved you and I need you to be on my side. Be my Empress and you can assist me in state matters. There's no one else I can completely trust, not even my father when he was alive. All he ever wanted was to use me to fight the Mongols, and I'll never forgive him for treating my mother like dirt. How I hated him! Sai'er, you have to support me! Together we'll make a great Empire of this nation."

"I may be young. But I'm not naïve," Sai'er snorted, unfazed. "Empress Xu had better not hear this from your mouth." *He's not lying about his birth mother's tragic fate, though.*

"I can have two Empresses. Who's to say no to that?" he clenched his jaw, looking offended. Then his face relaxed, and with an almost coddling voice he said, "I think I told you before that I couldn't love anyone else. It wasn't for love that I married the present Empress. Her father Xu Da was my father's most loyal ally. It was purely a political union, one to please my father."

"Ah, I didn't know the proud Prince of Yan had a need to grovel," she scoffed.

Sai'er now found herself embroiled in an internal struggle. She recalled Master Zhang saying that she might be able to guide this man back on the right track. She had dismissed the idea as too high-minded then. But what if there was such a possibility?

Could he have made this offer from his heart? Or was it another of his tricks? Not that she had the least desire of becoming his Empress. But if in that position she could make him listen to reason, wouldn't this be a chance to stave off further bloodshed, sufferings and chaos for her Shandong folks?

No doubt it would put her happiness on the sacrificial altar. But inciting a rebellion could easily end in abject failure and death, with unthinkable bloodbath and carnage on the side, including loss of her loved ones. Everything had a price. In the grand scheme of things, a little self-denial on her part would seem almost trifling.

"If I said yes, would you pardon my father, my grandfather and General Tie, and promise never to retaliate against the people of Shandong?" She knew she was driving a hard bargain, but wanted to test his margin of tolerance.

The moment stretched as he brooded. Finally he spoke, with slanting eyes, "Of course. Tang Wen and Tang Jun will then be my in-laws. How can I not pardon them? I'll grant them ranks and titles too."

She noticed he didn't mention General Tie or Shandong. But perhaps it was good enough for the time being. "Can you give me two days to consider your offer?" She was hoping by the end of two days she'd have recovered her strength, giving her more options in this tug of war.

Zhu Di wanted nothing more than to snatch her virginity, in order to cripple her North Star power. If she yielded, at least the lives of her Ba and Grandba would be spared.

Hanging in the balance were the lives of General Tie and Shandong people. How could she abandon them to their doomed fates? Also, if Zhu Di made an offhand promise at first, and then went back on his word, she'd be caught in a snare. Such a consequence would be no worse than a debacle.

It all came down to whether she could trust him to be a man of his word.

"You need two days? Umm, alright. I guess I could live with that," he said begrudgingly. "For my generosity, don't you think you owe me your gratitude?"

She glared at him with distaste.

Met with her stolid silence, he scooped her up into his arms like she was a pet kitten and carried her to his opulent bed chamber at the back.

Putting her down on the silk-quilted bed, he yanked away her cape and brazenly peeled off the flimsy silk gown. A frisson of fear shot down her spine as she whimpered, "Please don't do this. I will hate you for it."

"Did you think I would force myself on you?" he said with mock consternation. "Am I so crude in your estimation? Sai'er, I want my bride to come to my bed a virgin on our wedding night. But now, to celebrate our reunion, can you not at least let me admire you?"

His words said one thing, his sultry stare another. Those penetrating, vulturine eyes stripped her of all defenses. She felt like a crayfish prised out of its shell.

It reminded her of how in the hex he had taken pleasure in watching her cringe and squirm naked. *That's how he subdues – by evoking fear.*

But that was then. She had gone through fire since that time, even made a trip to the Bridge of Forgetfulness and back. By committing to the White Lotus cause, she'd declared to her followers that she was ready to stare down death at any time. If she still couldn't handle her own fear now, she was not fit to be their leader.

She bit her lower lip, determined to shake off the curdling dread. If he so much as dare make a lusty move on her, she would grab the dagger and slit his throat, or die trying. Binhong and Yinho would no doubt avenge her. Her death would at least empower the Sect's cause. Ba and Grandba would certainly be heartbroken, but they would understand.

"I'm not afraid of you," she glared at him with clenched teeth, tugging at her cape with trembling hands.

She saw his lips curl into a cryptic smile. He made a tut-tut sound with condescension. As she puzzled over what he was up to, he pulled on the bell string that hung down the side of the bedpost.

In a few heartbeats, Sanbao appeared at the doorway threshold. Sai'er's heart leaped to her throat at the sight of him. He seemed no less shocked than she.

She had never felt more ashamed in her life than at this moment. Instinctively she snatched the cape to cover herself. She wished she could just vaporize under the cape. Her cheeks blazed indignity.

"Come in, Sanbao. I wanted to share some good news with you," Zhu Di crowed with swaggering insolence. "Sai'er will soon be my Empress. Isn't she beautiful? Come closer and take a good look."

Awkwardly Sanbao took a few timid steps forward, his head drooping like a defeated soldier.

"Oh, I forgot. You've seen her naked before, haven't you?" He broke into a chilling guffaw. In one beat, his face warped into a wolf's snarl and he shot Sanbao a withering look, hissing, "I bet you've missed her. Don't you want to take another look now?" With a sharp tug he tore off the cape on purpose, and crowed over his denuded prize triumphantly.

She would have grabbed the dagger, had she not been aware that a full squad of Imperial bodyguards was pacing right outside the chamber. One false move and both Sanbao and she would end up being flayed alive. *I can't implicate Sanbao in this! It's not fair to him.*

A ridge of agony rippled across Sanbao's face. He dipped his head in crushing humiliation and dropped to his knees, wailing, "Your Imperial Highness, it's not in this lowly servant's place to even dream of it!" The veins in his temples were throbbing so hard that they looked ready to burst. Then a more visceral kind of hurt eclipsed his face. A stab of pain seized her.

Sai'er turned her head towards the wall to escape the torment. Tears started trickling down her cheeks. It suddenly became clear to her why Sanbao had pushed her away at that encounter in the open field of Jinan. He had always been aware of Zhu Di's obsession with her and did everything in his power to avoid gossip. She couldn't imagine the dire fallout if some of his jealous and tongue-wagging underlings started whispering about their liaison. Guilt wrenched her heart for all the times she had doubted his love.

"I thought not. Now leave us!" he growled in a hoarse rumble.

I must try to snuff out his suspicions.

She wiped away her tears and sat up with renewed fortitude.

"What did you do that for?" she pursed her lips, trying her best to act disdainful.

"To remind him of his place—" He trailed off, showing a tint of self-doubt.

"He's just a useless wimp. And of all people, you chose *him* to dishonor me. Ha!"

Looking a bit confused now, he whined with a pout, "I never meant for him to get intimate with you. But he said he loves you—"

"I can't remember how many times my admirers have said that to me. Am I to believe any of it?" A pause later, she said with a deliberate smirk, "Why would I love a stinking castrate?" She then sat up straight, tilting her eyebrows a little to feign the look of a snob.

"Do you love me at all? I want the truth." His gaze became less baneful now, almost benign. His face had reassembled itself into an innocuous pining look, like a child craving the attention of adults.

Sai'er could hardly believe her ears. *Is this hubristic, power-*

obsessed conqueror saying he needs love?

"You and I have a history. Much as you gave me reason to suspect your sincerity, I admit a part of me still can't get over you," Sai'er replied with measured words, fully aware she was treading a thin line. "But I have my doubts—"

"Didn't I already swear on my innocence in your Moon Palace that day? What more do you want from me?"

"I hope for your sake that you swore in good faith. The deities will hold you to your oath."

"Let's get back to my offer," he said with barely concealed irritation. Like a spoiled brat who was bent on having his way, he cajoled with a clear ultimatum, "My love, two days are as long as I can endure. You've made me wait long enough."

"I'm getting very tired now. Can you please let me rest?"

She believed a part of him truly desired her. But whether that desire was woven with even a shred of respect and care, or was purely animalistic and self-serving, was a question that kept taunting her to no end.

"Ma Huan, take Lady Tang to the side chamber," he shouted to his chamber eunuch. "Send four chamber maids to wait on the lady and serve her only the finest."

28

THE NEXT DAY, Sai'er woke up to a bevy of palace maids fussing over her.

They helped her try on a whole chest of newly made embroidered silk robes, and played with different hairstyles on her: chignons, single braid, coiled braids, each with matching jeweled hairpins.

Another group of maids brought in all kinds of rare fruits and snow fungus soup for her breakfast. She only took the fruits and dared not touch the soup, for fear it might be laced.

In late morning, they led her out to the Xuan Wu Lake Imperial Garden to enjoy viewing of cherry and plum blossoms and golden carp in the large lotus pond.

When she returned to the chamber, a sudden rush of homesickness surged through her. She removed the clam shell from her neck and placed it on the table and started telling her Ba's portrait all that had happened here. Ever since her mother's death, she'd never let this keepsake leave her person.

A palace maid came in and announced that Consort Xian requested to see her.

In sauntered a shapely young woman with a meticulously painted face. Narrow eyes strained to look rounder under arched brows, and leered over high cheekbones and an elongated nose with a bulbous tip. It was a face that would turn heads. Dressed in a peach color satin robe with a velvet sash tied under her bosom to accentuate her full breasts, she carried herself with an unabashed haughty air.

"Greetings, little sister," she curved her lips in a half smile, her glinting slits busy with sizing up Sai'er.

"I'm Consort Xian. His Imperial Highness has sent me here to train you in your upcoming duties as a concubine. These books are for you. If you find them helpful, you can thank me later."

Sai'er recalled having eavesdropped on the palace maids' gossip that Zhu Di was smitten with a Jurchen consort who was skilled at flute playing.

"Please be seated," Sai'er said out of involuntary courtesy, not bothering to rise.

"Is that a portrait of your brother or father?" The unwelcomed guest asked nosily when she spotted the clam shell. Sai'er didn't care to respond.

Lowering herself onto the chair opposite Sai'er, she laid down on the table several volumes of illustrations with gold thread stitch-binding, one of which was titled *The Maze Palace of Emperor Yang of Sui*.

One glimpse of that title and Sai'er knew what kind of training the Consort had in mind. Thumbing through the various volumes, she found nothing but pictures depicting sexual acts and erotic dancing, some suggestive with an artistic slant, others outright lewd.

Blushing to the nape of her neck, Sai'er simmered with resentment, "Let me get one thing straight, Consort Xian. I wouldn't be your 'little sister' if I ever consent to accept the Emperor's marriage offer. In case you haven't heard, my title would be Empress. And rest assured that I have no need for your help, now or ever."

Pausing to let her authority be felt, she flung back her lush black plait and ordered, "I'm sure you have other more important chores to attend to. So, please don't let me keep you."

Apparently taken aback by Sai'er's saucy ways, Consort Xian at first fumbled her answer, saying in her broken Chinese, "Well, you might be sorry—His Imperial Highness would not like a clumsy girl in bed." Then, lips curved in a sneer, she carped, "Empress, eh? What happens to our Venerable Empress Xu, I wonder?"

Now having composed herself, she glared at Sai'er's unbound feet with distaste, a feline smile spreading across her face, "If I were you, I would first learn to walk gracefully."

Sai'er took a quick glance at the woman's feet and was surprised to find they were small lotus feet. She'd thought Jurchens, being a nomadic tribe, would scorn the Han tradition of foot binding. Gossips abounded that Zhu Di had a taste for Jurchen and Korean women. So it was most likely that the woman's family had purposely groomed her to become an imperial consort, as a way to curry favor with the Zhu Court. *What wouldn't people do to pander to power?*

Was she glad that Putai was just like any other farming community where foot-binding had not caught on. Besides, she had wanted to train in kung fu as a child and her parents had always encouraged her.

"I'm sure none of what you said is any of your business," Sai'er quipped with restrained anger, eager to get rid of this officious guest.

For all she knew, this woman might well be acting on her own initiative. Just thinking of all the scheming and backstabbing inside the harem motivated by greed for power and petty jealousy was enough to sicken her. Her would-be life in the Palace didn't look at all pretty.

"As you please then," the woman snorted with injured pride.

Head tilting upwards and jaws clenched, she rose, whirled around and swayed her hips out of the chamber.

Zhu Di did not appear that day.

The following morning Sai'er shooed all the maids away. At last left alone, she spent the whole morning in meditation, invigorating the qi flow through her meridians until she felt strength return to her muscles.

In early afternoon, while she was taking a pear for lunch, someone knocked on the chamber door. Just as she was about to send away someone she figured was a maid, Sanbao's voice came through, "Please let me in."

"Ma Huan told me the Emperor is out hunting today," he said in a low voice as Sai'er opened the door. Quickly he slipped in and immediately bolted the door behind him.

She read the urgent question, "Did he hurt you?" in his heartsick tenebrous look. He clutched her in an anguished embrace and kissed her forehead tenderly.

Tears prickled her eyes as she uttered softly, "I'm alright—he didn't. He gave me two days to consider his offer." He let out an audible breath of relief.

As they sat down next to each other at the round curved-leg table, he took her hand and interlaced their fingers, holding her in his steady gaze.

Then he began to let her in on his story, starting with how Zhu Di had coerced him to act as a snitch to spy on her in Putai and Wudang and to despoil her. He explained how, after his Wudang days, Zhu Di punished him for his confession; and how he subsequently regained the master's trust through his battle merits. As of late, Monk Yao promised to help him secure the job of diplomatic envoy and he was studying hard to become a qualified ship captain.

With every poignant turn of his story, she sighed and squeezed his fingers in genuine sympathy, her eyes glazed over with tears. This honest sharing drew her closer to him than ever.

Those tears were like warm spring rain that fell on hard, frosted soil, reaching the stunted roots within. They nurtured his long wilted heart, now ready for a second chance to bloom.

"Remember I told you that I was sent to the Beiping Palace as a child slave?"

"Yes, I've been wondering what that meant exactly. Did they keep you in chains and force you to do hard labor?" Sai'er's innocent question made his face flush.

"It was much worse than that," his face twisted in pain as if someone had just punched his guts. Taking a deep inhalation, he guided her into the grimmest nook of his memory that he had kept tightly sealed off from light throughout his adult life.

With a quavering voice he began, "Zhu Di kept me and a few other pretty boys in the Inner Chambers. Every two nights he would pick one of us to go to bed with him. When it was my turn, he would toy with my private parts—during castration the drunken knifer had failed to cut the member—and would remind me how merciful he was in forgiving that oversight. Then he would roll me over.... Afterwards, he would send for a Court physician to tend to my wound. The next day, I'd receive expensive gifts from him." His voice cracked at this point and he took a long pause before resuming, face implacably twisted.

"One day, one of the other boys couldn't take it anymore. He tried to run away but was caught. He got a heavy dose of whipping, and later died from infections. From then on I had to fight my instinct to escape just to stay alive. Submission was the least painful path. This went on until I enlisted in the army."

The floodgate of tears crashed open with this revelation, letting out a coiling miasma of pent-up shame mixed with self-hate. He covered his face with both hands, his whole body convulsing in a storm of cathartic sobs.

The indelible malady of self-loathing that leaked from deep behind his eyes had from the first struck a chord in Sai'er. But now, after he uncorked this horrendous nightmare, a stab of pathos shook her to the core. At last she understood that ailment evinced a much more virulent pain than his castration alone could have caused.

Waves of empathic sorrow and anger surged through her. While gently enfolding his head in her bosom, she sniffled with an aching heart, "I'm so sorry you had to go through this hell." Then, looking into his eyes, she added with tenderness, "But the important thing is, you didn't allow the ordeals crush your spirit. You're a much stronger man now."

The image of Zhu Di taking sickly pleasure from mentally torturing Sanbao at will nauseated her. Sanbao was still no more than a human toy in bondage after all these years – a slave to be wrecked and crushed and dangled to keep alive just for amusement.

Such flossy, fastidious cruelty masticates your self-esteem into pulp and then makes you crawl to it on your knees. Killing men in battles at least gives him back a sense of worth.

She curved her lips in an attempt to give a coddling smile. "Sanbao, it's time to leave the past behind and move on. You now have a whole new beginning to look forward to. I believe Monk Yao really means to set you free. I'll pray to Guanyin everyday that you'll land that envoy job."

Looking into his wounded eyes through a mist of tears, she said with as much conviction as she could command, "Believe that the merciful Maitreya Buddha will not forsake you."

Even as those words came out, she couldn't suppress the pang of bruised sadness that foreshadowed their impending fate: the fate of parting.

Having quelled the emotional tempest in him, she then shared with him everything that was on her mind, from her miraculous recovery from the arrow wound, the setting up of the White Lotus Sect, to her kidnap by Lin San and Yusu, right up to the current bondage. She even bared her heart about her intent to accept Zhu Di's marriage offer, citing her conciliatory purpose for making such a decision.

"Sai'er, my life has few good things to boast of," he said, cuddling her in his warm gaze and fingering away her tears. "Having you as a soul mate is the best of them. Please know that whatever makes you happy makes me happy. I ask but one thing of you: whatever you do, please always remember you only live once. Nothing has meaning without life."

They gazed at each other for a long time, reaching into the private sanctum of each other's soul. He leaned in and pressed his lips softly on her slightly parted mouth. She opened her mouth wider. Their tongues touched and probed and roused, until both reeled from something that was inviolable and uniquely their own, born out of that intoxicating moment of butterfly wings beating in harmony.

He led her by the hand to the silk-quilted canopied bed. Sitting on the edge of the bed, she leaned back on the bedframe, her eyes gleaming with feverish desire.

Kneeling at the bedside, he gently loosened her coiled braids and hungrily drank in the fragrance of her silky black hair. As he slid off her silk garments one by one, his touch on her bare skin unleashed the pent-up thirst. Every fiber in her being reached out to him.

He bent down to imbibe her scent and caress her softness. Her face glowed as his tongue ambled along the curves of her body.He titillated the cleft between her firm thighs, making her shiver and gasp with delight.

Spreading her legs further apart, she begged for more with her watery eyes. In a transcending moment, his possessive tongue whisked her to the summit of the cloud and rain hill she never even knew existed.

Propped on her elbows, she arched her back and squirmed as he teased with a pause. Then, with his supple fingers he mounted another raid. Her panting and moaning crescendoed until an involuntary tremor tore through her body to the tip of her limbs. She dug her nails into his broad shoulders and broke down in tremulous sobs.

He smiled a subtle smile, planting tender kisses on her cheeks and breasts.

No sooner had the raptures of joy subsided than a feeling of emptiness set in. The spell of ecstasy felt brutally and unmistakably final. What she was left with was wistful yearning--the longing for another stroke of luck unlikely to happen any time soon,.

As if he could read her thought, Sanbao cupped her chin in his hands and said with fleecy tenderness, "My love, I will always starve for you — I need your light to live. Will you promise never to give up on us?" His warm brown eyes glinted with desperate hope.

"Did you have to ask?" She nuzzled her face in his wide protective chest to hide her churning emotions, realizing how little sway she had over her own future. *By tomorrow, my life will be out of my control.*

Then something stirred in her. She looked up and threw him a dubious glance, "Was this your first time?"

He covered her mouth with his thick hot lips before answering, "Not bad for a first-timer, eh?" Gazing into her deep pools of reflective light, he whispered, "One time I eavesdropped on other eunuchs bragging about how they do it with palace maids. I stashed it away in the back of my mind. Temptation pops up now and then, but the only woman I've ever wanted is you."

For all his naked vulnerability that was reflected in the sensitive dark brown irises, belied by his brawny physique, a glimmer of willfulness still sallied forth from behind those pain-stricken eyes, which might elude a lot of people. But not Sai'er. He'd die before betraying her. She regretted that she'd asked the silly question.

Her face shaded a rose hue, she shyly fumbled for his manhood. Imitating one of the acts in the erotic pictures she had seen the day before, she steadily swept him to the same empyrean heights of pleasure where she'd been just moments ago. Watching his face scrunch with pleasure gave her as much of a tingling thrill as the glaringness of doing this right under Zhu Di's nose.

I have Consort Xian to thank, she gave out a muffled short laugh.

They held onto each other tight as if there were no tomorrow, both pretending hard their moment of farewell was not pacing impatiently around.

As he budged at last to tear himself off, he said under his breath, "My precious, I swear this is not the end for us." Smoldering with passion, he pressed her hand on his chest and uttered with misty eyes, "You're in here with me wherever I go."

Before disappearing through the door, he turned around and said, his voice shadowed as much as his eyes, "I wouldn't do any deal with him if I were you."

In late morning the next day, Ma Huan came in with the Emperor's summons for her presence in the Audience Hall. The downturned corners of his mouth planted a seed of misgivings in her.

She flung the cape over her shoulders and followed the eunuch to the Hall, where she was offered a plush side seat on the dais, to the left of the dragon throne seat.

Secretaries and Court Officials stood grim-faced in two columns below the dais, separated by a wide central aisle.

Monk Yao was at the head of the right column, in formal attire with a celestial crane buzi sewn on the front of his robe.

Sanbao stood wan-faced to the right of the imperious-looking Emperor, who was decked in full regalia of a yellow silk robe embroidered with nine dragons and a formal headdress with hanging jade bead strands.

She had spent the previous night brooding over her options.

Suppressing every single thought about Sanbao, she had concluded that she would accept Zhu Di's offer in exchange for the immediate pardon of her Ba, Grandba and General Tie. Then she would request as a wedding gift the honorary title of Lady Protector of Shandong, in the hope this would pre-empt his retaliation plans against her people. In the event Zhu Di went back on his promise after the wedding, she would send a suicide note to Binhong and kill herself.

Sai'er was thinking that Binhong and Yinho would approve of such an arrangement. If it could erase past hatred and bring peace to all, she was willing to give up her North Star skill as a price to pay. At the back of her mind, though, the image of her lovemaking with Sanbao drew blood in her heart. He was the real ultimate price she would have to pay.

A commotion at the Hall entrance disrupted her thoughts.

Sanbao stepped to the front of the dais and announced in a raspy voice, "His Imperial Highness will conduct the trial of General Tie Xuan for treason. Bring in the prisoner now."

Sai'er's throat instantly constricted and her heart tumbled to the floor. Her instinct told her Zhu Di had planned to do this all along.

General Tie had aged decades since she had last seen him. His red-smeared grizzled hair tangled in an unsightly mess. Bound in iron chains, he dragged his bare, mangled feet along the aisle in great pain. A blood-splotched robe hung loosely on his skeletal frame that resembled the living dead. For all his pitiful outward look, his eyes still shone an iron beam of defiance.

The two guards that brought him in gave him a kick in the calves, making him drop to his knees.

"Prisoner Tie Xuan, I see that torture hasn't dented your will," boomed Zhu Di in an edgy voice. "I'm here today to give my own account as the chief witness to your heinous crime of treason. You and your allies obstructed my righteous campaign to eradicate my nephew's illegitimate reign and claim back my throne. I was there during the Yan army's attempted capture of Jinan in Shandong. You had the audacity to set up a trap to ensnare my army. Do you still have cause to deny your crime?"

"Few people would call your campaign righteous," the General said, spitting out each word in a succinct, coherent way. "Folks wouldn't have rallied around the Jianwen Emperor had they not thought him worthy of support. In a violent conflict, the victor is not necessarily the morally superior. If people are coerced into accepting such as their new ruler, there will be no peace. This is all I have to say. If my death will bring you closure, then please just grant me my death wish and let's be done with it."

"How dare you lecture me!" Zhu Di roared in a fit of frenzied rancor, bristling in hateful spite. "I ascended to the throne by right of Heavenly Mandate. What brazen disrespect! You want death? That'll come soon enough. But first, I have to teach you a lesson in deference. Guards, cut off his nose and ears."

His words sent a frisson of fright down Sai'er spine. Obviously Zhu Di feared the truth like the plague, as the truth skewered his conscience. Anyone who dared utter anything remotely close to the truth would inexorably become his archenemy.

Below the dais, a whip of the blade left dark cavities of cartilage and blood in the General's face. He stoically suppressed sounds that would come out as long howls of pain.

As if a demon had infested Zhu Di's soul, his face twisted into a canine smile and he spat out another sick order, "Feed the prisoner the severed parts."

Bile squirted up Sai'er's gullet and airway. She turned to the side and puked her guts out. Things were happening so fast that she completely lost control. Her hope for compromise had been founded on nothing but a puff of air. What was she thinking? How could she possibly expect Zhu Di to treat her Ba and Grandba any more leniently?

A sea of gloom, disgust and devastation drowned her. She was straining to raise her head to catch a breath.

"Tell me, does that taste good?" he growled like a blood thirsting animal.

"Why? An honorable general's flesh cannot but taste good," Tie retorted with truculent pride.

"Alright. I now declare Tie Xuan guilty of treason as charged. He is hereby sentenced to death by slicing, to be carried out right here, right now. His male descendants will be executed and his wife and daughters are to be indentured as brothel slaves." He was consumed with a venomous hatred that radiated from deep within him.

All the Officials and Secretaries cowered at the mad command. Bodies stirred with repugnance. Obviously, after the Fang Xiaoru case, Zhu Di had taken cruelty to another level. The executioner was called into the Hall.

"I hereby declare Zhu Di guilty of usurping the Jianwen Emperor's throne!" Tie declared, not to be subdued. "As a loyal subject to the Emperor, I will now turn my back on the usurper." Before he finished what he was saying, he about-faced, with his back fronting on Zhu Di.

"Let the slicing start, now!" Zhu Di bellowed at the top of his lungs. "Let's see if your body is harder than the blade." Tie had certainly poked a sore point on him.

Based on her judgment, Sai'er was certain he was going to ban the word "usurper", even decreeing its usage to be punishable by death.

Sprays of blood spattered the glossy marble floor. People below the dais swerved to the side to eschew the sight of horror.

Sanbao also averted his contorted face from the gruesome scene. He must be guilt-ridden for having a hand in this cruelty. The irony was, his life was always hanging by a thread around this volatile tyrant of a master. He had probably learned that clear conscience was at times the high price he had to pay for survival.

A sidelong glance at Zhu Di's beastly, verging on insane, expression convinced Sai'er to give up any shred of hope to convert him. The tragic fate of his birth mother might have induced his wrathful character, but he was haunted by too many ghosts of shadowy threats to ever be able to feel at peace with himself or value human lives for what they were.

The Deities' prophesy was not wrong after all.

Haunting shrieks of agony resounded through the Hall, like the shrill whining of a multitude of aggrieved ghosts. The sharp tang of blood suffused the space.

In Sai'er ears sprang up the echoes of gut-wrenching howls from an execution scene that she and her Ba had come upon in Yidu years earlier. The cacophony of past and present yowls mercilessly pounded her head. Her whole body throbbed like a leaf caught in a violent gust. The world turned into one bone-chilling blare of horror.

The bloody mass of flayed flesh refused to turn around.

"Bring in a cauldron of burning oil and throw him in it," he spouted another sick command.

When that was done, the deep-fried hunk still had its back facing the throne.

"Make him face me," he heaved like a raging beast. Junior eunuchs tried to pivot it around with wooden rods and had their hands badly burned by splashes of scalding oil. The seared hunk just wouldn't budge.

Zhu Di's face turned a ghastly white. He probably feared it was some sort of sign from the heavens. Perhaps the only thing that could make him cower was wrath sent down by the almighty Deities.

Sai'er realized she had been stunned into numbness by scene after scene of blood curdling atrocity. It suddenly became clear that there was no way out: she would be in a bind whether she accepted or rejected Zhu Di's offer. *I have to save myself*, the thought rudely jabbed at her. *Without life, nothing has meaning.*

Quietly, she fished out the dagger. Then leaping up from her seat, she bolted towards the throne seat, seized the Emperor's collar with one hand, and pointed the dagger at his throat with the other.

"Sai'er, what are you doing?" he croaked, startled into a jumble of words. "Don't you understand? Those who don't submit must die. Please don't do this — you're my Empress. I need you by my side — "

"You sick butcher! Do you think you can kill us all?" she quipped with blistering rage. Pressing the dagger harder on his skin, she demanded, "I want a horse brought to the Hall entrance, now, and all Southern Gates of the Palace opened at once. Give your order."

He fretted and tried to stall for time, "I have the Mandate of Heaven. All subjects must obey me..."

"Your cruel and twisted mind makes you unfit to hold the Mandate," she cut him short in a fit of raw disgust. "Now you have to obey me!"

She nudged the dagger tip deeper into his flesh, drawing trickles of blood. He yelped and hollered, "Bring a horse to the entrance. Open the Main Gates."

When she spotted the horse, she carved a red line on his throat with the dagger, saying in a loud unwavering voice, "Now tell your Guards to lay down their weapons and clear out with everyone else. Do it!"

"You fools!" he wheezed. "What are you still standing there for? Do as she says!" His dark face turned crimson with a frenzied scowl.

As the last of the crowd filed out, Zhu Di made a sudden jerk away from Sai'er's clasp, and managed to wrench the dagger from her hand.

He tried to skip down the dais steps, but Sai'er made a sideways flip to land ahead of him. With a flying kick she knocked him to the ground. Accelerating her qi circulation, she gripped his supine torso with her knees and planted her heated palm on his chest. As soon as her meridians locked with his, she began sapping qi out of him.

"This is to give you a taste of the North Star power," Sai'er said under her breath. "Too bad you squandered your chance to rob me of it."

His eyes grew wide with horror, as he wiggled futilely between her firmly rooted knees.

At that moment, she wanted nothing better than to snuff out

the life in him, ending his pathetic existence. All she needed to do was to continue to pipe his qi until he was totally drained of the life force.

But she hadn't forgotten the rule set by Master Zhang — that the practitioner must not use this skill to take lives. Or was she still clinging to the hope his deadened soul could somehow be salvaged?

Within moments, his eyes began rolling into the back of his head. When he was within a hairsbreadth away from asphyxia, she removed her palm from him. He had shriveled into a lame, flocculent pile, his mouth gaping like a half dead fish.

Picking up a long sword from the floor, she bolted for the Hall entrance, averting her eyes when she passed by the cauldron. With sheer will, she forced down the urge to throw up again.

29

MONK YAO had not shrunk away like other Court Officials.

He was waiting for her at the threshold, sheathed sword in hand. He ordered Sanbao and other eunuchs to tend to the stricken Emperor.

"I've long heard of your masterly Sword-as-Whip skill," he said with a steady voice. "Would you grant me the pleasure of witnessing it?"

Finally I get to fight you!

Up close, Sai'er saw his face clearly for the first time. His grizzled hair, pouched lids and sagging wrinkled cheeks made him look much older than Grandba. The bulk of his head seemed to fold over upon itself to create an overhang on his shoulders, almost too heavy for him to carry. His job certainly wasn't for the faint-hearted. Juggling political maneuvers in Court and the unenviable task of pleasing a mercurial and murderous master could drive any normal man insane.

"Likewise! I'd be honored to learn from the great Master Yao," she answered with aplomb.

She swept her eyes around the large terrace, which lay atop a flight of three-tiered white marble stairs fringed by sculpted balustrades and flanked by two horse ramps that ran right up to the Main Gates. Four arched stone gates, connected by three fortified barbicans, made up the Main Gates.

With an undetected swipe of his hand, Monk Yao unsheathed his sword, having already discarded his embroidered Court robe.

Sai'er threw the cape on the ground, lowered herself into a solid horse stance and worked up her qi, her sword pointing skyward.

"Young woman, you're in serious trouble," he said with a heavy frown and downward curling lips. "But, lest I should be accused of bullying a woman, I'll challenge you to a duel. If I win, you're to surrender to custody and punishment. If you win, you have my permission to leave the Palace compound. Any objection?"

"It's a deal," she said with incredulity, fully aware that even with her exceptional riding skills she couldn't possibly get past the archers in the barbicans.

Court Officials had re-appeared and gathered in a circle around the duelists to watch the fight, but mostly to gawk at the attractive woman who had the temerity to draw blood on the Emperor and hold him hostage.

A flurry of lightning fast strikes and dodges later, Sai'er judged that she was a close match for Monk Yao in sword skill, but at the same time she had a keen taste of his deadly qi force which underpinned that skill: his fathomless mastery of neigong. He might even surpass her in the North Star skill. No wonder Master Zhang had commended him as the best of his students. But she also had an edge over him. The Master had taught her the hexagram footwork, but not Monk Yao.

She must stay focused and be prepared for his offensive. She didn't even want to guess what Zhu Di might do to her if she was held captive again.

As she had expected, her archrival served her a series of lethal and precise blows with his qi-ignited weapon, forcing her to back right to the edge of the landing. Sharp whistling wind almost grated her face and arms when metal scratched on contact. It was best to feign retreat now, while searching for his weak point.

She met his second and third rounds of muscular strikes by hopping around in deceptive hexagram steps, conserving her energy while wasting his. As she studied his moves intensely, she noticed he never used the flying kick. She guessed he had leg wounds that hadn't completely healed.

After six more rounds of ferocious sparring, still the match was a tie. The winter sun was already crawling into the embrace of the cozy purple mountains. By this time, Monk Yao began to draw shallow, gasping breaths.

In the tenth round, Sai'er sidestepped a head-on blow, swerved to one side, fended off another blow by knocking her sword upwards. Catching the opening, she spun around with invisible speed to ram a flying leg into her opponent's right shin. It drew a yelp. He reeled back two steps. She didn't let off and jabbed the other leg right into that same spot again. He fell to the ground with a deep groan. She leaped forward to touch her sword between his eyes.

"Master Yao, I'm sorry if I've given offense," she said, retracting and sheathing her sword.

"This was a fair contest. No offense taken," he said, wincing from pain. "Master Zhang and Pearly had trained you well. I'm a man of my word. You can leave."

Turning to a junior eunuch, he ordered, "Send word to the tower archers to let the girl go."

"Thank you for this favor," Sai'er whispered. She understood the overt challenge was just an ostentatious display of his righteous outrage, a guile meant to give her a way out. With his severe leg wounds, he was also able to answer to his master without rousing suspicion.

She picked up the cape and vaulted into the saddle of the

waiting horse.

Once outside the Palace Gates, she galloped in a southbound direction, knowing Palace and City Main Gates were always in alignment with each other. If she just followed the main street, which was the north-south axis, she should hit the Imperial City Gates.

She was right. Once there, she waved the gold pass again to get through.

From there she threaded slowly through the maze of outer city streets.

Images of General Tie's kind demeanor and his booming voice flooded her senses as tears swelled in her eyes. Suddenly, his grisly torture and violent end pierced her like a knife thrust into her temple. The knife twisted and turned in her brain cells. His shrill wail of agony was chiseling at her every bone.

The torrent of tears and a giddy sensation blurred her vision so much that she made a wrong turn and promptly lost her way. Her stomach churned. She pulled the horse to a stop, dismounted and threw up on the street curb. *Curse eighteen generations of Zhu Di's ancestors!*

How she wanted to laugh aloud at her stupidity for thinking she could strike a deal with that rotten slug. She swore she would never waste another shred of kindness on him again.

Not far along the street fluttered a tavern banner in the hazy twilight. She decided she needed a rest. A cup of dark pu'er tea should calm her nerves. Having emptied her stomach to the last drop of ingested food, she could also use a hot bowl of soup. As it was getting dark and the Pier was likely closed, she might as well rent a room to pass the night. Fortunately Sanbao had thought of everything. She fingered the silver ingot in her cape pocket.

The street was still teeming with people at this hour, pervaded with sing-song voices, music and laughter. Lifting her head as she walked, she saw courtesans with painted faces dressed in colored silks leaning on verandah railings of two-storied houses that lined both sides of the street. Some were bantering with gawking male passers-by. Others were flaunting their pipa and singing skills.

On entering the tavern, she told the middle-aged owner at the counter that she wanted a room to stay the night. The double-chinned woman registered her name and said with a phlegmatic voice, "Twenty coppers for one night, meals extra. Pay in advance."

Sai'er handed her the silver ingot, saying, "Give me the change, please." Having never handled a silver ingot in her life, she had to make believe otherwise.

The woman's mouth twitched and she forced more courtesy. "Mistress, would you like to eat? I can take your order now." Sai'er nodded, counting the eighty coppers. She ordered pu'er tea and a bowl of spicy noodles in soup, and went into the small dining lounge. She picked a quiet table beneath the staircase.

While slurping her noodles, she heard a vague sobbing sound coming from a table in the far corner of the lounge, where a scholar-like young man and an old man with an eye mask stringed to his face were seated. When she looked that way, the old man quickly leaned over to pull up the young man's cape hood.

She turned her gaze away and took long sips of tea, faking lack of interest. When the owner came to clean the table, she looked around circumspectly and whispered, her eyes blinking fast, "Poor kid. His father was executed today in the Palace. Now he's on the run with his servant."

A pang of pity hit Sai'er. It didn't occur to her to question the owner's motive in passing on the information to her. All she could think of was her duty to offer any help she could to the fugitives.

So she went up to the young man and asked in a low voice, "Young Master, are you by any chance General Tie's son?"

He jerked his head up in a fit of alarm. The servant glared at Sai'er with bristling suspicion.

"Do not be afraid. I'm Tang Sai'er and I just escaped custody myself," she said softly, trying to calm them both down. "I had the honor of fighting side by side with General Tie in Jinan, and my father is a good friend of his. Look, I'm heading back home to Putai tomorrow. If you're in need of a safe hideout, I think I can help you with that."

"Thank you, Mistress Tang," he stammered as he rose from his seat and bowed, looking nervously at his companion. When the old man nodded approval, he went on with more confidence, "To tell you the truth, we are in desperate need of a hideout. You don't know how much we appreciate your kind offer."

"Why don't you come with me on the boat trip?"

"Of course we'd be happy to tag along if you don't mind."

The young man looked no more than twenty at most. He had a sculpted face and a svelte, verging on willowy, build. His sad, doe-eyed face looked like it could melt any womanly heart.

If one looked closely though, one might be able to detect a gleam of cold green light that glared from behind the dark watery eyes. Whether out of extreme fatigue or an overzealous desire to help, Sai'er let it slip past her scrutiny entirely.

"Good. Let's all have a good night's rest. Please meet me at the counter at dawn tomorrow. We'll catch an early barge at the Pier. By the way, I didn't catch your name."

"His name is Tie Fu'an," the one-eyed man interjected, his good eye sharp as a razor. "He's General Tie's eldest son. I'm his servant, Ah Luk. We're staying here for the night and we appreciate your help. See you at dawn then."

The raspy hostile voice sounded strangely familiar to Sai'er. But she couldn't connect it with anyone she knew, try as she might. *It's probably nothing important,* she persuaded herself.

Exhaustion caught up with her and, after saying goodnight, she dragged her weary body upstairs to her room to turn in.

As soon as Sai'er had left the lounge, a bunch of silver ingots passed into the owner's hands. The two guests quietly slunk out to the street.

On the journey, Sai'er spent most of her time inside her cabin practicing neigong. At meal times, she would go to the eating area to get food, always with the hood pulled over her head. Only at night would she go up to the deck to get some fresh air. She was probably being overcautious, as she didn't believe anyone would tail her after Monk Yao issued the release order.

Fu'an and Ah Luk were in the next cabin and they would always keep to themselves, for fear of being exposed. Ah Luk had placed orders with the kitchen crew for meals to be brought into their cabin.

Earlier, on their way from the tavern to the Pier, Sai'er had noticed posters with a sketch of Fu'an's face pinned up on street shop fronts. So she was also keeping an eye open for any suspects who might be on their tail. She was satisfied that no anomaly could be detected.

Midway on the trip, while alone on the windswept deck one night looking out into the unknown and immense darkness, Sai'er tried to come to terms with her feelings and take stock of where she was headed.

Zhu Di is one bloodthirsty tyrant, she mused.

Never could she understand why those with absolute power in their hands had to choose violence to eliminate dissidents and their innocent affiliated family members. Zhu Yuanzhang had been callous and brutal with people he had the slightest cause to suspect of treachery.

Both Yinho's and Binhong's parents had tragically perished as a result of his paranoiac and persecutory reign of terror, as had countless other innocents affiliated with alleged criminals. Ironically, the first Ming Emperor only ended up making recalcitrant enemies of millions more, like her two comrades.

Zhu Di obviously hasn't learned any lesson and is heading down the same path.

She couldn't imagine how many more Shandong people would be persecuted, either for having fought against the Yan army or being incriminated under the affiliation precept. General Tie and his relatives certainly wouldn't be the last victims.

She had thought she'd give him a redemptive chance, even after he had tried to browbeat her with the hex and after all his cruelty dished out to Fang Xiaoru and family and other Jianwen loyalists. Yet he was deranged enough to mete out even more monstrosity for no good reason. In a moment of weakness she had blinded herself to his duplicity.

I can't stand by watching my family and my people tumble down the monster's maw.

How glad she was that the trio had put in place foundational work for the White Lotus Sect! She was right after all to have set things in motion two months earlier. Her celestial mission couldn't be clearer to her now—armed aggression was the only way out. It was as much a moral duty she owed her loved ones and her people.

Having been away from home for so long, she just couldn't wait to be with her family and comrades again. She anxiously prayed to Maitreya Buddha and Guanyin for the timely delivery of Sanbao's message to Binhong, and for the safety of everyone in Putai and Yidu.

30

The Advisers arrived at the Tang cottage with a heavy heart at the start of the twelfth month.

Binhong quickly took out the note that Sanbao's uncle's maid had delivered on the last day of the eleventh month, a day after he'd sent out his report to the Advisers, and read it out aloud.

Having now learned that Sai'er had escaped captivity, the Advisers let out a big sigh of relief.

The note, however, had been sent prior to Sai'er's second capture by Yusu and her fraught stint in the Chaotian Palace.

To celebrate the good news that Sai'er had fled the Yao Residence with Sanbao's help, and to welcome the elders back home, Yinho volunteered to spin out a supper of culinary delight, one that they could still wrest out of their scant provisions.

The lotus roots and taro roots that he had reaped from Sai'er's cottage yards would make two separate savory dishes: lotus root stew and deep-fried taro root crisps. In his hands, even the most unappetizing of vegetables could turn out to taste scrumptious. He had kept a brood of chickens here in the Tang cottage backyard, so steamed chicken with dried mushrooms would make a delectable third dish.

Binhong was glad to see that intense qinggong training of all Assassins and Scouts had kept Yinho busy with coaching work. Their experience had informed them that good qinggong could save lives when they had to flee deadly perils. Such coaching had taken Yinho's mind off his grief and had put an occasional smile back on his face.

The Tang cottage hadn't seen a joyous event since Ah Long's death, and Binhong appreciated Yinho's gesture that was meant to bring a little cheer to everybody. Their only regret was that Yulan could not join them because she had to take care of her ailing father.

Decent meals were becoming a rarity these days, as aggressive hunting and trapping by villagers, refugees and bandits alike had almost scoured the county clean of all wild game, especially near the river and in the forest. Droughts had become more frequent in recent years and had made things worse. Millet gruel with root vegetables and eggs on the side was the usual fare for most households in the winter months.

Buoyed by high spirits, Yinho scurried off to buy fermented bean curd sauce, the spice for flavoring the much loved lotus root stew, and a jug of cooking oil for deep-frying.

On the Advisers' request, Binhong led them to Ah Long's grave in the nearby cemetery, where they paid their respects. They'd all loved the sprightly kid and his tragic and brutal murder had broken their hearts.

Then he gave them a tour of the millet fields outside Sai'er's cottage, and of the refugees' shanties near the foothills. Lastly, he took them to the Magistrate's Yamen compound and showed them how daily operations ran there under supervision of ten Strategists who reported directly to him. He also explained how the four Sect Units functioned under him and Yinho as Unit Heads.

"Binhong, you and Yinho have done an extraordinary job in Sai'er's absence," Tang Jun said. "I'm so proud of you two."

Binhong was a bit flustered and tongue-tied. His uncle was

habitually reserved and not one to give praise easily, especially to his loved ones. Yinho, who was fast becoming Uncle's favorite adoptee, said with humility, "Thank you, Uncle. We just did what we thought was the right thing."

"You two boys and Sai'er make a perfect team," chimed in Pearly. "We need young people with a dedicated sense of mission like the three of you. By the way, your Weaponry people are progressing well in their training at Rocky Ridge."

Binhong appreciated Pearly's support and praise, but nonetheless felt pressure mounting by the day, being all too aware that their cause was like pitching eggs against a hard rock.

"When do you expect Sai'er to arrive?" asked Monk Faxian absent-mindedly, who had kept quiet all this time.

"Boat trips from Yingtian to Putai usually take about a month," replied Binhong. "Sanbao's note is dated the fifteenth of the eleventh month. So, if Sai'er got on a boat that day, she should be here around the fifteenth of this month." He could see that Monk Faxian was anxious to see his granddaughter home.

Monk Faxian seemed too absorbed in his own thoughts to respond. So Binhong added, "Don't worry, Granduncle. We can trust Sanbao's word. He truly cares about Sai'er." He was in disbelief as those words slipped out. Never had he imagined he would speak in favor of his imaginary rival.

"I wouldn't worry too much," Pearly said soothingly. "With Sai'er's mastery of superior Wudang kung fu, and given her wits, she should be able to defuse any hazardous situation."

"You're right, Pearly, Binhong," Monk Faxian acquiesced in a flat voice, his face forcing a smile. "I often forget what a formidable martial expert my granddaughter has become."

Binhong guessed that Sai'er's near-death incident in Liaocheng must be haunting Monk Faxian still.

Since her disappearance, he also came within an inch of

madness worrying about her, until he got Sanbao's note. Praying was never his thing, but this time he succumbed to it with all his heart. After all, Yingtian was dangerous territory to be in, and as long as she remained there, she was not out of the woods yet.

When the fifteenth day arrived, there was still no sign of Sai'er. They had no idea that she had been held up at the Chaotian Palace for three days, and each passing hour felt like torture to every one of them.

After supper, Monk Faxian announced he wanted to take a stroll by the river and went into the bed chamber to fetch his overcoat.

Pearly said to Binhong in a low voice, "Better keep an eye on him. He's not quite himself today."

Binhong didn't find anything particularly strange about Monk Faxian. But usually women's intuition was more acute and shouldn't be ignored. He agreed with Pearly extra caution was called for in these unsettling times.

The riverbank was just a short walk away from the cottage, and years ago the muddy banks used to be the nestling grounds for water fowl like swans, geese, ducks, mallards and egrets.

Binhong knew the terrain like the back of his hand, as it was his favorite hunting ground. But now, not a single shadow of such fowl could be sighted on the grayish-black mud mixed with gravel and rugged stones that overlaid both banks of the river that bled into the Bohai Sea to the immediate east.

A full moon played hide-and-seek with scuttling clouds in the starless sky. Whistling gusts that hailed from the rough sea angrily scraped and scratched anything they touched.

In a heartbeat, a barrage of snow and hail mingled with a briny flavor volleyed from the raging sea. The hair on Binhong's skin stood up as he gazed at what looked like an army of white-clad ghosts mounted on chariots of gusts barreling into the river estuary.

Monk Faxian pulled his overcoat about him tightly as he stared out into the white vapor towering over the dark water.

"You love Sai'er, don't you?" He posed the sensitive question out of the blue.

Binhong had never expected anyone to discern his well-kept secret. Stumped, he faltered in his reply, "I—I love her like my blood sister."

"Ah, you can't fool me," the monk said as he shook his stubbly head. "I know how it feels to yearn endlessly for that special someone." His profile stood out sharp and poignant against the black-laced-with-white screen of the night.

A short pause later, he asked absent-mindedly, "Did you hear flute music inside the cottage?"

"No, I didn't," replied Binhong casually, preoccupied with inventing an argument that could prove he had no amorous inclination towards Sai'er.

From the corner of his eyes he spied a distinct white shadow floating in the haze on the wooden bridge to their right.

"That must be Pearly," he murmured. An idea hit him and he said, "Why don't I leave you to accompany her, so I can get back and do some paper work?" He thought the two would love to have some privacy to talk. Since they had arrived, he noticed his Granduncle's longing gaze whenever he set eyes on Pearly.

"If you find it too windy here, there's our lecture temple right off the bridge on the north bank. It should be empty at this hour. There're candles inside the altar drawers."

Monk Faxian looked pleased with the suggestion. "Thank you, Binhong."

By the time Binhong stepped inside the backyard through the postern gate, snow had started to drift down. He was worried

Pearly in her white robe was probably not dressed warm enough for this weather.

A waft of guqin music drifted from the lounge. When he stepped inside, he was aghast to find Pearly sitting at the round table, dressed in a warm purple cape and playing her guqin. Uncle and Yinho were seated around her, held captive by her music.

"I thought I saw you on the bridge just now," he said with rounded eyes.

"I never went out. You probably saw someone else," said Pearly. After a pause, she gasped in terror, "Could it be Yusu?"

"Oh no! I left Granduncle to greet her, thinking she was you!" He almost gagged at the belated realization. Blood started to pound in his head. "We must go to the lecture temple at once." He wanted to tear his hair out for acting so mindlessly.

"Yusu is an imposter with Pearly's looks," Yinho explained to Uncle, who looked puzzled on hearing the conversation. "She used to be Pearly's companion at Wudang and has long been infatuated with Monk Faxian. Monk Yao used Shamanist black magic to alter her looks."

"She had vowed to cast a spell on him," Pearly said with a deep frown, as she picked up her guqin from the table.

"Uncle, we'd better take our swords, just in case," Binhong urged. "Yinho, would you mind staying behind to guard the cottage?"

"No problem," he replied glumly. Earlier in the day they had heard from Yulan that her father had passed away that morning, which put Yinho in a dispirited mood.

The frigid air now choked with torrents of snowflakes as the threesome crossed the bridge.

As they approached the temple, Binhong saw Yusu in a white ermine cape seated on a rectangular stone bench underneath a willow outside the temple. She was playing on a bamboo flute. Monk Faxian was leaning on her, imbibing wine from a small bottle, with one arm draped around her waist. He looked flushed, staring into the mid-distance with glassy eyes.

"Wen, don't listen to the flute!" Pearly warned in a loud, ringing voice. She then turned to Binhong and explained, "It's the Shamanist love spell. But its power is weak. Monk Yao probably hadn't taught her the entire spell."

She stepped inside the candle-lit temple, sat on one of the low praying stools and began plucking forcefully on her guqin.

As the guqin music drifted out to break the flute spell, Monk Faxian slowly came to. He rose from the bench, confounded by what was happening. Looking at the Pearly with leering eyes on the bench, he cowered, "I—I didn't mean to cross the line."

"Come, you didn't cross the line," coddled Yusu, as she tossed off her cape and sidled up to him. "We're lovers, Wen. Please hold me. I'm cold."

She drew him close and curled his forearms round her waist.

Monk Faxian fidgeted with unease. Over her head he caught sight of another Pearly playing the guqin inside the temple. He flinched and immediately withdrew his arms, "Who are you?"

In a fit of paroxysm, Yusu dashed into the temple, pounced on Pearly like a wild cougar and tried to strangle her.

Angling her elbow, Pearly knocked her off with a qi-energized swat. Yusu flew to the ground and landed on her nose. With blood trickling down to her mouth, she lunged at Pearly again, yanking her hair with such bestial force that Pearly tumbled off the stool with a moan. Yusu reached into her boot to fish out a dagger. Before Pearly could rise, Yusu hit her head hard with the dagger hilt and straddled her, blade pointed at her throat.

Her eyes projecting a murderous glint, she cawed, "We'll settle this today once and for all." Turning to Monk Faxian, who was standing agape nearby, she demanded as if she had every right to, "Wen, tell her that it's me, Yusu, that you've loved all these years, not her!"

Binhong and Tang Jun watched helplessly as the tension-charged scene unfolded. Binhong sensed an ominous shiver in the air building up into a violent storm, as the grounds got buried under layer after mournful layer of white snow.

"Yusu, please — put down the dagger," Monk Faxian begged, his face drained of blood as he realized what Yusu was up to. "Look, I'm a Buddhist monk. My reason for following Buddha was to rid myself of all worldly emotions and to do penance for my past sins."

"You're lying. You're living under the same roof with this bitch, aren't you?" she gave out a bitter laugh.

After a pause, she softened her tone to a coax, "Wen, no one on this earth loves you as much as I do. This woman is a selfish whore who puts her own interest ahead of yours. She didn't even allow you to touch her and forced you into another woman's arms. Then the woman you married pushed you into the monastery. Neither of them deserved you. If you marry me, I'll show you what a real woman can give you — tenderness and pure, selfless love. It's not too late to let yourself be loved."

"Yusu, please understand — carnal love of this world no longer interests me. I beg you not to harm Pearly because of me. My decisions to marry Jun's mother and later to become a monk were entirely my own and I don't regret those decisions."

Binhong could see Monk Faxian was trying hard to tiptoe around the hard truth — that he had never loved Yusu — so as not to stoke her jealousy.

As if gripped by deranging fever, Yusu couldn't register even one word of what Monk Faxian said. With a shrill snigger, she pushed the blade deeper into Pearly's shoulder as if for fun.

"Why do you have to meddle now? Didn't you toss Wen away?" Pearly screamed from pain. "Yes, that's the sweet sound I've been dying to hear, you bitch!"

Monk Faxian lunged forward and tried to grapple with Yusu, but seemed too weak to wrench the blade from her. Yusu had likely laced the wine to weaken him. But he still managed to wrap his limbs around her like an octopus. As they rolled around, she said with a bitter laugh, her eyes emitting a manic gleam, "Wen, let's go to the next life together."

With the last word, she broke free from the tangle, bounced up and with both hands ran the dagger clean through Monk Faxian's ribcage. Then viciously she yanked it out with sinewy force. He gave out a gurgling moan, eyes wide with shock.

Tang Jun gasped, dumbstruck, then bellowed a long howl of pain, "Father!"

Monk Faxian went limp, blood spouting from his punctured artery. Pearly crawled toward him, circled her arms around the quavering body and squalled, her purple cape turning rusty with blood that kept squirting out.

Binhong skipped towards the couple. He crouched down to take Monk Faxian's pulse. It was so weak he could hardly feel any beat.

In his dying breath, Monk Faxian wheezed hard, "I love you — Pearly. Help Sai'er."

Yusu drew out another glinting dagger from her boot and snuck up behind Pearly. No sooner had she raised it than Tang Jun sprinted forward and lanced her with his sword.

Her eyes were wide open as she heaved, "Thank you for the send-off." Pausing to take a final breath, she added with malice, in shallow gasps, "Your daughter is the Emperor's whore now."

With a wicked smile lingering on her face, she succumbed to her fate.

Had she murdered Monk Faxian out of personal vendetta, because she couldn't inveigle him into being her love object? Or had she merely carried out Zhu Di's order and exterminated this 'traitor' who was on the Wanted List?

Binhong couldn't come up with an answer. What distressed him more than anything was that he had mistaken Yusu for Pearly on the bridge and had let Monk Faxian walk straight into Yusu's trap. He wouldn't know how to face Sai'er when she came back. He couldn't forgive himself.

31

THREE DAYS later, Sai'er and her two charges arrived at Putai.

They headed straight to the Tang cottage. Since she was bringing home strangers, she thought she should use the front entrance instead of the postern gates.

On approach, she was dumbstruck to see two large white lanterns hung from the beam above the front yard gates.

Frantically she banged on the gates with her clenched fist, shouting, "Binhong, Yinho—"

Ah Luk stepped up and said discreetly, "This doesn't seem to be a good time for us to intrude on your family. We'll go find an inn to stay in, and will call on you in a few days."

Sai'er just nodded without caring to bid them farewell, being completely overwhelmed with an acute sense of distress. The two men rode off quietly.

Binhong came to open the gates. He was clad and hooded in white mourning hemp, his chin covered in a thicket of stubble. Through the mournful, strangled silence droned the Buddhist monks' valedictory incantations. The front yard was imbued with smoke from the burning of joss sticks and paper offerings.

"Granduncle left us three days ago," he said, breaking the grievous news to her. He handed over a full mourning robe made of sackcloth that was reserved for family members. "Yusu killed him," said he with downcast eyes. "Then Uncle killed Yusu to save Pearly."

Her worst fear had come true! It was a fear that had haunted her ever since she had eavesdropped on Yusu's conversation with Pearly. It deepened when Yusu reiterated her intentions while on the Yingtian-bound junk. Since then she had felt in her bones that something tragic would happen. This was the worst scenario that could have unfolded.

His tight clasp on her bespoke the shared grief and his deep relief to see her home.

Ba looked like he had aged ten years. It broke Sai'er's heart to see his puffed eyes and sunken cheeks. He crouched by the large copper urn half filled with burning wood chips, and mechanically threw in paper offerings piece by piece. She trained her eyes, wordless, on his brownish fingers, stained from years of handling and mixing medicinal herbs.

Yinho was next to him fiddling with the stack of joss paper offerings: Buddhist sutras, monk robes, wood clappers and prayer beads. He looked up and greeted her with a brotherly look, his face grimaced with sorrow. Rising, he threw his arms around her and, as if sadness had robbed him of words, just mutely took her horse to the backyard stable.

Sai'er could see how hard this hit her Ba. Having been separated for decades, he and his father were reunited for only a short couple of years, and now the elder had left again, never to return.

When Ba saw her, he heaved a loud sob and twined his arms tightly around her, as if afraid she would suddenly take flight. She began to bawl her eyes out. Her crying set off more cathartic wails from her father.

She just didn't have the heart to break the news of General Tie's brutal death to him just then.

"Come inside and offer joss sticks," directed Binhong like

the big brother he always was. "We already buried the body yesterday."

"Granduncle died a violent death," he explained with tear-glazed eyes. "Local customs required that his corpse be buried immediately, to prevent the grievance-laden ghost from loitering around his home."

The lounge had been converted into a funeral hall with mourning wreaths and banners hung up on walls. They breathed a doleful white that was heart-wrenching to behold. The aura that pervaded the space was one of solitude, grief and regret. The Buddhist monks who squatted in rows on both sides of the lounge chanted in a low droning sound that gave her momentary escape from heartsick sorrow.

As she lit a bunch of joss sticks, in her mind's eye unspooled scene after scene of her Grandba's interactions with her ever since he had first entered her life in Madam Pu's guesthouse in Dengfeng.

The day she had flirted with death felt like it was just yesterday. The first thing she had seen when she opened her eyes was her Grandba's weeping and smiling face. That loving face would from now on only live in her memory.

Remorse wrenched her heart as she chastised herself for selfishly requesting him to stay and help with her cause. Having rescued him from captivity, she should have just let him live out his secluded life at the Lingyan Temple rather than involving him in the Sect.

And she hadn't even had a chance to hear his last words!

But no amount of regret or self-reproach would bring him back to life. She was now and forever robbed not only of his sagacious advice, but also of his lavish pampering love, which she would never have enough of. Nothing could substitute the deep familial bond that had spawned from their mutual desire to understand and trust.

It's so unfair! We hardly had enough time together, she wailed silently. She called to mind how Master Zhang's love for Pearly had sustained her on her chosen path of celibacy. That was how precious grandfatherly love was.

One thought kept gnawing at her. *How Pearly must be hurting! The butterfly is now crippled forever.*

At this moment, Binhong's voice came from behind, "Pearly is in her room recuperating from a shoulder stab wound. Yulan has been tending to her. It's her heart wound that's harder to treat."

It was not much of a consolation, but Sai'er was at least pacified to hear her coach was on the mend physically.

She knelt on a praying stool and bowed deeply three times, then inserted the lit joss sticks in the burner placed in front of the spirit tablet inscribed with Grandba's name. Silently she prayed to Guanyin to let her Grandba's soul pass smoothly from the Bridge of Forgetfulness into his next life, and to assuage Ba's and Pearly's grief.

"Tell me what happened," Sai'er tried to hold back her tears, with not much success.

"Come to my room and I'll tell you everything that happened since your kidnapping."

When Binhong recounted the tragedy that had happened three days earlier, Sai'er gnashed her teeth in a fit of maddening rage. It was all Yusu's fault. If that woman were alive, she would run the sword through her heart to avenge Grandba! How she wished she had killed her at the Yan camp in Jinan! Then this tragedy wouldn't have happened. Sometimes mercy was just wasted on evil people. With that thought she was seized with another storm of sobs.

Yinho came in to join them at this point. He and Binhong had been sharing the same room since the elders had moved back from Yidu. He put his arms around Sai'er in a fraternal hug and coaxed gently, "Don't cry, Sai'er. You're with family now. Whatever comes next, we'll shoulder it together."

Wiping away tears with the back of her hand, she then catered to their thirst with her yarn of hair-raising ordeals on the trip to and during her stay in Yingtian, leaving out only the feverish episode of her assignation.

"Serves that ugly toad right! No, what he deserved was a tortured death," Yinho seethed. Then, wrinkling his nose, he added, "Ah, Empress! So Zhu Di wanted to buy you out with status and privileges! How I wish you'd finished him off there and then! But then you wouldn't have lived if you had."

Sai'er was fazed to hear Yinho's pointed reasoning. How come she'd not seen through Zhu Di's scheming calculations at the outset? *Sanbao had good reason to warn me not to bargain with that turtle egg!*

She was glad Yinho made no attempt at chaffing her for her gullibility, as had been his habit. He was probably done with trying to dissemble with artificial humor.

"It was so close—I almost got trapped," she admitted with a long sigh, flinching at the thought that she could've been cornered by Zhu Di's subterfuge had he delayed General Tie's trial and execution to after bedding her. *I could have bartered away my life and self-respect, possibly the lives of others too.*

It was mere luck that she had managed to escape Chaotian Palace unscathed.

"Your anguish over Uncle's and Granduncle's safety got the better of your judgment, that's all," said Yinho, giving her a comforting pat on the hand.

After a moment's silence, with pinched brow he added, "I guess all along I'd been unfair to Sanbao. He must have steel nerves to survive in that hellish place!"

"The eunuch may have saved you once, but he's too close to imperial power to warrant our trust," Binhong interjected with a tinge of sourness.

Sai'er pursed her lips in silent protest.

With a deep sigh he added, "Sai'er, I don't want to see you get hurt. Just thinking Zhu Di could've harmed you on the first night gives me the creeps."

"Sanbao is my trusted friend and I don't want anyone badmouthing him in any way," she said in a barely audible hiss.

With a wry smile, she added, "I also have Monk Yao to thank for allowing me to escape. Time and observation are better judges than our casual take on a person's character." She remembered well what Ba had taught her.

An instant later, Binhong went on with his habitual stubbornness, "If Zhu Di is vicious enough to do what he did to General Tie, all bets are off. Vigilance is our operative word. Anyone connected to his camp should be viewed with suspicion, even Sanbao."

The air was thick with frigid silence.

Nothing piqued Sai'er more than when someone challenged her judgment of people, especially when that someone was Binhong, even if she normally respected his strategical mind. As well, sibling rivalry had never ceased between them since childhood and was rearing its ugly head now. On the topic of Sanbao, she just hated it that Binhong was too proud to trust her opinion.

"It's such an irony that General Tie declined rescue to protect his family, only to have all trapped in a brutal fate," Yinho tried to direct focus away from the subject of Sanbao. "Had he accepted rescue, they'd still have a chance of survival. The lesson here is: never trust a tyrant to show mercy — it's never wrong to assume the worst of him."

"I learned that lesson too late," Sai'er murmured in a shadowed voice.

When you're wrong, you're wrong!

"Almost too late," said Yinho with a quirk of his eyebrow.

A moment later, Binhong tried to soften his tone, with downcast eyes, "Sai'er, I have to take full blame for Granduncle's death. It was my fault that he walked into Yusu's trap—"

"Don't blame yourself," said Sai'er in an exhausted voice. Binhong was the last person she would pin the blame on for Grandba's death. Neither grief nor displeasure with his prejudice against Sanbao could steal away her sense of right and wrong. "That evil bitch could have tricked anyone."

"So, where are General Tie's son and his servant?" asked Yinho offhandedly, having now dispelled the stalemate.

"Oh, I almost forgot. They are staying in some inn. Ah Luk said they'd call on us in a few days," said Sai'er.

"Something's not quite right," Binhong said, his brow creasing into deep lines. "Didn't you find their appearance to be a bit odd, showing up as they did in the same dining lounge at the same time as you?"

Sai'er had always known he had a keen nose for smelling out oddities, but sometimes she just found his inquisitiveness a bit pestering, like now.

"Umm, I never gave it a thought. Sometimes coincidence is just coincidence," she began to search her memory for hints of doubt, but still couldn't come up with any. "Well, I was the one to approach them first. And I saw posters everywhere with Tie Fu'an's face sketch. They had such a desperate look. I can't see why else they would follow me home to this backwater."

"Maybe I was just too edgy," Binhong was quick to back off, not wanting to annoy her at this time of distress.

"So it looks like we'll be busy with preparing the Sect for some real action," Yinho said with moody anticipation. Sai'er could almost taste the bloodlust in his voice.

"By hurting Zhu Di with my North Star feat, I've burned my bridges," replied Sai'er, succumbing to an irrepressible yawn. "That might as well be. I'd been too naïve in the first place to assume compromise was possible. He'll take his revenge—that's a promise. I'm just glad that we had set things in motion two months ago. As leaders, the three of us must show grit and commitment to rally more support province-wide if our cause is to stand any chance of success."

Both her brothers gave firm nods.

Such an immense wave of fatigue coursed through her whole body that she wanted to immediately crash onto a bed. Those three agonizing days in Yingtian and the grievous loss of Grandba had drained her emotionally and physically.

"You boys have done a fantastic job with taking over and running Putai," she struggled to keep her swollen eyelids from drooping. "Aiyah, it feels so darn good to be home." She clapped her two brothers on the shoulder with heartfelt affection.

"Sai'er, you've walked through fire in Yingtian," Binhong said thoughtfully. "No one deserves praise more than you."

"I'm beat and can really use some sleep," she said, slightly abashed at the flattery.

"I hope you don't mind taking Granduncle's room, unless you want to go back to your own cottage."

"I'd like to stay in Grandba's room tonight." She was thinking of the unpleasant prospect of having to tell her mother-in-law about Lin San's death. "Right now, I can doze off standing up."

"Can you stay awake for a simple supper with us?" asked Yinho. "I'll make you your favorite taro root crisps."

That was the sweetest thing she'd heard since stepping into

the house. She choked back her welled up tears, overcome with gratitude, love and coziness of being with family again.

"My precious Flying Spear, I wouldn't miss supper if I had to sleep-walk through the meal. You don't know how much I've craved your cooking."

32

THE MOMENT Sai'er hit the bed, she dropped into a deep slumber.

At around the third watch, the sky outside suddenly turned a vermillion red amidst howling gales that whipped from the Bohai Sea, pummeling the quiet river and its banks. Reefs of thick dark clouds raced across the bright red sky. Angry white flashes of lightning streaked the vault that was painted in eerie black and red.

Sai'er in her dormant state saw Grandba standing at her bedside. He was dressed in a long gray monkish robe, with a strand of prayer beads hanging from his neck. His palms were brought together in praying gesture. He looked calm and spoke in a gentle, echoing voice.

"Sai'er, it is not the time to sleep. People need your help. Zhu Di has sent the Green Dragon here to wreck Putai. Do what you can to save lives."

With that last sentence he glided backwards, floating farther and farther away into thin air.

The mention of Zhu Di and Green Dragon jolted Sai'er awake. She sat straight up on her bed, only to catch a glimpse of the spirit's fading silhouette.

All of a sudden it hit her that Ah Luk had the same hoarse voice as the sorcerer in the hex. That chilling green light that shone from behind Fu'an's eyes! Her overzealous wish to help out General Tie's descendant had blunted her alertness. How could she miss those signs? Binhong was so right to raise questions. *I'm such an idiot!*

She scrambled out to the backyard barefooted, wanting to wake Binhong and Yinho, only to find them stumbling out of their room. Ba and Pearly were already in the yard checking on the stable's straw-thatched roof which, just a moment earlier, had been ripped off by fierce gusts, causing the mules to bleat frantically.

"Bad news! That Fu'an guy is the Green Dragon," Sai'er said breathlessly. "He's here to destroy Putai. Grandba came into my dream to—"

Before she could finish, hailstones the size of pebbles tumbled in an avalanche from the blood-red sky, like ice bombs shot from celestial catapults. Some large pellets punched holes in the cottage's reed-thatched rooftop to hit the clay-plastered floors.

Ba bolted back into his room and came out hugging a satchel to his chest. Sai'er knew that was the white jade Amulet she had left in his custody. "I better let you take this back to safe-keep," he said, handing her the satchel. She nodded with gratitude, and strapped it securely to her shoulder. He then went into his apothecary to collect his precious herbs and Pearly gave him a hand in packing them into cloth pouches.

"Binhong, can you mobilize our Sect members to help move villagers and refugees up to the hillside west of our millet fields?"

"Right, I'll send Zhuge Liang to take a warning note to the Yamen compound now," said Binhong. "Our Strategists will strike the gong to summon Sect members to the lecture temple."

Sai'er struggled to keep calm and riffled through her memory for clues that could shine a light on the Green Dragon's possible moves. Recalling that Zhu Di had once threatened to flood Jinan city, she murmured, "My best guess is that the Green Dragon will try to churn up the Bohai Sea to flood our river and plains."

"I'll go to the public granary to pack up the millet grains, and pick up Yulan on the way," said Yinho as he crouched on the vegetable patch trying to salvage half-grown jicamas before the hail pellets could ruin them all. "Then I'll meet you all at the temple."

"Good thinking, Yinho," said Binhong. "You might want to take Sai'er's horse and a couple of mules to carry the grains. Our three horses had been lent to the Scouts." He then spun around and dashed into his room to write the note.

As soon as Zhuge Liang flew off and Yinho left, the rest of the group headed to the lecture temple on foot, carrying in hemp sacks whatever essentials they could take along with them.

By now the avalanche of hail pellets had eased a little. But blizzards blowing in from Bohai Sea were still battering the county, uprooting trees and ripping off roofs and shattering loose farm structures, flinging debris in every direction.

As the group of four and their only mule braved the storm to trudge on frosty sludge towards the wooden bridge, an earth-shattering howl rose from the plane where the sky met the sea, just beyond the estuary.

Above the horizon surged a massive serpent-like beast with a rugged horned head and a bulbous scaly trunk, casting all of them and their surroundings in a dark ominous shadow. A series of thunderclaps exploded like firebombs across the sky. The world was instantly veiled in black. The Dragon's two glinting green eyes shot out razor-sharp beams that could slice anything into pieces.

This fiendish King of the East Sea appeared much more gargantuan and deadly than the one Sai'er had seen in the hex. She flinched to realize this was his true life-size form. What she had experienced in the hex was probably just an appetite-whetting, dream-like prelude for the vicious demon. For all she knew, he must have exulted over this chance to inflict punishing pain on her for daring to offend and hurt Zhu Di, his immortal twin brother.

The air crackled with a devilish energy that she had never felt before.

Taking a look at the worn-out bridge, she felt a numbing chill shoot down her spine. That bridge was the only connection between the north and south banks. For everyone who happened to be on the south bank at this point, that crossing was the only lifeline, as hills and uplands were all located north of the river. In this stormy weather, crossing the windswept river of churning sludge by sampans would undoubtedly be risky.

"We must hurry up," Binhong tried to shout over the howl of the wind, fully realizing the danger they faced. No one could read her mind as well as he.

As Pearly was still weak from her recent loss of blood, Binhong implored her to let him carry her on his back. Sai'er urged Ba to ride on the mule to keep away frostbite.

Finally they were on the wiggling bridge, clutching the railings as they inched along. Below them the river surged and eddied. Water was cascading onto the planks.

At this point, the rearing Dragon flicked his cutting gaze at the northern end of the beam-pillar bridge, severing a couple of beams and causing that part to totter. The whole bridge shook violently, its northern end teetering with only three transverse beams attached to the northern stone abutment.

The group was more than half way through now, and Sai'er shouted with an edge in her voice, "Let's move faster!"

Ba jumped from the mule and hauled it along towards shore. Binhong with Pearly on his back scrambled forward as fast as his legs could carry them both. Sai'er followed right behind.

No sooner had all landed safely onshore than the Dragon drew himself to its full height and flailed all his six talons wildly. Wall after soaring wall of water hurtled through the river estuary to block out the sky entirely, turning bleak dawn into night. Then in a beat they came crashing down onto the river and whipped up gigantic waves, instantly shattering the bridge. The former lifeline was now a massive heap of flotsam.

Just then they heard the clang of the Yamen gong. Moments later, terrified Sect members and villagers swarmed the south bank near the other end of the now ruined bridge, all flabbergasted at the sight of the wreckage.

"Use sampans to cross! Be quick!" Binhong shouted at the top of his lungs across the foaming river. "Once you reach this side, head west to the hills."

"Oh no! Yinho and Yulan—" Sai'er wailed, completely distressed and helpless. She had no means of fighting the East Sea Dragon. Her martial arts were useless against it. "Damn that turtle egg to the eighteenth level of hell," she cursed under her breath. Her best chance was to use the Xuannu Sword, but Nezha still had it with him. She fingered the jade tablet, but too bad no one could decipher the inscriptions to release whatever magic power it possessed.

"We have to hope for the best," Binhong tried to remain collected. "The river is rising fast. There's no point going to the temple now. Let's go straight to the refugees' shanties and help move them to the hillside."

"You're right," replied Sai'er. "I'll just swing by my cottage to take Mother Lin along. You three go right ahead. We'll catch up."

Ba insisted that he could manage the walk and to let Pearly ride the mule. Binhong couldn't argue with him.

Even as they spoke, swelling waves from the river had already breached the banks on both sides, raging in huge torrents through dry lands.

Sai'er waded through knee-deep water to reach her cottage. Mother Lin was weeping helplessly in the lounge, where the floor was already covered in ankle-deep water. A weak smile flitted across her face when she saw Sai'er coming for her. She had sense enough to have already packed up essentials in a cloth sack. Together they headed out to catch up with the others.

On the way, Sai'er told Mother Lin about Lin San's death and the events that led up to it. She seemed to be expecting such unpleasant news and didn't appear alarmed.

"Sai'er, I know you're a strong, good-hearted woman. My son didn't deserve you. And I hate to say this, but he probably had it coming," she said with a rueful frown. After a short pause, she added, "I'm just an illiterate woman who knows little about the ways of the world. But I can still tell right from wrong. I know you mean to do the right thing with the White Lotus Sect. Sai'er, please know that I'm proud of what you're doing. Also, consider yourself free to re-marry if you so choose; you'd have my blessing."

When Sai'er heard that, she felt like a load had been taken off her. She was wondering if her Ba ever had any feelings for Mother Lin. Women with an open mind like her were not easy to come by. But this was no time to think about these things. Too many things demanded her full attention now.

Once they were out in the open, they had to brave the blizzards and wade their way through the millet fields, which had now turned into a lake.

Mother Lin fell down a couple of times because her legs were too feeble. Sai'er caught her by the arm and propped her up both times. "Let me carry you," urged Sai'er. She then crouched down to let the shivering woman climb onto her back. At last they were able to move along and finally caught up with the others at the shanties site.

Sensible as always, Mother Wang had already gathered her people with packed belongings on their backs in a group, ready to follow Binhong's lead to trek up into the hills.

It was a good thing that Binhong as a child had scouted out hiking trails in these hills. Being a girl, Sai'er had been forbidden to follow him on those excursions. Right now, rather than begrudge him that unfairness, she was just grateful for his experience with the trails.

"There's a spacious flat landing about half a joss stick's walk up this slope," he announced, pointing to the shrub-covered access path a stone's throw away from where the group stood. "We can pitch our tents there."

After entrusting Mother Lin into Mother Wang's care, Sai'er turned to Binhong and said, "You go ahead and lead the people. I'll head back to find Yinho and Yulan."

Mustering up her stored qi, Sai'er leaped into the air and used qinggong to propel herself towards the bridge abutment.

Feeble rays of dawn struggled through crevices to throw a grayish light on the surroundings. The scene across the river was one of distressing chaos. Children were scared and screaming their lungs out. Abandoned horses and mules were bumbling around, bleating protests against their woeful fates. Adults were frantically searching for boats or sampans. Some were improvising rafts out of any logs or tree trunks they could lay hands on. The luckier ones were already rowing small boats across. But sometimes luck could be tricky.

The ruthless Dragon flicked his tail like a whip and sent mountainous waves up the river, and two boats immediately went bottom up, sliding helpless families into the dark maw of the river.

It was an agonizing sight to behold.

Perched on a huge boulder that jutted out of the flood water and squinting hard, Sai'er tried to pick out Yinho and Yulan from the agitated crowd. Her clothes were dripping wet and she was shivering from the assault of bone-freezing cold. The struggle to fight exhaustion that blanketed her began to feel like a lost cause.

Then she spotted them. Yinho and Yulan were at the head of a platoon of Sect members, some of whom Sai'er recognized as Assassins by the white bands they tied round their heads. Binhong had told her about that insignia. The rest should be Scouts and Strategists. He had also told her that Assassins and Scouts were mostly sword and spear fighters, now also well-trained in qinggong under Yinho.

One Assassin took an old villager by the arm and sprang into the air, hopping and skimming over the water surface like a pair of flying jacanas touching on lily pads. Such a feat required top-notch neigong and would burn up a lot of energy in the carrier. Other Assassins and Scouts just as bravely followed suit.

Yinho's intense coaching hadn't been wasted. But helpless villagers still far outnumbered rescuers. Assassins only totaled seventy and Scouts a hundred, but there were several hundred who needed help to cross the river.

While watching the ongoing rescue operation, Sai'er was suddenly hit with a thought that had all the time eluded her.

33

SAI'ER SPRANG across the river in a series of vaults and landed right in front of Yinho.

"Yinho, we need help from your Ah Long clones," said Sai'er with an edge in her voice.

"How has that escaped me?" he looked like a blow had just hit him. "I was racking my brain on how to transport the grain." He pointed to the horse and two mules, each laden with several heavy sacks.

"Quick, rub your gold wristband!" Yulan urged. She had Zhuge Liang perched on her gloved hand. On her hair she wore a woven white flower. She was in mourning for her father who had died from an incurable kidney disease on the same day Monk Faxian was murdered. Sai'er clasped her in a tight hug as a gesture of heartfelt condolences.

Just then, Yinho's face turned ashen white as he stared over Sai'er's head at something behind her. The air around her crackled with white shrieks of terror.

Sai'er whirled around and saw the Dragon towering over the entire south bank, having just slithered from the river onto land that was being deluged.

The screaming villagers started to scramble away from the gigantic beast, staggered by his sheer size and vicious disposition. The Dragon was known to them as a fearsome guardian of the elements. They had tasted the nasty droughts he had carelessly foisted on them from time to time. This was the first time they'd witnessed his overt wickedness.

Moving like a lashing whip, he aimed for the Tang cottage as if by design, and with his front claws repeatedly pummeled the thatched dwelling. The wood-framed structure immediately fell apart and splintered to pieces, like a junk wrecked by a violent tempest at sea.

Sai'er gasped as she watched her beloved childhood home collapse into shambles in a matter of moments. Her Ba had built the home plank by plank with his own two hands just before his marriage to Ma. This malicious razing would kill him.

"Yinho, call out the clones, now!" she said, heaving several deep, hoarse breaths.

Startled out of his daze, Yinho rolled back his sleeve and rubbed the gold wristband once. Thereupon, ten Ah Longs jumped out from the pouch that he kept strung around his neck.

"What do we do first, save people or fight the Dragon?" Yinho asked in confusion.

"Order the clones to save people first," Sai'er said, forcing calmness in her voice. "Then the grains. Leave the Dragon to me."

Immediately the clones went to work. Each could carry two persons in one go. Obviously they were not constrained by depletion of energy like humans.

Were she honest with herself, she would admit that she actually didn't have a clue how to tackle the demon. Panic was fogging her whole mind.

Then a sliver of light flashed in her head. She recalled that in the hex, the Dragon had needed the sorcerer to guide him once he got out of water, which meant the beast had poor vision on land.

The sorcerer must be somewhere nearby. She swept her gaze around. And there crouched the one-eyed servant Ah Luk in the alley that separated the Tang cottage from the adjacent hut. Sai'er recognized the wand that he had used in the hex. Cold sweat trickled down her back as the image of the sorcerer in the hex came back to her. That creepy hollowed-out socket had squawked at her.

She leapfrogged over the puddles to land quietly behind him. Accelerating her qi flow, she readied her palm for action. Just as he turned halfway around, she slapped her searing palm on his back. Before he knew what was happening, her major meridians had latched onto his and she started guzzling qi from him.

The picture of those families being devoured by the river rose in her mind, as did the scene of discovering Ah Long's brutal death and the image of her Grandba's murder. Her blood boiled. She felt a frenzied desire for payback. She didn't let go until her victim stopped breathing. The wand slipped from his hand.

She had killed in combat before. But this was the first murder with intent she had ever committed. Never had she envisioned such a deliberate extirpation of a human life could slip so easily past her conscience.

Picking up the wand she flashed it to get the Dragon's attention. He appeared disoriented and froze in his tracks.

Something that Caihe had told her but which she hadn't taken to heart now came back. In his deepwater habitat the beast could wield magic over rain, sleet, tide, storm, lightning and thunder. But on land his magic power was greatly abated. He was also forced to follow the sorcerer's wand due to his poor eyesight. Assuming a human form would give him good cover, but such feat would expend a lot of his dragon energy and so he would only use it sparingly.

Sai'er recalled that for some nights on the boat trip from

Yingtian she'd heard loud splashes that came from the deck. She'd thought it was just the crew dumping wastes into the river. She now realized what that was all about.

With the rescue operation at full throttle, it would be disastrous to let the beast slink back into the river. But what could she do to keep him ashore?

As she was dithering, the Dragon wagged his fat tail left and right out of boredom, and that single careless motion plunged several villagers into the ravenous river.

Remorse, guilt and rage surged through her guts in a series of intensifying fits. Because of her credulity, she had led the Dragon back here. Now because of vengeful reprisals that were meant for her, innocent villagers perished at random right before her eyes, not to mention she'd tragically lost Ah Long and her beloved grandfather, who, for all she knew, might've been killed on Zhu Di's orders.

Her insides were searing. When molten anger finally broke through, it was like an erupting volcano which, after singeing remnants of all other feelings into ashes, devoured her whole.

Who is to blame except that heaven-cursed Zhu Di?

Grinding her teeth, she leaped up the roof of the hut next to the heap of debris that had been the Tang cottage. With anger-charged courage, she brandished the wand right in front of the soaring demon.

The Dragon lowered his horned head to her level and cast her a tempered gaze. She stared back with unflinching confidence.

"I'm Chang'e incarnate and I want to make a deal," she shouted in a high pitch. "If you stop harming my people, I will convince Guanyin to persuade your daughter to return to the Crystal Palace."

In her desperation she had out of the blue recalled that Guanyin had adopted as an acolyte Little Dragon Princess who'd been banished from the Crystal Palace for pulling a few puerile pranks. She had heard that the Princess was the Green Dragon's favorite daughter, and guessed he could have regretted his harsh punishment of her, having hardly recovered from the painful loss of his third son, whom Nezha had accidentally killed. Perhaps he'd be amenable to striking a bargain with her, however ludicrous that idea might seem.

From the corner of Sai'er's eyes she saw the ten clones hard at work along with the qinggong experts, who together had delivered more than half of those trapped on the south bank to the other side of the river.

Her gaze then fell on Yinho, who was visibly shaking, apparently caught in an unexpected onslaught of sobs. Yulan kept patting his back to soothe him.

Sai'er could sense that his suppressed grief for Ah Long had at last exploded in one vehement outburst, no doubt triggered by the realization that the clones could not fill the void left by his beloved, one and only Ah Long. She felt for him in his grief. She also felt for Yulan, whose loyalty and love for Yinho was selfless and unwavering, but doomed to meet with an unresponsive heart. Only Yulan could judge if it was worth it. There was just no prescribed way to love.

The Dragon drew back with a pensive look and blinked, as if ruminating on what Sai'er proposed. She was delirious that her ruse had worked.

Sai'er knew she needed Lan Caihe's help on this one. But right now she had to feign utmost confidence and try to pin the Dragon down to a deal.

"Tang Sai'er, you hurt the Emperor badly and I'm here to punish you on his behalf for your brazen crime," the Dragon said with contempt in a deafening rumble. "Why should I believe you're Chang'e incarnate?"

"I know in your immortal life you were a Sky Wolf, and your twin brother was re-incarnated as Zhu Di," shouted Sai'er as loudly as she could manage. "You'd been separately raised by two fox nymphs. Only in this mortal world did you two reunite as brothers." Never had she been as grateful as now for the Pantheon stories Caihe had regaled her with.

The Dragon stayed immobile as he listened, his eyes no longer projecting deadly beams.

"I'll give you three days. But I doubt very much that that bitch Guanyin will let my daughter go. If she doesn't return to the Crystal Palace in three days, you can be sure I'll be back."

A short pause later, he added with a look at once crafty and covetous, "When I come back, I'll pick ten young and beautiful maidens for their delicious flesh to boost my dragon power — which I need for working magic. Have I made myself clear?"

The wicked terms of the bargain made Sai'er wince with nausea. She had no alternative but to nod her consent.

With those words and a thundering roar, the Dragon shrank to the size of a crocodile and waggled his way back into the river, soon disappearing into its murky depths.

Moments later, the boisterous river began to calm down. Blizzards stopped their angry howling. Gleams of light radiated from the rising sun to turn the sky aglow. But the flood waters would take a long time to recede from the banks and flat lands.

By late afternoon, all the rescued had assembled at the refuge landing on the hillside, now filled with raggedly makeshift tents.

Accompanied by Yinho and Yulan, Sai'er at last found the tent where Binhong, Ba and Pearly were staying. Binhong didn't hide his smile when he saw Zhuge Liang perched on Yulan's shoulder.

Once inside the tent, she couldn't help blurting out, "Ba,

the Dragon has destroyed our cottage!" She then went on with sniffles, "I'm sorry I wasn't able to stop him. But now my priority is to settle a bargain I've made with the Dragon. My end of the deal is to get his daughter, the Little Dragon Princess who is Guanyin's acolyte, to return to the Crystal Palace in three days. If I succeed, the Dragon will leave us alone. If I fail, he'll claim ten Putai maidens, to devour alive for a power boost."

Her audience gaped in horror at her words.

Even as she spoke, Sai'er harbored grave doubts about the Princess's willingness to return home. If she were the Princess, she wouldn't want to return to a prison under the restraining watch of a tyrannical father either. She shuddered at the eventuality of her failure: her hands would be soaked with the blood of ten innocent girls.

Binhong was the first one to detect her doubt. "Maybe we should prepare for the worst," he said with his habitual frown. "I would suggest that we move the villagers to the Rocky Ridge redoubt in Yidu as soon as possible. Day after tomorrow at the latest, regardless of whether your ploy succeeds or not. The sooner we set up in Yidu the better."

"That sounds sensible," Ba said after a moment's brooding. "It seems a good idea for us to use Yidu as our base from now on. The Rocky Ridge is a natural fort that offers us strong protection against both armed attacks and floods."

"I agree," Yinho said with confidence. "We were going to capture Yidu as a next step anyway. Our plan had always been to use Rocky Ridge as our command center. It makes sense to group all our members and supporters in Yidu county."

"But Ba, are you sure you want to leave Putai for good?" Sai'er asked, concerned that her father might find his emotional attachment to Putai too strong to sever.

"Sai'er, I've lost a father, a teacher and a good friend, but have gained Yinho as a son," he said with a reedy and choked voice. "You, Binhong and Yinho are my immediate family now, and the White Lotus Sect is my extended family. Wherever you choose to settle, it's good enough for me. Besides, I can continue with my lectures at the Bamboo Grove Nunnery."

When she heard that, she felt a lump in her throat. Ba had lost three loved ones to violent death in a short span of time. She couldn't imagine the pain he was going through.

"Pearly, what do you think?"

"Sai'er, for the rest of my life, my only goal is to honor your Grandba's dying wish. 'Help Sai'er' were his last words," Pearly said in a low voice, as a shadow of pain flitted across her face. "I'm happy to call Yidu home if you are." Sai'er went up to give her grief-stricken coach a warm embrace, her eyes prickling with tears.

"Yulan, what about you?"

"The day after my father died, I had a big fight with my brother Gao Feng," said Yulan with a heavy sigh. "He insisted on going to Yingtian to join the Embroidered Uniform Guards Unit. I wasn't able to talk him out of it. I have no family now. You're my leader, Sai'er. Wherever you go, I follow."

Sai'er gave Yulan a tight hug. Yinho and Binhong came up and clapped Yulan on the shoulder to show solidarity. Sai'er caught her two brothers exchanging a glance that smacked of apprehension. But she had too much on her mind to worry about Gao Feng now.

Much as Sai'er could exhale a temporary breath of relief about the big move, a dagger was hanging right above her. Now she had only three days in which to make her moves.

Turning to Yinho, she said, "For us to make the big move to Yidu, we'll need to cross the river again to get back to the south bank. I wish we'd asked the clones to build a bridge instead of to fly people across."

"Ah, I should've thought of that this morning," said Yinho, flushed with embarrassment. "Too bad we've used up the clones' magic."

"It is I who should take the blame," Sai'er readily owned up to the fault. "But it's hard to think straight when you're in a panic."

"You two, don't be too hard on yourselves," Binhong said soothingly.

"Binhong, I'm sorry I brushed off your warning —"

"No need to apologize," he cut her short. "You were just trying to save General Tie's son, and they preyed on your urge to help. Besides, the Dragon would've found a way here even if he hadn't tricked you."

34

MUCH AS SAI'ER believed that Little Dragon Princess would not agree to return to the Crystal Palace, she thought it might still be worth her while to talk to the Princess. *Who knows? I might get some insight about the Green Dragon.*

When everyone had retired, she sat on a tree stump by the bonfire, grateful to be left alone at last. The very thought that the fate of all of Putai's folks was in her hands weighed on her like a tub of lead. She must somehow get those who wished to leave for Yidu back to the south bank within three days.

But building a bridge was an impossible task, simply because they didn't have the knowledge or skill of bridge building, let alone doing it with time constraint. And the clones couldn't be called a second time.

Beset with anxiety and crushing fatigue, she looked up to the night sky and caught sight of the liquid full moon, which, as always, she was happy to drink in. She had little doubt her body had a natural need for the Yin qi that emanated from the moon. Having gulped all the Yang qi from Zhu Di and the sorcerer, she welcomed this new dose of Yin qi which would enhance the potency of her stored qi.

She wondered if Sanbao was looking at the same moon at this moment. The thought of his mouth on her breasts again induced a catch in her breath. She felt weak with yearning. But she must shut him out of her mind. Daydreaming was a luxury she couldn't afford right now.

Then memory of her last trip to the Pantheons jumped to the forefront of her brain. Quietly she mouthed Lan Caihe's name. Almost immediately, the familiar floral fragrance filled the frigid air around her.

"Did you want to meet the Little Dragon Princess?" The sprightly androgyne asked as it fluttered down to settle on Sai'er's shoulder, its favorite nook.

"Have you been watching over me all the time?" An abrupt feeling of embarrassment engulfed her as a thought hit home: the sprite had likely watched her making love with Sanbao!

"Don't worry. I won't judge you," the sprite winked with mischief. After a little brooding, it said with a hint of wistfulness, "Nothing's more beautiful than mortal love. The brevity of life makes it poignant and poetic, like an elusive rainbow that leads you on and vanishes. Yet, I'd still be a rainbow chaser if I had a choice."

"Caihe, I'm desperate for your help," Sai'er quickly changed the subject, breathing a heavy sigh, as pressure from the staggering onus of responsibility took hold again. "I need to talk the Princess into returning to the Crystal Palace, or else the Green Dragon will claim ten Putai maidens' lives."

"Alright, let's take a trip to the West Pantheon then," it responded with habitual insouciance. Dragging Sai'er by the sleeve, in one tug it hauled her up into the sheer black vault.

When they reached the Pantheons, the Thunderbolt Guards nodded at Caihe, who had resumed its normal celestial size, which was about the same as Sai'er's. In strict adherence to etiquette, the Guards waved them through after registering Sai'er's mortal name.

Upon reaching the West Pantheon, they passed through a peaceful maze of fragrant forests and fruit tree groves laced with crystal-clear springs and dancing waterfalls. Iridescent plumed birds were lilting back-and-forth with amorous songs. Rainbow-colored butterflies fluttered like flowers pirouetting through breeze-swept trees. Cicadas and dragonflies were cavorting in blithe cadence among green bushes mottled with pastel flora.

The bucolic scenery stirred nostalgic longing in Sai'er for the lovely Wudang Mountains. Those carefree days felt like a life time ago. She had since been broken to pieces. Those crumbled pieces were now taking one staggering step forward at a time, ever wary of further stumbles ahead.

Guanyin's Lotus Abode was a palace built on an islet in the middle of a large lake filled with giant white lotus flowers. Two bridges led from the lake periphery to the palace.

The Bodhisattva was ensconced in her seat made of huge lotus petals in the main lounge, deep in meditation. The Little Dragon Princess, a dainty little girl dressed in a pastel silk robe, stood serenely by her side, chanting Buddhist sutras. Her bright starry eyes exuded a vibe of childish innocence and wisdom.

"The Princess is in her early teens," the sprite whispered. "Much as she has the wisdom of an adult, she's entirely beholden to Guanyin. So my advice is: seek help from the Goddess of Mercy."

Sai'er stepped forward, went down on her knees and bowed to the ground. "This unworthy mortal Tang Sai'er pays the Honorable Perceiver of the World's Sounds her deepest respects."

Hearing that, Guanyin looked up, radiating beams of kindness that drifted around like balmy breezes. In a tinkling voice she said, "Welcome, Chang'e, Caihe! Chang'e, I know why you're here." Then, turning to the Princess, she asked softly, "My girl, would you be willing to go back to the Crystal Palace?"

After a moment's rumination, the Princess replied, "Honorable, my place is by your side, to learn to reach Nirvana. If I go back, my father will force me to marry the Sea Scorpion General and my life will be filled with miseries. Besides, my father is deep in sin. Only in my present place will I be able to accrue merits and earn atonement for his sins."

"You're a wise and devoted child," Guanyin said with a gratified smile. "I can't be happier to hear that you wish to stay with me. As for earning atonement for your father's sins, the sad news is that the Green Dragon is trapped in the vicious cycle of bitter hatred. If he does not of his own volition put a stop to his evil intents and deeds, there's little you or I or anyone else can do for him. Karma applies to each and every mortal. So there is no point worrying about your father. Now run along and play in the forest."

When the girl had scampered off, Guanyin offered seats made of green lotus leaves to Sai'er and Caihe. Then she spoke at length to Sai'er.

"Chang'e, I know the Green Dragon must have complicated things for your mission. As Caihe has told you, these former Sky Wolf twins grew up without love. When they were small, their foster mothers, the fox nymphs, had often used cruel punishments on them. That unfortunately scarred them for both their immortal and mortal lives. They erroneously believe that the use of brute power and violence could redress the wrongs done to them. But ten wrongs won't make one right. If mortals perpetuate their evil deeds on a wide scale, the Deities have no choice but to step in."

With a gentle sigh, the Goddess rose from her seat, went out to the lake and, with her willow sprig, flicked sacred water from her white jade bottle on the white lotuses. Then she came back and continued to patiently address Sai'er.

"But there is more bad news. Their immortal birth mother, the lynx nymph, was recently demoted to mortal status because of a misdemeanor. She was reincarnated as a mature, beautiful Jurchen noble woman who has become Zhu Di's favorite consort. I am not at liberty to disclose your mortal destiny to you except give you one word: Beware."

Oh no, I knew that Consort Xian was bad news. Had I known this earlier, I wouldn't have rubbed her the wrong way!

Caihe apparently detected what she was thinking, and gave her an understanding pat on the arm.

"Thank you for your precious advice, Honorable," said Sai'er in a dejected tone. "But the Green Dragon has vowed to come back in three days to take the lives of ten maidens. What am I going to do?"

"Ah, I can tell you that the Green Dragon's brutal deeds and deliberate neglect of his duties have angered the Jade Emperor," Guanyin said slowly after some thought. "As he had once belonged to the North Pantheon, I would advise you to seek help from Chief General Erlang Shen."

After thanking the Goddess of Mercy again, Sai'er and Caihe left the Lotus Abode to head to the North Pantheon.

At the entrance gates perched a straddling pair of huge black tortoises, the sacred guardians of the North Pantheon. Caihe was well prepared and it fed them each a stem of lingzhi, and the carapaced reptiles nodded their retractable heads in appreciation.

As they threaded their way through training halls and lecture rooms to the Marshals' quarters, they bumped into Nezha, who seemed to be in a hurry to head somewhere. When he saw Sai'er, he looked pleasantly surprised and said in a low-pitched and clear voice, "Ah, Chang'e! Just the person I wanted to see."

He wore loose cotton pants with a braided sash tied at the waist, and a vest woven of red ribbons on his upper body, with a glittering golden bracelet on the right wrist. On the other hand he carried the powerful Fire-Tipped Spear. But the daunting weapon belied the aura of his elegant charm.

On closer inspection, Sai'er discovered that he had porcelain white skin and a florid handsome face. She couldn't help but wonder how fierce a fighter he'd make.

Riffling through her memory she vaguely recalled that after Nezha had mutilated his own body and offered up his bone and flesh as atonement for his killing of the Green Dragon's third son, the Tao Immortal Taiyi had restored his life and had raised him to immortal status.

During her Pantheon days, she hadn't had any chance to get to know Nezha. It hadn't occurred to her until now that the life-restoring lotus petals had rendered him gentle and fragile, seemingly in complete contrast to the allegedly fractious and abrasive kid of his short mortal stint.

"Well, well! Look who's here. I've longed to speak with you too," said Sai'er with a grain of sarcasm. "If only you're not slippery as an eel. First, I have to ask you to return the Xuannu Sword to me. You know very well that I'm the rightful owner of the Sword and Yusu stole it from me. Second, I'd like to ask you to confirm something."

"Alright, would you two like to step inside the lounge so we can sit down and talk?" he said meekly, his clear limpid eyes radiating tender shyness.

Following his lead, Sai'er and Caihe stepped into a bright, spacious and modestly furnished lounge of the Marshals' quarters, where the left and right walls were lined with racks of shiny weapons ranging from spears, tridents, halberds to broadswords, long swords, sabers, maces and machetes. At the far end of the room was a door that led to the barracks.

They sat on carved agarwood chairs at a round table that

was placed in the middle of the lounge. A fox nymph maid came around to offer host and guests cups of snow lotus tea.

"Caihe has told you about the Green Dragon's demand that I work for Zhu Di as penance to settle his old grudge, right?" he started, his long black eyelashes fluttering ever so lightly. "What Caihe didn't know about was that I was under orders from Chief General Erlang Shen to use the opportunity to keep an eye on the renegade and his twin."

Pausing, he watched carefully for her reaction. Assured by the fact that she showed not the least doubt, he carried on in a more relaxed tone, "In other words, I spy on you and your friends for Zhu Di on the surface, but in reality I only pass on insignificant tidbits. To gain Zhu Di's trust, I'd offered to take him to the Pantheons on the Queen Mother's last birthday, because I knew he'd longed to talk to you before your descent to the mortal world. When Yusu needed help to get away from Wudang Mountains, I gave her help, to make her believe I was in the same camp as her. After that, she voluntarily handed me the Xuannu Sword to safe-keep. But I thought it best to stay out of her maneuvers she used on you, knowing you could well wiggle your way out."

Well, here's news for you — I was almost done for! But I always believed you weren't a real menace.

"Yusu is no longer our problem now. But we have a bigger problem — in three days' time the Green Dragon will return to Putai and will want to have ten maidens slaughtered, as I've failed to hold my end up and persuade his daughter to return to Crystal Palace. I need to protect the Putai folks. Guanyin has asked us to seek Erlang Shen's help."

"As a matter of fact, I've just come back from a meeting with the Chief General," Nezha said softly in reply. "The Jade Emperor has told him he's decreed punishment for the Green

Dragon. Both our Pantheon Ruler and the Chief General have endorsed the decision."

Sai'er couldn't be more pleased to hear that, as it meant the high ranked Deities had taken matters into their hands. Then her thought shifted to one of her two urgent questions.

"But why haven't you returned the Xuannu Sword to me all this time?"

She threw Caihe a sidelong glance, and found that the androgyne's eyes were dopily fixated on Nezha, its face tinted in rose.

"Ah, that's because the Sword, having been entombed in the Wudang mountain tunnel for many millennia, needed to be re-energized with the Warrior Goddess's divine power. Worldly soil has the effect of draining spiritual power from celestial objects. Just now I said I wanted to see you. The purpose was to tell you that the Sword is now ready for use. Xuannu said you'd need it to fight the Green Dragon."

"What? Am I supposed to fight him?" Sai'er asked with a gaping mouth.

Just then, a white light flicked and Xuannu appeared carrying the Sword in its emerald-inlaid scabbard. She floated towards Sai'er, her crimson long robe and gauzy shawl billowing after her.

This was the Sword that belonged to Xuannu the Warrior Goddess, which she had once granted to the Yellow Emperor to help him defeat Chi You the Ogre King in the cosmic war millennia ago. It was the same Sword that Sai'er, Binhong and Yinho had unearthed from the mountain tunnel. Master Zhang had presaged in his farewell letter that she'd need to use the Sword and the Amulet in her mission in due course.

Sai'er realized that she had earlier misspoken when she blurted out that the Sword belonged to her. She thought it was sweet of Nezha not to upbraid her for this insolent brag.

When her eyes fell on Xuannu, she was struck speechless by her blinding, mystical beauty. In a great panache of ice-of-flesh and jade-of-bones splendor, the Warrior Goddess radiated a magical glow of prismatic colors and an aura of dreamy sensations that pulsated freely in the air. Anyone who got caught up in the vibe couldn't but feel like being whisked away to the euphoric Nine Heavens.

When she spoke, the sounds of her words tinkled like a strand of pearls broken loose in a jade bowl. "Chang'e, take this Sword and use it well. It's destined to tame Dragons in the Demonic and Mortal Realms. The Jade Emperor has just passed a guilty verdict on the Green Dragon. You are to bring him back here to be tried and punished by Xuan Wu, the North Pantheon Ruler."

With those words the Goddess placed the sheathed Sword in Sai'er's hands.

"But, Honorable, with all due respect, this is an impossible task for me. I'm way out of the Green Dragon's league!" Sai'er said with a clearly audible edge in her voice, utterly confounded and anguished by the newly imposed assignment. In a fit of exasperation, she added with a wry smile, "He's a mighty demon that wields insuperable magic power, not to mention his leviathan heft."

Sai'er whispered to Caihe, "Who is the Dragon of the Mortal Realm?"

"Haven't you guessed? The Ming Emperor Zhu Di of course," the sprite humphed.

"You have to believe in my Sword and in your sword skills," said Xuannu as her luscious lips spread in a beguiling smile, silver-bell voice ringing with an undertone of steel resolve. "I've asked Erlang Shen to lend Nezha out to help you. He'll guide you to the undersea world."

Caihe pressed a finger to its lips to warn Sai'er not to nag. *Why me? I was hoping the Deities could rid us of the Green Dragon! And Nezha really looks like brittle porcelain. I'm going to die!*

"Venerable, may I ask you what magical power the White Jade Amulet holds?" She was thinking she needed to arm up with all the magic available to her. "If you don't mind, I would be most grateful if you could decipher the inscriptions for me."

"Ah, the time has not yet come for the use of the Amulet," came the insouciant reply. With that terse remark, Xuannu whirled around, her long robe and shawl flowing in graceful cadence, and she glided out of sight like a red feathery cloud. Soft as her appearance was, the air throbbed with her feral power and authority from her brief presence.

Sai'er slumped in her chair and let out a long sigh, dreading what was about to befall her.

"It's not that bad," the forever optimistic sprite cheered her on. "The Xuannu Sword is a formidable weapon. You have to try it to know its true might."

Throwing Nezha a stealthy glance, the smitten sprite added with a flushed face, "Besides, Nezha has had experience fighting the Green Dragon in his mortal life. He'll be an invaluable aide to you."

As on previous occasions, the immortal friend's wise words made her feel a lot better.

Unsheathing the Sword, which had a slit in the center of the blade and felt light in her hand, Sai'er was for a moment blinded by the icy blue green glare that uncoiled from the extremely thin, clear and translucent blade. It emitted an aura of serene frigidity. Its lightweight design seemed especially suited for Sword-as-Whip flourishes. The blade slit could allow the wielder to easily snag an opponent's sword and wrench it off the grip.

A rush of thrilling joy raced through her, as she made a

strange connection with the Sword spirit. It felt like the Sword spirit had identified her as its master.

When she brandished the celestial weapon, it crackled like a current of lightning. The cutting wind that swished from the blade barely grazed a porcelain vase that was on a side table, and for a moment nothing stirred. Then the vase cracked into a spray of tiny shards, followed by a series of sharp tinkles as they hit the ground. Everyone present gasped.

She quickly sheathed it, secretly awed by the Sword's deathly beauty.

Nezha was twiddling a strand of stray hair between his index and middle finger. Any onlooker would get the impression that his mind was somewhere else. But the moment he opened his delicate mouth to speak, Sai'er could tell that he'd listened well.

Sounding surprisingly collected and poised, he said, "Let's face it: the Green Dragon will definitely return to Putai. If you want to protect your county folks, you can't shirk this fight. "

Turning his steady gaze on Sai'er, he continued, "Between you and I, we can take him down if we coordinate well. Your mastery of the Sword-as-Whip feat will come in handy."

"You make it sound like a walk in the garden," Sai'er said with a forced smile, hoping Nezha would live up to his acclaimed valiance.

"Oh, before I forget," Sai'er added, suddenly remembering an important question. "I was going to ask you to verify something. You see, Sun Wukong told me that you were an eyewitness to Sky Wolf's rape of two fox nymphs. Is that true? Sky Wolf swore to me on his immortal life that it was Wukong who had committed the crime and had framed him. Which one of them told the truth?"

Even though she already had an inkling of what the truth was, she was still eager to get Nezha's affirmation.

An intense look overshadowed the Senior Marshal's young chiseled face, as he said with a low but steady voice, "With my past crime of killing the third Dragon Prince, I just didn't want to get into trouble with the Green Dragon ever again. So I didn't come forward as a witness during the Jade Emperor's trial of his twin Sky Wolf. But even without my testimony, Sky Wolf still got the guilty verdict and was demoted to the mortal realm as Zhu Di. That at least eased my conscience."

"So you're saying that Sky Wolf did commit the crime and did try to frame Wukong?"

"If he swore that Wukong was the culprit, he's a brazen and devious liar! I caught him red-handed."

It was the answer that Sai'er had been expecting. Now she could throw any remnant of illusion about Zhu Di to the winds, not that she would admit there was any in the first place, after what she'd experienced in Yingtian.

"Nezha, would you mind telling me what led to the deep rift between you and the Green Dragon, and what kind of a character he is?"

Sai'er thought it crucial to learn as much as possible about an enemy before she faced him in a life-and-death combat. Besides, as her soon-to-be co-fighter, Nezha was also an object of intense interest to her. The more she understood him, the better she could coordinate with him. Her intuitive feeling was that his story was far more complicated than what appeared on the surface.

"Yes, please tell us your whole story," Caihe chimed in, its dark eyes sparkling with burning anticipation.

35

The year Nezha turned thirteen in his mortal life, something happened that would turn his world upside down.

It was a sweltering summer day in the seaside fortress town of Chentang Pass, Nezha's birthplace. The town nestled alongside the Nine-Bend River which flowed into the East Sea, home to the Dragon King's Crystal Palace. Nezha lived with his parents and two elder brothers in a modest courtyard house located about a li from where the river mouth opened to the sea.

Before this day, Nezha had been the most pampered son of his mother and the much cherished little master in the Li Jing household. He was clever, jaunty, friendly and gifted in martial arts. There was not a soul who didn't love him, except, maybe, his father. Perhaps no one doted on him more than his mentor and coach, Taoist Immortal Taiyi, who had trained him in spear-wielding and magic since he was ten.

In fact, his birth was something like a lush drama of magic. It was said that his mother had carried the fetus for three whole years before finally giving birth. At the time of his emergence, an exquisite fragrance permeated the whole bedchamber, which was then lit up by a flourish of sparkling red lights.

The father was dumbstruck to see a child-size infant burst out of a rolling ball of fire. He had a long strand of red ribbon looped around his tiny body, and on the right wrist flashed a golden bracelet. Both the ribbon strand and the bracelet were celestial objects, as a Taoist monk would later reveal.

When Li Jing placed the child in the mother's arms, she was overwhelmed with tears. This bundle of pride and joy was going to be more precious than her life. Nothing made her happier than cradling the oversized infant in her loving arms.

She was so glad to get her husband off her back at last. He had been nothing but a moping pest throughout her uncomfortable pregnancy years. But alas, instead of feeling joy, he was now obsessed with the thought that the child was some kind of evil that the heavens had sent him, and he tended to regard this son with hostility.

Just then, the Taoist Immortal Taiyi appeared in the human form of a Taoist monk at the doorsteps of the Li house. When he was ushered inside the lounge, he made a request to Li Jing to adopt the child as his acolyte. He was going to train the child in spear-wielding and working with his magical objects. Li Jing could sense that the monk was someone with immense supernatural power and found no reason to reject such a generous offer. He at once gave his consent.

Taiyi asked what hour the child was born. When Li replied it was the Hour of the Ox, the monk did some divination with his fingers and said, "For the child's protection, I'd suggest we name him 'Nezha'. This name has heavy earth content, and can neutralize any ill effect that the water element could bring, because water subdues fire, and his birth's fire element makes him vulnerable to water. The Sky Earth Bracelet and the Sky Red Ribbon that were found at his birth are celestial weapons for his personal use."

Before Taiyi left, he warned, "Nezha is destined to be a nemesis of dragons, because dragons typically have an innate metal element, and fire naturally quells metal. When he turns ten, send him to me at my abode in the Golden Light Cave on Sky Mountain."

"Whatever you say, Master Taiyi," Li Jing replied with nonchalance.

That day was inordinately hot. Nezha was a kid who hated the hot season, because heat always irritated him immeasurably and it made him sweat profusely.

After telling his mother that he was heading out to the seaside to cool himself off, he left the house and gamboled all the way to the beach, accompanied by a house servant as insisted by his mother. He was secretly rejoicing that his stern father was away in the battlefield suppressing a riot and was not expected back home for another day, affording him the rare chance to play as much as he wanted without fearing punishment.

Since his return from apprenticeship with Taiyi, he felt like his wings had been clipped. Life in the Li household was a stifling bore. His father made him learn ancient Chinese classics and practice calligraphy every day. How he loathed that! His only relief was a couple of hours in the late afternoon of spear practice in the courtyard. Still, the old man had to make it a stupid rule that he had to complete his daily assignment of rote-learning and writing in exchange for those precious two hours of pleasure. If he didn't finish on time, that one piece of recreation would be snatched from him.

Very often when his mother saw that he was struggling with his assignment, she would help him finish his work. For this, and for all the doting love she freely showered on him, he was drawn ever closer to her while being progressively distanced from his austere father. His older brothers were posted to military garrisons far away from home and it didn't help to ease his ennui.

How he missed the carefree days during his apprenticeship on

Sky Mountain! He was at liberty to roam about the fragrant pine forests for hours on end, forage in copses for the most delicious fruits and mushrooms, fish in the scatter of streams and creeks, bathe in the crystalline shallow lagoons, and just lie on the grass at night to gaze at the infinite lattice of stars.

His coach and mentor Taiyi was always happy to cook whatever he brought in. Mentor and acolyte would share simple and happy meals every day. Taiyi was easy-going except when he gave morning spear lessons each day. Clever and adroit as Nezha was, the child just lapped up what he was taught with the least effort. Taiyi was more than pleased with his progress and didn't mind showering him with praise from time to time.

Sometimes he felt that his mentor cared more about him than his own father.

That feeling came up again when Nezha saw a father playing cuju with his two little boys on the beach. His father would never do such a thing with him. If he played this game in the courtyard, he could get a good scolding from the old man, or denied supper if he was in a grumpy mood.

The sweltering heat was really getting to him. To his great joy, his servant found a shady willow grove about fifty yards from the sun-drenched beach and waved him over. Swaying willows lined the rocky banks of the Nine Bend River estuary which fed into the sea. He found a smooth rock to sit on and took off his dripping tunic, while dipping his feet into the water to cool them off.

From where he sat, he had a good view of the whole beach. Other than the father and his two boys, three small girls were chasing each other for fun, giggling aloud, their father quietly looking on.

In a beat, a giant octopus slithered onto the shore, its sinewy tentacles grabbing one of the small girls. Screams of horror crackled in the air. The father of the girls scooped up the other two in a fit of paroxysm, while gaping helplessly at the caught girl. The boys and their father rushed forward and tried desperately to disentangle the girl in distress, but the tentacles held too tight a grip. The girl shrieked at the top of her lungs.

Nezha leaped up and bolted towards the octopus. He knew by instinct that it was a sea demon in disguise. Taking the gold bracelet from his wrist, he bashed it twice on the octopus's head. Instantly the creature loosened its grip and dropped the girl. It then transformed into a yecha with a dark green face and fang-like incisors, wielding an axe and yelping in pain.

"How dare you hit me? Do you know who I am?" the yecha growled. "I'm the Chief Guard from the Crystal Palace of the East Sea!"

"I don't give a whit who you are. You were bullying a defenseless little girl."

"I'm under orders from our King to capture girls for his elixir concoction. You'd better mind your own business." The yecha threatened Nezha by brandishing his axe.

"Your King is a hideous monster. I think I need to send him a message."

"Scram before I hurt you bad," the yecha hollered in a snotty tone, while lunging his axe at Nezha, who nimbly sidestepped the blow.

In the flicker of a moment the yecha turned back into an octopus, flailing its six arms and two legs all at once. In swift motion, it chased after the three girls and the father who were scuttling away for their lives.

Nezha chanted a prayer and pointed his finger to the Sky Earth Bracelet, which instantly grew five times in size. He tied it to his Sky Red Ribbon and threw it out like a lasso noose. The Bracelet trapped the octopus's head in it. Then he chanted again,

ALICE POON

and the Bracelet tightened and tightened, choking the yecha to death. Nezha then picked up the corpse and flung it back into the sea. That was the message he wanted to send to the Green Dragon.

The girls' father bowed repeatedly to Nezha to thank him for his heroic act, and the family of four left the beach, their faces still blanched with terror from the near tragedy.

The boys' father came up to Nezha and said, with fear in his eyes, "This wasn't the first time this has happened. A month ago, two little girls were caught by the octopus while playing here by themselves. The next day small bones were found floating near the shore. The three girls and their father are probably from out of town and hadn't heard about that terrible incident."

A fit of righteous anger came over Nezha when he heard the story. "The Green Dragon must be punished for this heinous crime," he murmured.

"Some time ago, a Taoist monk told us that the Green Dragon Ao Guang has been trying to boost his magic power by concocting an elixir using girls' flesh. He's been neglecting his duties as a rain dispenser, and our town has suffered long bouts of drought."

"It was for a crime that his immortal being, a Sky Wolf, had committed in the Pantheons that he got sent to the underworld to do penance in the first place," said Nezha, recalling the story of the twin Sky Wolves that his mentor Taiyi had once told him. "If he continues with his vile ways, someone has to stop him."

The boys' father shook his head in despair, exhaling a long sigh.

"For many years, Ao Guang and his three sons were in the habit of disguising themselves as handsome young men when they ventured ashore, and every now and then they would hoax their way into homes and snatch away young maidens. They would claw out the guts of any man who dared put up a fight. Now they send up yechas to do the job. How can we humans possibly guard against these vicious demons?"

Nezha was dumbstruck on hearing such an atrocious account.

At this time, thick ominous clouds swarmed the sky and blocked out the sun. The sea heaved up rolling swells that crashed onto the beach with an angry roar. Seagulls screeched in fright in the midst of the thundering howl of gales.

The father said a hasty goodbye and scurried off the beach with his sons.

"Young Master, we'd better get back home now," the servant pleaded, fearing his young master might get into more trouble.

Just as they began strolling away, a young lad with wiry hair and scaly skin riding on the crest of waves hurtled onto the pebble beach with a loud splash.

"Stop! You mother-fucking son of a whore!" the lad yelled rudely. "You have some nerve killing our Chief Palace Guard!"

Nezha had never heard anyone use such crude profanity regarding his mother. Acerbic anger surged through his veins. He spun around and glowered at the cantankerous lad.

"What did you call me?" he snarled, eyes spewing flames.

"Son of a whore! Only a whore could've bred a piece of scum like you! My King father has sent me to dole out punishment."

Without another word, Nezha enlarged his Sky Earth Bracelet and smashed it on the lad's head with violent force. The lad shrieked and transformed into a green dragon the size of a small crocodile, writhing and wheezing, "How dare you? Don't you know I'm Ao Bing, the third Dragon Prince?"

"Oh yeah? And I'm Nezha, the third Prince of the Li Jing household," he snorted in a cutting riposte. "To me, you're a bum who doesn't know right from wrong. Your father is a depraved demon who murders girls on a whim."

"So my father wants to brew an elixir with maiden flesh. What's wrong with that? Girls in your world are worthless anyway," Ao Bing sneered.

Fury bubbled up in Nezha's guts. He snapped up the reptile by its scaly trunk and used a knife that he carried in his boots to make a deep laceration along the dragon's ridge. The reptile thrashed and writhed. But no matter how hard it lurched and jerked, it couldn't escape Nezha's powerful grip. Then with his thumb and forefinger he pulled out a stringy tendon from the beast. It squealed piteously from the agony.

Unwinding the Sky Red Ribbon from his waist, he twined it around the dragon's trunk to have it bound tightly.

"Now, how does that make you feel, you cruel pest?"

Not realizing the superhuman brawny force that he had used, he was unknowingly cutting air out from the beast's gills and suffocating it. When he untied the dragon, he thought it had just passed out.

"Young Master, we must leave now! We've been out for too long!" urged the house servant in agitation.

"Alright! Let me wash my soiled Ribbon in the river first," he answered with insouciance.

36

By the time Nezha and his servant arrived home, it was late evening.

The maidservant told them in a low whisper that the old master had returned home a day earlier than planned as he had won an easy victory in the riot suppression.

Nezha tip-toed quietly into the back of the house, and, once inside his bedchamber, he quickly changed into clean clothes and got ready for supper.

After having supper, he went back to his chamber under pretense that he wanted to read, feeling lucky his escapade of the day had remained unremarked. His mother always knew what not to reveal to his father at the dinner table.

Just then, a loud and urgent knock on the front gates shattered the peaceful ambience of the house.

Moments later, a bout of furious squabble between his father and a visitor could be heard coming from the lounge. Nezha left the chamber door ajar to try to listen in. Picking up most of the conversation, he was aghast to learn that the hostile exchange had something to do with the death of Ao Bing that afternoon.

Apparently, the enraged visitor was Ao Guang the Dragon King in human form, making an eye-for-an-eye demand that Li Jing kill Nezha as compensation. He even threatened to take the matter to the Jade Emperor for a fair settlement.

Li Jing, believing that Nezha had stayed home all day, tried vehemently to defend his son and dismissed Ao Guang's allegation out of hand. Feeling indignant about the absurd demand, he gave an ultimatum for the guest to leave at once.

As soon as Ao Guang left, Nezha went out to the lounge and, kneeling down in front of his father, made a full confession of what had transpired that afternoon.

"I knew you'd bring the family trouble," Li Jing growled in a fit of exasperation. Looking accusingly at his wife, he added, "Look what a jinx of a son you gave me! This is a disaster!"

This last remark cut deeply into Nezha's heart. He couldn't bear to see his mother verbally abused this way. "Father, this is all my fault. It has nothing to do with Mother! Please whip me all you want, but don't blame Mother."

Tears welled up in his mother eyes, as she stroked his hair tenderly and pleaded for Li Jing to calm down and listen to what his son had to say.

Mustering up his courage, he tried to defend himself like a man, "Ao Guang has been ordering the capture of girls so he can flay their flesh to use in brewing an elixir. Two girls were captured and killed a month ago. For a long time Ao Guang and his sons have been snatching girls from our town at random for that purpose. If I didn't stop these atrocities, who else would do it?"

At heart, Li Jing was not an unreasonable man. Now that he had the whole picture, he knew his son was not the one at fault. But he also was not so naïve as to entertain the wishful thought that Ao Guang would let this pass without exacting revenge. Nezha was, after all, his own flesh and blood. How could he kill his own son? He was irredeemably caught in a quagmire.

What made matters worse was that Ao Guang had the support of the other three Dragon Kings: the Red Dragon of the

South Sea, Black Dragon of Lake Baikal in the North and White Dragon of Qinghai Lake in the West.

For a long time Ao Guang had total sway over these subordinate Dragons through a combination of bribing and coercion, such that even the Jade Emperor had no way of verifying that his regular work reports actually stated true facts. Thus Ao Guang's long-time impudent abuse of power, neglect of his assigned duties and brazen vile deeds against humans were all under wraps.

Such a background history Nezha had heard Taiyi mention in passing during his apprenticeship. But it wasn't until this day that he personally heard plaintive recounts by locals and actually witnessed a real case of egregious crime unfolding.

Nezha was feeling as anguished as his father, if not more. He tossed and turned the whole night brooding on his possible course of action.

When the first ray of dawn pierced through the lattice window, Nezha rose from bed and sneaked out of the house. He was headed to the Golden Light Cave to ask for his mentor's advice.

"My dear child, you've landed yourself in deep trouble," said Taiyi with a worried face as soon as his apprentice showed up in the Cave. He moved his thumb on the inside of the middle and fourth finger, his brow furrowing into deep lines.

Nezha dropped to his knees and wailed, "Teacher, I've come to seek your help. I didn't mean to kill Ao Bing—it was an accident! It's true I had killed the yecha, but I was only trying to save a girl's life. With Ao Bing, all I wanted was to curb his conceit and let him taste pain."

"Don't you think I know?" said the mentor, letting out a long sigh. "No one knows you better than I. For all your pranks and petulance, you're by nature a good-hearted kid. But now the fact remains that Ao Bing died because of your fight with him, and the Green Dragon will not let you off the hook until he sees you dead."

After a moment's mulling, Taiyi leaned over and whispered his advice into Nezha's ear. Before he left, Taiyi handed him a sharp-bladed saber and a pouch of poppy seed powder.

Later in the day, Nezha approached Chentang Pass with a heavy heart. Knowing there wasn't any better alternative to what his mentor advised, he was still fighting against that advice as he felt strongly that Ao Bing and the yecha were the real culprits in the whole matter. He had merely wanted to see justice done.

The sky had turned pitch black with bursting rain clouds. Flashes of lightning cleaved through the air, accompanied by deafening claps of thunder. Heaving swells from the sea assaulted the seashore and ran amok inland. From a distance he could make out that the seaside town was inundated in a combined deluge of torrential rain and impinging sea water. *This must be that turtle egg Ao Guang's good work,* cursed Nezha inwardly.

No sooner had he stepped into the front courtyard of his house, which was covered in ankle-deep water, than the house servant cried out to him, "Young Master, the Four Dragons came this morning and took Old Master and Madam away—"

Nezha blanched in shock. "Do you know where they've taken Ba and Ma?"

"They said to tell you to meet them at the Heavenly Gates to the Pantheons."

A mix of anger and frustration assailed Nezha. Much as he wanted to be tried by the Jade Emperor, he felt he wouldn't get a fair trial because the Four Dragons would collude to give a false statement, and the Jade Emperor would be pressured to give a biased judgment against him. Besides, the conspirators were holding his parents hostage to warn against any defense he might be contemplating. The chances of getting exonerated were close to nil.

Looping the Sky Red Ribbon around his body, he made a series of leaps and within moments was propelled through blanket after thick blanket of grey clouds. The brush of cold wind on his face cleared his foggy mind. The only feasible way out of this quagmire was to die, as his mentor had suggested, for the sake of his parents and hometown. That was the conclusion he'd reached when he landed in front of the imposing Heavenly Gates.

Flanked by his three Dragon King brothers, Ao Guang stepped forward in a swagger, with a smirk on his rugged face. "What took you so long?" he asked with insolence.

"May I make a proposition?" Nezha tried hard to press down his bubbling fury.

"Let's hear it!"

"First I sincerely offer my apologies to you for my grave blunder of accidentally killing Ao Bing," said Nezha with candor. "It was never my intention to take his life. For my serious wrongdoing, I'd like to offer up my flesh and bones as penance and in exchange for the immediate release of my parents. I'd proffer that my death will be the final settlement of our dispute. You must also stop flooding Chentang Pass."

"A life for a life—it sounds fair enough," said the Black Dragon with apathy. When he realized the other two Dragons kept mum, he looked a bit embarrassed.

Ao Guang responded with a sullen glower at the Black Dragon, then said dourly to Nezha, "You're wise not to ask for a trial by the Jade Emperor. Your death is a must to pay for Ao Bing's life. If you want your parents released, you'd have to fight me in a duel first. But even if you win, you'd still have to stick to your promise of self-destruction."

Alright! You asked for it, thought Nezha with secret mirth. "I accept."

Ao Guang in human form wielded a heavy trident and jabbed it with brute force at Nezha, who dodged the blow with ease. At once he enlarged his Sky Earth Bracelet and, after a flurry of strikes and counter strikes, swung it at Ao Guang's head with precision and hefty force, landing a direct hit on his protruding snout. He lurched to the side from the hit, then reeling two steps back.

Years of idle debauchery had slackened Ao Guang's muscles and sapped his alertness. Despite having the obvious advantage in bulk, he was not half as nimble as Nezha. In terms of strength, Nezha, who had been endowed with superhuman energy at birth, was every bit an equal match for the mutable beast, if not superior.

Nezha seized the opening to launch a flourish of hammering strikes aiming at Ao Guang's badly bruised snout before he could steady himself. At least two blows hit the target spot-on, sending him into a vertiginous spin, the trident slipping off his hand. The last blow transformed him back into his Dragon shape as he wriggled and writhed on the ground.

With one hand, Nezha grabbed the Dragon by his long neck and with the other he reached for the celestial saber that Taiyi had given him. He used the sharp blade to shear off a bunch of scales from the Dragon's thick trunk. The demon bellowed in total prostration, floundering helplessly in the pool of his blood.

The other three Dragons stood flabbergasted as they watched the fight come to an end. None dared make a move.

Nezha's intense gaze roved across their faces as he said solemnly, "I beseech Your Eminences to be my witnesses: I'm going to destroy myself right here, right now." Turning to the Green Dragon, he added, "I trust you to keep your word and release my parents immediately."

While scaling the Dragon's trunk, Nezha had secretly swallowed the poppy seed powder. With his senses now mostly numbed, he first severed one arm, then both legs, and then disemboweled himself. The ultra sharp saber slid through muscles, bones and tendons as if they were mere cardboards. Taking a last breath, he swung the saber at his throat and sliced off his own head.

As soon as the Four Dragons left, Taiyi showed up to collect Nezha's head in a hemp sack and his spirit in a small pagoda-shaped bottle and immediately flew back to the Golden Light Cave.

Meanwhile, Li Jing and his wife were released by their kidnappers and returned safely to their half-wrecked home. Grieving deeply for Nezha, Madam Li couldn't refrain from giving her husband an earful of how wrong he'd been about their youngest son. Li Jing had nothing to say to defend himself, feeling only deep remorse over the whole matter.

On Sky Mountain, Taiyi's immortal pet, White Crane, had earlier plucked the petals and leaves from two fresh stems of lotus in the nearest lagoon and had placed these on the low stone table inside the Cave.

From cylindrical tubes made from rolled-up green lotus leaves, Taiyi first built a human skeleton. Then he affixed the pink lotus petals to the bone frame and put Nezha's head at the top. As he chanted incantations, he released the spirit from the bottle, directing it to settle on the human form.

Two more days of incantations later, Nezha's eyes flicked open. His resurrection was complete. The first thing he did after assuming this new life was to visit his parents and to let them know of his reincarnation.

After receiving a full report from Taiyi of Nezha's story,

the Jade Emperor granted him immortal status and appointed him Marshal of the North Pantheon. Taiyi gifted him with the Fire-Tipped Spear for fighting demons and the Wind-and-Fire-Wheels for transport on air and sea.

Later he was promoted to the post of Senior Marshal. His father Li Jing, through his own merits, also achieved immortal status, and father and son were finally reconciled in the Pantheons.

When the Green Dragon heard of Nezha's new immortal status, he felt cheated and pressed him to help Zhu Di with spying on Sai'er and her allies, as a way to settle the old score.

37

That was the Nezha now sitting in the Marshals' quarters of the North Pantheon talking to Sai'er and Caihe.

"You don't care much to socialize, do you?" Caihe asked, its eyes dreamy with infatuation. "I wish I'd known you sooner."

Nezha blushed and said in a soft voice, "I don't like crowds. People may find me boring." He threw Caihe a furtive sidelong glance, which the sprite caught with a smug smile.

"What? Boring? I'd long with bated breath for any story you'd care to share!" asserted the coy Caihe.

Having heard Nezha's story and his mortal clash with the Green Dragon, Sai'er now took a genuine liking to this spear-wielding florid lad. She knew intuitively she could trust him as a fighting partner.

"Seems the Green Dragon hasn't changed a bit," said Sai'er pensively, as if to herself. "And twins do share common traits. Both are so vicious and vindictive."

"I have to warn you, though, that since our last altercation at the Heavenly Gates, Ao Guang has not ceased his habit of devouring young girls to boost his dragon power. So we have to be prepared for surprises. Also, his Sea Scorpion General is a fierce fighter..."

"We've been here long enough. It's time to get back to earth," Caihe cut in anxiously to warn Sai'er.

"Sai'er, I'll look for you in Putai on the day the Green Dragon is due to appear," said Nezha as Sai'er and Caihe said their farewell.

As Sai'er and the sprite swam through clouds to make their descent, suddenly Sai'er thought of the broken bridge.

"Monkey Sage! I've forgotten all about the bridge! How can we move the villagers back to the south bank?"

"Not to worry. I know your Magic Peach was used up," Caihe said with a confident smile. "Remember I have an unused one? But you must take note that after I've rebuilt the bridge, my Peach is good for only one more use, as I had told you before."

"Yes, yes, I know. Oh, Caihe, you're a life-saver! I can't thank you enough."

As Caihe used its Peach's magic to repair the tattered bridge, Sai'er wended her way through mud and sludge back to the camp site on the western hill.

While time had stood still in the Pantheons, time on earth had marched forward by two days since she left for the Pantheons. She must get her group ready to cross over to the south bank for the exodus today. The next day would be the day of the great combat.

It was late morning. The air was freezing cold. The world was draped with a thick black fog that heralded heavy snowfall.

As she skittered up the slope, a premonitory feeling choked her throat.

Yulan was starting a cooking fire outside her tent when she saw Sai'er climb the steps to the landing. She looked relieved and asked,

"Where have you been? We were worried about you."

"Sorry, Yulan, I had to make a trip to get the Deities to help. Look, we have to get going in a few hours. The bridge is being repaired. Could you please round up those who want to leave for Yidu as soon as possible?"

At this time Binhong and Yinho emerged from their tent.

"Where's Ba?" Sai'er was hit with an ominous thought.

"He said he was going to cross the river by sampan to take a look at our wrecked cottage," Binhong replied. "Ah, I see you've found the Xuannu Sword!"

Sai'er was too preoccupied to respond. "When did Ba leave the tent?"

"About half a joss stick's time ago," Binhong answered, sensing something was wrong.

"He seemed a bit off this morning," Yinho added with concern. "Last night he was sleep-walking. Just like you at that time when Zhu Di had cast a hex on you. I thought it was strange."

Suddenly it dawned on Sai'er that Consort Xian had most likely filched her clam shell. That morning when the Jurchen woman paid a visit, Sai'er had put the clam shell on the table. After she'd left, it was nowhere to be found. Then she had become too caught up in dramatic events to give the matter another thought.

"If a woman had a portrait of Ba and wanted to cast a hex on him, could she do it?" she asked Yinho in deep angst.

"Yes, a portrait is all it takes, even if predator and prey have never met." Yinho confirmed with a frown. "If the predator also knows the prey's birth date and time, he or she could put the prey into a trance and order the prey about like a puppet. Black magic hexes are most commonly used to scare and unsettle the prey, like in your case, or to subject the prey to the predator's will, as in a love spell or an enslaving spell."

He now could guess what had transpired. "You said 'woman'. Did you mean that Jurchen Consort?"

She gave the slightest of a nod, as blood pounded in her head and breadths whooshed from her airways, forming bereaved swirls of white fog.

"Ah, many Jurchens are Shamanism believers and some know how to work Shamanist black magic," said Yinho with a glum expression. "As the hex creator is a woman, only female Deities could be called upon to subdue the hex. Too bad my sorcery ability is limited to invoking the power of North Pantheon Deities."

Her shoulders slumped in a fit of morose despair.

"Let me go and search for him on the south bank," volunteered Binhong, his face knotted in deep angst.

But Sai'er's instinct told her it was too late.

[The story continues in
Book 2 of Sword Maiden from the Moon.]

GLOSSARY / TERMINOLOGY

add oil to the fire: Chinese idiom (火上加油) that means to exacerbate a bad situation.

celestial crane buzi: A buzi is a square patch sewn onto the front of a Court Official's formal robe to indicate his rank. A celestial crane buzi represents the highest civil rank.

cloud and rain hills: Chinese idiom (雲雨巫山) to describe sexual pleasure.

Embroidered Uniform Guards: A secret spy squad established by and reporting directly to the Emperor. The Hongwu Emperor was the founder. The aim was to weed out traitors/dissenters.

Eight Immortals: In Taoist beliefs, the Eight Immortals are deities of the East Pantheon. They are: Lu Dongbin, Iron-Crutch Lee, General Chungli, Fruity Cheung, Water Lily Nymph, Minister Cao, Lan Caihe and Flutist Han. Lu is the leader of the group.

Eight Immortals Rod technique: A spear/rod wielding martial skill that originates from the Wudang School.

First Hour of the Dog: 7:00 pm – 8:00 pm (戌時)

First Hour of the Rabbit: 5:00 am – 6:00 am (卯時)

flowers in the mirror, moon in the water: A Buddhist saying (鏡花水月) which means worldly belongings are illusory. The saying is attributed to an East Jin Dynasty Buddhist monk named Huiyuan (慧遠法師).

Hour of the Ox: 1:00 am – 3:00 am (丑時)

Hour of the Rabbit: 5:00 am – 7:00 am (卯時)

ice-of-flesh and jade-of-bones: Chinese idiom (冰肌玉骨) to describe the exquisite beauty of a woman.

joss stick's time: In ancient China, a common way to tell time was to gauge how long it took for a single joss stick to burn. Standardized joss sticks were manufactured and calibrated for specific time measurements: an hour, a half hour etc. When referred to in this novel, a joss stick's time indicates one hour.

kung fu: The pinyin Chinese term for martial arts.

lianliu: A shrub with long willowy branches that's native to Shandong. The branches can be woven into baskets, thatch mattings and sunshades.

meridians: Channels inside the human body through which qi flows.

needle wrapped in cotton: Chinese idiom (綿裏藏針) that means hiding power or strength under a disguise.

neigong: (a.k.a. qigong). Internal martial arts using qi as a major defending or attacking force. It is said to be a Wudang School specialty.

North Star Qi-Extracting technique: A deadly neigong technique inspired by "北冥神功", an arcane feat acquired by the protagonist Duan Yu (a Dali Kingdom prince) from Jin Yong's novel *Demi-Gods and Semi-Devils* (天龍八部).

'Peach Blossom Spring' utopia: *Peach Blossom Spring* (桃花源記) is the title of a famous Chinese narrative poem written by Eastern Jin dynasty poet Tao Yuanming, depicting an otherworldly milieu with ethereal landscapes and an idyllic community.

pear blossoms drenched in rain: Chinese idiom (梨花帶雨) to describe a beautiful woman in weeps.

qi: Internal energy or life force. The word is commonly used in the fields of Chinese medicine and Chinese martial arts.

qinggong: In martial arts fiction, "qinggong" is a unique style of kung fu where the practitioner can walk in air or glide on water surface. The Wudang School of Martial Arts is believed to be well known for this special style.

Ren and Du Meridians: The two overarching qi channels inside the human body.

sanqi root powder: Sanqi root (a.k.a. tianqi root) is used in Chinese medicine to stanch bleeding from wounds.

Second Hour of the Rooster: 6:00 pm – 7:00 pm (酉時)

shifu: A respectful Chinese form of address for a master of certain skills who teaches his/her skills to apprentices.

turtle egg: A Chinese epithet that is equivalent to "bastard" in English.

Wave Treading technique: A zenith-level qinggong technique inspired by "凌波微步", an arcane qinggong feat acquired by the protagonist Duan Yu (a Dali Kingdom prince) from Jin Yong's novel *Demi-Gods and Semi-Devils* (天龍八部). This term first appeared in Cao Zhi's prose poem titled *Ode to the Goddess of River Luo* (洛神賦) to describe the graceful way the Goddess of River Luo walks on the river.

Wudang Mountains: A massive mountain range (now a landmark) in Hubei Province known for its huge array of temples built under the Ming Yongle Emperor's reign.

Wudang neigong: In the martial arts world, it is believed that Zhang Sanfeng (張三豐) founded and led the Wudan School (武當派) which specialized in neigong (or qigong), and that Taiji kung fu evolved from this School.

Yamen: The bureau of an administrative body at the county, prefectural or provincial level, usually with annexed residences for senior officials.

Yu the Great: Yu the Great (大禹) was a legendary Sovereign of pre-dynastic times in China who successfully introduced flood control methods that included dredging riverbeds and redirecting the flow of water into oceans. He is believed to be the founder of the Xia Dynasty.

ABOUT THE AUTHOR

After a childhood spent devouring Jin Yong's wuxia (or martial arts heroes) novels, Alice Poon has, over the years, fed herself a steady diet of modern wuxia/xianxia and historical C-dramas, Chinese history and mythology masterpieces.

Since the release of her two historical Chinese novels: *The Green Phoenix* and *Tales of Ming Courtesans*, nostalgia for the magical world of wuxia has spurred her desire to write in the Chinese fantasy genre. Her writing has been inspired by the wuxia/xianxia media, Chinese mythology classics and period history.

She lives in Vancouver, Canada and wishes to indulge herself in putting her imagination on the page.

https://linktr.ee/alicepoonauthor
http://twitter.com/alicepoon1
https://www.goodreads.com/alice_poon
https://alicewaihanpoon.blogspot.com
https://www.instagram.com/alicepoonauthor

CPSIA information can be obtained
at www.ICGtesting.com
Printed in the USA
BVHW040804070123
655722BV00019B/1587